Braving Strange Waters

Sarah Hanks

Praise for
Braving Strange Waters

Three friends get swept up in the adventure of a lifetime when they embark on a girls' trip together, not knowing that they would experience time travel, face their greatest weaknesses, find love, forge healing, and encounter Jesus calling them deeper into trust and intimacy with Him. Readers will find a piece of themselves in each woman, being offered the opportunity to walk the path with them, letting go of mindsets, behaviors, and assumptions that keep us shackled. Once again, Sarah Hanks uses her incredible storytelling gifts to jar us out of the status quo and into a higher, more excellent Way. Pick up *Braving Strange Waters* if you like relatable characters in high-stakes situations, women's fiction with a bit of love and a lot of faith, and twists and turns that keep you on your toes.

Heather Wood, author of the Finding Home series

Once again, Sarah Hanks masterfully intertwines dual timelines, bringing together brave friends separated by over a century yet communicating through an antique mailbox. Her storytelling is captivating, offering a beautiful narrative of friendship and the profound journey of living out God's calling. Enjoy.

Kristine Delano, award-winning writer and soon-to-be Tyndale author

Sarah Hanks captured my attention from the beginning with her unique concept of time sailing which presents a new and interesting twist in the genre of split time stories. In Braving Strange Waters, Sarah proves once again she is never one to shy away from the hard topics. In her masterful way, she weaves the threads of the past and present timelines to tell a compelling story.

We journey with each of the characters as they struggle to overcome their own issues with insecurity, fear, and identity. We are left with a new and different spin on time travel which opens a world of possibilities for more characters and stories that I hope Sarah will continue to tell.

Andrette Herron, Author

A Case of God-given Identity: A Workbook for Finding Purpose and Fighting Fear

In *Braving Strange Waters*, Sarah Hanks takes us into the hearts of three women struggling with fear and self-doubt. We cheer them on as they struggle with friendships, faith, and finding a man to share their lives with. Hanks's characters come alive on the page, showing us much of ourselves as they stumble and fall short, only to get back up again. And we, along with them, learn to see ourselves as God sees us.

Sherry Shindelar, author of *Texas Forsaken*

What could be more fun than a light story about a group of girls getting together for a cruise to celebrate an upcoming wedding with a little time travel tossed in for good measure? This is the perfect beach read, but not for the reasons a passive observer might expect at first. Beneath the surface of fun and adventure, Sarah Hanks weaves a story that will touch readers' hearts on so many levels. All three of the girls have secrets and failings they've tried to hide from one another that will be tested by the events in the story, both in the past and the present, and will reveal their true characters to themselves and one another. Each will be given a choice: to persist in deception and continue past mistakes or to be open and vulnerable with one another, allowing Christ to shape them into the women they were created to be. Don't miss out on this stunning timeslip novel. You won't regret diving beneath the surface.

Sarah Everest, Author of *One Week in November* and
the *Darkening Dragons Trilogy*

Edited by Joanne Biscoff
Cover by Samantha Fury of Fury Cover Designs
ISBN 979-8-9854789-5-2

Chapter One

Stella stared at the text, her thumbs hovering over the screen in indecision. A simple *Have fun. I love you,* from her fiancé should be the most natural message in the world to respond to. But guilt at what she'd done—or rather hadn't done—ate at her.

"Hey, Stella, come look at this view!" Wendy called to her.

Without responding to the text, Stella locked the screen and slid the phone into her pocket. She'd handle it later. Right now, her friends deserved her sole focus. She jogged to where Wendy absorbed the ocean view.

Stella leaned against the cruise ship's pristine top railing, stretching her arms wide and grinning. "Hello, vacation." She'd needed this for so long.

The sun beat down hot as the *Comfort* drifted from the Seattle shore. Party music emanated from the pool area below them, along with cheers at the blast of a horn.

"Come on, ladies, let's take a selfie." Stella waved her two best friends to the front of the boat.

Wendy readily complied, but Claire seemed lost in her own world. Stella stifled a giggle as Wendy's curly chestnut hair whipped her face from every direction.

"I swear," her friend said while batting curls out of her eyes and pulling a strand from her mouth, "wind is overrated." But once Wendy found her place next to Stella, the breeze hit just right, blowing all the offending strands over her shoulder, and setting them up for the perfect shot.

Stella laid her head on her friend's shoulder. "Thanks for this trip."

This fifteen-day bachelorette getaway Wendy had organized and funded for her was more than generous. There was nothing Stella wanted more in this moment than carefree time away with her friends.

Stella snapped a picture of the two of them, then called Claire over again. But Claire didn't budge.

Wendy joined in. "Come on, Claire. Quit scoping out cute guys and take a picture with us."

Claire pulled her attention from her perusal of the pool deck below, tucked a strand of her auburn hair behind her ear, and sauntered over. "Happy last hurrah before your big day, Stells."

She scooted in on the other side of Stella, dropped her oversized white sunglasses an inch down her nose, and angled her ginormous sun hat to the right. Stella reached her arm out as far as it could go but couldn't get all three of them fully in the shot. She lowered the phone camera an inch. No, that was worse. She raised it three inches. Better, except now their arms looked huge. And the way the sun glinted on her fair skin and hair made her look washed out.

Claire sighed. "No, you have to …" Claire tried to maneuver Stella's arm to the correct angle. "Actually, just let me take it." She reached into her bag.

Stella readjusted slightly down and to the right. "There. I think I have it."

"Yeah, that's great," Wendy said holding her pose.

But Claire was already pulling out her phone. Thrusting her phone in front of them, she bumped Stella's arm. Stella's phone fumbled and fell from her grasp, crashing onto the deck and sliding across a freshly mopped section of flooring.

After a gasp in unison, all three of them scrambled after it as it slipped under a table and past a lounge chair toward the edge of the railing.

"Oh no." Stella lunged for it, bumping one bystander's arm and nearly tripping another.

She strained her fingertips as the device teetered precariously on the ledge. At the slightest touch, the balance tipped, and it careened downward several flights until it clanked against a railing far below, where it busted, splaying what looked like little pieces of metal confetti before plunking into the ocean.

Stella's gaze snapped to her friends' horrified faces. Wendy gripped her stomach as if she were going to be sick.

Claire's hand covered her mouth, her face pale. "Oh my gosh, I'm *so* sorry."

Stella looked overboard again to the spot where her phone had disappeared. She waited for her stomach to sink. Waited for panic to rise. Yet the feeling that ambushed her senses was … relief. Her shoulders relaxed.

She was free.

Claire wrapped her in a hug. "I feel horrible. I'll make it up to you. I'll buy you a new phone when we get to Hawaii."

Stella shook her head. "Wouldn't that be crazy expensive? Besides, there's no way I'd want to waste a beach day at a cell phone store."

"But how are you going to get by without it?"

"I didn't buy onboard Wi-Fi anyway. Everett was aware I'd be out of contact once we got out to sea." She shrugged.

Claire needed social media to build her business. Her YouTube sensation friend wouldn't understand how being without technology could be cathartic. But for Stella? What a relief to be completely untethered from her boss. No need to send vague replies to his cringy texts. No need to politely remind him she was on vacation. The only downside was not being able to text Everett one last time before they went off-grid and then connecting with him again at ports. But she could always borrow one of her friends' phones to shoot a quick text.

"It'll be fine. Really."

Her friends exchanged a worried look with each other, and Wendy wrung her hands, but at least neither lost their lunch over the ordeal.

She took a deep breath of salty air and smiled. "You ready to take that selfie, Claire? Only let's do it sitting on that couch over there." She pointed to a cushion-lined wicker sofa a safe distance from any railings.

Claire tilted her head. "You sure?"

"Absolutely."

After more than a dozen pictures of several different poses, they were back to laughing, the incident seemingly forgotten. When Claire tucked her phone away, the trio stood.

Stella swept in between her friends, wrapping an arm around both their shoulders as she guided them toward the elevator. "This trip is going to be perfect, ladies. I've been looking forward to spending time with my two favorite people for months." She gave them a squeeze. "I've missed you this past year."

Claire scrunched her nose. "Gosh, yeah. It has been that long, eh?"

Two years since college graduation. One year since they'd converged in Kansas City to celebrate surviving as adults. Stella adjusted Claire's twisted pink bikini strap for her, then slid the matching cover-up over her shoulder. "You know what they say."

"Time flies when you're having fun." Claire grinned.

She shrugged. "If you can call it that."

Claire may have had one killer of a time, but Stella had been trudging through mud, counting down the days until this trip and then until her new start with Everett. A fresh beginning after her grandma's diagnosis, decline, and death, and after a bumpy start at her new job.

"Where are we going?" Claire cast a glance behind her to the sparsely populated lounge chair–strewn deck. "I wanted to work on my tan."

Stella stepped forward, engaging the automatic door to the interior. "There'll be plenty of time for that. I'm hungry."

"I hope they have salad." Claire scrunched her nose. "I'm not about to gain five pounds on this trip."

Wendy patted her stomach. "I'm fully prepared to gain ten."

"Seriously?" Claire frowned. "You won't be able to fit into your bridesmaid dress."

Stella smiled. "That's why I scheduled alterations for after the trip."

Stella pushed the down button for the elevator and studied the map of the boat while they waited. It would take her a while to find her way around. Even though this was one of the smaller cruise ships, as a first-time cruiser, the layout intimidated her.

"Hey, what happened to the thirteenth floor?" She pointed to the floor listings as Wendy came to look. "We're on floor fourteen right now, and then it skips to twelve. There's no thirteen."

"Hmm. Strange."

"With my luck, that's where I'll end up. Murphy's Law and all." Claire tucked her sunglasses on top of her head. "You'll be wondering where I went, and I'll be wandering around the unlucky thirteenth floor."

Stella rolled her eyes. "Would you stop? There's no such thing as luck. You know that."

No luck and no coincidences. All three of them believed that, didn't they? They'd bonded in college over their Christian faith. Women with three completely different majors who wouldn't normally mingle in the same circles, but at the campus Bible study, they'd found a sisterhood.

The elevator finally pinged and opened, and the three friends slid inside. Wendy pushed the down button to take them from viewing the pool from above to dining beside it. "Don't worry about a thing. Let's just enjoy this time together."

Stella would toast to that. Having time to connect with these people who loved her despite her flaws was like a cool drink of water on a scorching hot day.

The elevator opened, and the scents of grilled onions and cumin from tacos and burgers tangoed in the air. Sunlight shimmered off the pool. Perfect. Forget luck. Forget Murphy and his law. Freed from all contact with her life back home, this was going to be the best vacation of her life.

~

With a plate overloaded with tacos, Wendy maneuvered through a sea of people in various states of dress—from swimsuits to one man in a three-piece suit—toward the poolside table Stella had commandeered. Her best friend was already scarfing down a burger, apparently with no thought of her fitted wedding dress. Good. At least the two of them would fully enjoy their girls' trip while Miss Health Nut nibbled on rabbit food.

A glob of ketchup dripped onto Stella's sleek black cover-up. Well, at least it added some color. Wendy was no fashion expert, but even she could tell when someone with bleached blonde hair and eyelashes so light they were nearly nonexistent without mascara wore black, it only accentuated their pale features. Hence, why Wendy had chosen mint green for the color of the shirts she'd purchased for the three of them to wear on their first day at sea tomorrow. Never mind she'd look ghastly in it. This trip was about Stella, and she'd endure looking like an Easter egg if it gave her bestie a chance to shine. Claire? Well, Claire would look good wrapped in brown paper. The brat.

Speaking of which … Claire stood a few feet away from their table, salad bowl in hand, chatting with a hunk of a shirtless guy. Wendy slowed as she neared so she could catch their conversation.

The man shook his head as though puzzled. "No, that's not it. But I swear I know you from somewhere." His eyes lit, and he pointed at Claire. "Oh wait, you're the yoga girl from YouTube!"

Claire's coy smile didn't fool Wendy. Her friend was likely shuddering on the inside from the man's blunder.

"Pilates, but yes. I have the Claire-ity Fitness Channel. I'm surprised you recognized me without my mat."

Wendy couldn't walk any slower without being uber awkward, so she passed the flirty couple and sat across from Stella, who'd already devoured half of her burger.

"Good?" Wendy stole a fry from her friend's plate.

Stella swallowed before answering. "Excellent."

Wendy hadn't taken more than a bite of her first taco when Claire plopped into the seat next to her with a huff. "What? Things go south with Mr. Hunk-o-licious over there?"

"Yes! And here I thought we had some sort of connection. Then he says, 'Oh, my girlfriend loves your channel.'" She wagged her head while mocking his voice. "And said girlfriend sidles up wearing a white bikini. Apparently, my workouts have done her good." She shrugged. "At least he recognized me. Even if he can't tell the difference between yoga and Pilates."

Wendy nudged Claire playfully with her shoulder. "I keep telling you that a cruise is not the place to find the man of your dreams. I know you're eager to find Mr. Right. I am too. But …" She let the sentence hang.

Surely, Claire could fill in the rest. *This trip isn't about us. It's about celebrating Stella.* Their time would come. Maybe one of Claire's other five hundred thousand YouTube followers would hunt her down and propose on the spot. She nearly snorted at the thought.

"It doesn't hurt to look." Claire forked leafy greens into her mouth.

Stella pointed a fry at her. "It might. What would happen if you did hit it off with someone? What are the chances he'd be from Indiana? Or even the Midwest?"

"I'd move in a heartbeat for the right person."

"Just so you didn't have to hear the song?" Stella's eyes sparkled as her gaze met Wendy's.

"Don't you dare." Claire's mouth firmed into a straight line.

Too late to stop them from belting out the song from *The Music Man*. "'Gary, Indiana. Gary, Indiana. Gary, Indiana.'"

Claire slumped low in her chair as her friends sang in unison. "Stop." But playfulness lilted around the edges of her command.

Stella's smile brightened. "Speaking of musicals, isn't there a show one of these nights that features numbers from Broadway? We should go."

Wendy snatched her phone from the table. "Let me find the itinerary." No need for the bride to stress about any of the details. Wendy had pieced the trip together so the only thing her friend had to do was board and bask. "Here it is. Tell me what sounds interesting to you."

The girls went through the activities listed each day and debated about which ones to participate in. When at last Wendy thought they had their schedule locked down, Claire sighed. "I don't know. I thought we'd spend more time relaxing in the sun and less time at shows and the piano bar."

Wendy wrinkled her nose. "Most of the activities are in the evening. You'll have plenty of time to work on your tan."

"I'll probably hit the gym too."

The gym? That was definitely not on her itinerary.

"And I told you I want to film a few videos for my channel, right? When we get to the beaches."

Um, no. She'd failed to mention that. "You just said you wanted to relax. Now you're talking about working while on vacation."

Her expression spoke innocence. "It's not work when you're doing what you love."

Wendy snorted. "Hey, I love my middle schoolers, but let me tell you, teaching is work. A whole lot of stinkin' work." And yes, she needed a vacation. Only not a permanent one. *Lord, please. I can't lose my job.*

Stella nodded. "I love my job too. Seriously, it's been my dream to be the editor of a newspaper. But I'd have to agree. Loving what I do doesn't mean I don't need a break from it."

Wendy's throat burned with the story of what had happened two weeks ago. She did not keep secrets from her best friend. And yet, she couldn't ruin Stella's celebratory trip with her own issues. She swallowed the urge to speak.

Claire shrugged. "To each her own." She took another bite of rabbit food before her eyes sparked with mischief. She leaned in and whispered, "Hey, check out that guy. He's a cutie."

Wendy and Stella both rolled their eyes, but honestly, thank goodness for the distraction. Leave it to Claire to keep things light.

~

Claire forced a smile as she wedged between a mass of people in line for coffee and another exiting the lounge where trivia had just wrapped up. An elbow jabbed her ribs. She winced and glanced behind her. No apology came. She rubbed her side and cast a longing glance toward the sun-kissed deck.

When would they get to the relaxing portion of this vacation? Apparently, the three of them needed to tour every square inch of this massive boat first. She sighed. If her stress level got much higher, it'd seep out her pores and create noxious fumes. Then she'd have zero chance of pretending all was well.

Stella talked over her shoulder as she entered the lounge where the cruise line would host the comedy show in the evenings. "Isn't the retro décor fun? What is it, like 1960s?"

Wendy smirked. "Somebody wasn't a history major."

Claire would have bristled at the remark, but Stella laughed. "No kidding. So, expert, what's the time period?"

Wendy scanned the area. "Looks antebellum to me."

Okay, she was either making up words or showing off. Claire crossed her arms and lifted a brow.

"Pre–Civil War," Wendy explained. "It reminds me of the old steamboats that used to cruise up and down the rivers. I read a book about them once, and I went to a museum featuring one."

Of course, she did.

Claire sucked in her bottom lip and, as she'd done in each room they'd toured so far, surveyed the lighting and angles for possible social media pictures and reels. She hadn't planned on the retro décor of the ship, but she could find a way to make it play. Perhaps she could focus on history. Yes, that was it. The history of Pilates. Of course, the fitness craze didn't date as far back as the horrid décor, but it would make a good conversation starter to discuss the origins dating back to the 1920s.

Her stomach soured. No. It wasn't compelling enough. Not to snatch the attention of Fit TV. She had to come up with something that would wow the producer–and quick. They'd only be watching her social media for one more week to see if they'd take a chance on launching her career. And her first impression last week had been less than impressive.

"Claire?" Stella's voice seemed to echo through Claire's haze of thought.

Her attention snapped to her friends, who stood across the room at the exit. "Sorry." She scurried to catch up.

What was wrong with her? She needed time to think. Or a distraction. They passed the salon, and her steps slowed. A massage. Yes. She needed a massage for the golf ball–sized knots in the back of her neck.

Her gaze fell upon the price list. Yikes. Never mind. This trip had already stretched her budget, and since she still hadn't been able to find a steady job in her major as a dietitian, her YouTube channel provided her only stream of income. For now. But if Fit TV picked her up—no, *when* they slotted her on their channel—everything would change. No more stressing about money. No more striving for every like and share.

"Stop staring at the hunk and come on." An edge of irritation sneaked through Wendy's sassy smile.

The hunk? Claire blinked. *Oh.* Next to the price list hung a billboard featuring a shirtless man with a towel wrapped around his waist. Wendy thought she was gawking at that? She fought the urge to roll her eyes. She'd be the first to admit her piqued interest regarding men, but it wasn't so she could drool over their glistening pecs. Was it so horrible to not want to journey through life alone? To yearn for someone to know her so completely he could finish her sentences and see beyond the exterior to the depths of her heart? She was bone tired of going it alone. But whatever. Let Wendy think she was boy crazy. What did it matter? Little Miss Perfect was bent on misunderstanding her.

She forced a saucy grin. "Can't blame a girl for looking."

Wendy scoffed.

The edges of Stella's eyes crinkled with her smile. "We've almost seen everything. Ready for the pool?"

That got Claire moving. She reached her friends in two steps. "Am I ever!"

They passed a candy store, jewelry shop, and art gallery before nearing the elevators that would take them poolside.

"Take a look at that mailbox." Wendy ran her fingers across an old-fashioned mailbox nestled into the corner across from the elevators.

"Wow. It fits the décor perfectly," Stella mused.

The arched doorway leading from the corridor to the deck outside of where they stood would make a great photo backdrop. It was wide enough to do wall Pilates moves on if she could find an opportune time with little to no foot traffic and decent lighting.

Behind her, Wendy and Stella went on about the mailbox. "I think it's real. Like an antique."

Seriously, who cared? The pool was calling! "Come on, ladies."

But Wendy's attention didn't waver. "Hold on. There's an inscription."

This time, Claire didn't fight the eye roll.

"I was right." Wendy flashed a smile as if she'd won the lottery before turning her attention back to the old mailbox. "This postal box was in use in the 1800s. How cool is that?"

Claire utilized a controlled breath before replying. "Super cool." Just not as cool as glistening water and the sun's caress.

Stella cocked her head. "Kind of odd. The placement of it by the elevators." She peeked inside, then yanked her hand back. "Yikes. I got a shock."

"You okay?" Wendy asked.

"Yeah. It was nothing."

Claire cleared her throat and took a step toward the elevator.

Wendy let out an exasperated sigh. "Okay, okay. We're coming."

Stella laughed. "Guess we won't take you antique treasure hunting."

"Yeah, I'll sit that one out."

Wendy lifted a brow. "Sit it out? Or will you pass for an hour on a Peloton?"

"They have those here?" The gym was the only area of the ship they hadn't toured.

"Ugh. You!" Wendy bumped her shoulder good-naturedly.

But seriously, did the gym have Pelotons? Because Fit TV made it clear they were only interested in people in peak physical condition. She couldn't afford even a half inch to creep up on her midriff.

Stella hit the up button for the elevator, and they waited to the sound of the mechanical whir. "What floor again?"

"Thirteen," Wendy and Claire joked simultaneously. Their chuckles blended with the ding of the door opening.

"Guys, seriously."

"Four," they said again in unison.

The corner of Wendy's mouth lifted. "Great minds think alike."

Only they didn't. Not at all.

Chapter Two

The next day, Wendy stepped out of the bathroom wearing her navy one-piece bathing suit, her arms smeared with sunscreen. "Can you get my back?"

"Sure." Claire strode forward, palm held out for a squirt.

Wendy had been talking to Stella, but her bestie sat on the bed, fingers flying rapidly across the phone's keyboard. Since it was Claire's fault Stella's phone had gone overboard, Claire had offered to let Stella use her phone for a while. Claire would have to do as a sunscreen buddy.

When had the dynamics between them shifted? Stella had always been the glue that held their friend group together. Wendy was friends with Stella. Claire was friends with Stella. Therefore, Wendy and Claire were friends by extension. If not for Stella, it was unlikely Wendy and Claire would cruise together.

Although that had always been the case, Claire and Wendy had gotten along much better in college, hadn't they? Wendy couldn't remember their friendship ever requiring such effort. They'd met at the campus Bible study, but their camaraderie hadn't been confined to Wednesday nights in the chapel. The next year, they'd roomed together, and it had gone well. Late nights of laughter and genuine conversation.

Wendy shivered as Claire rubbed the cold cream onto her shoulders.

Had Claire been this shallow then? Or had her obsession with her YouTube channel taken her down a more worldly path? Wendy's mouth twisted as she considered this. Claire had always been boy crazy. Fond of makeup, manicures, and hair styles. But her insights into Scripture had proven profound. She'd had depth—at least back then—hidden beneath layers of fluff. That was what had attracted Wendy to the friendship in the first place. But she couldn't see it now. All she could make out was a pretty face, perfectly sculpted abs, and a driving desire to make it big as a YouTube sensation. Was the friend she had found years ago still in there?

"There you go." Claire patted her moisturized shoulder. "Will you do mine?"

"Yeah. Turn around." She squeezed a blob of sunscreen on her palm and began to rub Claire's well-toned back. "Did we decide if we're going to lounge by the pool or on the top deck?"

Stella looked up from the phone, golden feather earrings dangling. "The pool looked pretty crowded when we passed by after brunch."

"Yeah. I vote for top deck." Claire rolled her head from side to side. Her shoulder muscles were tight beneath Wendy's fingers.

Stella sighed. "A text came through from Everett, but when I tried to text him back, I couldn't get a signal."

Wendy winced. She should have paid for at-sea Wi-Fi for the three of them, but the trip had already cost a pretty penny, and with her job hanging precariously in the balance …

Claire tilted her head. "I purchased Wi-Fi service. I wonder why it's not going through."

Wendy's circular motions on Claire's back slowed. She'd bought her own Wi-Fi? Why? So she could keep up with her Claire-ity Channel and the social media she obsessed over? Irritation rose within her. This trip was for Stella, and their friend deserved their undivided attention.

"It's fine. He knew I wouldn't be able to communicate during the trip, and it's not an emergency."

Claire shrugged. "Okay. Let me know if you want me to look at it. Maybe it's not connected correctly."

"Finished." Wendy's pat to Claire's back sounded more like a slap. Oops. Harder than she'd intended. "You ladies ready?"

"Yep." Stella rose. "Let me grab my bag."

Stella went to hand the phone to Claire, but Claire shook her head. "Keep it for a while. I'll get it back when I find something worthy of posting."

Stella wore a cute floral sundress over her bathing suit while Claire wore a stringy black cover-up that did little to cover up. Wendy pulled her maroon cotton cover-up from the bathroom hook and slipped it on. "Let's go."

The three of them made their way to the elevators, chatting about the comedy show last night. Several other people waited for the elevator as well, and the friends crowded on.

Stella's fingers grazed her ear. "My earring. I lost an earring."

A woman in front spoke up. "I saw a dangly gold earring down the hall a ways. I put it on the side table in the B foyer."

"That has to be mine." Stella shouldered past a couple to get off. "Excuse me, please."

Wendy and Claire moved to follow, but Stella waved them off. "Go ahead. I'll meet you there. Floor fourteen."

She stepped off, and the elevator closed.

Wedged in the back, Wendy stood stiffly as the elevator stopped at every floor—save the nonexistent thirteenth—before opening to the top deck. She and Claire spilled out into the foyer. She gaped out the window.

What a gorgeous day. Picture perfect. Only a few puffy white clouds dotted the bright blue sky. The lap of gentle waves crested to her ears. The swirl of a soft breeze. Oh yeah. Sunbathing on the deck would be paradise. Once Stella got there.

"Should we grab chairs?" Claire stepped toward the deck. Couldn't she wait even a minute for her friend?

"You go ahead. I'll wait here for Stella."

Claire adjusted the bag on her shoulder. "No, it's fine. I'll wait too."

Only it didn't look fine. She shifted her weight from foot to foot, impatience emanating from her like heat off the deck.

The elevator dinged, and a flood of people streamed off. Wendy scanned each face, but Stella wasn't among them. Wendy bit her lip. "Hopefully, she found her earring okay."

"I have a similar pair she can have if she didn't." Claire's flippant tone grated.

"Those earrings were from her grandmother. The one who just passed away. They're irreplaceable."

"Oh." Now she had the nerve to sound hurt, as if Wendy had done something wrong.

The elevator opened a second time, but again, no Stella.

Claire sidled up next to Wendy. "It was a beautiful funeral, wasn't it? Her grandma's?"

Her stomach wobbled. She *so* didn't want to talk about this. "Yeah."

"And Stella's poem." Claire put a hand over her heart. "Powerful."

"For sure."

She glanced around, as if Stella could have snuck by without them noticing. She needed a change of subject. Something. Anything. "How's your YouTube channel going?"

"Fine. Great." Claire's smile looked forced.

Is that all Claire was going to say about her absolute favorite topic? Apparently, because minutes of awkward silence followed.

More people exited the elevator, and still no sign of their friend.

Wendy sighed. "What's taking Stella so long?" There was only so much of Claire she could take by herself.

Claire shifted her weight. "Maybe she went back to the room for something."

Wendy checked her phone, even though she knew a text likely wouldn't go through. Unlike Claire, she hadn't purchased onboard Wi-Fi. "She might have gotten lost."

"But she knew we were coming to the fourteenth floor. She said as much."

"True."

So where was Stella?

~

Stella stepped onto the elevator, pressing the send button on her text to Everett. From the looks of it, she still didn't have service. It wasn't a big deal, really. She'd only texted *I love you, too*, and he knew that already. Of course, he did. They were getting married next month for goodness' sake. But the drive to enhance her text with pledges of love and loyalty pressed upon her.

Everett didn't know about the comments her boss had made or her subsequent silence. If she had it her way, he'd never know how she'd thrown him under the bus. But if he did find out—*Oh, Lord, please don't let him find out*—she needed him to understand that she *did* love him. She was just afraid. And she wasn't sure she'd ever overcome this monster of fear.

"Fourteen," she said without looking up from her phone. She rechecked the connection settings until silence wrapped itself around her. Why wasn't the elevator moving? A glance up and she had her answer. She was the only one on the elevator. Odd with as crowded as the lobby had been. When she hit the button for the top floor, static electricity zapped her finger. Strange. She returned her attention to Claire's phone. Maybe if she tried a messenger app instead of text. But no. Still an error message.

A jolt shook the elevator. Stella yelped. What in the world? But the elevator kept moving. Her shoulders relaxed. Thank God she wasn't stuck on the elevator. What a nightmare that would be. A soft ding announced her safe arrival. Maybe now the text would go through.

She pressed the send button with more urgency–as if that would help–and nearly collided with a woman. Stella stumbled back, her breath catching in her throat.

"Pardon me." The woman's delicate teacup clinked against the saucer in her hands. Her long blue dress billowed around her ankles. As she took Stella in, her eyes widened, and her mouth parted. Color rose in her cheeks.

Stella gaped. "Sorry. My fault. I wasn't looking where I was going." She must have pushed the button for the wrong floor. This wasn't the top deck. Wherever she'd accidentally chosen must have a costume party in progress. She scanned the room and its costumed participants. Men in suits and suspenders sat at tables, puffing on cigars, and playing cards at one side of the room. Women wearing large hats and dresses with high necklines sat at the other side of the room, sipping from teacups and talking. Had they toured this floor? The décor was similar to what she'd seen earlier, but not exact. The room certainly wasn't as wide as the lounges they'd toured, and the lighting was much dimmer.

One by one, people took notice of her, gesturing to those sitting beside them with soft gasps. Everyone stilled and stared at her for a moment as if she was on center stage with a spotlight trained on her. It was obvious she hadn't been invited to this party. She attempted a smile, and hushed conversations resumed, though glances continued to flash in her direction.

The woman blinked back at her, still looking flushed. Was it because the poor girl wore a long-sleeved, high-collared dress on a stiflingly hot summer day? Or perhaps it had more to do with Stella's attire. She looked at her sundress. It matched the woman's gown in length but definitely not in style, and the slit down the side would have been scandalous in that time period. "Oh, I'm not dressed for this."

"Indeed." Her brow furrowed. "Did you purchase deck passage?"

Deck passage? Stella stepped backward. "Uh, I meant to go to the top deck."

"The hurricane deck?"

Is that what it was called? "Yes."

"The stairs are bow side." She pointed warily to the front of the boat while raking her gaze up and down Stella with pursed lips.

"Oh, I'll just take the elevator." She turned in the direction she'd come from, but there were no elevators. Only a wall. She must have been really distracted when she got off and wandered farther than she thought. A strained giggle clamored out of her mouth. She turned back to the lady. "Where are the elevators?"

The woman tilted her head, squinting. "Elevators?"

Stella forced a swallow down her dry throat. Which direction was the café? She could use a cool drink. She took a few steps, looking around for anything familiar, anything to show her how to get back to where she needed to be. But each direction she peered in left her more confused. Her knees wobbled.

The woman stepped to her side, placing a hand on her elbow and eyeing where the slit revealed Stella's leg. "Let me fetch the steward for you. You look unwell." She guided Stella to an ornate, plush chair and motioned for her to sit. "I'll only be a moment."

Man, these people did an excellent job staying in character. Were they part of the Broadway show? If so, it was sure to be entertaining.

Sweat beaded at the back of Stella's neck, and she waved her hand in front of her face, suddenly warm despite the cool temperature of the room. She looked again at the wall where the elevators should be. Strange.

In the corner, she caught a glimpse of the antique mailbox. Oh, thank God. She thought she'd been going crazy for a moment there. At least that was something familiar. But wait … Wasn't the mailbox next to the elevators? And she'd been on the floor with the mailbox. The sixth floor, right?

But she most certainly hadn't been on this floor before. Goosebumps prickled her skin. Was there more than one mailbox?

A moment later, the woman returned with a man in a black suit and tie. His dark skin reminded her of Everett, a familiarity that comforted.

"How can I help you, miss?" Though he directed his question to her, he didn't bring his gaze up to meet hers. Was he shy, or had she embarrassed herself more than she realized by crashing this party?

She smiled to put him at ease. "I need to get to the top deck. I seem to have gotten turned around."

"By all means. I'll direct you to the hurricane deck."

She stood and followed the man, who was perhaps an inch shorter than she, through the gaudily carpeted room. She prepared herself for a burst of hot air as they stepped outside, but instead a cool breeze greeted her. How strange. He gestured to a set of stairs.

"Right up there, miss."

She looked up the dozen steps, then back to him. "Only one level?"

"Yes, ma'am. You were on the boiler deck." He shifted his stance. "You did purchase first-class passage, didn't you, ma'am? You have a stateroom?"

Her mind stumbled over his words before finding its footing. "A room? Yes. Room 1113."

"Very good." His brow wrinkled, but he bowed, then disappeared.

Man, she was out of it. She must have gone to the twelfth floor. Or—she chuckled at the thought—maybe *that* was the thirteenth floor Claire had talked about. Down one level from the top deck. Everyone played their part perfectly. What a trip.

She ascended the dozen or so steps while rehearsing the story she'd have to tell Wendy and Claire, but when she reached the top, her stomach plummeted.

She was at the top of the boat all right, but instead of the ocean as far as the eye could see, there was a flowing river and a muddy riverbank.

~

Claire lowered the lounge chair head and flipped from her back to her stomach, soaking in the sun.

Next to her, Wendy checked her phone for the fifth time in two minutes. "Okay, I'm officially worried."

"I'm sure she's fine. She must have changed her mind and gone to grab a bite to eat or something." Perhaps Stella needed space from Mother Hen's constant hovering. "Can I borrow your phone?" Claire's hands itched for her own phone, still in Stella's possession. She hadn't checked her socials in over an hour. Was she still trending?

Wendy handed her phone over, lay back for half a second, and then shot up as if ready to spring into action. "We should look for her."

Claire stifled a groan. "She's a grown woman. She can take care of herself." She tapped her fingernails on the lounge chair as she waited for Wendy's snail-paced internet to load. If this cost Wendy in roaming charges, Claire would just have to pay her back. She was desperate. Yes, she continued to trend on Instagram, though she lagged a bit on TikTok. Facebook stats looked decent, but a video would really help boost things.

"What if something happened to her?"

"What's going to happen on a cruise ship? Seriously, stop worrying. This is vacation. If she's hungry, there's a plethora of food at her fingertips. If she's tired, she could be sleeping in our room. If she's bored, she might be reading in the library. Who knows? And if she needs anything, there's a whole staff of people here to help."

"Do you think they'll page her for us?"

Oh. My. Gosh. She would not let up. "Listen to yourself. You're not her mother. She knows where to find us when she's ready. If we go tromping all over the boat, she might come up here looking for us, and we won't be here. If you page her, she'll think it's an emergency. You'll give her a heart attack by making her think something is wrong with Everett."

Wendy snapped her fingers. "Everett. Text Everett and see if he's heard from her."

Claire closed her eyes. "You know she couldn't get ahold of him."

She plopped onto her back and slung her arm over her face. "I hate not being able to do anything."

"Why is this bothering you so much?"

Her voice came out whiny. "This trip was supposed to be perfect for her."

"I'm sure it is."

"No. Nothing is going right."

Claire lifted her head to view the picture-perfect day. "Everything's fine. I'm sure she's having the time of her life." She poked Wendy's arm. "You didn't answer my question. Why do you care so much?"

Wendy let out an exaggerated sigh. "I'm trying to make things up to her."

"What things?"

"Big things."

Talk about cryptic. "Oookay. Well, don't forget to breathe yourself. This is your vacation too."

Wendy huffed. "And don't you forget to work on your tan. Oh wait. You won't. Because all you think about is you, you, you."

The spiteful words smacked Claire in the face. Her mouth parted. That was what Wendy thought of her. Nice to know.

Wendy recoiled. "Sorry, Claire. I didn't mean it. I'm stressed. I—"

Claire put her hand out to stop the excuses. "I, uh, think I'll go check our room for Stella." She stood and grabbed her bag before her stinging eyes could betray her with tears.

"Claire, I'm sorry." Wendy rose and put a hand on her shoulder, but she shrugged it off.

She needed to find Stella before she was forced to spend any more time alone with Wendy.

Chapter Three

Stella opened bleary eyes to a bright blue sky. A cool breeze tousled a strand of her blonde hair across her face. She exhaled. Right. She was on the top deck. Cruising with Wendy and Claire.

"Excuse me, miss." A man's worried face hovered above her, marring her view of the sun-kissed sky.

She startled.

"I sent the steward to fetch the physician. You seem to have had a fainting spell. Are you unwell?"

She squinted up at him, and his details came into focus against the brilliant backdrop. He wore a top hat, wire-rimmed glasses, and a suit with a vest that had some sort of chain attached to the second button. It all came flooding back. The costume party. The disappearing elevators. The river. She groaned. "I'm still dreaming."

"I would advise against succumbing to sleep until Dr. Duncan gets here."

She rubbed her aching temples. "Dunkin'? Like the donuts?"

"Pardon me?" His rigid mustache twitched.

Her dreams were getting stranger the closer she got to her wedding. "Never mind."

She pressed her eyes closed as pain radiated through her head. Stranger and more realistic. How could a dream be so painful? Maybe her imaginary donut doctor could give her an imaginary ibuprofen.

She forced her stiff muscles to propel her upward so she could sit and take in the view. Instead of salty sea air, a fishy smell assaulted her nostrils, along with exhaust. Two towering smokestacks belched out black sooty puffs. The boat moved at a snail's pace past tree-lined riverbanks. An occasional modest house peppered the landscape, smoke billowing from the chimney. A man and two small boys fished from a dock. The scene before her was almost languid. Something seemed to be missing.

What was it? A bird flitted in the air as if looking for a place to land. Telephone poles or wires. That was it. There were none as far as she could see. Were they way out in the boonies?

She stood and walked to the railing, staring down at the murky water. She turned back to Mr. Top Hat. "What river is this?"

"Why, the Missouri, of course." His brow creased. "Perhaps you should lie back down."

She shook her head and opened her mouth to ask where they were traveling from and to, but a bell clamored from somewhere close beside her. She stumbled backward and plugged her ears with her fingers. Could a dream make her go deaf? When the horrid ringing stopped, she pulled her hands down. "What was that?"

Mr. Top Hat frowned. "The bell to warn of snags, of course." His tone sounded as if she'd lost her mind.

She nodded. "Yeah. Of course. Snags."

She needed more sleep and less stress. Maybe then she'd have normal dreams about returning to high school or giving a speech naked.

"Ah. Here's Dr. Duncan now."

She turned to see a middle-aged man with a ring of bushy hair surrounding a deeply receded hairline. His striped tie hung askew on his rumpled shirt, and his physician's bag thumped against his thigh with each step. His keen, gray eyes reminded her of boiling water. Something simmered in them, and when they focused on her, she felt more seen than she ever had before.

Mr. Top Hat rushed to Dr. Duncan, pumping his free hand. "I found her lying here on the hurricane deck. I didn't see her faint. No one did. But the steward said he had left her here only moments prior."

"I see. I see." Dr. Duncan set his bag down and motioned to a wooden deck chair. "Would you please sit, Miss …"

She backed into the chair. "Lindy. Stella Lindy."

He smiled in a fatherly way. "Please sit, Miss Lindy." He pulled a stethoscope from his bag. "Who are you traveling with? Should I have the steward fetch your husband?"

She waved him off. "I'm not married yet."

"Is your mother with you? Or another relative or chaperone?" the doctor asked while listening to her lungs.

She shook her head.

Mr. Top Hat shifted his weight. "Highly unusual," he muttered.

"Excuse me?" What, in particular, did he find unusual? Because this whole thing fit into that category for her.

He straightened his suspenders. "It's highly unusual for an unmarried woman to travel unaccompanied."

"I came with my friends. I don't know where they are."

Mr. Top Hat hovered inches from her sweaty head. Dr. Duncan moved the stethoscope to the other side of her back.

If she knew she was dreaming, why couldn't she awaken? She shook her hands in front of her, then slapped her cheek. Hard. "Wake up," she mumbled.

Mr. Top Hat stepped away from her as if she were diseased, then swiped his hat from his head and mopped his forehead. "Does she have it? Is it the traveling sickness again?"

Dr. Duncan straightened. Paused. "Would you excuse us, please, Mr. Simon? Miss Lindy may indeed have the traveling sickness, but in order to make an accurate diagnosis, I'll need to ask questions of a more personal nature."

"Of course. Of course." His mustache twitched again as he replaced his hat and backed toward the stairs.

"Thank you kindly." Dr. Duncan offered a polite nod.

"If you need anything—"

"I'll have Gus fetch you straight away." Dr. Duncan motioned toward the steward, now positioned across the deck, out of earshot.

With a nod, Mr. Top Hat disappeared down the steps.

"Now." Dr. Duncan sat on the deck chair next to her. Propping his elbows on his knees, he laced his fingers together. "Can you tell me precisely what happened, Miss Lindy?"

She shaded her hand over her eyes against the sun's glare. "I was supposed to meet my two friends on the fourteenth floor, but I must have pressed the wrong button on the elevator. I ended up at some costume party on a riverboat, and the elevators disappeared."

His eyes narrowed, the intensity in them a contrast to the relaxed atmosphere on the boat. "May I ask what year you were born?"

"In 2000."

He puffed out his cheeks. "And the boat you hailed from, it had fourteen floors, you say?"

"The cruise ship? Yes. Fourteen."

"Mr. Simon guessed correctly."

"The traveling sickness?"

He pulled a handkerchief from his breast pocket and dabbed his forehead. "'Tis not a sickness, but that's what I call it for the benefit of the other passengers. I've seen only one other case on the Missouri River but half a dozen on the Mississippi."

"So, this traveling not-sickness gives you weird dreams?" She chuckled to herself.

"You're not dreaming. You're time-sailing. The year 1856 called to you across the waters, across the years, and you answered."

How could she not snicker at that? "The year 1856? It called to me?" Her shoulders shook with her laughter.

Dr. Duncan didn't so much as crack a smile. "Yes. And you answered. You're here."

"Here?" She pointed to her hard wooden chair. "You're telling me I'm in the year 1856?"

He put a glass thermometer under her tongue. "Yes. The dizziness and headache should remedy themselves momentarily." He frowned at her dress. "We'll have to fetch you more appropriate attire."

"Because this"—she gestured to his suit, speaking around the thermometer—"isn't a costume party. It's how people dress. In 1856."

She studied her slitted floral sundress. Her scandalous sundress. Wait, was she actually going along with this nonsense? She needed to wake herself. She pinched her forearm. Nothing but pain.

He removed the thermometer and studied it, then placed it back into his bag. He stood and consulted a pocket watch. "Your stateroom should be ready for you now, but it will have items from your other time in there, not items appropriate for this time. We'll have to search for what you need among the cargo. Secretly, of course." He ran a hand through his tufts of hair, making them stand on end. "I'll elicit McDonald's help."

She quirked a brow. "McDonald's? Like the restaurant?"

He threaded his hands together behind his back and rocked onto his heels, ignoring her question. "McDonald is Irish, but we can trust him."

"Okay, you lost me at stateroom."

"Yes, your stateroom. Go there now and change into the most modest frock you have in your possession. At sunset, meet me on the boiler deck outside your back door, lantern trimmed."

She squinted back at him. "You want me to what?"

He exhaled slowly. "Go to your stateroom—"

"What stateroom? How would I have a room on a boat I've never been on?"

"You told the steward your room was 1113. I assume that was your room number in your other time. Your room number in this time should be 13. Check your bag for the key."

Her bag? Her gaze fell to the bag at her feet that she'd brought with her into the elevator. She thrust her hand inside and heavy, cool metal grazed her palm. Seriously? She pulled out a brass skeleton key and turned it in her hand. "Go to my stateroom," she whispered.

Dr. Duncan's voice gentled. "Change into a modest frock."

"A dress. A long one." Had she packed any other ankle-length dresses? She couldn't remember. "Then … something about a light?"

"Meet me on the boiler deck with a trimmed lantern."

"That's like a candle?"

He patted her shoulder. "Do your best." Bag in hand, he stepped toward the stairs but turned. "It was nice to meet you, Miss Lindy. You must be special to be chosen as a time sailor."

She jumped up and moved toward him, tucking a windswept strand of bleached blonde hair behind her ear. "Dr. Duncan, why would 1856 call me? Why me?"

His smile held a smidge of playfulness. "I wager we'll find out soon."

~

Wendy wrung her hands as she maneuvered through the fourth floor, her eyes sweeping every inch for a glimpse of Stella. *Lord, please! Help me find her.* After Claire had left the top deck for who knows where—taking Wendy's phone with her, the brat—Wendy had checked their cabin first, but there'd been no sign Stella had returned. From there, she'd started with the stern end of the first floor and searched the right side, then the left. Followed by the second floor, and now the third. She'd make her way through all fourteen stories if she had to. She would have tried texting too, despite the poor cell service, if only she'd had her phone.

She suppressed fears of worst-case scenarios like sex trafficking and serial killers and checked her watch. It'd only been two hours. Not the lifetime it seemed like. She'd find Stella somewhere ridiculous like the candy store or casino—the most un-Stella-like place of all—and they'd hug and laugh about doing crazy things before leaping into marriage. It'd make for a great story to tell someday when her stomach wasn't in knots.

But if she didn't find her, what then? Her teeth chattered as she thought about news stories she'd read. She'd have to go to guest services and report her friend missing. They'd page her on the intercom, then search the boat themselves. They'd review security cameras, call the coast guard. Sweep the ocean for her dead body.

Heavens, no. No, no, no.

She couldn't allow her mind to go there.

She had to plow ahead. Keep searching until she found her best friend. And she would find her. She would.

Things got trickier on the fourth floor when, instead of rows of cabins, she stepped into a mass of humanity lounging around the pool and weaving around the food vendors. Stella's near-white hair would make her stand out in a crowd, but looking for her in this muddle of shifting humanity felt a bit like playing "Where's Waldo". Stella was never loud. Never brash like Wendy. Never pretentious like Claire. How easily she could fade into the background.

With no sign of her around the pool, among tables, or in lines, Wendy continued through the air-conditioned cafeteria. Her steps were slow and careful, her gaze roaming every inch in much the same way she approached word searches, systematically going from left to right, line by line, hunting for the word's first letter.

Her gaze snagged on something on the deck to her right. Not Stella's pale blonde hair, but a familiar brunette with red highlights. Claire. Wendy stepped closer to the window, and her jaw dropped. Claire on her yoga mat? Doing Pilates? And … Wendy's gut churned as her eyes zeroed in on that blasted phone screen. *Her* phone screen. Claire had stormed off with Wendy's phone and used it to film a video for her channel? The nerve!

While Wendy was frantically searching for *their* friend, Claire was focusing on likes and shares? Any remorse Wendy had felt for calling Claire out on her selfishness burned in the fire of her indignation. How could anyone be so self-serving?

Wendy marched to the side door, inches from where Claire lay pumping her perfectly sculpted arms, and flung it open. "What do you think you're doing?"

Claire's eyes widened, and her body froze in a crunch. Then she turned her head and smiled at the camera. "And exhale. Now, turn to your left side—"

"Are you kidding me?" Wendy could nearly feel the vein bulging from her temple.

"We're going to do leg circles. I want you to concentrate on—"

"For the love, Claire! Stop it!" Wendy swatted at the mini tripod that held the phone, causing it to topple to the deck.

Claire scrambled for it. "What's wrong with you? Now I have to start over."

Oh, she could scratch Yoga Girl's eyes out. Her ears burned hot. Fury laced her words. "Poor baby. You have to redo your video. By all means, do that while I continue to search for our missing friend!"

"She's fine, Wendy." But Claire's admonition lacked its previous confidence. Her lips trembled. "I'm sure she's fine."

"She's been gone for two hours."

"I know." Claire's voice dropped to a whisper. Still on her mat, she wrapped her arms around her knees. "I looked for her on the serenity deck, at the salon, the coffee shop, and the pool. I quickly realized it's going to be nearly impossible to find her with so many people. We're going to have to wait for her to show up."

Wendy rolled her eyes. "And in the meantime, you'll get a video in? Give me my phone back." She held her hand out.

Claire handed it over. "Staying busy helps me not to worry."

Something in Claire's eyes gave Wendy's judgment pause. She *had* searched those popular areas. Plus, her words made sense. Wendy often buried herself in grading and lesson planning whenever something stressful loomed. A niggle of guilt wedged itself under her ribs. She shifted her weight to dislodge it. "You could stay busy by helping me look for Stella."

Claire's frown transformed into more of a scowl. "Forgive me, but I'm not super eager to spend buddy-buddy time with someone who hates my guts."

Wendy stepped back. "I don't hate you, Claire." Sure, they didn't see eye to eye, and they got on each other's nerves, but hate? "You're my friend."

"Yeah, sure." She gestured toward the toppled tripod. "That's how friends treat each other."

Her stomach twisted. Apparently, she didn't know how friends treated each other. That was why she was here, wasn't it? To make things up to Stella. A kind of penance for letting her friend down, for not being who Stella had needed her to be when she'd needed her. Only she couldn't exactly do that if Stella wound up kidnapped.

Wendy dropped down and sat cross-legged next to Claire on her mat. "I'm sorry. I suck at this friendship thing."

Claire shook her head. "You're a good friend to Stella."

If only.

For a few moments, they looked out over the lapping waters. Wendy picked at her cuticle. "What if she went overboard?" Her throat tightened around the last word.

Claire put her hand on Wendy's, stilling her anxious movement. "Unlikely. I'm pretty sure most cases of people going overboard on cruises occur when the person's intoxicated. That's not the case with Stella."

"True." Her eyes filled with tears. So unlike her. "Should we alert customer service? Or keep looking ourselves?"

Claire pressed her lips together. "Have you tried showing people her picture and asking if they've seen her?"

Wendy straightened. "No. I hadn't thought of that." Not that she could have done so without her phone anyway.

"Let's do it. We could split up. If you emailed a picture to yourself and printed it off at the printing station—"

"No." Wendy squeezed Claire's hand. "Let's stick together." Something strange was going on. Better to be safe and not lose anyone else. Not even exasperating Claire.

~

Claire ascended the last stair, drained of all but a few drops of hope. They'd searched every floor, flashing Wendy's phone in front of passengers' faces, asking if they'd seen the woman in the picture. A few said they had, but when they'd talked further, the sightings were from the day before. Not helpful.

Had their friend finally made it to the top deck?

They'd agreed if Stella wasn't there, they'd march straight to customer service and report her as a missing person. When Wendy had used the restroom, Claire had borrowed her phone to search news stories of disappearances on cruise ships. Not a good move. Most searches proved inconclusive. Sometimes, dead bodies were found in the water. Sometimes, law enforcement found nothing at all. She didn't read about any happy endings.

They emerged into the blinding sunlight of what should have been a picture-perfect day. Claire slid her sunglasses on as she and Wendy approached a couple sunbathing.

Wendy smiled sweetly. "Excuse me, I hate to bother you, but can you tell me if you've seen this woman?" She held the phone out.

The couple gave it a cursory glance.

"No. Can't say I have," the man said.

The woman shook her head.

"Thanks anyway," Wendy said.

Used to such answers by now, they moved toward the next group, but a man in khaki slacks and a loose white button-down that billowed in the breeze stepped to them. His gray eyes seemed as fathomless as the ocean around them. "Excuse me. You're looking for someone?"

Claire's heart leapt. "Yes."

Wendy thrust her phone at him to show a picture of Stella right before she boarded the ship. "Her. Have you seen her?"

He put out his hands. "No, no."

Her heart sank.

"But I might know what happened."

"What?" Wendy and Claire asked in unison.

The man looked around, then leaned forward, voice low. "Perhaps we can talk somewhere more private." He nodded toward the front of the boat, which was empty of passengers.

Wendy moved to follow him.

Claire clutched Wendy's arm.

Wendy's gaze snapped to hers, and she mouthed *What?*

Claire whispered in Wendy's ear, "What if the guy's a psycho? What if he pushed Stella off the boat, and now, he's about to do the same to us?"

Wendy's lips twisted as she looked at the man who'd stopped several strides ahead of them. He stood waiting with his hands in his pockets. Well-manicured toes peeked out of his sandals. The wind tossed his thinning gray-brown hair in all directions, but he didn't seem to mind. He looked more like a young grandpa than a psycho, but what did a psycho look like?

"We'll stay away from the edge," Wendy whispered. "And be ready to scream and run."

Sure. That sounded like a perfectly safe plan. But she sympathized with the pull in Wendy's eyes. If this man knew what had happened to Stella, how could they not hear him out?

They followed him with cautious steps until they were out of earshot of other passengers, but they didn't dare go near the railing. Just in case.

He withdrew a hand from his pocket and extended it toward Wendy, then Claire. "Allow me to introduce myself. I'm Dr. Rodney Duncan."

"I'm Wendy. That's Claire." Wendy nodded in her direction. "Now what do you know about Stella?"

His gray-speckled eyebrows bunched. "She went missing, you say? Without a trace?"

"Yes." Claire took a step forward. Wendy didn't need to take charge of all conversations. "She was supposed to meet us here hours ago, and she didn't show. We've looked everywhere for her. We're about to report her missing—"

He held up a hand. "You've checked her room?"

Wendy frowned. "Yeah. Of course. We're sharing a room, and it was the first place we looked."

"How long ago?"

"About a half hour after she didn't show. Why?"

Hands once again in his pockets, Dr. Duncan rocked back on his heels. "Check again. If my suspicions are correct, all her things will be gone."

Claire shot a panicked glance to Wendy and inched backward. Lunatic on board.

Wendy, however, cocked her head as if interested. Had she not watched any crime shows? This was the time to get away. "Gone? Like poof. Gone."

He rewarded her skepticism with one curt nod. "The question is not *where* your friend is. It's *when* she is. I've heard of numerous similar occasions, and the time sailor's items always cross waters with them. They're connected on a cellular level."

Claire tried to catch Wendy's gaze with her wide eyes. She nodded toward the doors behind them. Why wouldn't Wendy look at her? They had to get away from this crazy man. Any minute now, he might pull out a weapon. Or a gag. Or a blindfold.

"Time sailors?" Wendy pinched her lips together. "Tell me more about that."

On second thought, maybe Wendy wasn't interested in the Duncan guy's nonsense. She studied him as if memorizing every detail of his face. Perhaps she was absorbing information in case she needed it for a police report. That would be a Wendy thing to do.

"Time sailors cross waters to another time and place when there's a need for them. The mission calls to them across time. When they finish their mission, they cross back over the waters to the present, as long as they're on a boat. It's quite fascinating."

"You think a mission called to Stella?"

"It's possible."

"What mission? Where? Or when?"

"No telling. Were there any causes she was particularly passionate about?"

Wendy finally met Claire's gaze, questioning. For a minute, Claire forgot about the utter lunacy of the moment and racked her brain for a specific cause that mattered to Stella. Her friend was a journalist, and as such, she loved to uncover a good story, but it didn't seem that there was any particular kind of story that mattered more than others. Stella desired to see wrongs made right, but nothing stood out as fuel for her burning heart. Goodness, was she buying into this nonsense? She winced.

"I don't know," Wendy said.

Dr. Duncan sighed. "Then the only way to find out is to ask her."

Claire nearly choked. "Ask her?" Were they on *Candid Camera*? Was this a big joke? "How in the world would we ask her if she's not here?"

He scrubbed at the five o'clock shadow lining his chin. "Using the mailbox, of course."

"The mailbox?" Wendy's brows raised.

"Yes. The antique mailbox located on the sixth floor by the elevators. Drop a letter to her there, and if she responds, you'll have your answer." A small smile broke through his serious demeanor.

"Oh." Claire nodded. "Makes sense." She took giant steps backward and motioned for Wendy to follow. "We'll drop her a line and ask her what year she's in. Thanks for your help."

With a wave, she turned, hooked her arm through Wendy's elbow, and jetted away from the mysterious man.

Chapter Four

Stella's hand trembled as she slid the key into the keyhole of room 13. She glanced over her shoulder again, half expecting to see a burly man scowling at her for trespassing. Her heightened senses told her this wasn't a dream, but how could it not be? The lock clanked as she turned it, then the door swung open. Her breath caught. She stood frozen in the carpeted hallway.

Should she go in? Of course, she should. Why else would she have unlocked the door? But her stomach quivered. What would she find inside? Fear shackled her feet.

"Is there a problem, miss?" An ebony woman in a black dress and white ruffled apron came up behind her, startling her.

"No," Stella croaked. "No problem at all."

The woman offered a tentative smile, revealing one missing tooth on the bottom right and highlighting a small scar to the side of her left eye. "If you need anything, I'm Leela, your chambermaid."

Chambermaid. Sure. Stella nodded.

"The ladies' bath house is bow side, but I've already supplied you with a pitcher of water."

Stella's return smile wobbled as she stepped timidly into room 13, closing the door behind her.

She blinked. Stared. Could this be happening? Was it real? A strained, nervous giggle tumbled up her throat. Upon a single bed sat her modern clothes, folded in neat stacks. Sweatpants, jeans, leggings, and several pairs of shorts. A few knee length skirts. A colorful pile of T-shirts. Her throat burned at the sight of the green one near the bottom. She pulled it free and held it in front of her. In embellished lettering, it said *Cruising with My Besties*. She hugged it to her chest. Wendy had gone to great lengths to make this trip perfect. And now? What in heaven's name was going on?

She refolded the shirt and replaced it on the pile. Right on top of her blue Jayhawks shirt. All three of them had packed their college T-shirts. Her extra swimsuit sat on top of a stack of underwear. Ah, and two longer dresses. Thank goodness. Next to the bed were her tennis shoes as well as a pair of strappy sandals. Her Bible and notebook lay on the bedside table. It looked like the most natural thing until her gaze swept the rest of the room.

A washstand with a porcelain bowl of water and a towel stood in the corner. Another table with a pitcher and teacup were nearby. A small dresser. A plush-looking velvet chair. But no bathroom? Perhaps that was what Leela had meant by "bathhouse." She scrunched her nose as she spotted something sticking out from under the bed. A chamber pot? Gross. As long as the bathhouse contained some semblance of a toilet, she'd keep that pot stowed under the bed. At least the silky scarlet curtains, etched glass windows, and ornately patterned rug gave the room an air of luxury.

How long would this be her reality? Her heart constricted, and she swallowed a wave of panic.

In two long strides, she made it to her bedside table. She sat on the bed, picked up the Bible, and found comfort as the weight of it settled in her hands. Just the feel of the soft leather against her fingers had a calming effect. She thumbed to Psalm 23.

> *The Lord is my shepherd; I shall not want. He makes me to lie down in green pastures; He leads me beside the still waters. He restores my soul.*

It was her favorite passage. Her go-to. A promise of peace and safety—two things she coveted. He would lead her by still waters.

At that moment, a bell sounded, and the boat jolted, nearly knocking her from the bed. What had the man said? A snag? What *was* a snag? She'd landed in a foreign place without knowing the language. It sure didn't seem peaceful. It sure didn't seem safe. The room appeared darker now, yet lively music was suddenly playing from somewhere above. Could this get any stranger?

Lord, help me. Tears pricked her eyelids. *I don't know what I'm doing.*

Voices outside seized her attention. The sound came from behind another door on the opposite side of her room. Surely, it led to the balcony, or boiler deck as Dr. Duncan had called it. She laid her Bible to the side and went to investigate. Hand on the door handle, she hesitated.

The tense voices lowered to a hush. A secret? If she barged out there now, they'd most likely stop talking. Instead, she pressed her ear to the door and strained to hear.

She couldn't make anything out clearly, only snatches of words. *Arms. Weapons. Kansas. War.* She shuddered. What were they planning?

She scoured her brain for everything she'd memorized in her history classes and came up woefully short. If only Wendy, the history expert, were here. At least Stella remembered the Civil War began in 1861, so it hadn't started yet. Were the men outside rumbling about the beginning of the war? Ugh. She should have paid more attention in those classes. She didn't recall anything about Kansas from the units on the Civil War. They'd covered the big battles of Antietam, Shiloh, and Gettysburg. All conflicts that happened far from where she lived and worked. They seemed far removed from her everyday existence.

Oh gosh. Talk about in over her head. She needed to speak to Wendy. Bad. Why couldn't 1856 have called *her*?

The voices faded, and Stella peeked out onto the deck. The sun lowered on the horizon, creating a sleepy haze on the riverbank. Wait, sunset? How had it gotten so late so fast? She tried to appear casual when looking to her right and left for the men who'd been conspiring outside her door. Two men walked side by side. A tall, broad-shouldered blonde in a full suit towered over a far shorter man with greasy-looking black hair that brushed his shoulders. She couldn't make out any further details due to the distance and the glare from the setting sun.

She'd commit those men to memory in case she needed that information later. For now, she should probably find a lantern and figure out how to trim it. Darkness would fall soon, and she needed to be ready for whatever Dr. Duncan had in mind.

~

Wendy jetted down the hall to their room.

"Wait up." Ironic how fitness-minded Claire panted behind her. "Why are you in such a hurry? You don't think that whacko was telling the truth, do you?"

"Only one way to find out." Curiosity itched at her, propelling her forward.

Claire grabbed Wendy's arm, stalling her. "Am I in Crazy Town?" She raked a hand through her hair. "You're taking him seriously? A time sailor. Really?"

Wendy puffed her cheeks out. "We've got no leads. Stranger things have happened."

"Stranger things? Like what? Alien abductions?"

Wendy rolled her eyes and continued down the hallway. "When we checked last time, we only looked for Stella. Not her things. It doesn't hurt to check before we report her missing."

"Maybe it does hurt to check first. Maybe that nutso killed her and is distracting us so he can get away with the crime."

"Unlikely."

"You might be the expert on history, but I think I've watched more crime shows."

Claire had her there, but she wouldn't admit it. As they neared their room, she took her key card from her lanyard and slid it in. "You've always said I could read people, right?"

"Like a book, but—"

"He's not a psycho."

"How do you know?"

"Same way I knew Ryan was a jerk from the moment you met him." She shrugged and ignored the flash of pain that sparked in Claire's eyes at the mention of her ex-boyfriend. "I get a feeling about people." She couldn't explain it. With Stella, she wouldn't have to.

"Not sure I want to put my life behind one of your *feelings*." Claire used air quotes.

The dismissiveness rankled. Whatever. Some people couldn't understand intuition. And just because she believed he wasn't harmful didn't mean she was confident he was correct. "We'll see."

But they both stood on the threshold, staring at each other.

Finally, she forced a deep inhale, said, "Let's do this," and pushed her way in.

At first glance, nothing seemed amiss. Ricardo, their steward, had been in to make their beds, and he'd folded a towel into a stingray and placed it on Stella's bed. All trash was gone. Everything neat and orderly.

Claire opened the third dresser drawer. "Wendy." Her gaze snapped up, filled with alarm.

Wendy looked into an empty drawer. She flung open the other drawers. Her clothes were exactly as she'd left them. Claire's clothes as well. But no sign of Stella's. "The closet."

Claire wrenched open the closet. "Her dresses are gone!"

"What?" Wendy rushed over and riffled through the hangers. Claire was right. No sign of Stella's dresses or skirts.

Both women stared at one another for a moment before apparently having the same idea. They stumbled over each other to the bathroom and knocked facial cleanser, moisturizer, and sunscreen into the sink looking for Stella's toiletries.

Claire's voice shook. "It's all gone."

A wave of dizziness nearly knocked Wendy off her feet. She backed up until her legs hit the edge of Stella's bed, then she sank down. She picked up the stingray and absentmindedly held it in her hands.

"Wendy." Claire looked deathly pale. With a trembling finger, she pointed to the spot next to Wendy near where the stingray had been.

Stella's phone. It must have been hidden by the towel.

Wait? Stella's phone? Wendy catapulted from the bed as if it were on fire. She grabbed Claire's arm. "What the heck?" They'd both seen Stella's phone plumet into the ocean after crashing into the railing below.

"Maybe it only looks like hers." Claire's voice squeaked.

Okay, possible. Tons of people had bejeweled giraffe phone cases, right? Still didn't explain what it'd be doing on Stella's bed, but … "You check."

Claire had more experience with phones. And scary movies. And scary movies featuring phones.

Claire bit her lip, then stepped forward to pick up the phone. She handled the item as if it were antique china, using slow, cautious movements while flipping it around. She pushed the power button and gasped as Stella and Everett's picture appeared on the lock screen.

Wendy rubbed sweaty palms on her cover-up. "Is this really happening?"

Claire continued to stare at Stella's image. "Maybe that Duncan guy is a serial killer. He came and cleared her things from our room after he kidnapped her. Then he planted this phone that looks like Stella's."

Wendy shook her head. "He would have to be a serial stalker to pull that off. I didn't see him on deck when her phone went overboard, and how would he have gotten the picture?" Besides, how would he have known which clothes were Stella's? And her gut feelings had almost always been right on track, causing her to trust the Holy Spirit to lead her intuition. If her friend was in danger, wouldn't she know it? Surely, her internal warning signal would be blaring.

"Maybe it didn't really go into the ocean. Maybe we were mistaken, and the phone ended up on level one."

Wendy raised her eyebrows. "We all saw it sink into the water."

"You think she's in a different time?" Claire plunked her hand on her hip.

Wendy paced—as much as she could in such a small space. "I don't know what to think." Could such things happen? Crazy things happened in the Bible all the time. The walls of Jericho collapsed to the sound of trumpets. A donkey talked to Balaam. A man leapt from the grave when Elisha's bones touched his. How could she say this was impossible?

"I guess …" Claire nibbled her lip, twisting her hands together. "I guess we could try to send a letter through the mailbox and see what happens."

Wendy straightened a section of her hair. It rebounded. "Yes. Let's try. Worst-case scenario, nothing happens, and we report her missing."

"How long do we wait? And how do we get her reply?"

"No idea. But we have to start somewhere." She bounded for the door. "Let's go buy stationery from the gift shop."

But if Stella had traveled to a different time, would she be able to return to the present? How? When? Her wedding to Everett loomed a month away. Would the dazzling bride walk down the aisle to her groom? Or would Wendy and Claire disembark at the end of the trip alone?

~

What to write? Wendy had tapped her pen on the notepad for a solid five minutes before passing it to Claire.

Now it was on her to come up with the perfect words for a letter sent through time. No pressure.

"What about: *Hey, Stella, where are you? When are you? We're worried sick. Write back ASAP.*" Claire grimaced as she said it. It sounded woefully inadequate.

But Wendy shrugged. "Sure. That'll work."

Okay, she hadn't been expecting agreement. She jotted the words onto the page. "Should we sign it?"

"No. Stella will know it's from us. No need for anyone else to."

Made sense. They didn't need to leave evidence of whom to cart off to the psych ward if this plan was, in fact, crazy.

She slid the note into an envelope and scripted Stella's name on the front. "Now to deliver it." They only had to slide it into a just-for-show mailbox located in a busy lobby. No biggie.

Wendy stood and rummaged through her drawer. "Let's change. I feel ridiculous walking around in my swimsuit all day."

Everyone wore swimsuits on a cruise boat, but no need to protest. "Sure."

"You brought your KU shirt, right? Let's wear those. A show of solidarity." She pulled out the blue T-shirt with the Jayhawks mascot plastered on it.

"Yeah. Okay." Claire wouldn't argue. It was much more pleasant when the two of them got along.

Once dressed, they left their room arm in arm, as if they'd face whatever came together. It was a nice thought, but their bond still felt tenuous at best. It would take more than matching shirts to unite them.

They exited the elevator and stepped into the bustling sixth floor lobby. Claire zeroed in on the mailbox and stepped toward it.

"Miss Booker!" A preteen girl rushed to Wendy, eyes alight. "Oh my gosh. I can't believe it's you."

Wendy broke into a smile. "Allison. Great to see you." But her smile dimmed as she looked around, hand flittering to fidget with her hair. "You're here vacationing with your family?"

"With my mom. She's around here somewhere." Allison glanced over her shoulder.

"Well, I won't keep you. Have a great cruise and a fun summer." Wendy grabbed Claire's arm and led her away from Allison and away from the mailbox, into a crowded corridor.

"Where are we going?"

"I'm going to grab a latte first." Wendy shuffled into the line at the coffee shop.

What in the world? "Who was that?"

"Who?" Wendy's pink cheeks didn't help her plea of innocence. "Oh, Allison? She's one of my students."

"Why did you run away from her like she had the plague?"

"What? I did not. I love Allison."

Seriously? She was going to be like that? Claire pinned Wendy with a narrowed gaze. "Come on." It was a demand, not a plea, but a bubbly voice beside them interrupted the interrogation.

"Wait, are you Claire? From YouTube?"

Claire turned to find an attractive twenty-something blonde looking starstruck. "Yeah." She smiled. "I'm Claire from the Claire-ity Fitness Channel."

"No way. I can't believe it." The girl put her hands on her cheeks. "Can I get a selfie with you?"

Wendy scoffed. Rude, but Claire pretended not to notice. "Sure."

The two posed for several shots.

"Make sure to tag me on your socials." That would help. A lot. Fit TV was watching her social media, and today was sure to disappoint. Due to the Stella situation, she hadn't posted a thing. But if this girl tagged her, it'd show up. That was something, at least. If only Wendy hadn't ruined her video.

Claire had to make a living. The juxtaposition of normal life and goals jolted her back to their crazy situation. If Stella really did travel through time, would she return to them? And if she did, would life continue as normal? But if Stella didn't return, what then? Would Claire fade into poverty because nothing would matter anymore?

Stella wouldn't want that for her. Her friend had never fully understood her fitness "obsession," but she'd always supported it, always supported her. Stella had been one of her biggest fans and one of her first followers. If Stella knew about the Fit TV opportunity, she'd undoubtedly want Claire to go for it. But Claire hadn't found the right opportunity to tell her before everything happened, and now things were complicated. Now Fit TV had to take a back seat to helping her friend. What did that look like? Ditching Fit TV? Or perhaps just doing less to secure her career than she'd originally planned. She couldn't fathom Stella being okay with Claire allowing her dreams to wither and die.

If she wanted a chance at all, she had to get content out there right away.

Once Wendy had her latte in hand, they wove their way back to the mailbox. Wendy seemed on edge. Jittery. The girl—was it Allison?—was nowhere in sight.

Claire bent toward Wendy's ear. "Pretend to admire the mailbox. I'll sneak the letter inside."

"Got it." Wendy trailed her fingers over the mailbox's molding, leaning forward as if to inspect it. "Isn't this interesting? It looks like an antique." Her voice echoed over loud. She obviously wasn't a drama teacher.

"Wow, yeah. Look at this plaque." She read it out loud, then opened the lid and discreetly slid the letter in. "Amazing how old this is."

They strolled around the corner casually, but then Wendy froze and stepped back. "Let's take the elevator back down. Or up. Somewhere."

Claire narrowed her eyes. "Why?"

"Allison's mom," she mumbled, and shook her head. "Just go."

She nudged Claire in the direction of the elevators, casting one last glance over her shoulder. Okay. This needed an explanation, and as soon as the opportunity presented itself, Claire would demand one.

Chapter Five

Lantern burning, Stella opened her creaky door to the boiler deck and stepped outside. Her emerald dress swished around her heels. Far from fitting in with the time period, the slit reached midcalf, and her leg remained scandalously exposed. But this was as close to a *modest frock* as she was going to get.

Dr. Duncan stood a few feet away, peering over the railing, presumably observing the river's current in the moonlight as if it were a normal night. When he turned to her, he gaped, then pinched the bridge of his nose. "Don't you have a shawl you can don?"

"I have a hoodie." She'd meant to pack her silk wrap in case the air-conditioned dining room made wearing her sleeveless dress uncomfortable, but she must have forgotten to do so.

He huffed. "Never mind. Follow me. If anyone asks, you're helping me fetch medical supplies for an ill passenger."

She crossed her arms. "I'll come with you, but I expect answers."

He had the nerve to tap his foot as if put out. "Answers to what questions?"

"Dozens. First being, what the heck is going on? What is time-sailing? And how do you know about it?"

He gave a slight shake of his head, then plowed forward. So, he was going to be like that, was he? She'd pried many stories out of people who weren't forthcoming with information. The direct approach didn't work with everyone. Stealth was needed to uncover some necessary morsels. Stealth, cunning, and patience.

She followed him past numerous staterooms on their right. To their left, the river glistened. Crickets chirped. The water lapped softly. No one else was in sight, but laughter emanated from the other side of the boat. He led her to the front of the ship where they descended the stairs. As they did so, an unpleasant odor met her. She brought her hand under her nose.

"It's the animals," Dr. Duncan said. "Well, mostly the animals."

Animals? On the boat? But as they rounded the corner, she saw them. Pigs, chickens, a couple of mules, and a horse. They stood in a thin layer of hay and stomped through their own excrement. She gave them a wide berth as she studied the area around her.

Piles of cargo towered at the center of the deck, taking up most of the expanse, with open space around the edges. Unlike the floor above, there were no interior walls or rooms. Only an open-aired surface stuffed with wooden boxes and barrels, hay and—she stood on her tiptoes to get a better view—were those stoves? It appeared they were shipping appliances upriver too.

People of all sizes scattered about the open deck area. Only a few feet away from the animals, several Black men rested against hay bales.

Dr. Duncan nodded toward them. "Deckhands."

As if that explained everything. "They work on the boat?"

"Yes, ma'am. On this deck."

"They sleep here? Out in the open?"

The corner of his mouth twitched. "Yes, of course."

"Even the women?" Call her nonprogressive or whatever, but for some reason, picturing a man sleeping in the elements was different than picturing a woman. She shivered.

"There are no female workers on the boat, save the chambermaid, who has her own quarters. But all deck passengers sleep exposed to the elements: men, women, and children.”

“Passengers?” she spit out. “Paying passengers sleep out here?”

His eyes widened. “May I remind you to keep your voice down?” He scanned the area before returning his attention to her. “Yes. Deck passage costs far less than cabin passage. The ship provides no meals or rooms for deck passengers. Only transportation.”

Thank goodness when 1856 had called her, it had provided her with a room. She couldn’t imagine sleeping on the dirty floor of this boat, exposed to the elements and the eyes of all the other passengers. The smell was beginning to make sense. It wasn’t only the animals. Unwashed bodies joined the mix.

“This way.” Dr. Duncan’s whisper redirected her focus.

As they walked past stacks of wooden crates piled high, she kept casting glances to the open deck. Two small girls huddled against their mother as the threesome attempted to sleep while sitting propped against a sack of something. Not far from them, a couple of men played cards by candlelight. One man lay on his back snoring loudly, a mostly empty bottle of whisky tipped over next to him. These people were likely far poorer than those on the floor above. What an interesting study in class distinctions of the nineteenth century. The journalist in her itched to dig for a story.

The spirited music began again, and Stella craned her neck to see where it was coming from. “What’s that?”

“It’s the calliope playing the polka. They play most nights and every time we come ashore for wooding.”

“Wooding?”

“To get fresh wood for fuel.”

“Ah.” But then, she asked, “Calliope?”

“It’s like a steam piano.”

Okay, two mysteries solved. Many more to go.

Dr. Duncan greeted a man with a newsboy’s cap and suspenders. “Ah, McDonald. Thank you for meeting us.” He kept his voice to a whisper. "We'll need to procure appropriate attire for Miss Lindy."

McDonald nodded to her. "Follow me."

He led them to piles of cargo. Boxes upon boxes lined the boat, all with handwritten labels. Hats. Dishware. Shoes. Hardware. Furs. Pipes. Barrels and sacks also interspersed the area.

"Here we go." She hadn't noticed McDonald carrying a crowbar, but he used one to pry open a wooden crate, then he left them.

"Hold the lantern close so we can see," Dr. Duncan said.

She brought it near to reveal dozens and dozens of dresses in blue-and-brown-checkered patterns, some with flower designs intermingled.

"Choose two or three that suit you." Dr. Duncan stepped back, allowing her space. "Quickly."

She looked around. No one was up and about this far into the cargo area, but her nerves still skittered. "But it's stealing, right?"

Dr. Duncan's mouth twisted. "If time-sailing bends the rules of time, I consider it moral to bend other rules to accommodate the time sailor. Don't you?"

Oh my. But what choice did she have? She'd never fit in with her current wardrobe. Maybe she could return the clothes before she went back to her real time. She wouldn't need them forever. She fisted a dress in her grip as her gaze snapped to Dr. Duncan's. "Please tell me I won't be here forever."

He managed a slight smile. "Every time sailor I've encountered has returned home after they accomplished their mission."

That should have brought her relief, but heat burned in her chest, and she snapped. "What mission? How can I complete a mission when I have no clue what it is?"

"You'll discover it in time." He spoke as if with ancient wisdom, but it only grated on her nerves.

She wouldn't get any information out of him. She ought to stop trying, at least outright. She dug a palm into her forehead. How would she ever get home? Everett's kind eyes and knee-weakening smile flashed through her mind. Longing swelled. She hated being separated from him, and now she was over a hundred and sixty years away with no way to make things right between them. She had to get back. God forgive her. She'd do whatever she had to do.

She dug through the dresses, holding each up to check the sizing. She chose a blue-and-white plaid one, one with a delicate green flowered pattern, and a plain brown one. If Claire were with her, she would have spent more time figuring out which dress would look most fashionable. Stella only concerned herself with which would fit comfortably. She frowned. If only Claire and Wendy *were* here. Her friends would make this freak happening seem more like an adventure and less like a punishment. But no. She'd have to brave this alone.

"What else do I need? A bonnet or something?"

But Dr. Duncan was preoccupied with crates farther down and didn't hear her. She turned and held the lantern up to the crates near her to see what their labels proclaimed. One was marked with a simple A. She pulled at the top board, but it didn't budge. Of course, it wouldn't. She blew an errant strand of hair from her face and scanned the area for a hammer to pry the nails loose. Or was that McDonald's crowbar propped against a nearby barrel? He must have left it for them. She'd never used one before, but it couldn't be that hard.

"What in the blazes is all the racket?"

Dr. Duncan reached her as she heaved the board free with a final grunt.

Her mouth went dry. Guns. Lots of them. Were they simply cargo for people to sell out west? The two men she'd caught whispering outside her door earlier came to mind. *Arms. Weapons. Kansas. War.* Goosebumps broke out on her arms as a shiver slid down her spine. Telltale signs she was on the track of a breaking story.

He slid the board back into place. "Nothing to see here." His fingers twitched.

"Why is it marked with an A? All the other crates are clearly labeled."

"A for ammunition." He took the crowbar from her hands but wouldn't meet her eye. "I found reticules and bonnets over there." He started to walk back to where he'd come from, but when she didn't follow, he stopped. "Don't ask too many questions, Miss Lindy. Sometimes, it's better—and safer—when you leave things be."

She straightened and tilted up her chin. "I'm a journalist, Dr. Duncan. Asking questions is what I'm trained to do."

Asking questions. Making observations. These were the parts of her career she excelled at and adored. Diving headlong into conflict to get a story? Not so much. But she had to find out her mission. Asking questions was a must. Diving into conflict? Hopefully not.

He paused, seeming to consider her. Then he broke into a conspiratorial smile. "Maybe you're precisely the person we need."

~

Claire bit her tongue to keep from crying out as she smashed her leg against the desk. Oh great. Fit TV would love an ugly purple bruise marring her leg. Foundation might help, if it came to that. Their room was far too small for both of them to pace, but where else could they go? What could they do?

"So now we just wait? For what exactly?" Claire failed to temper the irritation in her voice. It wasn't even Wendy irking her anymore. She was like a caged animal. Helpless. Frightened.

"How am I supposed to know?" Wendy shot back before nearly colliding into her yet again. "It's not like I've ever been in this position before."

Claire threw her hands up. Obviously, their nerves were frazzled. Neither one of them were at their best. The tension in the room reminded her of finals week during their senior year. Maybe they should resort to what brought them peace then. "Look, I don't know how this works, and neither do you. But we do know the only One who has a clue what's going on. Can we pray about this? Together?"

Wendy huffed, sending a curl flying. It landed in the center of her forehead. Claire tucked it behind her ear.

"You're right." Wendy plopped onto her bed. "I don't know why I always try to solve things on my own first, then go to God as a last resort."

Claire settled across from her. "I know, right?" She held out her hands in invitation.

Wendy took them and bowed her head. "Heavenly Father, we come before You today to ask—"

Claire's phone pinged from her back pocket, and her head shot up.

Wendy's eyes cracked open.

"Ignore it." Claire bowed her head again.

Wendy cleared her throat. "We ask You—"

Another ping.

"Sorry. Let me turn my phone on silent." Claire pulled it out, trying not to look at the notification. But a message from her agent glared at her.

While Wendy was buying stationery earlier, Claire had given Trenia Stella's number to contact for updates. Plus, she'd stopped by customer service to upgrade Stella's Wi-Fi plan. Why did she feel guilty about that now? She'd bumped up Wendy's plan too. She was a good friend. No reason to feel shady. Now, she froze for half a second before fumbling to put her phone on silent, but it was long enough for Wendy to pounce on her hesitation.

"What is it? What's more important than this prayer right now, Claire?"

Claire shook her head. "Nothing." She turned the sound off and slid it back into her pocket. "Continue."

But before Wendy could say a word, her phone buzzed. Shoot. Apparently, she'd turned it to vibrate. She shivered under Wendy's icy glare.

"Look, I'm sorry. What if we both get some air, take a bit of time away from each other, and meet back here in an hour? I'll take care of this." She waved her phone in the air. "Then I'll be ready to reconvene without distraction."

Wendy's mouth twisted. "Fine."

Her defenses rose. "It's just … we're both tense. Some space would do us good."

Wendy crossed her arms "I get it."

"Okay, then." Claire catapulted to her feet, snatched her bag, and thundered out the door.

Her eyes burned, but she wouldn't give in to tears. She stomped toward the elevators. Too bad she wasn't dressed for the gym. Pivoting, she headed toward the stairs instead. She could burn through this irritation with exercise. Working out always proved the best way for her to suppress emotion.

Yet, by the time she reached the sixth floor, moisture gathered in the corners of her eyes despite her best efforts. Ugh. Why did Miss Perfect hate her? It was like she was looking for reasons to disapprove of Claire, and man, did she find them. Around every corner. People who were critical were only unhappy with themselves, right? Surely, it had nothing to do with Claire. Not really. Wendy was unhappy with Wendy. Claire was merely a scapegoat.

How come that didn't make her feel any better?

Halfway to the seventh floor, Claire's heavy footstep missed the stair entirely. Her shoe slipped, and she stumbled backward.

"Whoa." Strong arms caught her from behind. "Are you okay?"

She turned and found herself looking into chocolatey brown eyes framed by long lashes. Wavy tendrils of matching hair brushed a brow wrinkled with concern. She sucked in air. What an utterly beautiful man. Her gaze lowered to his hands gripping her upper arms. This utterly beautiful man was touching her. She wobbled on unsteady feet.

Something flashed in his eyes. Recognition? Did he know who she was? But it was gone in a blink, replaced with tenderness. Her paranoia must have conjured it up.

"Are you okay?" he repeated, bending a bit lower to meet her gaze.

She nodded, not trusting her voice. But the kindness in his expression caused the tears barely below the surface to overflow their banks. They trickled down her cheeks.

"Oh gosh, are you hurt?" He bent to examine her ankles.

A few people walked around them, casting curious glances. No one else offered to help. No one but this kind man.

"Can I help you to a chair? There's a lounge right above us."

Us. Her heart pinged at the word. Maybe what she saw in his eyes was unadulterated attraction, because it pulled her like a magnet. She nodded again.

"Here." He held out his arm. "Grab ahold of my elbow." She did so, and she made her way up the stairs, leaning heavily on him. She didn't analyze whether her ankle warranted such assistance. It was beside the point. Likely, the only thing injured was her pride. But might this be *the* story she told someday? Of how she met *the one.*

She was getting ahead of herself.

But how could she not? She'd never seen a kinder face.

He guided her to a leather wingback chair, then settled into the one next to it. In the background, someone played *Georgia* on the piano.

"Better?" he asked.

Again, she nodded. She could smack herself. He was going to think her mute if she didn't say something. She forced words out of her tight throat. "I don't know how to thank you. I'm Claire."

"Neo." His smile sent a thrill tingling through her. "I'm glad you're all right. You seemed to be attacking those stairs. Something on your mind?"

She'd forgotten about the texts from Trenia. Her shoulders sagged. "A lot, actually."

"Want to share?" He sat forward, elbows on his knees, and threaded his hands together. As if there were nothing more important in that moment than her. She shouldn't blab her personal business to a stranger. But the way he looked at her … She'd waited her whole life for someone to look at her that way. Like he'd hang on her every word.

She couldn't help but tell him the whole mess with Fit TV. Which led to how Wendy viewed her. Which inevitably led to Stella, but how could she tell him about her friend's disappearance without appearing insane?

She ran her tongue over her teeth.

"There's something else, isn't there?" Attentive *and* perceptive. Somebody pinch her. He'd scooted closer to her as she'd poured out her soul. Perhaps it was so he could hear her over the music, or perhaps he felt the connection between them as much as she did.

"Yes," she admitted. "My friend—my other friend—she had to leave for a mission of sorts."

"A mission?" His question held curiosity, but not judgment.

She bent forward, lowering her voice. "We don't know the details. It's … secret. But I'm nervous for her. I'm afraid she's in danger." That was as close as she could come to confiding in him without lying.

"Wow. A secret mission. Sounds important."

"It is." Claire managed a weak smile.

"I'll say a prayer for her."

She straightened. "You're a believer?"

"Yes." He cleared his throat. "Yeah. Come from a praying family all the way."

Her conscience twinged. How long had it been since she'd left her room? She probably needed to get back to pray with Wendy. Only she couldn't seem to draw her gaze away from Neo's.

"So," he continued, "I'll say a prayer for your friend."

"Thank you. She's a very important person."

"So are you." He was so near now that his breath warmed her cheek. He smelled of coffee and coconut. Her belly warmed.

She dared to inch closer, her knee brushing his. He reached out and tucked a strand of hair behind her ear. His hand lingered at her chin. When he tilted her face up, a question hung in his gaze. He was a kind, chivalrous, fellow believer? That was all the permission she needed.

She answered by brushing her lips against his in a kiss, tender and tentative. He threaded his hands through her hair and deepened the kiss. Soft and satisfying. Dousing and igniting flames all at once. Claire surrendered to it. This. This was what she'd been waiting for. Hoping for. Praying for.

Praying for?

A gasp grappled through the euphoric haze. Claire untangled herself from Neo's arms and stared into the horror-stricken face of her friend.

Wendy shoved her hands in her pockets and stepped backward. "You didn't come back when you said you would. I was scared. After what happened to … I was scared." She rubbed her forehead with her palm before returning her hand to her pocket. Her voice shook. "But obviously, you're fine."

"Wendy, I—"

"I'll see you in our room." Wendy turned and disappeared around the corner.

Claire stood and moved to follow.

"Wait." Neo took her hand. "Will I see you again?"

She squeezed his hand. What if when her perfect guy finally crossed her path, the timing wasn't right? With Stella's disappearance, falling in love should be the farthest thing from her mind.

She smiled sadly at him. "I hope so."

The tips of Wendy's ears burned as she stormed down the corridor. The nerve of that girl! To think Wendy had been full of contrition when Claire brought up praying together. A godly solution. Oh, how it smarted that Wendy hadn't thought of it first. For a moment, it had almost felt like the two old roommates had connected on a deeper level again. That deeper version of Claire that'd seemed to be missing resurfaced like a buoy bobbing on the water. And like a drowning fool, Wendy had fallen for it.

But no, it was merely an illusion. A mirage. Claire was as surface-level as ever, more concerned with cute guys than with her missing friend. She wasn't interested in turning to God. No. She wanted to make out with strangers in between checking her texts and social media.

Unforgiveable.

Hot breath puffed out her nostrils as she jammed the down button for the elevator. *Okay, okay.* Nothing was beyond God's forgiveness, so eventually, the Lord would help her forgive selfish Claire. But she sure wasn't ready yet.

"Wendy, wait up."

But Wendy didn't turn at the hand on her shoulder. Instead, she stepped forward onto the elevator as if she hadn't heard Claire speak.

Claire pressed her hand into her side. "You're surprisingly fast."

Wendy quirked an eyebrow, though she didn't turn. Insulting much? Just because she didn't spend an hour a day on a Peloton didn't mean she was out of shape.

"Look, I'm sorry. I lost track of time."

Claire attempted to swivel Wendy in her direction, but she didn't budge. She clenched her jaw. "Not here." No need to make a scene.

They rode the elevator and walked back to their room in icy silence.

As soon as the door shut, lava bubbled from Wendy's mouth. "Time isn't the only thing you lost track of. What about your mind? What were you thinking, locking lips with a random guy? He could be a psychopath!"

Claire folded her arms around herself. "He's not a psycho."

"You don't know that. What if he trafficked Stella, and now, he's set his sights on you? These things happen."

"I know they do." Claire rolled her eyes. "But it's not like that with Neo."

"Neo? Are you kidding me? Are we in the Matrix?" She gave a humorless laugh. "I can't believe this. Instead of going to God, you fall all over yourself for some guy you know nothing about. Are you *that* desperate?"

"Yes!"

The tears that sprang from what seemed like nowhere shocked Wendy into silence. They filled Claire's eyes, then spilled onto her cheeks, dripping off onto the carpeted floor. Had she ever seen Claire cry? Not that she could remember.

The sight of it—the mere thought of glib Claire feeling gut-level pain—flooded her with remorse. She hadn't known such protective walls existed around Claire's heart. To see them tumble nearly took Wendy out.

"Yes, apparently, I *am* that desperate. Because if I had tonight to do over again, I'd probably kiss him sooner. And if all this hadn't happened with Stella, and I could do something crazy like elope with some guy I just met, I might be desperate enough to do it. Because then, I wouldn't have to spend another day with this yawning chasm of loneliness."

She finally swiped at her wet cheeks, but the damage had been done. Wendy couldn't unsee Claire's vulnerability. She couldn't unhear her confession.

"I know I'm pathetic." Claire's voice was small. A turtle sneaking into its shell.

Wendy forced words out of her parched mouth. "I've been a jerk."

"No."

For the first time in a long while, pathetic was the furthest word from Wendy's mind. More like *real. Authentic.*

Brave. Claire had bared her soul amid friendly fire. That took guts.

Advice swirled on Wendy's tongue, but she trapped it in her mouth. She could tell Claire how no guy would ever satisfy the ache inside, how the Lord alone could heal her heart and bring fulfillment and joy. She could serve platitudes on a platter. Let go and let God. There's a reason for this season. God won't give you more than you can handle.

The thing was, Claire already knew the truth. Her friend didn't need a sermon. She didn't need cute words with a pretty bow. She needed the Lord to heal her hurting heart like only He could. Maybe at some point, she could use a reminder of the truth, but right now, what she needed from Wendy was prayer.

What had happened to Claire to shatter her heart? Wendy didn't need to know the answer to that question to pray. She stepped forward and wrapped her friend in a hug.

Claire clung to her and wept as she prayed. Perfectly put-together Claire, perfectly broken.

But why?

Chapter Six

Stella had just changed into her KU shirt and a pair of jean shorts when a knock sounded at the door. Shoot. Dr. Duncan said he'd have the items she'd picked out delivered to her room, but she hadn't planned on wearing any of the stuffy period clothing to bed since she wouldn't see anyone until morning. Clearly, she hadn't thought this through.

"Who is it?"

"It's Leela, ma'am. Your chambermaid. I have a delivery for you from Mr. McDonald and a letter."

Stella cracked open the door, but the maid held a box half her size. Leela couldn't slip the package through the crack. She'd have to let the woman in. Oh well. It wasn't like several other people hadn't seen her in scandalous clothing today.

She stepped aside and motioned for Leela to enter.

Leela's mouth dropped open as she scanned Stella from foot to head, then her eyes alighted back on Stella's T-shirt. She quietly closed the door and then set the box by the washstand.

Stella's stomach growled. She hadn't eaten since breakfast, and that was well over a hundred sixty years ago. Or ahead? Whatever. Did they have 24/7 ice cream on this boat? Doubtful, but she could ask about the food situation. She opened her mouth to do so, but Leela spoke first.

"Oh, miss. This is too good to be true." She clapped her hands together.

"Excuse me?"

"You a Jayhawker?" She pointed to the Jayhawks mascot—or was it the lettering—on Stella's shirt.

"I went to KU. Go Jayhawks." She raised her arms in a little cheer. Wait, how old was KU? Certainly not this old. How did this woman know about the university?

"It's good to have a lady like you on our side." Her face shone with admiration.

What in the world was she talking about?

Leela's gaze drifted to the novels on Stella's bedside table. "All dem books yours?"

"Yes." Stella's cheeks heated at Leela's visual perusal. They were all clean—no smut—but they were beach reads, fluffy and light, perfect for vacation. Would Leela think less of her because of it?

"Can I touch them?"

Touch them? Well, that was odd. Then again, she was on a riverboat in 1856. An awkward giggle spilled forth. "Okay."

"Forgive me for being so bold." She lowered her gaze. "I only ask 'cause you a Jayhawker. I thought maybe you let me."

"Go ahead." Stella motioned toward the books.

She fingered each cover with reverence. "I've always dreamed of reading me some books. I've never seen any like these." She rapped her knuckles on a protagonist's face. "Why are these covers not hard?"

What? Had paperbacks not been invented yet? Stella sucked on the inside of her cheek, considering her answer. "Something new they're trying. It's called paperback."

Leela gave a happy little sigh, clearly enamored.

"You can borrow one if you want. I won't be able to get through all of them. I don't know why I brought so many. I always overpack."

Leela's eyebrows bunched. "What would I do with one of dem books?"

"Read it?"

Her shoulders drooped. "I can't read, miss. Can only recognize a few words Pa points out in the paper. Jayhawker. Runaway. Auction."

Couldn't read? Stella's eyes slid shut as everything fell into place. Of course. Leela was likely a slave. In some states, it was illegal for slaves to learn how to read and write. Was that the case here?

Leela dropped her voice to a whisper. "Maybe you could teach me."

"Teach you?" Stella's eyes flew open, and her hand covered her heart. Her? Teach someone to read? Wendy was the teacher. Not her. She wouldn't know how. Besides, it was probably illegal, and there would be stiff penalties for teaching slaves how to read. What if she got caught?

"We could have lessons late at night here in your stateroom." Her eyes brimmed with hope.

Stella's gut twisted. "I could get in a lot of trouble, couldn't I?"

Leela narrowed her eyes. "You ain't a stranger to the risk though, is ya?" She pointed again to Stella's shirt.

"I don't know." Stella threaded her thumbs through her belt loops to keep from fidgeting. "I'll have to think about it."

Leela's gaze once again fell, and she resumed a demure posture, hands together, head down. "Yes, ma'am. Will there be anything else tonight?"

"No. I don't think so." Her stomach rumbled again. "Wait, yes. Can you tell me when I can get something to eat?"

"Breakfast will be served at seven in the morning in the social hall, ma'am."

That was what she'd figured. She had to wait until morning for a meal.

Leela had turned to leave when a thought occurred to Stella. "Do people normally tip you? You brought that huge box here."

Leela shook her head. "Passengers tip the free Blacks, but not usually us slaves. I only get tips when they can't tell the difference." A hint of a smile graced her face.

"That hardly seems fair." Stella grabbed her purse from the chair in the corner and dug in her wallet. Her modern money surely differed from the currency used in the 1800s, but how much so? It had to still be usable, didn't it? "All I have is a ten."

How exorbitant of a tip was that? She handed it to Leela.

Leela stared, gaping.

"Are you okay?"

Leela cast wide eyes at her. "I ain't never seen a ten-dollar bill before. You a rich lady."

Stella laughed. "Hardly."

"I don't feel right, taking this much money from you."

"No worries. It was a big box. You deserve it."

"Thank you, ma'am." She folded it carefully and slid it into her apron pocket, then turned to leave. "Oh! Your letter."

She pulled an envelope from her apron and handed it to Stella.

Stella's pulse thudded in her ears. On the front was her name. In Claire's handwriting.

The envelope trembled in her hand. She barely registered Leela's bow and exit.

She backed up until the back of her legs brushed the edge of the bed and lowered herself onto the mattress. Part of her clamored to rip it open, but another part was afraid to. As if opening this letter would make this all real somehow. And if she didn't, she could go on playacting in this role she hadn't rehearsed for.

She had to open it. Of course, she had to. But something inside warned her there would be no going back once she did.

She peeled open the seal and slipped a piece of paper out.

> Hey, Stella, where are you? When are you? We're worried sick. Write back ASAP.

Oh no. Why hadn't she thought of it before? To her friends, she'd simply disappeared. No explanation. No Dr. Duncan to help them understand. She'd told them she'd meet them on the top deck and then … didn't. What were they going through right now? Her stomach roiled. Maybe it was best that she hadn't eaten.

But wait. She read the short note again. *When are you?* They knew she'd traveled back in time. How? And if she was to write back, how could she deliver a letter to the future? How did her friends get this note to her?

She had to try, even though questions swirled through her mind. The thought of Wendy and Claire pacing around their room, worried to their core, propelled her into action. She sprung from the bed and riffled through the desk drawer for the stationery she'd spotted there the day before.

Everett.

Did he know she'd disappeared? He'd be beside himself with worry. She had to set everyone at ease.

She grabbed a book to write on, sat cross-legged on her bed, and began to write.

> Wendy & Claire,
> So good to hear from you. How'd you get this letter to me? How'd you know I traveled through time? I'm okay. I'm on the steamboat *Arabia* in 1856. I'm supposed to be on some mission, but I don't know what it is. Tell Everett I'm okay and that I love him. Please help me figure out how to get back so I can marry him.
> Stella

She had a hundred more questions about the time period she could ask Wendy, but she ought to first make sure this letter reached them safely. If she poured out her heart and the letter ended up in someone else's hands, she'd be mortified and quite possibly deemed insane. How should she address it? She studied the envelope she'd received. It had nothing on it but her name, and it had been delivered to her hands. She'd do the same. She scrawled her friends' names on the front.

Now what?

Since Leela had delivered the letter to her, perhaps she could deliver one from her? Stella slid into her flip-flops and out the door in search of her chambermaid.

Low flickering light from a couple of crystal chandeliers cast a dim glow onto the main cabin—the social hall, as Leela had called it. Inky darkness seeped through the skylights surrounding the space. Unlike the cruise boat that housed rows of rooms on the lower floors and corporate gathering areas above, the steamboat's cabins surrounded one large room that extended the entire length of the boat. Folding doors sectioned off an area at one end. At the other end stood a bar that had been crowded with men earlier. Now all was quiet. Near the bar to the side was a washstand and what looked akin to a barber's chair. Where was Leela? Stella hadn't a clue what a chambermaid's other duties were. Might she be in the kitchen? Wherever that was.

Stella headed toward the bar—maybe the kitchen was behind it?—but then stifled a gasp when someone moaned underneath her feet. What in the world! She'd stepped on someone. Had they passed out drunk? She squinted to make out the scene in the dimness. No, the man she'd stepped on wasn't the only person lying on the floor. She counted at least fourteen lying on mats, blankets pulled to their chins.

Leela rushed to her, sidestepping the sleepers. Where had she come from?

"What you need, ma'am? Can I get you something?"

"Why are they on the floor?"

"Staterooms are full, miss. When they're full, passengers sleep on the floor." She waved to Stella's shirt. Then she lowered her voice to a whisper. "I wouldn't be wearing that where others can see you. You never know who be on this ship. Best keep your allegiance a secret."

Ugh. She should have asked Wendy what all the fuss was about her KU shirt. Oh well. Next time. There would be a next time, right?

She fidgeted with the letter, then held it out. "Can you mail this for me?"

"Yes, ma'am. Anything else?"

"No. Thank you."

Leela hustled away. Where would she take it? Her breath caught as Leela approached the familiar antique mailbox and dropped it inside.

So that was why the unique postal box was strategically positioned on both boats. It was a portal of some sort. Wild.

Careful not to step on any more passengers, she tiptoed back to her room and went to sleep without reading a page of her novel. She had more interesting things to contemplate than a beach read. Her life had become a mystery. Or was it an adventure?

Time would tell.

~

Wendy rolled onto her left side and checked the time on her watch. Two in the morning. She couldn't sleep. The tumultuous evening with Claire had left her insides feeling as topsy-turvy as a rowboat in a storm. She couldn't stop thinking about Claire's tears. Her declaration that she'd elope with a stranger if she had a chance. Wendy's heart squeezed.

She'd overreacted. Again. She'd had no right to lay into Claire like that. They were on a cruise, for goodness' sake. People hooked up all the time on cruises. Not good, Christian girls like them, but plenty of others. What if the spark that had ignited the bonfire of Wendy's rage hadn't been indignation but rather jealousy?

When she'd seen Claire in the arms of a handsome man, the first thought to gut-punch her had been the realization she was utterly alone. Stella had Everett. Claire now had Neo. Wendy had no one. She was a fifth wheel.

She flopped onto her back and stared at the ceiling. Ridiculous. She didn't need a man to complete her. She wasn't boy crazy like Claire. She had no inner romantic like Stella. Hopefully, she'd find Mr. Right someday, but she wasn't in a hurry. Let the other girls fall all over themselves pining. She'd wait until the boys grew into men and could appreciate all of her, uh, eccentric qualities.

Her foot tapped in beat with her racing mind. *Ugh.* There'd be no falling asleep now. She might as well get up and walk the deck. Admiring a starlit night at sea sure beat staring at a white ceiling.

Careful not to disturb Claire, she rose, slid on her sandals, and slipped out the door. She ended up on the top deck, staring out at inky waters in her pajama pants and Bristol Middle School T-shirt. Claire wouldn't be caught dead in public looking like this, but who did Wendy have to impress? Her boss and school board were miles away. No one here had any stake in her future.

Well, Allison. More specifically, Allison's mom. But they wouldn't be wandering around in the middle of the night.

"Was I correct? Did she time-sail?"

The voice beside her made Wendy yelp. She pressed a hand to her thrashing heart and gaped at Dr. Duncan. "You scared the bejesus out of me."

A soft smile played on his lips. "I apologize. Not my intention." He joined her at the railing and rested his elbows on the white metal bar.

She stepped slightly to the side, putting a bit more distance between them. "Who are you, anyway? How'd you know?" As before, she studied him closely, committing his features to memory in case he ended up being a creeper, and she needed to relay details to the police.

"I already told you my name."

"I don't care about your name. I want to know why you said her stuff would disappear."

His mouth parted. "I only suspected it might. Stories passed down from my great-grandfather. I always thought them tall tales."

She crossed her arms. "What stories?"

His smile broadened as he peered wistfully into the distance, as if he were viewing the past. "All sorts of stories. Time sailors. Time travel over the waters. His father told these stories after hearing them from his father, and so on. A long line of oral tradition." His smile dimmed. "But seeing as how I'm an only child with no wife or children, it seems like that tradition will end with me."

"But you didn't think the stories were true. Only now you do?"

"You tell me."

"I think it's true." She turned and faced the sea again. "Her stuff disappeared."

He laughed. "Well, I'll be." He shook his head. "I always believed as a child. When I began to doubt, it was like losing the magic of Santa Claus, only it felt like losing a piece of my great-grandfather as well."

"Well, now you have him back." She offered a weak smile. "We're still waiting for a return letter. That will tell us for sure. There could be some other explanation." Though she had no clue what it could be. "Everything was gone except her phone. Why not that?"

A frown dimpled his chin. "I don't know. Was it with her other things?"

"No. It was at the bottom of the ocean. It dropped overboard the first day."

"Ah. It must have missed the window if it needed to reassemble and relocate."

Her brain hurt. She opened her mouth to ask him to expound but thought better of it. Why expend energy trying to understand these crazy time-sailing rules? The only *how* she needed to concern herself with was how to get Stella back.

"Time sailors," Dr. Duncan said again, as if to himself.

"Tell me more. What else do you remember? When will she come back? How?"

He squinted as if wringing out his brain for details. "I wish I could remember. I know he said time sailors return after accomplishing their mission. And that time works differently when time-sailing. Something about different rules."

Different rules? "What's that supposed to mean?"

He shrugged. "Great-grandad died when I was seven. I didn't think to ask too many questions. My grandfather thought the whole thing nonsense and didn't carry on the tradition of telling those stories."

She released a small growl. How was she supposed to help Stella get back with such little information?

"I wish I could help you more," Dr. Duncan said.

"Maybe you'll think of something else. If you do, will you let me know?"

"Of course. How?"

She hesitated. Her intuition told her he was trustworthy, but common sense said not to give a random man with questionable sanity her room number. But if his sanity was questionable, so was hers. And if he'd wanted to harm her, he'd had ample opportunity to do so in the middle of the night on the top deck.

"We're in room 1113."

He nodded. "If anything comes to mind, I'll tell you. I'm in room 3434 if you need me."

"Thanks."

He began to walk away but turned back. "Will you do me a favor?"

She quirked an eyebrow in response, not about to promise anything before knowing details.

"Will you tell your children about the time sailors? Since I can't tell mine."

Who knew if she'd have children, but she said, "Of course," anyway. If she ended up meeting Mr. Right and having babies, she'd start her own oral tradition and stress that it be passed down for generations. She wouldn't just do it for Dr. Rodney Duncan. She'd do it for Stella.

~

Claire awoke to the soft click of the door. Her eyes fluttered open to find Wendy's bed empty. She checked her Fitbit: 2:30 a.m. Strange. Where had she gone? When trying to fall back asleep didn't prove successful, Claire got up, changed into workout clothes, and headed to the gym. Nothing like a middle-of-the-night workout to untangle the mess of emotions inside her. Especially since her workout on the stairs had been interrupted.

Her cheeks heated. Interrupted in the most delightful way. Lips tingling at the thought of Neo's kiss, she hopped onto the exercise bike and pedaled.

Was it ridiculous for her to have kissed him? True, she didn't know the guy, but Wendy didn't either. She hadn't been there to see the tender care Neo had shown in escorting Claire up the stairs or checking her ankle. Wendy hadn't seen his chivalry. Hadn't heard his sweet concern during their conversation. Hadn't seen the depth of his chocolate brown eyes as he'd listened—truly listened—to her.

Claire had never met anyone like him.

He didn't treat her as just a pretty face. Didn't talk to her as if she were dumb. He acted like she was worth knowing. Unlike Ryan. Unlike Troy. Unlike Blake.

Ugh. Blake.

Blake the Snake. Is that where her insecurity stemmed from? That stupid group project? Back in science class during her freshman year of high school.

She could have been stuck doing a project about rocks or winged insects, but this time, she had a green light to do a project involving health and nutrition. What amazing luck.

The moment the words of approval left Mrs. Acre's mouth, a dozen possibilities bubbled up like geysers. How the rise of technology had negatively impacted exercise trends in America? No, too obvious. The dangers of trans fat?

Even more obvious. No. This needed to be far more meaningful. Her eyes roamed around the room as Mrs. Acre assigned the last few groups. Her classmates were clueless about much more than who was dating whom and what people were wearing to prom. She could educate them. Make an impact.

Food deserts? That was more like it. Or the effects of unsanitary drinking water in developing countries? She'd wager not one of the freshmen in Mrs. Acre's general science class thought to thank God for clean water that morning. They all took it for granted, but she'd read a heartbreaking article earlier in the week that had twisted her insides. Those poor children with sunken, glassy eyes stared at the camera holding an old, dirty milk jug full of contaminated river water. The very thing they reached for to keep them alive was killing them. Now *that* would make a compelling project.

She pulled her sleek hair into a ponytail. Time to get to work. On her notebook, she jotted a list of tasks and began to delegate them to each member of the group. Blake Adams and Penny Narcaster had practically dislocated their arms volunteering to be in the group with her. And why wouldn't they? They had to know the topic of health and nutrition was her passion. Blake was a goof-off, and Penny went with the flow. Claire was the obvious group leader for this one.

Mrs. Acre finished her instructions, and around Claire, desks and chairs began to shift. Blake and Penny scooted their desks against hers.

Blake plopped down with an easy smile. "Here's what I was thinking. We take a picture of hottie here"—he pointed to Claire—"with food from each of the food groups and slap it on a poster. Easy A. Can you wear leggings and a sports bra?"

She stared at him, her brain struggling to jump tracks from unsanitary drinking water to posing with a celery stick. What the heck was he talking about? Food groups? Seriously? They weren't in third grade anymore.

She pressed her lips together for a second before speaking. "Actually, I was thinking—"

He grimaced. "No need for that. Do what you do best. Look smokin'." He turned to Penny. "I figured you can type the report. A few paragraphs on the healthiest foods in each food group. Sound good?"

Penny shrugged. "Sure. No problem."

Her mouth fell open. No problem? Penny didn't have a problem taking on the brunt of the work for this farce of a project? Apparently not, because she was assumed to be the smart one. Claire, however, was only a pretty face devoid of a brain.

What use was there in arguing? They obviously didn't care about what she had to say. They only wanted an easy project. An easy A. So much for wanting to be in her group because they valued her input. Maybe they thought it was the easiest subject. Or Blake only wanted to exploit her body.

Nothing to offer. It was clear she had nothing to offer. At least, nothing that went beyond skin deep. Not here. Maybe not anywhere.

Claire's pulse pounded as she pedaled faster and faster as if she could out cycle the memory. How stupid that she could even recall the silly project from way back when. It didn't matter anymore. Not now, when she had a hit YouTube channel with half a million followers. She clearly had something to offer that many found valuable. People tuned in from around the world to learn how to get toned and healthy, which helped them to live more fulfilling lives. She did important work.

Yet a niggling voice taunted her, reminding her of the lewd comments some posted, the crude offers. It suggested she wouldn't have such a following if she didn't have a pretty face and gorgeous body. Her looks were what secured her position in stardom, not her brain. Not her personality. Not who she was on the inside. Heck, she couldn't even get a real job. This was her only shot, using the beauty God had given her to create a living for herself.

If she screwed it up, then what?

She couldn't screw it up.

What was that parable about the servant who buried his talents in the ground? The master rebuked him, yet he rewarded the servant who invested his talents. That was what she was doing. Investing her talents. Growing them. Starting with ten followers, gaining ten more. Starting with one hundred thousand followers, gaining one hundred thousand more. Starting with a YouTube channel, gaining a TV slot. No matter how Wendy disparaged her work, this was Biblical stewardship.

She started her cooldown and worked through a reel she could post on the importance of stretching. Yes, she'd do that and schedule it to post in a few hours.

She wasn't about to miss this chance. She'd not bury her talent.

Chapter Seven

Stella awoke in a cold sweat. She'd dreamed of those men who'd spoken of weapons outside her room. She'd dreamed of them breaking into homes, shooting those weapons, killing men in cold blood. She shivered and wrapped the quilt tightly around herself. There was another part of the dream. She struggled to remember it. As she sat still and concentrated, it came back to her. She'd written on the crate with the weapons. Instead of an A, she'd turned it into CARPENTER'S TOOLS.

Such an odd dream, but her skin prickled with awareness. It meant something. What if this was her mission? What if 1856 had called to her for this purpose? To change the label on the crate so that … what? So the men wouldn't be able to find their ammunition? So they wouldn't use those guns to murder?

None of this made sense. She should go back to bed. She lay back down, but she couldn't shake the impression she needed to go back to that box.

Ridiculous. By herself? How would she even find it, much less relabel it?

Well, she did have a black Sharpie. Overpacking to the rescue. She could make the current A part of CARPENTER'S.

No. That was crazy. Sleep was what she needed. A lot more sleep.

Only, what if this premonition was the Lord speaking to her? She could at least ask Him. She should. But she didn't want to hear His answer if He told her He wanted her to get out of her comfortable bed and go poking around the dark boat for a box of weapons that scary men wanted. Surely, she wasn't the only person who shirked prayer when she wasn't positive she'd like God's answer. She buried her face in the feather pillow and groaned.

Coming up for breath, she whispered a prayer. "Lord, You don't want me to relabel that box, do You?" She didn't wait for an answer. "And besides, even if You did, I'm too afraid to."

The Lord knew her through and through. He had to be aware of what a coward she was. And He loved her anyway, right? He knew what He was getting into when He chose her for His kingdom, and He still chose her. So, it was kind of His fault.

A light rap at her outside door made her jump and stifle a scream. Good golly, who in the world would be knocking at her door at this hour? She rubbed her clammy arms. Was it the two men who'd been talking about weapons? Had they come to use those weapons on her?

She told herself to answer the door, or at least check who it was, but her feet wouldn't budge from underneath the covers.

"Miss Lindy?" Dr. Duncan's voice came as a whisper through the crack of the door frame. What was he doing here?

She padded to the door and cracked it open.

His forehead puckered at the sight of her. "You're not ready."

"Ready for what?" She brushed a strand of hair from her face, then combed the rest of her bedhead with her fingers.

"How can you ask that? *You* dream-summoned *me*. I arose from a perfectly fine night's sleep to come, and now you're not ready." His hair, too, stuck out in all directions, but instead of taming it, he stuffed his hands into his pockets, frowning.

"I what?"

"You dream-summoned me."

"How did I do that, exactly?"

He pulled out his pocket watch and made an exaggerated gesture of checking the time. "If you'll excuse me, Miss Lindy, the hour is quite late. Are we or are we not going to relabel the box?"

She gasped. "My dream. You had it too?"

He huffed. "You gave it to me, Miss Lindy. You used it to inform me of the next action you wanted to take."

That certainly wasn't the case. But maybe she could do this if Dr. Duncan was beside her. And she was already wide awake with little chance of falling back asleep. Might this be God's guidance after all?

"Okay, let's go." She rushed to slide on her flip-flops and returned to the door.

He scanned her outfit. "You intend to wear that attire?"

She'd fallen asleep in the KU shirt and sweat shorts. "Not quite a modest frock, huh?"

He hesitated, then sighed. "We don't have time for you to dress. We must hurry if we want to return before the cabin staff awakens."

She nodded, grabbed a Sharpie and lantern, and closed the door behind her.

They walked in silence to the stairwell. Water sloshed beside them. Frogs croaked and crickets and cicadas chirped along the riverbank, but the night was otherwise serene. No lurking shadows clawed at her. She could almost forget her dream and imagine she was merely out for a moonlit stroll on the deck.

When they reached steerage, they walked with purpose toward where they'd seen the box of ammunition. Holding their lanterns close, they inspected each crate's label until Dr. Duncan whispered, "Here."

He then held the lantern out so she could see clearly enough to write stencil-shaped letters. She'd just finished the S on TOOLS when a voice behind her made her yelp.

"What are ya doing here?"

She spun around, hand clasped over her mouth. Her breath rushed out of her in relief. McDonald. Dr. Duncan had said he could be trusted.

His brows lifted as he took her in. "Why are ya trouncing about in your bloomers and underthings, missy?"

Bloomers? Her face heated. He must mean her shorts. She should have taken the time to put on a dress. She scrambled for an excuse for her attire but came up short.

Dr. Duncan answered for her, ignoring the last question. "This crate was suspiciously labeled. We needed to remedy that."

"Aye. And you think doing such will help us sneak it into Kansas, do ya?" McDonald crossed his arms over his chest.

Wait. *Us?* "You mean this is *your* box?" Not the scary men from outside her door? A jittery chuckle escaped before she could suppress it.

McDonald raised a brow. "Ya got this missy workin' for ya without her knowing a thing, do ya, Duncan?" His gaze dropped to her shirt. "Or does she know more than she be lettin' on?"

"Okay, what is it with my shirt?"

"Quite bold of you, proclaiming yourself to be a Jayhawker for anyone to see." His mouth tipped in a smile, revealing crooked incisors.

She cast an exasperated glance to Duncan, who only shrugged. Seriously? Would no one tell her what a Jayhawker was?

"Ya better get back now. Wouldn't want anyone to suspect this pretty miss is involved." McDonald winked.

"Involved in what?"

McDonald's snort was the only reply.

What had she gotten herself into? Something that required boldness and risk, apparently, but she didn't deserve any accolades for courage. If these men only knew how adverse to conflict she truly was.

She turned to go, but McDonald stopped Duncan with a hand on his arm. "Introduce her to the man from Massachusetts. They be kindred spirits."

"I shall." The men shook hands.

Kindred spirits? Her mind spun. They'd better not be trying to set her up with anyone. Her heart belonged fully to Everett, even if she'd done a poor job of standing up for him.

As she followed Dr. Duncan up the stairs, she whispered her questions. "What's going on? You're involved with that box of weapons? What are they for? Who's this guy from Massachusetts?"

He let out a low chuckle. At the top of the stairwell, he turned to her and grasped her shoulders. The breeze blew his wild hair about like wheat waving in the wind. "I'm a freedom fighter like you, and yes, I'm working with a group of people to get that box to Kansas."

"A freedom fighter?"

"Yes. A Jayhawker. A freedom fighter. An abolitionist."

Abolitionist. Finally, something she understood. "Against slavery."

"Yes."

"But why does Kansas need weapons?" She shuddered, images from her dream vivid around the edges of her mind.

"To defend themselves against Border Ruffians."

"Border who?"

"Pro-slavers from the Missouri border. Violent men who want Kansas to be a slave state instead of a free state."

"Oh." She'd been touting herself as an abolitionist without knowing it. Which was fine, right? Because, of course, she was against slavery. Naturally, she'd want to help Dr. Duncan with whatever he had in mind. But violent Border Ruffians? Was that who those men were outside her door? Was she putting herself in danger weeks before her wedding?

She curled and uncurled her fingers. "And the man from Massachusetts? Is he a Jayhawker too?"

Moonlight reflected off Dr. Duncan's smile. "The best of the best."

"Okay, then. I look forward to meeting him." She had a few questions for the man. She glanced down the deck toward her stateroom. The long night was beginning to catch up with her. Exhaustion pulled at her limbs. "I'd better get back."

"See you at breakfast."

"Yeah. I'll wear a modest frock." She turned and walked to her stateroom, flip-flops slapping the deck with each step.

~

The next morning, Wendy awoke with a start to Claire shaking her and shouting. She peeled up the bottom of her sleep mask. "For the love, Claire, what is it?"

"A letter!" Claire shook an envelope in her face. "We got a letter under our door."

Wendy sat up and flung her mask off. "From whom? Stella?" Or Dr. Duncan masquerading as Stella?

"I think from her. Maybe." Claire plopped next to her, causing the bed to bounce slightly. "I mean, that's her handwriting, isn't it?" She angled the front of the envelope with their names on it toward her.

"Yes!" Oh, my goodness. It worked. It actually worked. They'd sent a letter through time and gotten one in return. "Go on. Open it."

Claire started to daintily split the top of the envelope with her fake nail.

"Oh my gosh. Give it to me." Wendy snatched it, ripped it open, and read it out loud.

"Wow." Claire looked at her with rounded eyes. "This is real? Like, really real."

"The *Arabia*. How come that sounds familiar?" Wendy twirled a curl around her finger, searching her memory.

"It doesn't ring any bells for me." Claire took the letter from Wendy's hand and reread it.

The *Arabia* steamboat. She'd heard of it somewhere, which was odd, considering steamboats weren't her particular area of historical interest. The image of a paddle wheel flashed in her mind. Wait.

She grabbed Claire's arm. "I've been there."

"Where? On the *Arabia*?" Her brows nearly reached her hair line.

"Yes. Well, no, of course. Not on the antebellum boat. But there's a museum in Kansas City called the Arabia Steamboat Museum, and I've been there on a field trip with my class."

"Why would they have a museum dedicated to a steamboat?"

"Because it sank." In her mind, she walked through fragments of memories from the tour. If only she could remember more. "It hit a log and sank with all this cargo on board. Then, many years later, these guys discovered it buried in a field or something, and they dug it up. The museum had the artifacts they found on board."

Claire's panicked voice broke through her haze of memories. "Stella's boat is going to sink?"

Oh shoot. "Quick. Look it up, will you? Steamboat *Arabia* sinking. When did it happen? My mind is fuzzy on the details."

Claire whipped out her phone. Or rather, Stella's phone. Since Stella had taken Claire's phone back in time, Claire'd been using her friend's phone to stay connected. Her fingers flew across the keys with impressive precision for someone with two-inch nails. "September 5, 1856."

They stared at each other in stunned silence for a minute before Wendy nudged her. "Read more."

"It says on September 5, 1856, on a routine trip, the *Arabia* hit a tree snag near Parkville, Missouri. The snag ripped open the hull, and the lower deck rapidly filled with water. The upper decks stayed above water."

"And no one died, right? Am I remembering correctly?"

"It says the only casualty was a mule."

"And by the next day, nearly the entire boat had sunk into the mud?"

"Yes. All but the smokestacks and pilot house, whatever that is."

"It's the …" Never mind. It wasn't important. "The good thing is, even if Stella is on the boat when it sinks, she's probably not in mortal danger."

Worry lines still creased Claire's forehead. "Yeah, but if there's no boat, there's no mailbox. No way to communicate. And doesn't she have to be on the water to cross the water back into our time?"

Wendy sucked in her bottom lip. Good point. "Okay. We need to figure out what month Stella is in. We might find out we've got plenty of time."

Claire's frown proved she wasn't relieved.

"Then we have to figure out what her mission is and how we can help her accomplish it. It seems like that's the only way to get her back here with us."

"Oh yeah. Easy-peasy." Claire blanched. She looked like she might be sick.

"Let's take it one step at a time. Step one: write her back."

Claire nodded. "I can do that."

She rose to get a pen and paper and then returned to sit next to Wendy. "First, to answer her questions."

Wendy scooted close to see what Claire was writing.

> Stella,
>
> We put our letter into the antique mailbox at the suggestion of a man named Dr. Duncan. He's the one who told us you had probably traveled through time. He called you a time sailor and said you'd likely traveled across the waters to accomplish some mission. We thought he was crazy, but your things

disappeared from your room, they had traveled to the other time with you like Dr. Duncan had said. When we checked the room, they were gone. Do you have any idea why this happened?

What month are you in? Wendy has been to the Arabia Steamboat Museum in Kansas City, and she knows a little about the boat. I hate to tell you this, but your boat is going to sink on September 5. We have to figure out a way to get you home before then.

Everett doesn't know you're gone. No one knows but us. And Dr. Duncan. Please give us any clues you have as to what your mission could be.

Claire & Wendy

"Sound okay?" Claire asked.

"Yep." But she snatched the letter and wrote *PS: We love you.*

Claire raised a brow. "I think she knows that."

Maybe. Maybe not. Wendy sure hadn't done a great job showing her over the past year. "Doesn't hurt."

Claire folded the letter, placed it in an envelope, and sealed it. "Ready to go inconspicuously admire the mailbox again?"

Wendy chortled. "Our acting skills are top notch. We make quite a team."

"Yeah. Lucy and Ethel."

They both threw on clothes, and Claire ran a brush through her hair while Wendy finger-combed hers into a messy bun.

"Wait, which one is which? Am I Lucy or Ethel?" Wendy asked as Claire applied eyeliner. The brat better not even think of mentioning weight.

"I'm Lucy, of course. I have red hair."

Wendy snorted. It was dark red. More like brown with rich red highlights. Nothing like Lucy Ricardo, but whatever.

Claire swept eye shadow over her lids. "Did you know I'm naturally blonde?"

Wait, what? "No way." After all these years, not even a hint of blonde roots had shown. "Why'd you switch?" The beautiful blonde persona fit Claire much better.

"I read that brunettes and redheads were perceived as more intelligent. I wanted people to take me seriously." She glided ruby lipstick on and puckered.

Surely, she couldn't change how people perceived her as easily as choosing a box of hair dye from the drugstore. "Did it work?"

"Obviously not. I'll forever be the pretty girl without a brain." Claire scooped her makeup into the handbag she took with her everywhere. As if she'd need a lipstick touch-up while they were out delivering the letter. But her efforts came across differently now. Was her apparent shallowness really a mask for insecurity?

"Oh, Claire. You're so much more." Flashes of who she'd known her friend to be in college came rushing back. Not one to give glib answers. Searching the Scriptures to find truth. The first to offer to help someone who needed it. Even when they didn't deserve it. And no, she might not have been in high-level classes, but it probably wasn't because Claire wasn't smart. She certainly knew a lot about health and fitness. She was the best person to have around when you were sick or aching.

But Claire waved her off. "Anyway, enough about me. Let's deliver this letter."

~

Claire scanned yet another article on Stella's phone, searching for more information on the *Arabia*. She and Wendy sat at an outside table in view of the mailbox, just in case anything crazy happened, like someone waltzing out in period attire. Or Stella rushing to greet them. Not that Claire would see any odd happenings as Wendy had tasked her to research info on Stella's steamboat while Wendy wrote everything she remembered from the field trip.

Wendy was the history buff, not her. Some of the articles had words she didn't know, and the ones she understood all said the same thing. She wasn't learning anything new.

A text from Trenia popped onto the screen. Good thing she'd had the sense to turn the phone on silent. Part of her ached for the freedom from technology Stella was experiencing now. Maybe she shouldn't have given people this number. But pressure from this new opportunity pressed in on her until she could see no other way. She tapped the message and read.

> Where are you? Have you fallen into the ocean? If you want a shot at F.T., get back on social media pronto.

Her stomach churned. So, this was how it felt to watch your dream career slip through your fingers. But what was she supposed to do? Excuse herself from vital research to do a Pilates video by the pool? Oh, the judgment that would seep through Wendy's pores at that one.

She needed something, though. Some sort of presence.

"Miss Booker!" Allison waved at Wendy. She was walking next to an older woman who had to be her mother.

Wendy's gaze shot from her notebook to the pair. "Oh, hi." Her voice sounded strained. "Allison. Mrs. Gardenia. Nice to see you."

Allison's mother smiled stiffly, her shoulders rigid. Allison didn't seem to notice as she bounded closer. "Are you working? You're supposed to be on summer vacation."

Wendy chuckled nervously as she shut the notebook and poked the pen through the spiral. "No, not working. Just researching for fun."

Mrs. Gardenia made a little noise in her throat. It sounded somewhat judgy.

Wendy stood so abruptly her chair nearly toppled backward. "Actually, I was about to leave. It was nice seeing you again."

Leave? Leave where? Allison and her mom said goodbye—the girl with a grin, the mother with a scowl. Claire stared up at Wendy for answers.

She bent low and whispered, "I'm going to the library for a while. Maybe I can find information there."

Claire tried not to let her relief show. "Okay. Good idea." Hopefully, Wendy didn't expect her to come.

As soon as Wendy was out of sight, Claire took the phone back out and pulled up her socials. She spent a few minutes liking and replying to comments. An idea struck her. She could be present on social media and get research done at the same time. And yes, thank goodness, her signal was strong here on the deck.

She found the best angle for the camera, reapplied lipstick, put on her brightest smile, and went live.

"Hi, everyone! It's Claire from Claire-ity Fitness. I can't wait to give you some great tips and tricks in a few days from the beach! But for now, I'm wondering if you can help me out. Does anyone know about the steamboat *Arabia* that sailed the Missouri River in the 1850s? If you can give me any information I can't find on Wikipedia, I'll send you a free Claire-ity Fitness water bottle! Thanks, everyone."

She waved and signed off.

Now to wait.

Chapter Eight

Stella stepped out of her stateroom into an uproar. The social hall brimmed with chaos as passengers huddled about, handkerchiefs pressed to taught, pale faces. The captain stood on a stool and read from a letter. The tumult drowned out his words. What was going on?

She'd awoken to the blast of a whistle. The boat had slowed, then stopped. In a rush, she'd pried open the box Leela had delivered the night before and sifted through bonnets, hats, and undergarments until she found a golden-brown dress. She'd slipped it on, struggling to button it herself. It was slightly big on her, but with some contorting that rivaled a circus performer, she managed to do it. She'd stick with her underthings from her century and dig through the rest of the items in the box later. She needed to find out why the boat had stopped.

All she could gather was that something was horribly wrong.

Dr. Duncan stood a few feet away. She wove her way to him and whispered in his ear. "What's going on?"

"Someone found a letter dropped by a Mr. Start from Massachusetts"—he gave her a pointed look—"that says there are weapons on board destined for Kansas."

Her throat went dry.

"We're about to dock near Lexington. Captain Shaw is notifying the authorities." His tone and expression remained as neutral as if he were giving a weather report, but thick tension radiated from him. "We need to move the crate to a more inconspicuous place. Quickly." His eyes flashed a warning. "Before they search for it."

She pressed her hands to her middle as a wave of nausea rose. "We?"

He nodded, nostrils flaring slightly. "Please. Your assistance would be much appreciated. It's hard to maneuver on my own."

What if her mission was to help get this crate to Kansas safely? Failing would mean—What would it mean? Remaining here in 1856? That was not an option.

"I expect everyone to cooperate," Captain Shaw announced.

"Of course, he does," a man beside them said. "He knows he could be hanged for this."

The woman near him tsked. "It's not the captain's fault. It's the man with the letter who should hang."

Someone else chimed in from a few feet away. "Him and whoever else had anything to do with these weapons."

Goosebumps flecked Stella's arms. Dr. Duncan took her elbow, searching her eyes.

Could she truly hang for helping him with this? But if she didn't help, she might risk not returning home at all. She fingered the base of her throat, imagining a noose. But then she pictured Everett waiting for her at the end of a wedding aisle.

She squared her shoulders. "Let's go."

Ducking her head, she allowed Dr. Duncan to steer her away from the social hall and toward the boiler deck. As they passed through the door, she cast a nervous glance over her shoulder to find narrowed eyes peering back at her. Shoot. Some man had noticed their exit. Was he wondering where they were going?

With hurried steps, they made their way to the stairwell and bounded to the cargo hold. A chilly breeze swirled around them. Her nerves leapt as something clattered on the floor above them. What was that? She put a hand to her racing heart. She had to focus. She couldn't get distracted.

"Come now," Dr. Duncan whispered, reaching the crate. "Heft your side. We'll move it back behind the cargo hatch and place another crate on top."

She bent to hoist it, but her biceps screamed in protest at the weight. She wasn't strong enough. Why did Dr. Duncan think she could do this? Why hadn't he asked someone else? Someone stronger, like McDonald?

He peered at her, his stormy eyes narrowing with intensity. "I need you to summon all the mettle you can muster."

She clenched her jaw and, with a grunt, lifted the box a few inches off the ground. It nearly slipped from her sweaty fingers, but she grappled for a firmer grasp. The wood dug into her palm, and she bit her lip to keep from griping. They made it merely a foot before her muscles gave way, and she had to set it down.

A series of thuds sounded above them. What was that? Stella looked up, shivering as if at an approaching storm.

Dr. Duncan rushed to the deck's edge, scanning the area above where the commotion was coming from. All color drained from his face. "Border Ruffians have boarded," he whispered. "Hurry."

Once again, they hefted the crate and maneuvered it a few feet farther back before thundering footsteps halted their progress. Dr. Duncan's eyes widened, and he guided her with his gaze to a small haven behind nearby barrels. He slipped behind a stack of lumber.

Rough-looking men clomped through the cargo, armed with crowbars and pistols. They busted open crates and rifled through the contents, spilling beans and buttons all over the deck. A sea-blue glass bead rolled near Stella's foot as she huddled behind a barrel of cheese, breathing as shallow and quietly as she could, watching their every move. She'd make a run for it if she had to, not that it'd do her much good. Surely, they were faster than her. They were certainly bigger. Their muscles bulged through their buttoned-up shirts and open vests.

She sucked on the inside of her cheek as she waited, counting the seconds. *Lord, keep that crate away from these dangerous men.* Why had she taken part in something so foolish? She never did things like this. Never jumped into something haphazardly without calculating the costs. Yet here she was. The whole time-sailing thing remained a mystery, but if she died in the past, she couldn't expect to live in the future. Couldn't expect to marry Everett and have her happily ever after. *Oh, God! Don't let me die.*

But after dumping out the contents of the nearby box, they came to the crate Stella and Dr. Duncan had failed to hide. Her naive hope crumbled with the sly grin spreading across the leader's face.

"Found it!" he shouted, so close Stella could have reached and untied his shoe. "Over here. Says Carpenter's Tools."

Stella slammed her eyes shut in a heavy blink. Her shoulders slumped. All that for nothing. They'd found the crate anyway. What was the point of risking her life? Had she failed at her mission? What would that mean?

The voice called, "Maybe a hundred Sharps rifles."

A hundred of them? No wonder the crate was so heavy.

More commotion ensued to her right. Other ruffians dragged the captain down the steps. He winced but didn't make a sound, even as his leg banged against the railing.

One man got in the captain's face. "Do you resign these weapons peacefully?"

Captain Shaw stood stoically, not backing down, not pushing for a fight. "Indeed."

"Then we won't have a problem, will we?"

"I think not."

The ruffian spit on the deck near the captain's shoe. "But if we ever find weapons on your ship again, we'll hang you. You and anyone who brought them on board or had a thing to do with them. You hear me?"

"Clearly."

Four men worked together to lug the crate off the boat. Another walked the captain back upstairs. She remained as still as stone, listening until all footsteps retreated. Was it safe to come out? Fear froze her in place.

Soft rustling sounds made her teeth chatter. Dr. Duncan's face popped into her periphery, and she startled.

"It's safe for us to reemerge. May I help you up?" He extended his hand.

She allowed him to assist her to stand. As she accompanied him back to the social hall, she couldn't stop shivering, despite the muggy morning. She rubbed her arms to ward off the bone-deep chill. The breakfast bell sounded, but the thought of food turned her stomach.

Hanged. She could have been hanged. If someone would have seen her writing on the crate, they would have assumed she had intimate knowledge of the entire scheme. She'd narrowly escaped execution in 1856.

"Thank you for your assistance." Dr. Duncan's voice was quiet. Resigned.

"A lot of good it did."

"Valiant efforts are never wasted ones, Miss Lindy." Dr. Duncan gave her a sympathetic pat on the shoulder before motioning toward the interior of the boat.

She preceded him inside to the cadence of loud voices. While cabin members scurried back and forth, setting the table for the morning meal, several men argued and jeered at each other. Or perhaps at one man in particular.

Air whooshed from her lungs as she recognized the man in the center of the debate. He loomed above the others in the group, taller and broader than anyone else. A beam of sunlight reflected off his blond hair. One of the two scary men outside her room the other night. One of the men from her dream.

She clutched Dr. Duncan's elbow. "Who is that man?"

He spoke low in her ear. "It's best not to introduce you now. Too dangerous. But that, Miss Lindy, is the man from Massachusetts McDonald and I spoke to you about."

She recoiled. "Him?"

"Yes."

"But he's—" She stopped herself from saying *dangerous*. "Never mind."

"Maybe," he said as if she'd spoken her thoughts aloud. Could he read her mind, or did he guess from experiencing her dream? "But we all fight for freedom in our own ways."

Okay, she was officially freaked out. She probably couldn't trust the man from Massachusetts. Could she trust Dr. Duncan? He'd been nothing but helpful and kind. Besides, what choice did she have? But the company he kept was questionable. Or perhaps she had no clue what was truly going on.

Writing on the crate or hiding it couldn't have been her mission, her reason for being here. If it had been, she'd be back in the present right now. Not to mention, it had accomplished nothing.

But Dr. Duncan's words echoed in her head. *We all fight for freedom in our own ways.*

She hadn't fought for freedom. Ever. She'd never taken a stand against injustice, despite multiple opportunities to do so. Her heart squeezed at the memories. She'd been silent when she should have spoken out.

But there was something she *could* do. Now.

She could teach Leela to read.

Anticipation ignited in her at the thought. Could she be so bold? So brave?

Yes. She could, and she would. Starting tonight.

As the servers bustled back and forth, placing dishes and then food at the table, the tantalizing scents teased her. Perhaps she could eat after all. Eggs, muffins, pancakes, rolls. At least this part of the journey seemed up to par with her planned vacation.

She moved toward an empty chair. But then Leela walked across the room, and Stella stilled. She couldn't get distracted from her mission. She caught Leela's gaze and winked. The edges of the chambermaid's mouth turned up. Did they have an understanding? A shared secret?

Stella's smile spread. She'd finally become a freedom fighter.

Another bell tolled, this one much harsher than the breakfast bell. Oh no. A snag. She clamped her hand onto the back of her chair, expecting a small jostle. Instead, a large bump thrust her forward. She knocked over her chair and jammed her elbow into the woman next to her. Hats tumbled off heads and onto the eggs and muffins. Shouts and cries rang out. And then, all went black.

~

Wendy plodded into the library and collapsed onto an armchair. A curl bounced against her forehead. She blew it to the side.

Talk about a smooth getaway. She could have skated all the way here on the iciness of Mrs. Gardenia's glare. If Claire hadn't been there, perhaps she would have addressed the issue between them. But Claire didn't know Wendy was on probation at work. And she didn't know why.

All Claire knew was that Wendy's students loved her. Though she had a reputation of being a "hard" teacher, she had an equal rep of being a cool one. She didn't take any crap. Students knew not to expect their excuses to fly with Miss Booker. In her class, you worked hard, you owned up to your mistakes, and you accomplished more than you ever thought possible. Her no-nonsense style was a turnoff to some, but most of her students respected it because she balanced it with fun and snark, two things middle schoolers loved most.

That snark didn't go over as well with parents.

It certainly didn't go over well with Mrs. Gardenia.

And to think they'd once been friends, or at least on friendly terms. Come to think of it, Marilyn Gardenia probably found out about this cruise because Wendy shared about the great deal she'd snagged. Maybe that was the problem. Wendy had felt a bit too comfortable around the woman who frequently volunteered in her class. So comfortable she must have shed a layer of professionalism along the way. Let her guard down and been too much of herself during those spaces of time without students in the room. One morning, it had become clear as the atmosphere chilled when Marilyn reminded Wendy to call her *Mrs. Gardenia*. Something she'd said must have caused the shift between them. Whatever it was, Marilyn had gone to the principal and then the school board about it.

Did Allison have any idea? She couldn't. She'd be devastated if she knew her favorite teacher was in jeopardy of losing her job because of her mom's ruffled feathers. Apparently, Wendy couldn't figure out when to keep her mouth shut, even when it mattered most.

What would she do if she lost her job? She loved her students. Lived for teaching in a way that made her wonder if she should get a dog or take up tennis or something. If Bristol Middle School fired her, would she be able to get a job anywhere else? She had no backup plan.

"Is it that bad?"

Wendy startled at the voice coming from the armchair across from her. She'd been in her own pathetic world and hadn't paid attention to her surroundings. The man sat with an open book in his lap. His honey-brown hair was shaved on the sides and crested on the top of his head like a wave. His trimmed beard and mustache lifted with a small smile. Amber eyes shone at her from behind matching glasses. He wore jeans with a black V-neck T-shirt. He exuded an aura of edgy and cool. *My word.* Her students would gravitate to this guy like fans to a football game.

"Excuse me?" She couldn't rein in her return smile.

He closed the book, using a finger to keep his place, and leaned forward. "It can't be *that* bad, can it? You look like you've lost your best friend."

Her smile dropped. "I have."

He covered his mouth. "Oh no. I'm so sorry." He ran a finger over his forehead. "I'm forever sticking my foot in my mouth."

She couldn't let this poor guy think her best friend had died, but how else could she explain this mess? She puffed out her cheeks. "She's not dead. She's … missing."

He rested his elbows on his knees. "Missing?"

She shook her head. She couldn't talk about this with a stranger. "Don't worry about it. Everything will work out." She forced a small smile.

His frown didn't vanish, but he made no move to argue. "I'm Grayson."

"Wendy."

"Nice to meet you. Did you come here to get away from your father, who is driving you certifiably insane, or is it just me?"

That flipped her insincere smile into a sincere one. "Must be just you. I literally fled from one of my student's mothers."

His eyes brightened. "You're a teacher?"

"Yep. Middle school."

"No way." He sat back and crossed an ankle over his knee. "I'm a high school history teacher."

Her ears perked. "History?"

He nodded. "Crazy, right? I actually enjoy the subject that puts many of my students to sleep."

Oh, she doubted any of his female students fell asleep watching him. She scooted to the edge of her seat. "Do you know anything about antebellum steamboats?"

His eyes squinted at the edges. "I've got to say, that's one question no one's ever asked me before."

"The *Arabia*. Have you heard of it?"

He brought a knuckle to his chin. "Wait, wasn't that the one that sunk near Kansas City? There's a museum about it. I went there when I was in school."

"Yes!" She nearly jumped out of her chair. "Yes, that's it." When his eyes flew wide, she tempered her enthusiasm.

"That's the one. I took a group of my students there for a field trip a couple of years ago. I was sick this year, so they went with the sub."

He chuckled. "Poor sub. They have a hard enough job corralling the kids inside a school building."

She played with a curl. "I hadn't thought about it from her end. I was just bummed I didn't get to see it all again. Fascinating."

"I know, right? Do they still show the same old video of the excavators, where one of them talks about eating the pickles they uncovered from the boat?"

"Yes." She scrunched her nose at the thought of eating one-hundred-year-old pickles. "In fact, that same man was our tour guide when we went."

"No way!" He smacked his knee. "One of the originals? He's got to be getting up there by now."

"For sure. It was hard to understand him, but he had incredible insight."

For a full minute, they stared at each other. The silence didn't even inch into awkward territory until after the thirty-second mark. His eyes were gorgeous. They shone outward and drew her inward at the same time.

What were they talking about again? History. Teaching. Stella.

Her spine straightened. *Focus, Wendy. Focus.*

"Anyway." She forced herself to study her plain, boring nails. Anything to keep from getting pulled into those honey-rich orbs. "A friend of mine was given an assignment that depends on her knowing as much about the *Arabia* as possible." She chanced a glance. Heaven help her.

Grayson's brow furrowed. He was skeptical, wasn't he? Of course. She sounded ridiculous.

"Her assignment is top secret, so I'm afraid I can't share details." She winced. That had made her sound more crazy, not less. "I don't even know many of the details myself. What I do know is any information about the *Arabia* would greatly help my friend. If you could—"

He gave a decisive nod. "Of course, I'll help. Anything you need."

"Really?" She'd only just met this guy. He knew next to nothing about her. She quirked a brow. "Why?"

He flashed a grin. "We teachers have to stick together, right?"

She rolled her eyes. Cheesy.

"Besides, I told you my dad is driving me up a wall. Any excuse I can conceive of to get a break from his company is more than welcome."

She couldn't hold back a smirk as she threw his opening words back at him. "Is it that bad?"

"Yes." She loved the way his facial hair framed his smile. "My dad is a compulsive complainer. He can't help himself. He opens up his mouth and negativity spews forth." He gestured the spewing motion with his hands.

"What's there to complain about on a cruise ship?"

"Oh, you'd be surprised. The food is too bland. The cabin air is too stale. The loudspeaker is too loud. The waitstaff is too slow. The water too warm. The children too rowdy. The women too scantily clad. The men without manners. The alcohol too plentiful. The entertainment too few." He gestured around. "And this library has too many stinkin' books."

She was laughing so hard tears formed in her eyes. "You've got to be exaggerating."

"Oh no, my new friend. You wait and see. You meet Sam Hill, and you'll know I haven't disclosed the half of it."

She nearly choked on her laughter. "Sam Hill? Your dad's name is Sam Hill?"

"The one and—wait, no. Not the one and only, but yes." He held up a finger. "And in case you're wondering where the saying 'what in Sam Hill' comes from, it was taken from a Michigan surveyor by that name in the 1800s who cussed so monstrously his name became a euphemism for foul language."

She could. Not. Stop. Laughing. She tried to catch her breath but only ended up wheezing on air before dissolving into giggles again. She couldn't remember when she'd had this much fun talking with someone.

Finally, she patted her eyes dry and calmed enough to speak. "With a namesake like that, you should be thankful he isn't worse."

"True."

She worked to keep her mouth in a straight line. "Also, with a last name like Hill, you should be thankful your parents named you Grayson. There are much worse possibilities."

"Like?" He mirrored her straight face.

"Rocky." She inhaled through her nose, using all her self-control to keep her lips from turning upward.

"Sandy." He didn't so much as twitch a facial muscle.

"Cliffy." She couldn't breathe, or she'd crack.

"Bill." He stared back.

Something else. Something else. She couldn't think of another witty thing to say.

When he started to hum, at first, she thought it was the *Jeopardy!* theme song. But no. He was humming "The Sound of Music."

She burst into laughter again. "Oh my gosh, stop!"

"You started it. Making fun of my name."

She rubbed her sore ab muscles. "I haven't laughed that hard in years."

His smile dimmed slightly. "That's unfortunate."

She mirrored his expression. "Yeah. It is."

Again with the staring at each other, looking into those beautiful brown eyes. What was she doing? Turning into Claire? She shut her eyes, blocking out the distraction.

"Anyway, yes, I'd love your help with finding information about the *Arabia*. Anything you can remember or find. I don't suppose they'd have anything about it in here?" She opened her eyes to scan the bookshelves.

"Unlikely, but I'll take a look." He stood to peruse the shelves to the left of the room.

She went to the right side. Starting at the top left of the first bookshelf, she scanned each row left to right, top to bottom, looking for any title that would hold even an ounce of hope for information. The books weren't categorized. Fiction titles stood next to nonfiction, a Stephen King horror next to an encyclopedia on birds next to a Jamie Ogle historical fiction. Her fingers itched to make sense out of this mess, but she suppressed the urge. Passengers borrowed a book and then returned it to a shelf, and wherever they stashed it was where it stayed. It wasn't like the ship paid a librarian.

When nothing of consequence turned up on the first bookshelf, she moved to the second. A recipe book, a whole shelf of smut, a few World War II novels, a book about hunting. How ridiculous to dream they'd have a book about some random Missouri steamship from the 1800s. What information was she even hoping to find?

When she met Grayson in the middle, they were both empty-handed.

She shrugged. "Thanks anyway."

He slid his hands into his back pockets. "Hey, don't give up. I visited that museum years ago, and I can't remember much off the top of my head, but I'll give it some thought. I didn't spring for Wi-Fi, but my old man did. After he conks out tonight, I'll search online. See what I can find."

Okay, all hope wasn't lost. Still, prospects looked bleak. She managed a wobbly smile.

"Meet me here tomorrow afternoon? Say, two o'clock?"

Her smile broadened. "Yes. I can do that."

"Until tomorrow." He gave a little salute and took two steps backward toward the door.

She moved to the exit as well. "Until then." When he held the door open for her, she slipped out. "Rocky."

He turned left. She turned right. Yet his laughter followed her down the hallway. She hummed "The Sound of Music" all the way back to her room.

~

Sweat beaded on Claire's shoulders as she pushed through the last hill on her elliptical's sprint workout. Her muscles screamed to quit, but she silenced them with each forward motion. Cardio always made her feel alive. In control. She could master most anything that came against her in the gym with sheer determination and good form. This was her domain to reign.

Her phone pinged, and her hand flew to it instinctively. Stella? No, that was impossible. No way her friend had cell service in the 1800s. But man, she missed hearing from her. How was she? Was she scared? Grossed out by the lack of sanitation? If only she could hug Stella's neck right now.

The text was likely from Trenia, and no, she wouldn't look. She could check the notification during cooldown. Only a few more minutes. She also needed to remember to take a sweaty selfie for social media. Those always went over well.

When Wendy hadn't returned after an hour, Claire had contemplated sneaking in a video. But she could imagine setting up and getting through her first set of reps only to have Wendy barge in and throw another hissy fit. They'd only just made up. How could she risk such a tenuous bond? Plus, Wendy had a point. Stella was most important here. Their focus. Doing videos for her channel made it seem like she was ignoring the fact her friend was lost in the 1850s with no way to get back. But she hadn't forgotten about Stella. Not a chance. But she'd go mad thinking about something she could do nothing to change. Better to focus on something productive. Surely, Wendy couldn't fault her for going to the gym. She'd watched a twenty-minute YouTube video on the *Arabia* while working out. Which unfortunately hadn't helped much.

A string of dings fired from her phone until she couldn't resist any longer.

> What was that? What does some steamboat have to do with your brand? You're way off track.

Claire's steps faltered. She nearly stumbled off the machine. She hit the emergency button and grasped the handle for dear life. Blood pounded in her ears. Her legs shook.

> Better rein it in, or you'll lose your shot. Fit TV needs more from you.

Her chest burned, burned, burned. She gulped water as if she hadn't had any all day. Some dribbled down her chin. She swiped at it with her shaking arm.

> Bring it, Claire. This is a huge opportunity. Don't screw it up.

No, no, no. Pressure squeezed her temples as she read the texts again. And again. And again.

She'd messed up. Big-time. And she might pay for it with her career.

Maybe she could take the post down? Too late for that. Wincing, she pulled up the live video. A lot of views. Few likes. Even fewer comments. If someone had offered helpful information, it would all be worth it. At least her career suicide would have done something to help Stella. She could go to bed at night after working at some minimum wage job, feeling good about herself as a human being. She held her breath while checking the new comments.

> Looking good, Claire.
> You're a hottie on land and on water.

Claire groaned. It was all for nothing. She'd murdered her chance at Fit TV for absolutely nothing.

Her phone chirped and buzzed in her hand. Another text. This time from Wendy.

She slammed her eyes shut. She could not deal with Wendy's judgmentalism right now. Maybe she should confess everything that was going on with Fit TV. Wendy might be more understanding if she had an idea of what was at stake.

No. More likely, she'd think Claire was more pretentious than ever. She probably thought a big TV deal was ungodly or something. Better for Christians to make their living serving others in more acceptable ways, like teaching or running soup kitchens or scrubbing toilets for orphanages. In Wendy's mind, good Christians lived below the radar.

She'd keep this mess to herself. She'd figure it out.

She stepped back onto the machine to pose for a selfie before all the sweat dried. She tried to make her smile look genuine and unforced, but each picture she snapped rang false. No use trying any other angles. One of those would have to do. She typed a blurb.

As she posted it with the picture, the lies coated her mouth like bile. Keeping it real? What hypocrisy. Which part of her was real? The part of her who cared about helping people be healthy or the part who obsessed over the image she so carefully crafted for the public? Having a blast? Yeah, right. *Lord, where are You in all of this? Where is Your hand in my life?* For a few moments, she stared back at her image now gracing the feed. A bright, alluring face with hauntingly dismal eyes.

Chapter Nine

Stella winced at the pale light streaming through sheer curtains on her deckward door. Light? Sunrise? She sat up, inspecting the space around her. A normal morning on an 1856 steamboat to be sure, but she didn't remember going to bed. She ran through yesterday's events, recalling the escapade with the Border Ruffians in bone-chilling clarity. Then, while waiting for breakfast, a snag had thrust her forward, causing her to bump into another passenger, who had knocked over a chair, and …

Nothing.

She couldn't recall a thing afterward.

Now it was morning again? Did she bump her head when the boat hit the snag? Perhaps she had amnesia. What about her resolution to teach Leela to read? She'd meant to start last night. She massaged her temples. Just when she thought this time-sailing thing couldn't get any stranger.

Someone knocked on her interior door. She rose to answer, thankful she wore the same dress she'd put on the day before. No need to hide from whoever stood outside.

A voice spoke before she could open the door. "It's your chambermaid, miss. I have a letter for you."

Another letter from Wendy and Claire? She flung the door open. But instead of Leela, a different woman stood before her. This one was curvier and younger with large, soulful eyes and a small birthmark on her right cheek.

The woman curtsied. "Good morning, miss. I have a letter for you." She placed the envelope in Stella's waiting hand.

"Thank you, but where's Leela?" Stella smiled to soften her question. She didn't mean to be unkind.

"Leela, miss?" Her forehead creased.

"Yes, the chambermaid who was here yesterday."

She kept her head lowered, gaze hovering near Stella's bare feet. "I've been on board since June, miss."

Strange. She hadn't seen her before. "Okay, but what about the other maid. Leela."

"I'm the only maid on board. This ship is too small to warrant more than one chambermaid."

This woman was either lying or confused. Hard to tell which. Stella studied her for a moment. Not so much as a twitch or flicker to betray a lie. "What's your name?"

"Bridge, miss."

"Bridgett?"

She brought her chin up a notch as if to be clearly heard. "Just Bridge."

"Thank you for this, Bridge." Stella waved the letter. "Are you a slave as well?" The question tumbled out before propriety caught up. It was probably rude of her to ask. Why did it matter, anyway? She was only curious.

"No, miss. I'm a free Black." The corners of Bridge's mouth pinched as if she were holding back a smile.

She bit back a smile of her own. There was something about this woman she liked, though she couldn't place what. "Could you please let Dr. Duncan know I'd like to talk with him on the deck?"

She curtsied again. "Straightaway, miss."

Stella closed the door and rested against it. Something odd was definitely going on. Rather, something odder than the lunacy of traveling back in time.

She swatted away all thoughts of chambermaids and disappearing days from her mind and tore open the envelope. Before even reading a word, the sight of Claire's handwriting comforted her, then her eyes dropped to Wendy's cute postscript. Oh, she missed them. She hugged the letter to her chest, then pulled it back and read it.

Wait, what?

She scanned the third paragraph again. This boat was going to sink? Suddenly, she felt every unsteady shift in the water, heard each creak. This boat that seemed unfaltering would be underwater soon. Gone. Images from the movie *Titanic* flashed through her brain. She shivered. She had no clue what month it was. How long did she have?

She had to get back to Wendy and Claire and Everett. She had some sort of mission to accomplish to return home. This wasn't new information. But now the tick of a clock beat in time with her heart.

There was a deadline. This journalist knew about deadlines.

Another knock came, again at her deck side door. It had to be Dr. Duncan. She rushed to answer it, letter clutched in hand. She flung the door open and didn't give the doctor a chance to wish her a good morning before plowing outside and verbally pelting him.

"What in heaven's name is going on? What happened yesterday? We were in the social hall waiting for breakfast and then what? Did I hit my head or something? Did someone sneak something into my drink? Do they have those kinds of drugs in 1856?"

Dr. Duncan gave her a tight-lipped smile. "Miss Lindy, I do ask that you lower your voice to a more socially acceptable level for a lady of your standing."

She narrowed her eyes. Suppressing her volume, she threw her next words like hard balls. "Answer my questions."

"As to what happened yesterday, Miss Lindy, I believe you are referring to what happened on March 9. Yesterday was August 16, and you weren't …"

"I wasn't? Wasn't what?"

"You weren't in August 16, 1856."

How infuriating! She could shake the man. "You aren't making any sense."

"I may have failed to explain something to you."

"You think?"

He fiddled with his collar, then his tie. "Every time the boat hits a snag, a time sailor will jump forward in time. A small snag causes you to jump forward perhaps a minute or so. It's inconsequential, and you'll likely not notice. A slightly bigger snag can lurch you forward hours. But Miss Lindy, the snag this boat encountered on March 9 was a large snag. It lurched you all the way to August. The date is now August 17."

She backed against the railing, needing the support. She recalled that night when the men had talked outside her door. The snag bell had sounded, there'd been a bump, then it'd suddenly gotten much darker outside.

"Leela?"

"No longer works on this boat, unfortunately."

She'd missed her chance.

Someone had come to her asking for help, and she'd refused. She'd been too frozen in fear to do the right thing, just like before. And now it was too late.

Did she miss her mission? Her chance to return home? Her palms grew clammy.

She swallowed as the date clicked in her mind. "It's the end of August?"

"Yes."

"What about the present time? My real life? Has time leapt forward there as well?" Had she missed the entire cruise? Her stomach dropped. She couldn't have missed her wedding.

"Your other time is proceeding as normal. Snags only affect this era. Your other era moves forward only when you are fully present in this one."

"So, I have until the end of the cruise to figure out what my mission is, complete it, and get back home?"

"Yes, my dear. Nothing to worry about."

If only. The boat was going to sink in twenty days. Should she tell Dr. Duncan? All the movies she'd seen about time travel warned of telling other people the future. Something about messing with the time continuum. She'd better not, at least for now. As long as there were no more snags, she'd be back in present day before the sinking.

If she hadn't already missed the chance to complete her mission.

Oh, God, don't let it be too late.

A breeze ruffled the letter in her hand. "What about this?" She smoothed it out, stepped next to Dr. Duncan, and pointed to his name in print. "You've talked with my friends? You're in my time too?"

He cocked his head, frowning. "Can I see that?"

"By all means." She gestured again to the incriminating evidence, then crossed her arms and stared him down.

"This isn't me." He handed the letter back to her, brow creased.

"What do you mean it's not you? How many Dr. Duncans are there?"

"Perhaps he's a descendant of mine. Might you ask his Christian name? Or his features?"

"His Christian name?" Was he Catholic or something?

"His given name, rather."

"Oh, his first name?"

"Yes, yes. That's it. I'm Joseph Duncan. Without disclosing my first name, inquire of this other Dr. Duncan's full name, as well as what he looks like. I'm sure we can clear up any misunderstanding."

Nothing was clear about this mess, other than that she had to get out of it. And she was running out of time.

~

Wendy caught sight of something white while stumbling to the bathroom in the middle of the night. Another letter? Suddenly, her bladder didn't seem so urgent.

She snatched the envelope, excitement coursing through her at the sight of Stella's handwriting on the front. Claire looked to be sound asleep, with one foot hanging off the bed and her arm draped over her face. Still, she whispered Claire's name to be sure. No movement. Should Wendy wake her? There'd be no waiting until morning to read this letter. She had to either wake Claire or read it by herself and let Claire read it in the morning.

Claire would probably be angry, but Wendy ducked into the bathroom, closed the door, and flipped on the light. If she pried the envelope open carefully, perhaps she could reseal it, and Claire would never know. But she ripped it in the process. Oh well. She'd ask for forgiveness later.

> Wendy & Claire,
> I found out something interesting. Whenever this boat hits a snag, I lurch forward in time. It was March, but now it's August. The boat will sink in twenty days, but it shouldn't affect me, right? Our cruise is only fifteen days, and I have to be back before it's over.
> I thought I knew my mission, but that mission isn't possible now. I'm still trying to figure things out. There's a lot I don't understand. Everyone here freaked out over my KU shirt. Apparently, the term Jayhawker means something very different here. It's an abolitionist, right? They think I'm one because I wore the shirt. Maybe I am, but it seems like a dangerous thing to be, at least here and now. These people called Border Ruffians came on board the ship and threatened to hang people with abolitionist sympathies. Care to explain any of this to me?
> I have questions for you. First, what is your Dr. Duncan's first name? And what does he look like?
> These questions are probably for Wendy: How am I supposed to brush my teeth? What did they do for deodorant in this time? I miss

Wendy itched to reply. She checked her watch. Two in the morning. There was no way she'd be able to fall asleep with the answers to Stella's questions formulating in her head. She knew most of the answers, though she'd need Google's help with converting the tip amount. She tiptoed out of the bathroom and used her cell phone's flashlight to search for paper and a pen. Then, she returned to the bathroom to write.

side. Those years were violent and vicious between the two states. It's when the name "Bleeding Kansas" was coined. Many say it was this conflict that essentially erupted into the Civil War.

Dr. Duncan's first name is Rodney. He's probably in his early fifties. He has thinning brown hair with gray at the temples. He has a freckle next to his right eye, thin, pale lips, and a square jaw. He didn't wear a wedding ring. He knows about time-sailing from stories his great-grandfather told, which were passed down through the generations.

No, you can't use your money. Sorry. And that tip was around $380. No wonder she thought you were being super generous, huh?

I hope that helps. Please let us know what you uncover. We'll do everything we can to get you back here.

Wendy & Claire

PS: No one dies in the *Arabia* sinking. Except a mule.

Wendy folded the paper, stuffed it into an envelope, and licked it closed before she could second-guess herself. The words had flowed from her. She hadn't been able to stop them. And now, with a complete letter, what was she to do? She couldn't tell Claire she'd written a letter back without her. She snuck out of the room and made her way through the quiet halls. An occasional bout of drunken laughter wafted past her, but her path was clear of most everyone but staff members. She popped the letter in the mailbox without anyone chancing upon her, then returned to her room.

What should she do with Stella's letter? If Claire saw it, she'd be angry that Wendy had already replied. But the only thing more she'd learned about Stella's predicament was the problem of the snags. They still didn't know her mission, or how to bring her home. None of the information Stella had shared was vital for Claire to know. Would it be so bad for her to remain ignorant of the letter? It seemed like Claire had other things on her mind anyway.

Wendy tucked it under a book in the bottom of her suitcase.

~

Claire awoke with a gasp the next morning, blinking her nightmare away. In the creepy dream, Stella had been there with them, then she'd disappeared into a murky mist. Now, Claire pressed her thumb onto the pulse on her wrist and willed it to slow. It was just a dream. In real life, Stella was safe. At least, hopefully, she still was. But how could they be sure?

Claire made a living from calm, relaxed breathing and movements. She knew better than to let herself get worked into knots over something she couldn't control. She bent into the child's pose and focused on what was true. God was with her here and now, and He was with Stella in 1856. He promised to never leave them or forsake them. Neither of them were alone. Her heart rate evened out. She sat up. No going back to bed now. Might as well eat.

Wendy didn't flinch when Claire flipped on the light, so she went to breakfast without her. Perhaps she'd had a rough night. Did she have nightmares as well? If there was anything Claire had learned from rooming with her for years, it was not to wake Wendy except in case of an emergency. Claire's growling stomach didn't qualify as such.

She took the stairs two at a time and made it to the breakfast buffet with a raging appetite and accelerated heart rate. She scooped Greek yogurt into her bowl.

"Excuse me," she asked the waitstaff behind the bar, "is this fruit organic?"

But she didn't hear the answer. Across the room, she spotted wavy brown hair and that perfectly chiseled profile. Neo. She froze for a second. Should she shout out his name or duck behind a pillar? Her lips tingled as if they had a mind of their own. That utterly delightful kiss. But no. She'd better stay clear. Nothing good could come of entangling herself with a summer romance when her friend's future hung in the balance. Not to mention Claire's career.

She ducked her head, scooped mangos and pineapple onto her yogurt, and moved to a table on the opposite side of the room, angling herself away from the handsome man. She used the Wendyless time to check her social media stats and respond to comments. The stretching reel had gone over well, thank goodness.

"Look who it is."

Neo's voice set Claire's belly aflame. She flipped her hair over her shoulder and shot him a sassy smile. "Hey, stranger."

"Hey." A world of meaning contained in a single word. A greeting. A question. An invitation.

She had to get out of there. Away from this temptation.

She stood, dish in hand. He didn't back away, and now she couldn't help but look into his chocolate eyes.

"I, uh, have to go. I need to check on my roommate." She pointed a thumb over her shoulder as if Wendy was on the deck behind her and not sleeping three floors down, oblivious to everything but her dreams.

She stepped to her left, ready to return her bowl and jet out of there, but Neo blocked her path.

"I haven't been able to stop thinking about you." An adorable dimple appeared on his left cheek. Oh my.

"I should go." Her protest came out as a squeak. Her feet refused to budge.

He trailed a finger down her arm. "Don't run away, Claire." He hooked his pinky finger around hers. "Don't be afraid."

She wasn't afraid. Not of him. Only of being a horrible friend and terrible person. Of putting herself above others who needed her. Of bad timing. How could she explain it?

He took the bowl from her hand and went to deposit it, then returned. "You know, they'll get your dishes for you if you leave them at the table, but you're too considerate for that, aren't you?"

Her lip trembled. Too considerate? If only.

"How about a walk around deck?" He took her hand and led her out of the air-conditioned dining space into the fresh air.

She could protest. But the reasons why kept fleeing from her mind.

"How's it going with Fit TV?" Once again, his voice hung heavy with concern. He cared. Unlike everyone else in her life.

"Horrible. I screwed up. Did a Live that wasn't part of my brand. Trenia—she's my agent—chewed me out last night. I've got to up my game, but I don't know how. Not with Wendy breathing down my neck and Stella gone. I have to focus on her. She's most important. I can't be doing videos every twenty minutes." She relished the feeling of Neo's hand in hers. Soft and tender. Warm and inviting. What a relief to finally be able to be honest with someone about what was really going on.

"What is Fit TV looking for exactly? What do they want from you?" They stepped aside to let a group of older people pass. Neo pulled her close to him as they waited. Her arm connected with the solid muscle of his chest and abs. Delightful. Was that coconut scent from his sunscreen or shampoo? Wherever it came from, she couldn't get enough. She inhaled with her eyes closed.

Far too soon, the group passed, and Neo led her on. What had he asked again? Oh yeah. What *did* Fit TV want from her?

"A strong presence, mostly. An engaged community. That means I must keep posting regularly. To keep trending, you can't fall off the face of the internet."

"How long does it take to do that? What's the grace period?"

She twisted her mouth. "Maybe five hours without any word from me."

"How can I help? What can I do?"

She stopped. Turned to him. Searched his face. Was this guy for real? "You seriously want to help me?"

His smile broadened. "Of course. Tell me how."

But how could he help?

"What if I took pictures of you? I could post them to your page, or you could. Maybe a combo. Wendy wouldn't even have to know."

She smirked. "Sneaky."

He raised a shoulder. "You could look at it like your own secret mission."

She ran her thumb over his. "*Our* own mission."

He rested his forehead against hers. His minty breath teased her senses. "Ours."

When he met her lips in a tantalizing kiss, she lost all sense of where she was. All she knew was warmth and exhilaration.

Winded, she pulled away, tracing the pulse in his neck with her index finger. So, she had an effect on him too. Nice to know.

"I really do have to go," she whispered.

He brought both of her hands to his lips and kissed them. "I understand. I'll be watching you. Taking pictures. Make sure to flex." He winked.

"I will." She started to back away, but he pulled gently on her hand again.

"Wait. I don't have your number."

"Oh yeah."

He handed over his phone so she could input her cell number. "I have Stella's phone right now, so this is her number. Whenever I get my phone back, I'll have to give you mine." They would keep in touch, right? This couldn't be only a cruise ship romance.

No, Neo wasn't like the others. He was worth holding on to.

Chapter Ten

Stella smiled at Mrs. Atlee next to her as she took the platter of fried hominy—whatever that was—from the plump woman's hands. Hopefully, it was as good as the excited proclamations around her declared it to be. She eyed the portion size on nearby plates and scooped an equivalent one onto her own before passing the platter to the teenager to her right.

"Where do you hail from, Miss Lindy?" the stout Mrs. Atlee asked.

"From Washington, originally, but I went to college in Kansas and then settled in a small Midwest town nearby."

"Did she say she hails from the nation's capital?" the woman's husband next to her asked.

The peacock feather extending from the lady's hat nearly poked Stella's eye as she turned to answer Mr. Atlee. "I believe she did."

DC? Stella opened her mouth to correct them but remembered Washington was one of the last territories to become a state. Apparently, it hadn't happened yet.

"College, you say?" Mr. Atlee angled forward, straining to see her over his wife's ample form. "College in Kansas territory?"

Oh my. She stifled a giggle. She needed to think before she answered any more questions. She kept forgetting what was Midwest to her was very much the Western United States for these people. She had to steer this conversation in a different direction. Time to ask questions.

As the broiled kidneys came around, and then the stewed chicken, Stella didn't offer the Atlees another chance to corner her in a faux pas. Between tentative bites, she let the inquiries fly.

After the perfunctory questions regarding where they were from and where they were going to, she ventured asking about what she really wanted to know.

"Are you familiar with Dr. Duncan?" She suppressed a grimace as she forced oily meat down her throat.

"We were introduced only yesterday, isn't that right, dear?" Mrs. Atlee looked to her husband, and her feather danced under Stella's nose with the movement.

"Two days ago, I believe," Mr. Atlee said.

She whipped her head back around to Stella, leaving bits of feather drifting in her wake. "Two days ago." A small piece floated into Mrs. Atlee's hominy. She took a bite without noticing.

Waiting for the woman to say more, Stella sipped her dingy-looking water. Straight from the river. Yum. At least there were over a hundred years' less pollution in this time. The thought didn't make the water taste better.

"It is comforting to have a trained physician on board, is it not? With so many outbreaks of disease, it only makes sense."

She nodded her assent. After gladly accepting a roll from a passing waiter, she returned her attention to her neighbor. "Had you heard of Dr. Duncan before this trip? I'm curious as to whether he's developed a reputation as a physician."

"I can't say that I have." She patted her mouth with a napkin. "Then again, with hundreds of steamboats traveling the rivers, who can keep track?"

Mr. Atlee let out a hearty chuckle. "I can barely keep the boat names straight. What with each lasting a few years, only to be replaced by another. I only know the *Arabia* came highly recommended."

"Only a few years?" Considering the grandeur of this boat, that seemed odd. Why put so much work into exquisite furnishings and beautifully painted murals if it would be in service for such a short while?

"Traveling by river is far more pleasant, I daresay." Solemn lines etched around Mrs. Atlee's mouth. "But, of course, it's more dangerous. Not a day goes by when we don't read of one incident or another in the paper. A boiler explosion, an Indian attack, a sinking."

Stella's stomach wobbled.

"That's why I brought my mother's lucky broach with me. It wards off wayward happenings." She gestured to the jeweled tulip pinned to her collar.

Stella smiled. "It's lovely."

She forced another swallow of murky water. If the woman happened to be sailing on this boat on September 5, she'd better be wearing the beloved broach, or she'd lose it. All the luggage would end up encased in mud at the bottom of the river. A precious keepsake gone forever.

But, of course, Mrs. Atlee wouldn't remain on the *Arabia* twenty days from now. The couple's trip would be finished. But would Stella's? Would she be on this boat when it sank? Because she didn't seem any closer to discovering her mission. Was she in danger of losing her possessions to the Muddy Missouri?

Instinctively, Stella's fingers went to where her grandmother's earrings dangled from her earlobes. To think she'd almost lost one of them. To think that's what had started this whole mess.

Grammy Rose. Oh, how she missed her. Her throat burned as a wave of grief crested. She rode it out, going through the motions of eating with the others while her mind filtered through memories. Grammy teaching her to ride a bike. How to braid her hair. How to kiss a boy using their hands to practice on. What a riot.

Her favorite memory was Grammy running through the sprinkler with her when she was a girl. When Stella had forgotten her swimsuit, Grammy had told her their backyard was secluded enough that she could strip to her underwear. When Stella balked at the idea, Grammy had shed all but her own underwear and bra and had run through first, clearing the way for an afternoon of giggles.

What an ugly thing cancer was. What would Grammy Rose think of this crazy adventure Stella was on now?

"Excuse me, Miss Lindy." Dr. Duncan interrupted her bleak thoughts. He stood in his full suit, hands clasped behind his back, face drooping in a somber expression. "May I request your assistance?"

She narrowed her eyes at him. "Assistance?"

"If you are quite done with your meal."

The waiters hadn't dished out dessert yet, but the greasy meal and her melancholy mood left no room for bread pudding. "Yes, I'm finished." She placed her napkin on her plate and stood.

"It was nice conversing with you, Miss Lindy." The Atlees waved politely at her.

"Yeah, you too."

She followed Dr. Duncan onto the boiler deck.

"Yes, you as well," he whispered.

"What?"

"You addressed that couple far too informally. To avoid raising suspicions, you must act as a woman of your breeding."

"Yeah, okay."

He stopped and eyed her.

"Yes, I quite understand your sentiment," she said with what she imagined to be an aristocratic accent.

He stalked forward, straight-faced and purposeful.

"Where are we going?"

"I need your help labeling crates of medical supplies."

"My help? Why?" He seemed perfectly capable of labeling his own crates.

"My penmanship is atrocious."

She did have neat handwriting. But still. "Okay, but why would crates need to be labeled? Don't they come on board already labeled?"

"Most do. Some are labeled *incorrectly*."

She lifted a brow. "And why is it a doctor's job to remedy that?"

He scrubbed his chin. "I am, shall we say, a jack-of-all-trades. And some crates have"—he paused as if fishing for an answer—"supplies of a medical nature."

"You are incredibly cryptic." She pointed a finger at him. "People who are cryptic have something to hide."

And she meant to find out what. The response this morning from her friends had assured her they were not talking about the same Dr. Duncan. Was it a strange coincidence? Could the cruise ship Dr. Duncan be a descendant of her Dr. Duncan? But what were the odds they'd both end up on these boats, one on the Pacific Ocean, one on the Missouri River?

She hadn't shared the news with her Dr. Duncan yet. She'd spent the time before breakfast eavesdropping in the ladies' cabin. She'd also done a lot of journaling and some futile brainstorming for how to get back home. Bridge had gotten her fresh hair from a horse's tail in steerage so she could brush her teeth. Now *that* was an educational experience.

Dr. Duncan turned his head so she could hear him while they descended the stairs. "There are numerous crates of, uh, medical supplies. I'll tell you what they are, and you can pen the name."

It still didn't make any sense, but if she went along with it, perhaps she could discover what he was hiding. They were all the way to the boxes before she realized she didn't have a Sharpie. "What am I to write with?"

"I brought a pen and ink down earlier."

Oh, joy. Another new experience. Writing from an inkwell.

They came to the first unlabeled crate, and he asked her to write Herbal Remedies. She did so, though it took her several tries to get the hang of how to keep the correct amount of ink on the metal tip. The first few letters were misshapen. Dr. Duncan didn't seem to care. He asked her to label the next crate Stomach Bitters and the one after that Ointments. When she finished, she shook her hands out to relieve the cramping.

A small, muffled cry came from somewhere nearby. Very nearby. She raised her brows. "What was that?"

"What?" He carried a small notebook and pencil and seemed to be taking inventory of supplies.

"I heard a cry. It sounded like a young child."

He shook off her question as if it were a pesky fly. "Must have heard one of the deck passengers. There are many women with children on this trip, going to join their husbands out west."

She peered at him. Liar. If the cry came from a deck passenger, it would have come from the other direction and would have been far fainter.

Just then, a rustle came from maybe three crates down. It almost seemed like the box moved. Then a shushing sound.

"Duncan," she warned, but she didn't wait for him to explain. She stepped to the crate in question and peered through a crack in the boards. Two sets of wide, frightened eyes stared up at her.

She gasped.

"Miss Lindy—" Dr. Duncan inched toward her as though she might attack.

"Don't Miss Lindy me," she hissed. "There are *people* in that crate. You'd better tell me what's going on. Quick."

He neared her and fear swarmed her senses. What if he was a psycho who stuffed women in boxes? She looked for a weapon. Something. Anything. The only thing she could possibly use to defend herself was the pen in her hand and the ink just out of reach. Why hadn't she taken Claire up on that self-defense class? She held up the pen, ready to stab if necessary.

He stopped at the tip of her pen, mere inches away. Her hands trembled despite her best efforts to keep them steady. He dropped his voice, so faint she had to strain to hear it. "That woman and her child are slaves. I'm helping to transport them to freedom in Kansas." His eyes softened in sympathy. "Please, Miss Lindy, have compassion on these poor people. Don't jeopardize their chance to escape oppression."

Her lip quivered. "They're living in that crate?" That cramped, dark, stuffy place. How long would they have to endure that existence?

He nodded.

"But how do they eat? Drink?" She thought about bathroom usage, but her neck heated at the thought of asking.

"I'll show you." He walked in a slow circle first, as if to ensure no one was watching. Then he came around the side and wiggled a loose board. It slid to the side. "I've been providing them food and water through here, as well as emptying their chamber pot. Late at night, of course."

Stella bent to see inside. The stench of human waste assaulted her. She worked to school her features and not show her revulsion at the smell. Her eyes adjusted to the dimness inside. A woman sat, knees crunched nearly to her chin, with a little girl tucked to her side, thumb in mouth. Perspiration beaded their foreheads and dribbled down their necks. Such little space. So little air. How could they bear it?

"Can't they blend in with the deck passengers?" she whispered. Desperation to free them from this cage clamored in her chest.

"Have you taken note of the deck passengers, Miss Lindy? They are all White. Not one Negro among them. Only the workers are colored. All men. Authorities have posted notices, and their owners are offering a hefty bounty to anyone who returns them. We cannot take the risk."

"But can they survive in there?"

Dr. Duncan offered her a small smile. "Their will to survive exceeds anything you or I could imagine. Now, will you please label this crate Frozen Charlotte Dolls?"

She pinched the bridge of her nose. "Frozen what?"

"Frozen Charlotte Dolls. They're quite popular and made from porcelain, so one would know to treat the crate with care, and it would explain the large size."

She'd have to ask Wendy what a Frozen Charlotte Doll was later. For now, she worked on labeling the box with a steady hand. Best not to give any reason for someone to pause at this crate to examine a misshapen letter.

"We thank you for keeping our secret," the woman whispered.

"Of course." She straightened and stretched her back. "Are we done here?"

Dr. Duncan nodded.

As they wove their way back to the stairway, she whispered, "Pretty bold to do this work in the daytime, isn't it?"

"It'd be mighty suspicious to label crates at night, wouldn't it, Miss Lindy?"

"I guess so."

"No one paid us any mind doing so in the morning." At the top of the stairwell, he offered a slight bow. "Thank you for your assistance and discretion."

He took a step toward the hurricane deck, but she stopped him with a question.

"Did you mean for me to know? Was it a ploy to show me what was in that crate?" She still didn't fully trust the man. What were his motives?

He lifted a brow as if impressed by her question. "Precisely as I suspected, Miss Lindy. You are exactly the person we needed."

With that, he retreated to the upper deck, and she hurried to her cabin to write another letter to her friends.

~

When Claire returned from breakfast and her rendezvous with Neo, Wendy remained asleep. Seriously? That girl must have had one hard night.

Claire settled onto her bed and pulled out her Bible, reading chapter two of Philippians to the sound of Wendy's gentle snores.

Therefore, if you have any encouragement from being united with Christ, if any comfort from his love, if any common sharing in the Spirit, if any tenderness and compassion, then make my joy complete by being like minded, having the same love, being one in spirit and of one mind.

Oh man. How could Scripture do that? Cut her to the heart so thoroughly. She looked to Wendy's sleeping form. They definitely weren't one in spirit and in mind. Not by a long shot. Like-minded. How could two people who were so different be like-minded? *Oh, Lord. I need Your help on this one.* She chuckled to herself. As if she didn't need His help with everything. She continued to read.

Do nothing out of selfish ambition or vain conceit. Rather, in humility value others above yourselves, not looking to your own interests but each of you to the interests of the others.

Wendy obviously thought Claire was full of selfish ambition and vain conceit. Was she right? Was Claire obsessed with her own interests and oblivious to everyone else's? Or did she value other people above herself? In the end, Wendy's opinion of her wouldn't matter. Only God's assessment stood. What would He say about her life? About her heart?

"What time is it?" Wendy's groggy voice interrupted her musings.

"Almost ten."

"Oh, my goodness." Wendy sat up and stretched. "I haven't slept that late in ages." She yawned. "You're probably starving. I'll get ready, and we can grab breakfast."

Should she mention she'd already eaten? Wendy assumed Claire had waited for her. Probably because if Wendy awoke early, she would have waited for Claire. She did a far better job at the whole "not looking to your own interests but each of you to the interests of the others" thing. She clamped her mouth shut. She could not confess her selfishness right now. She'd work on doing better. Next time, she'd do better.

Wendy emerged from the bathroom in shorts and a T-shirt, hair in a messy bun. "Ready?"

Claire jumped up and checked her reflection in the mirror. "Almost." She glided on lip gloss. "Yep. Let's go."

They'd missed their appointment in the dining room, so once again, Claire found herself in the café. This time, she opted for an omelet. She wouldn't eat the whole thing, of course. She found a table and waited for Wendy, who joined her a few minutes later with a plate overflowing with pancakes, hash browns, and breakfast meats.

"Is that all you're eating?" Wendy scrunched her nose.

"I'm not too hungry."

"You're making me feel bad. Hold on, I forgot coffee." She disappeared toward the beverage station.

Good. Wendy saved her from having to scramble for a reply. She cut her omelet into small bites but waited for Wendy to return before eating. That was the unselfish thing to do, right?

From out of the corner of her eye, she spotted Neo leaning against a pillar several tables away. She almost waved, but his slight headshake reminded her to play it cool so Wendy wouldn't catch on. Wendy returned with her coffee, and Claire pretended not to notice Neo over her friend's shoulder.

He winked and took a picture as she pierced the egg with her fork and lifted it toward her mouth. The brat better not get a shot of her chewing. She straightened and made sure each movement was poised and fluid as she drank her water and took small, polite bites. This wasn't exactly what she'd had in mind when he'd offered to take pictures of her, but she'd roll with it.

"I'm going to the library at two this afternoon," Wendy said.

Claire nodded. "Yeah, okay." She paused with a bite halfway to her mouth. "Wait, why two? That's specific. Do you have an appointment or something?" She'd never been to a library on a cruise and didn't plan to.

"No, it's just … It's what I decided."

"Ooookay." Strange, but this was Wendy. She had her idiosyncrasies.

Neo had moved forward a table and to Wendy's other side. She couldn't help but smile as he took another picture. Wendy's gaze remained on her meal.

Claire refocused her attention on her friend. "Did you find anything out yet?"

She sighed. "Not really."

"Me neither. But to be honest, I'm not sure what we're looking for." Her nightmare flashed in her mind's eye, accompanied by a shiver. What kind of information could they possibly unearth that would bring Stella back to them? She was out of her depth. Big-time.

Neo motioned for her to go to the beverage station. She questioned him with her gaze, but he only pointed in that direction.

She gulped the rest of her water. "I need a refill. I'll be right back."

Neo met her at the water station, just out of Wendy's view, with a silly grin. "You're beautiful."

"You're a nut."

He planted a tantalizing kiss on her lips. Too quick. It was far too quick a kiss.

"How am I doing so far?" He flipped through his gallery, revealing several decent shots in between a few awkward ones.

She pointed to one in particular where she looked the epitome of happy and healthy. "This one's great."

"Want me to post it?"

"No. Send it to me, and I'll post it. You post"—she flipped back through and found another one taken from farther way—"this one."

"Will do. Now do a push up or something. Bench press your friend."

She chuckled. "Wendy said she's going to the library at two. Meet me on the top deck then?"

"Absolutely." He leaned in for another kiss.

His camera clicked as she walked away. So, this was what it felt like to be uber famous. She could get used to it. She tossed a glance over her shoulder and smiled for the camera.

When she approached the table, she found Wendy craning her neck. Her friend's gaze swept the room as if searching for someone. Definitely not Claire, as the beverage station was in the opposite direction.

"Who are you looking for?"

Crimson crept up Wendy's neck and mottled her cheeks. "Hmm?" She twirled a curl and forked a bite of egg into her mouth without looking Claire in the eye.

Claire crossed her arms. "You seemed to be searching for someone." Was it that Allison girl?

"What? No." Wendy's headshake sent hair flying around her shoulders. Far too adamant. She stacked her dishes. "You done? I'm done." When she stood, a fork clanked to the floor.

Claire bent to retrieve it. "Sure."

She eyed her friend. Wendy was hiding something. But what?

~

When Wendy entered the library, nearly breathless with anticipation, Grayson already stood leaning against a bookshelf. Grinning.

"You're never going to believe this." Was it her imagination, or did his eyes light up when she entered the room?

"What?" Her question came out on a giggle. She sounded as juvenile as her sixth graders. What was wrong with her?

"Check out this shelf." He pointed, somehow maintaining his relaxed vibe while emanating excitement. How'd he pull off that paradox? The same way he pulled off those khaki shorts and sky-blue polo. He made it irresistible with his aura of cool.

Twisting her lips, she scanned the area near his index finger and gasped. "Shut up." *Steamboat Disasters of the Lower Missouri River.* She pulled it from the shelf. "You planted this, didn't you?"

His laughter bubbled. "I swear I didn't."

She smacked his chest and had to fight the urge to let her hand linger on those muscles. "You had to."

He threw his hands up as if pleading innocence. "What? You think I carry random books about steamboats in my vacation luggage?"

She narrowed her eyes. "You *are* a history teacher. No telling." She pointed a finger. "Maybe you had it delivered."

His eyes danced. "How? By dolphin?"

Okay, good point. "But how did it get here? It certainly wasn't here yesterday."

"Someone must have borrowed it and then returned it." He shrugged. "That's kind of how libraries work."

Yeah, but a book about steamboats? Unless … what if it was Dr. Duncan? If he randomly encountered time-sailing situations, he might be one to bring along a book about steamboats. But why leave it in the library for her to find?

She'd given him her room number. Why not give it directly to her?

He gently took the book from her hands. "Let's not waste time trying to figure out how it got here and instead see if it has any helpful information."

"You mean, you haven't looked through it?"

"I wanted to wait for you."

How sweet. "Thank you."

She found a table in the corner and sat. He chose the seat next to her and opened the book between them. They were so close that their knees brushed. She tried not to notice, but the back of her neck prickled with awareness.

He flipped to the index. "*Arabia.* Look! Lots of entries. This is great."

The first two entries yielded nothing helpful, but on the third, they found a jackpot. An entire section on Stella's steamboat.

"It sinks on September 5." Wendy caught herself speaking in present tense. For Stella, it was present tense, but for Grayson, they were researching a past event. She had to remember that. "I mean, I knew it sank on September 5 near Parkville. What I couldn't seem to find out was when it left St. Louis."

"It says it took seven days to get from St. Louis to Kansas City."

She looked up from the book straight into his eyes. "Isn't that wild? It's a three-and-a-half-hour drive now. Can you imagine spending seven days on a boat to get somewhere only three hours away?"

His smile tipped. "I'm from St. Louis."

"No way. I'm from Kansas City."

"To think, all this time, we've only been one disastrous steamboat trip away from each other."

She tucked her bottom lip between her teeth, but it didn't keep her smile at bay. "Actually, I think the *Arabia* made it to Kansas City fine. It was after it left KC that it hit the snag. Right?"

His attention returned to the page. Fine by her. It gave her a chance to study his profile. This man made studious sexy. Her cheeks heated at the thought. She needed to reel it in. She'd met a new friend. He'd be pleasant, and helpful, company for the remainder of the cruise, but nothing more. She wasn't one to fall all over herself for a guy, no matter how good-looking. And they had work to do. She inhaled deeply and grounded herself in her present reality. She was researching to help her best friend return from time-traveling to the past. Or time-sailing. Whatever it was called, it left little time for anything else.

Grayson turned the page, and a painting grabbed her attention. She traced her finger over the image of the boat her friend was on right now. Unreal. Stella was *there*. What was she doing? *How* was she doing? She'd written back to Stella, again without Claire's knowledge. Too much to explain. No going back now.

The bottom painting showed the boat sinking. Wendy's chest squeezed. Knowing everyone made it out alive did little to alleviate her worry. Everyone history knew about had lived through the ordeal, but history didn't know about Stella. There were no guarantees. Could history be changed?

"The rest of this is about the excavation. Do you need any info about that?" Grayson asked.

She shook her head, still engrossed in the picture. "How does the *Arabia* compare to this boat?"

He flipped the page back, then returned quickly to the picture. "It says it was a hundred seventy-one feet long. This boat is over eight hundred fifty feet, I think."

"Wow. Less than a fourth the size."

"But steamboats were glamourous for their day. Floating palaces." He nudged the book toward her. "Do you want to read the firsthand accounts. Sorry for hogging it. I do that without realizing it. Often."

Funny. She had the same habit.

She took in the testimony of a passenger and an officer regarding the sinking. Though it did sound chaotic and dramatic, she felt better after having read it. "It does sound like it ended okay."

"No one died, you mean. Whatever luggage didn't sink ended up stolen, but they made it out with their lives."

"Yeah." Something still didn't sit right, though. "But you know what bothers me?"

"What?"

"They lied about the mule. They said the mule died because it was too stubborn to get off. That they tried to lead it off the boat, and it wouldn't come. Yet, when the boat was uncovered, they found the mule had been tied up. They outright lied about the stinkin' mule."

"And?"

"What else did they lie about? What else were they hiding?"

He laced his fingers behind his head and tilted back in his chair, accentuating his pecs. "There's so much about history we'll never know."

But she could know more about this mystery. She might learn much more.

Only at what cost?

Chapter Eleven

Stella was sitting on deck the next day, rocking and fanning herself from the midday heat, when the snag bell clanged again. She dropped the fan into her lap, clutched the rocking chair's armrests, and braced herself.

The boat careened to the right, sending her chair sliding toward the railing. She cried out and squeezed her eyes shut. Then with a thud, she was deposited onto something soft like a bed. She opened her eyes to find herself back in her room, the faint light of morning sneaking through the curtains.

She bolted upright. It had happened again. She'd lurched forward in time. How far? Where were they now, and when? And how long did she have before the boat sank and her chance to get home was gone forever? She threw the blankets off and thundered out of her room and onto the deck. She had to find Dr. Duncan. She walked the length of the deck with no sight of him, then peeked inside the main hall. He wasn't there either. Perhaps he was down with the escapees.

She descended the steps and snaked through the cargo but didn't see him anywhere. Passing to the place where the woman and child had been, compassion pulled at her as she remembered those wide eyes staring up at her. She should check on them. Make sure they were okay. But as she searched the crates on board, she couldn't find any that said Frozen Charlotte Dolls. These said Furs, and there were fewer of them. This was the right spot, wasn't it? Maybe she was turned around.

But as she continued to look, she found no sign of the slaves.

"They're not here."

She jumped at Dr. Duncan's voice behind her. She spun around and pressed a hand to her thundering chest.

"The Frozen Charlotte dolls were safely delivered as planned." His knowing gaze bored into hers. Her shoulders relaxed. The woman and child were safe. They'd made it. They were free.

"Good." She inhaled deeply. "Where are we?"

"We're finishing the trip downriver from Sioux City. We're almost to St. Louis." He laced his hands in front of him.

Finishing the trip. The trip was nearly over, and she'd missed more than half of it. Her shoulders sagged. She'd labeled the crate convincingly enough those slaves didn't get caught in their escape, yet she remained in 1856. That hadn't been her mission either.

"When are we?" Defeat seeped from her voice.

"It's August 28."

Her chest constricted. August 28? That close to September 5? She would be on this boat when it sank if she didn't hurry up and finish her mission. She tugged on the high neckline of her dress, but she still couldn't seem to take in enough air. She truly was running out of time. "Are we landing in St. Louis? Then what?"

He rocked back on his heels. "We'll dock there while they unload and load cargo. Then she'll be off again. This time, to Nebraska."

This boat wouldn't make it to Nebraska. She had eight days until the morning the boat would sink. Heaven help her.

"If you'll excuse me." She gave a little curtsy before scurrying to the stairs. What was that about? Perhaps the time period had rubbed off on her, at least a little.

As she reached the first step, another thought occurred to her. She spun around to find Dr. Duncan a few steps behind. She startled, then regained her composure. "We'll get off the ship? In St. Louis, I mean."

"Yes. We'll disembark when the ship arrives."

"But I can get back on. I have to get back on."

He nodded. "I'll re-embark as well."

"Won't that seem strange? Me getting off and then getting back on?" She couldn't imagine it not arousing suspicion.

He shook his head, smiling at her as if he were amused at a young child. "Once you step back on the ship, no one from this journey will have any recollection of you. Stepping away from the water for any length of time has a resetting effect. It's the way time-sailing works, my dear."

"No one will remember me?"

"Not a soul. Save one." He pointed to himself.

Her suspicions rose. "How are you the exception? What makes you special?"

A shadow crossed his expression. "Another tale for another day."

Oh no. She would not let him get off that easy. "Nice try. I think you owe me an explanation. Why don't things reset for you?"

His mouth firmed into a straight line, though his eyes remained soft and kind. "My story belongs to me, Miss Lindy. I will choose when to tell it and to whom."

His soft rebuke landed like a pebble in the lake of her heart, rippling outward. Reverberating through her core.

She couldn't keep her voice from betraying how shaken she was. "Fair enough." She turned and sped to her room, shutting her door, then leaning against it.

She wrung her hands. She was a journalist, for goodness' sake. Her superpower was digging deep to pry people's stories out of them. She went after scoops, no matter the cost. She wrapped her arms around herself and slid to the floor. *No matter the cost.*

Everett.

She'd been trying to keep her mind from wandering to him. To his saucy smile and intelligent eyes. When he'd sat next to her in their gen ed science class, she'd forgotten how to breathe. Then, when he asked her to join him for coffee, she'd said no. She'd blown him off. Despite the accusation, it hadn't been because of latent racism. She'd just been too nervous. She hadn't known how to interact. She'd been too afraid of blowing it, of saying the wrong thing.

But he'd been persistent. And far too good for her.

Maybe this whole thing was God's way of saving Everett from making the biggest mistake of his life. Shove the bride back in time so the groom doesn't throw his life away on the wrong woman. On a coward who can't seem to stand up for her man.

She pressed the heels of her hands against her misting eyes to keep the tears from flowing. She couldn't feel sorry for herself. A lot of good that would do. She needed to focus on how to get out of this mess.

Lord, forgive me. Help Everett to forgive me.

It was the same prayer she'd prayed a hundred times before. How come she didn't feel forgiven? Why did she still wallow in guilt and shame?

Make me brave, God.

She needed a transformation. She couldn't change herself. God was going to have to do something inside of her.

Change my heart. Heal me from the inside.

With a sniff, she looked around her room. What did she expect? A literal sign to drop from heaven? Nothing had changed except … was that a letter on the floor in front of her door? She crawled to it.

It was another letter from Claire and Wendy! Another one in Wendy's handwriting.

> Stella,
>
> The Frozen Charlotte dolls are super interesting and kinda creepy. Supposedly, there was a song that went with them about a girl who took a ride to a ball without taking a blanket or wrapping up in something warm, so she froze to death in the sleigh. The dolls were made of porcelain and were given as a

reminder to listen to your parents and wear your coat, I guess. Can you imagine singing a song to your sweet little child about a girl freezing to death? You're living in a crazy time, Stells.

We're both fine. Missing you, of course, but fine.

Yes, it's likely our Dr. Duncan is a descendant of your Dr. Duncan. Highly likely.

Maybe labeling the crate as Frozen Charlotte Dolls was your mission, and you'll be back here with us soon? If not, any other ideas? We're trying to find information but haven't gotten far. Keep in touch.

Wendy & Claire

PS: How's that toothbrush working out for you?

PPS: Is the drinking water as murky as Mark Twain said it was? Do you really have to wait for the sediment to settle on the bottom?

Stella smiled at the thought of her friends hovering over the stationery, penning the letter. She could almost hear the cadence of their voices as they bantered back and forth. She pulled out her own pen and paper.

Wendy & Claire,

Do you know of anything fun to do in St. Louis in 1856? I'll be there for at least a day or so. Oh, and I lurched forward in time again. Now it's August 28. Trying not to freak out.

Why do you say it's highly likely our Dr. Duncans are related? What do you know, Wendy? Spill it.

My Dr. Duncan says when I step onto the boat
again everyone from this trip will forget I
existed except for him. He won't tell me why
he's the magical exception. Does your Dr.
Duncan know? I wonder if I get stuck in this
time if everyone in the present day will forget I
existed as well. Maybe Everett would be better
off that way.
Love always,
Stella

She almost scratched out the part about Everett. Too
mopey and depressing. Too vulnerable. If only she'd written
in pencil. And a twinge of guilt crept up her neck at the part
about Dr. Duncan. If it was his story to tell, why was she
trying to pry it from someone else? Couldn't she be patient
and let him confide in her when he was ready? She could
trash this letter and write a new one. Only she was short on
time, and curiosity spurred her on. She folded the letter and
slid it into the envelope.

She didn't have time to second-guess herself. She had
nine days to discover her mission, accomplish it, and get
back home.

No matter the cost.

~

Wendy swooped into the library, letter from Stella in
hand. Her search for Dr. Rodney Duncan had proved
unfruitful—he hadn't been in his room or on the top deck—
so she'd missed the chance to pelt him with questions about
who he was and if he'd planted that book. Now it was
Grayson's turn to endure an inquisition.

She couldn't keep from breaking into a grin when he
came into view. Shoot, he even knew how to wear pink well.
The V-neck T-shirt was the most casual thing she'd seen him
in thus far, and it nicely accentuated his muscular build.

Somehow, he made what she had previously considered a girl's color look all man. And from the heat that rose in her face, her cheeks likely matched his shirt. *Cool, Wendy. Really cool.*

She refocused. "Have I got a question for you."

She held up the letter, then realized she couldn't exactly show it to him. He didn't know—couldn't know—the entire ordeal of Stella's situation. Trying to cast a casual vibe, she tucked the envelope into her back pocket.

"What's that?" He sat forward, eyes alight with interest.

"A letter from my friend. She asked if I could tell her about things to do in St. Louis in 1856." She clicked her tongue and pointed to him. "I thought you'd be the perfect person to ask." Wendy had found the letter again in the middle of the night and snatched it before Claire could see it. Stella's response wouldn't make sense to her when she knew nothing about the letter Wendy had sent.

Only there was that curious bit about Everett being better off without her. Was it prewedding jitters that made her say such a thing? If only she could shake some sense into her friend. This was the kind of thing Claire and Wendy should gang up on Stella for—to convince her of her worth. But, well, she'd write back when she had an answer to the other questions.

He chuckled. "I wish I knew more about the history of my city."

Her excitement dimmed. "You don't have any ideas? I mean, you love history, and you live in St. Louis. I thought …"

"It's a good thought." He scrubbed his beard. "It's funny how a lot of people research a slew of things other than what's in their own backyard."

She tucked a curl behind her ear. "Yeah. I guess that's true." Though, she knew a thing or two about Kansas City.

"I actually had a thought for you."

"Yeah? Shoot."

"You said your class went to the steamboat museum this year without you, right?"

"Yep."

"And you mentioned one of your students is here on this ship."

"Allison. Why?"

"Might she have pictures from the field trip that could be helpful? Or am I the only one who takes pictures of the historical info from the plaques and whatnot?"

Oh, my goodness, what a brilliant man. Instinctively, she threw her arms around his neck. "You're a genius!"

Did she imagine his intake of breath? The stiffening of his muscles under her touch? She winced. She probably shouldn't have been so forward. He chuckled and patted her back. Awkward. How to extricate herself gracefully?

She rose, tossing her hair over her shoulder as she'd seen Claire do a million times. "I'll go see if I can find her. Will you let me know if you find anything about St. Louis?"

He tilted his head, all business. "I would, but"—his eyes flashed a playful glint—"I don't have your number."

"That's easy enough to remedy." She held her hand out for his phone and typed in her number. She handed it back, nodded, and turned to walk out, mustering as much grace as she could. Her ears flamed. Why'd she have to embarrass herself like that?

She'd barely made it out the door when her phone dinged.

> Tomorrow, same time, same place? Longer visit?

She ran her tongue over her teeth, formulating her reply.

> If this is Keanu Reeves again, no can do. Stop stalking me.

She smiled to herself.

If this is Grayson, see you then.

A minute later, a reply came.

Glad to know I'm edging out my competition. ~Grayson

She covered her open mouth. Was he flirting? Was she? Her stomach flipped. She *should* work to keep this thing with Grayson carefully categorized into the friend zone in her mind. Were they sticking their toes into another territory entirely?

No. Of course not. She was fooling herself if she thought someone so suave and hunky would be interested in her. She wasn't supermodel gorgeous like Claire. She didn't even have Stella's ethereal beauty. She was loud, obnoxious, and a little pudgy around the edges.

But what if he *was* interested?

Her toes curled.

Okay, okay. She had to focus. After doing everything she could to avoid Allison and her mom, she now needed to try to hunt Allison down. Minus the mom.

~

Two o'clock couldn't come soon enough for Claire. If she had to reread those same three pages of that steamboat book again, she'd scream. As soon as Wendy excused herself, Claire changed, touched up her makeup, and jetted to the top deck, scanning the crowd for a gorgeous hunk.

When her gaze tangled with Neo's, his camera was already pointed at her. She sashayed toward him as he clicked away. Way to make her feel like a runway model. People had complimented her beauty her entire life, but never before had it seemed like a good thing. An utterly delightful thing. Not until now. Perhaps because with Neo, her outward beauty seemed to be only one of many things that drew him to her.

She could be imagining everything, but the way he listened to her, the thoughtful way he tilted his head when taking her in … He gave her far more consideration than she was accustomed to.

Yes, she could definitely get used to this.

He sauntered toward her. "You ready for active shots?"

"Almost." She met his soft mouth with an eager kiss.

His hands cradled the back of her head as he drank her in. He trailed his thumb along her jawline.

"Okay. Ready now." She stepped back and perused the deck for an open space. "There, in the corner." She pointed, then went to lay her mat down.

"Great. Do your thing. The lighting is excellent behind you."

Wonderful. Who needed Photoshop when you had gorgeous days at sea? She got into a side-lying plank position. Her core tightened, and her confidence soared. Finally, she was in her zone. Here, she knew how to succeed, and soon she'd do so on a much larger scale. She switched into a forward plank and didn't miss the glimmer of admiration radiating from Neo's grin. She'd worked hard to get to this point in her career. Before long, it'd all be worth it. She moved to a crunch.

"Wait, are you Claire? From that YouTube channel?" A woman with wispy white hair hunched close, an awed smile adorning her wrinkled face. She had to be in her eighties, at least.

"Yes, I am." Claire bounded up and shook the woman's frail hand. "Do you watch my channel?"

"Me and the girls work out with you every Thursday morning before bingo. You're a hit at the retirement home."

That was a first. "Oh, wow." She nodded and caught Neo's eye. He looked to be trying desperately to contain his laughter. "What an honor."

"How about a picture of you two?" he asked.

The woman brightened further. "Will it go on the Face magazine?"

Claire looked to Neo in question.

"Facebook?" he interpreted. "Yes, it will go on Facebook."

The woman clapped. "Oh, my grandkids will love that."

She sidled up next to Claire, and they smiled at Neo.

After a friendly goodbye, Claire returned to posing on her mat. This time, leg lifts. Neo had barely gotten three shots when a group of teenagers interrupted her again.

"Claire? It's you, right?" the ringleader asked. They turned to each other and giggled. "From Claire-ity Fitness."

"Yeah." Okay, this was wild. Sure, she'd been recognized in public before, and yeah, the context of the mat probably helped things along, but it wasn't like she was a celebrity. Even if Neo had made her feel like one.

"We want a picture too. We saw you take one with that lady."

"Of course." She scrambled up.

"How should we pose?" They handed their phones to Neo.

"How about with a flex?" Claire bared her bicep, and the girls followed suit.

Neo took a picture with his camera and then with each of the girls' cameras. That would make a super cute picture for her page. Wow, oh, wow. Fit TV was sure to be impressed.

"I can't wait to tell our friends." The girls tittered as they went off.

Once they were gone, Claire did a few more poses. Was she glowing? All the attention had energized her. No faking smiles now.

Neo swiped through pictures. "These are good, but a little … stiff. How about trying a full Pilates routine from start to finish. The pictures will be more natural that way, less staged."

She glanced around. It felt a bit awkward, but it would help her keep in shape. Though she'd carved out time to work out in the gym, she'd done nothing for her core. Her gaze dropped to her exposed midriff. Did her lack of exercise show? What if Fit TV could tell? They were professionals, after all.

"Yeah, okay." She lowered onto her mat.

"Excuse me." A woman from a nearby lounge chair looked over her sunglasses and spoke in Claire's direction. "I didn't mean to eavesdrop, but did I hear you say you were going to do a Pilates routine?"

Claire blinked back at her. "Yes." Was that against the cruise ship rules?

"Do you mind if I join in? I go to classes at the Y at home."

"Of course. Feel free to join me."

"I don't have a mat. I guess I could use my towel."

"If that's comfortable for you."

"Hey, guys." The woman waved over a group of other women from where they sat at a table. "Want to join me in an impromptu Pilates class?" She turned to Claire. "You don't mind if my friends join in, do you?"

"Not at all."

As the women prattled among themselves, deciding whether to exercise on deck, Claire shot Neo an open-mouthed gape and mouthed, *Can you believe this?*

He covered his mouth with his fist as if trying to contain a bout of laughter.

Minutes later, Claire was doing her thing, not only in front of a camera in typical fashion but also with a handful of women. A few more spontaneously joined in along the way. Endorphins flooded her system. This was her happy place. It hadn't clicked before, but so much of her career included living behind a camera. Away from the very people her videos influenced. She rarely got to connect with others as she worked. She was the pretty face on a screen, replying to comments on a keyboard. No wonder she was lonely.

When the workout finished, each participant thanked her profusely. Neo took pictures of her with the group before they scuttled away, chatting about what an amazing experience that was.

Claire took a step toward Neo, intending to wrap her arms around him and let him kiss her senseless, but she stopped, frozen in her tracks.

Wendy stood a few feet away, arms crossed, frown pronounced. "This is what you've been doing while I've been researching? While *I've* been trying to help Stella?"

Claire thrust a hand on her hip. How dare Wendy hunt her down to fling her judgment. "What was I supposed to be doing?"

"I certainly didn't think you'd throw a fitness party with your superfans. Not with everything going on." Wendy paused and closed her mouth. She lowered her eyes for a moment. Was she about to back down? Soften? Admit she might be overreacting? But no. When she brought up her gaze, it was full of fire. "I thought better of you than that."

"Give me a break. No, you did not. When was the last time you thought good of me?"

Wendy shook her head and turned, as if contemplating leaving.

"Not everyone has a job with summers off. Some of us have to work."

Wendy rolled her eyes. "You're on vacation."

"My job doesn't give vacation time."

"Your 'job' is whatever you make it." She had the audacity to use air quotes. "You're the boss. You set the rules."

If only. "Shows how little you know about social media influencers."

Wendy stormed off in a huff.

When Claire turned back to Neo, he was nowhere to be found.

Chapter Twelve

Stella gaped at the city of St. Louis outside her door, looming before the docked boat. The busy sounds of voices, steamboat whistles, and carriages swirled through the air. This was no small town, even considering this was so far in the past. The city looked massive and full. Nervous butterflies tumbled inside her. How would she mingle among the inhabitants for two full days as if she belonged in this time? The limited scope of the steamboat afforded her a semblance of safety, but unleashed into the wide world outside, a host of things could go wrong.

The only money she had was unusable. Where would she go? What would she do? She kept saying ridiculous things, like she'd studied at Kansas University. What if she put herself in a dangerous situation due to her careless words? Or what if she accidentally altered history?

No time to worry. She had to get ready. As she went to freshen up in the washbasin, a letter on the floor near her front door caught her eye. Thank God. Wendy and Claire must have written back. She pried open the envelope.

> Stella,
> The St. Louis riverfront was busy at that time. Here are a couple of places that might be of interest: Frederick the Great Coffeehouse and The Screaming Peach Restaurant.
>
> There are plenty of boarding houses and hotels. Do you have money for those?

There's also a plethora of stores. Toys and fancy goods, clothing stores, confectioneries, dry goods, drug stores if you need any medicine, wagonmakers, cattle dealers, shoemakers, blacksmiths, tailors, and watchmakers. Central High School, the first public high school in St. Louis, was just built last year. You can see it on the corner of Olive and 15th Street. And the old courthouse is there, only I guess it's not old to them. The west wing is being remodeled right now. The famous Dred Scott case will be heard there the next year.

Oh, I'm so jealous. You have an opportunity to walk around a real living history museum. Enjoy every minute and remember all the details so you can share them with me. (Wendy, of course. I think Claire is less enthused about the history part, though she'll want to hear about the fashions of the day and what "fancy goods" are.)

And dear, sweet Stella, we don't want to hear you say Everett would be better off without you ever again. You are his dream come true. He loves you, as he should. You are the kindest, most compassionate, most loving person we know. Plus, you're beautiful. He's a lucky man. Come back and make him your happy husband.
Love always,
Wendy & Claire

A tear escaped as she read the last paragraph. If only they knew. Their high praise wasn't warranted. Still, it comforted her to know their love stretched across the miles, across the years.

Underneath the text, they had drawn a crude map with street names and some hotels and boarding houses highlighted. Stella smiled. Thank God for her friends.

She'd just dressed for the day, washed her face, and brushed her teeth when someone knocked on her front door. She opened it to find Bridge waiting with an eager smile and an envelope. Another letter?

Bridge handed it over. "From Dr. Duncan."

Oh, good. He hadn't forgotten about her.

With a bounce to her step, Bridge breezed through the room to open the curtains.

"You look especially chipper this morning. Any special plans for your days off?"

The woman nearly glowed. "I have family in the city. And a beau."

That explained it. The anticipation of seeing loved ones lightened her load.

"That's wonderful. Enjoy."

Bridge smiled her thanks. "Do you need anything this morning before you disembark?"

She needed a friend in the city. A guide. But she wouldn't impose on this lovely chambermaid. The dear woman worked hard and deserved a couple of days off. No need for her to be obligated to entertain and serve another white woman.

But before she left, Bridge tilted her head. "What are you going to do in the city?"

Stella shrugged.

"Well, if you get lonely, stop by The Screaming Peach. My uncle's the cook there, and he and my auntie live next door. I'll be staying with them."

The Screaming Peach? Wendy had mentioned it in her letter. "I'll check it out."

Bridge nodded before ducking out the door and closing it behind her.

Stella opened the envelope to find a note and several bills and coins tucked inside.

Muscles in her shoulders and neck relaxed as she tucked the cash into the little purse Dr. Duncan had given her the other day. What had he called it again? The name eluded her. Now with money, a map, and the odd name of a restaurant, she should be able to make it as a stranger in a strange land for a couple of days.

When she stepped off the boat, her mouth fell open at the sight of dozens upon dozens of steamboats lining the riverbank. She'd never imagined so many of them. Stacks of flour sacks lined the wharf along with lines of barrels, all ready for loading. Pigs, chickens, and mules surrounded crates of various sizes. Horse-drawn wagons clicked along the cobblestone street beyond.

"Excuse me, miss." A dark-skinned boy, who couldn't be older than eleven or twelve, looked at her expectantly. "Do you need help with your trunk? I can carry it for you."

"Nonsense, Eli." A redheaded man with an Irish accent swaggered up behind the kid and gently nudged him out of the way. "The lady's going to need a carriage to take herself and her trunk to wherever she fancies. Ain't that right, miss?"

She hated to concede when he'd treated the young boy so rudely, but without knowing how far away the hotel was, how could she say? "Could you recommend a hotel or boarding house nearby?"

"I'll take ya right to one." Without waiting for confirmation, he hefted her trunk and placed it in the back of his wagon.

The boy's countenance fell. Poor dear. She fished out a dime from her, uh, bag and placed it in his hand. What was that worth to him? It must have been something because the corners of his mouth twitched up, and he thanked her before dashing away.

She followed the redhead and climbed in beside him on the wagon seat. As he drove, she stared at the scene before her in wide-eyed wonder. Wendy was right. It was like a living history exhibit.

"Here we are." He pulled the carriage onto Fourth Street in front of a limestone building occupying an entire block. The sign boasted it to be the Planter's House Hotel. Rows of windows glistened down on them. "The finest hotel in the city."

She nearly choked. "I-I." She banged on her chest as she coughed. "I don't need the finest." Why had he brought her here? Could she afford it?

"Nonsense. Only the best for a lady like you. Four stories tall with one hundred and fifty bedrooms. Two dining rooms. The second-story grand ballroom was modeled after the Temple of Erectheus in Athens." He tucked his thumbs under his suspenders and grinned. "Isn't she a beauty?"

"Yes, but I would have been happy at a simple boarding house." She certainly didn't need any luxuries.

"You just got off a floating palace. I figured I'd take you to a landlocked one." He winked, then unloaded her trunk and handed it off to a bellman.

She sighed. "What do I owe you?"

He told her, and she paid, then went inside to the reception desk where the clerk informed her $4.25 would get her a room for the night as well as four meals that she could either take in her room or in one of the dining rooms. Four meals! This was more decadent than the cruise, and her stay in St. Louis would cost her less than ten bucks. Good thing, because Dr. Duncan had given her ten dollars and change.

On her way to her room, she gaped at the spiraling staircases and the orchestra platform suspended seven or eight feet above the floor. Her shoes sank into the plush carpeting as she walked long passages with skylights topping each door. So, this was what it meant to live like a queen in the 1850s. Not bad.

She was even more delighted to see her room. With venetian shutters adorning the windows and a cool-looking coal grate for heat, it was like she'd stepped into an antique B and B. And hallelujah for indoor plumbing!

After using the room's call bell to request her midday meal be brought to her room, she lay back on her bed and relaxed. What had she been nervous about? The bellman delivered her trunk, then a waiter delivered her food. Trays and trays of it, accompanied by a menu. Fried oysters, broiled grouse, saddle of antelope. Maybe living like a queen wasn't quite as amazing as she'd thought. None of that sounded appealing. But the dessert tray included three types of pie—apple, plum, and pumpkin—so all was not lost.

She pulled a novel from her trunk and tried to read for a while, but her wandering thoughts kept distracting her. How could she spend time in a fictional world when she had the opportunity to stroll through history right outside her door? She shut her book and consulted the map, finding the intersection of Fourth and Pine. She pulled out a pen and wrote Planter's House Hotel there, then traced a path to The Screaming Peach.

It was time for an adventure.

~

Wendy stuffed the rest of the sad taco in her mouth and pulled her gaze away from a group of friends laughing around the table next to her. This was pathetic. What was she doing eating lunch by herself? This cruise wasn't going anything like she'd imagined.

She should apologize to Claire. These long hours of ignoring each other were getting old. She was being juvenile. So what if Claire had led a fun workout session with a gaggle of her adoring fans? It didn't mean she didn't love Stella.

It might mean Wendy was a dull loser in comparison.

Was that why it bothered her so much?

Her phone buzzed, and she pulled it out of her back pocket to check the text.

> Did your friend find the info on St. Louis helpful?

She smiled to herself. She couldn't be that much of a loser if Grayson kept texting her.

> I think so.

Meaning, she hoped so, but she had no way of knowing. Not yet, anyway. His thoughtfulness to do that research to help her—well, Stella, but also her—warmed her insides. He'd continued to send her info late into the night until she'd finally told him that was enough and to go to bed. Then she'd delivered a letter to the mailbox.

A familiar profile passed by, and Wendy jumped up so fast, her chair toppled backward. "Allison," she called, then stopped to place the chair upright.

"Oh, hi, Miss Booker." Allison turned, plate with burger and fries in hand.

"Do you have a minute?" Wendy gestured to the seat across from her. "I was looking for you yesterday but couldn't find you." Instead, she'd found something else entirely. "Where's your mom?"

"Yeah. Sure, I have a minute. My mom is somewhere around, finding something healthy to eat." Allison settled at the table and took a bite of a fry. "What's up?"

"I'm wondering if you can help me with something. You went on the field trip to the *Arabia* museum, right?"

Allison nodded, downing another fry.

"Did you take any pictures? That you might have on your phone?"

Her mouth twisted. "I think so. Hold on." She whipped out her phone, her fingers flying with expert precision. "Yeah, here's some. Want to see them?"

"Yes!" Wendy nearly yanked the phone from her grasp.

"Stick to the field trip pictures, okay? I don't want my teacher creeping around on my phone."

"Will do." She thumbed through pictures of gold-rimmed china, brass spoons, earrings, beads, and porcelain buttons. She gasped, nearly giddy. "A Frozen Charlotte doll!"

"Miss Booker, no offense, but you're acting weird." She twirled a fry in her ketchup. "What are you looking for anyway?"

What *was* she looking for? She couldn't answer because she didn't have a clue.

"Do you miss teaching *that* much?"

Wendy tossed her a sassy smile. "Maybe." She didn't want to think about how much she'd miss teaching if she lost her job for good. "Mind if I text these to myself?"

"Go ahead."

While Allison munched on her burger, Wendy went to work sending herself each and every picture—except for the selfies and pictures of Dillon Lane, the boy Allison apparently had a crush on. She still didn't know how they'd help, but maybe she'd end up needing them at some point.

"What's up with you and my mom?"

The question startled Wendy from her task. So, the girl had noticed. She worked to keep her expression innocent. "What do you mean?"

"She told me to stay away from you."

Wendy winced. "She did?"

And here Allison was, disobeying her mom. Wendy likely looked complicit. Mrs. Gardenia might even think she'd encouraged the rebellious behavior.

"At first, I thought she didn't want me to bother you while you were on vacation, but the angry way she said it makes me think there's something else."

No way would she wade into this mess with the woman's twelve-year-old daughter. "Grown up stuff." Best to leave it at that.

"Whatever. I know it's something about an advocacy group. I'll pry it out of Mom."

That didn't make Wendy feel any better. What would Mrs. Gardenia say about the situation? About her? And what was she talking about regarding an advocacy group? She'd heard a handful of parents had started a parent advocacy group, and there were concerns about the educational system trampling parental rights, but she had nothing to do with that. She was the last person to side with the state over the parent. Allison had to have misunderstood.

"Shoot. There she is. Gotta go." Allison ducked her head, grabbed her phone and plate, and bailed.

~

At the sound of her phone's ping, Claire lifted her head from the massage table, careful not to disrupt the seaweed body wrap, and reached to check her text. So what if she couldn't afford a spa day? At this point, her mental health trumped her dwindling bank account. And with this being only day six of a fifteen-day cruise, she needed to offload a chunk of stress if she wanted to make it back home without ending up in handcuffs for assaulting her roommate.

Propped on her elbows, she read Trenia's text.

> Way to up your game! You're turning things around. Those pictures yesterday were hot, and you've been getting great engagement on them. Fit TV is pleased. Keep it coming.

She'd clap, except her body was slathered in brown goo and wrapped in cellophane. Finally, some good news. Thank God for Neo. If not for him, she'd still be scrambling to right her previous wrong.

If not for him, this would be one downer of a trip.

Wendy wasn't talking to her. Talk about petty. Were they in middle school or what? Claire had considered apologizing, but what for? She hadn't done anything wrong. There was nothing she could do to help Stella find her mission or get back home. Stella hadn't sent more letters to give them a clue as to how to help her, and Claire wasn't smart enough to figure any of that out on her own. She'd taken the plunge and attempted to aid Stella using her superpower and look where it had gotten her. It hadn't helped her friend, and it had really hurt her.

She was just about to lower herself onto the towel again when another text from Trenia came through.

> You're going to post videos tomorrow, right? They'll upload in Hawaii. You need a lot of videos to make up for the lack.

She sighed. She didn't have the backlog of videos planned. Not since Wendy had ruined the first one and hijacked most of her time, making Claire feel like she had to sneak around like a rebellious teenager. She'd planned on doing a video a day at each beach for their four days at Hawaiian ports. Would that be enough? She nibbled her lip and winced as moisturizer got into her mouth.

The attendant came toward her, tsking. "You're supposed to be unwinding."

She cringed and slid her phone back onto the table. "I know. I know. It shouldn't be this hard."

The woman chuckled. "Five more minutes and I'll start your massage."

Claire laid her head down and focused on relaxing her shoulders, then releasing the tension in her jaw. She inhaled deeply of the strong lemon scent in the room. The essential oil blend, seaweed mix, and Cellutox were supposed to detoxify her system while she marinated. Why, then, did she feel as tense as ever?

Only five minutes? She should text Neo and see if he could help her film a video. She grabbed her phone, smiling at the string of texts from yesterday and that morning.

> Claire: Why'd you run away?
> Neo: Your friend is scary!
> Claire: True.
> Neo: Seriously, didn't want you to get in more trouble with her if she saw me with you.
> Claire: When will I see you again?
> Neo: I'll be watching for you. Smile for the camera.

But she hadn't seen him since Wendy had blown up on the top deck. Had he been looking for her and been unable to find her? Had he taken pictures of her without her noticing? She'd have to check her page later to see if he'd posted any, but for now …

> Hey, I need your help. Meet me tonight to film a video?

His reply came almost instantly. Interesting. Was he as eager to see her as she was to see him?

> Where and when?

Good question. She needed somewhere indoors for the lighting. And it needed to be after Wendy went to bed.

> The piano bar lounge? 12:30?

He replied right before the attendant returned.

See you then.

That bit of resolution helped her enjoy the rest of her spa treatment and move on with her day with far less stress. But at 12:30, the lounge remained full of people. She met Neo outside the doors.

He crossed his arms over his toned chest. "Need a new plan?"

She blew out a breath, sending her bangs flying. "Yes."

"Let's walk around and see if we can find a good space."

She itched to hold his hand, but she couldn't while holding her mat and water bottle, so she walked close enough to him for their arms to brush. They strolled around the whole boat but couldn't find anywhere roomy enough with decent lighting. The gym didn't have enough room for floor work, and groups of people were scattered through all the other lounges and areas, filling the spaces with drunken laughter.

"We could always use my room. I have a suite and no roommate."

"I don't know." Claire slowed, considering.

Neo had been nothing but a gentleman. He'd given her no reason to think he'd be otherwise now, but still. Hanging out with a handsome guy she was insanely attracted to late at night in his room didn't seem like the best idea.

"Let's check the piano lounge again. Maybe the crowd has dispersed."

But from several feet away, the raucous laughter told her the group remained.

Neo gently put his hands on her shoulders. "I would never take advantage of you if that's what you're concerned about."

She was far more concerned she would be a willing participant and violate her values. What to do? How important were these videos? Maybe she could do three or four videos on each beach to compensate for it. But no. Variety was key. Fit TV would probably not be impressed with her cramming. She could always leave if she felt tempted or if Neo made a move she wasn't comfortable with.

"Okay. We can try it."

His smile should have sent a tingle through her. Instead, it unsettled her. But why? He was a fellow believer, right? Maybe he hadn't talked about his faith at all, but then again, she'd hardly mentioned hers. There was nothing to worry about. She stuffed down the feeling and followed him into the elevator and to his room.

Chapter Thirteen

Stella had a blast meandering past shops of all kinds on her way to The Screaming Peach. Filled with druggists and blacksmiths, clothing boutiques and livery stables, banks and barbershops, the city buzzed with life. It wasn't until she neared the square between Main and Second Streets that the ethnic makeup of the neighborhood shifted. White faces had become the minority, and dark-skinned men, women, and children filled the streets and alleyways. Had she stumbled into the Black portion of the city? Suddenly self-conscious, she wrapped her arms around herself. Would she be welcome here? Bridge had told her to come.

She found The Screaming Peach easily and entered through the heavy wooden door. A couple of dozen dark faces turned and took in her arrival.

She forced a nervous smile to the surface. "Hello. I'm a friend of Bridge."

A beefy man behind the bar lifted a brow. "Bridge? Some lady's here to see you."

No one spoke as Stella clasped her hands in front of her and waited for Bridge to appear. Patrons sat at rectangular tables, a bowl of peaches upon each as a centerpiece.

Bridge rushed down a stairwell tucked off in the corner. The woman's face lit when their eyes met. Relief washed over Stella at the welcome.

"Miss Lindy, glad you could come." Bridge came near and curtsied before her.

Stella took her hands and squeezed. "Please, call me Stella."

Her head dipped in concession. "All right, Miss Stella." Close enough. "Come sit. Uncle Marty will fix you up something to eat."

"I don't need anything."

Bridge led her to a table, then continued toward the kitchen as if she hadn't said a word. "Marty, bring her peach cobbler."

She'd sampled three different pies not more than an hour earlier, but the mention of peach cobbler made her mouth water. One-hundred-and-fifty-year-old calories didn't count, did they? Conversation resumed at the table beside her, though at a hushed level. Her experience as a journalist had taught her how to eavesdrop inconspicuously, and she put that skill to use.

Bridge set a glass of milk and slice of cobbler in front of her. "On the house."

"Thank you." One bite and her taste buds sang. "This is delightful."

Bridge smiled, settling across from her. "You're welcome. Uncle Marty is the best cook this side of Main."

The men at the next table piled bills in between them. One man counted them as he puffed on a cigar. "Looks like we have enough."

Cheers rang throughout the establishment. Bridge clapped, beaming. "Praise be."

Stella straightened. "Enough for what? What's going on?"

Cigar Man cast Bridge a warning look, but she crossed her arms and nodded in Stella's direction. "I trust her."

His eyes narrowed farther as he paused for a beat, but he nodded his consent. "Go ahead."

"They're selling my nephew Jimmy at the courthouse today. His owner died last week without a will. We've been saving our money with hopes of purchasing his freedom, and now we have the chance."

Cigar Man sat back in his seat and puffed. "I only hope they let Marty make a bid."

Stella looked back and forth between their faces, now etched with concern. "What do you mean?"

Bridge worried her lip. "Last time Marty tried to bid on another relative of ours, they wouldn't let him near the courthouse. A rich white lady ended up buying my cousin, and there wasn't a thing we could do about it."

"This time, though, he got a tuxedo." Cigar Man nodded as if that solved everything, but his eyes remained worried.

"A nice one," another woman interjected. "I ironed it."

Anxiety hung in the atmosphere like heavy fog on the river. What would happen to the boy if Marty went to purchase him and was turned away? Would this family member be lost to them forever? If only there was something she could do, a way she could assert the privilege of her skin color and class for good.

Wait a minute. "You said a rich white woman purchased your cousin?"

Bridge's frown deepened. "Yes'm."

"What if I purchased your nephew?"

Her brows knit together.

"Not really purchased, but used your money to buy him off the auction block and set him free for you?"

She splayed her hands on the table. "Truly? You'd do that?"

"Of course. Why not? It's legal, isn't it?" And free from any dangerous repercussions. A shiver ran down her spine at the memory of those Border Ruffians rummaging through the crates.

"Yes, indeed."

Cigar Man squinted at her. "How do we know we can trust you? What if you make off with him. You'd have legal right to, and we wouldn't have any way to stop you."

She pursed her lips. How could she convince these people she was trustworthy? They'd be placing a loved one's life into her hands, not to mention their hard-earned cash. Her hands went to her grandmother's earrings dangling from her ears. Perhaps a little collateral would do the trick?

She removed the earrings and placed them into Bridge's palm. "These are extremely special to me. A family heirloom. If I don't bring your nephew to you, they're yours to keep."

Bridge studied them thoughtfully. "I never seen anything like them."

Stella smiled at Cigar Man. "Now, where and when is the auction?"

Hours later, she hustled toward the east door of the courthouse, little purse thingy in her hand. Her ears felt strangely naked as she stumbled a bit on the cobblestone street. She edged her way through a crowd of men dressed in bow ties, vests, and suits. For the second time that day, conversation simmered to a whisper as curious glances took her in. This time, she matched them in skin color. It was her gender that was out of place. She was clearly the only woman in attendance.

"Good day, gentlemen." She gave a nod with a tight-lipped smile.

A man wearing a black cape and carrying a cane ambled up to her. "Might I ask what business you have here, miss?"

She pushed the words out on a wave of nausea. "I'm here to purchase a slave." Just saying the dreadful thing made her skin crawl.

The man's mustache twitched as he looked around her vicinity. Was he searching for her husband? "It's highly unusual for a woman to come to an auction unattended."

Apparently. Why hadn't Bridge mentioned as much? She scrambled for a justification and spit out the first thing that came to mind. "My husband's been detained. He sent me in his stead."

"Detained?"

"Rheumatism." That was a thing in the 1850s, right?

The man's chin dimpled with a sympathetic frown. "How unfortunate. Well, best of luck to you, then." He shuffled off to join a group of other men, leaving the muscles in her neck to unknot.

Until a group of a dozen Black men, women, and children were paraded by with shackled ankles. Her throat dried. Three women, four girls, two grown men, two boys, and a baby. Jimmy had to be one of the two boys, likely the taller one, since Bridge had said he was eleven. The backs of her eyes stung, and she pressed her lips together to suppress her emotions. She couldn't allow sorrow at what would have been a completely normal sight in this day to give her away or keep her from securing Jimmy's future.

The next couple of hours lanced her heart as a trader forced each of the enslaved to strip down to nearly nothing and allowed prospective buyers to inspect them as if they were purchasing animals. Stella schooled her features, gritting her teeth to keep from crying out against such inhumanity. Her chest burned at the way the men perused the women's nakedness. How could this have ever been normal? An average afternoon of bidding on a human being in the streets of an American city. If only her money worked in this time. She'd be rich enough to purchase the freedom of several of these precious people. Instead, she could only watch helplessly as one after another was sold to the highest bidder while she waited for Jimmy.

By the time Jimmy stood on the auction block, nearly half of the crowd had dispersed, already having made their purchases and seen what they came to see. Jimmy was the second to last sale. The gentleman she'd spoken to earlier made the first bid, but when she outbid him, he relented. Likely, he felt sorry for her husband in his condition. No one else countered. Were they not interested in the boy, or did they not wish to get into a bidding war against a woman? No matter the reason, she ended up walking away with a deed of sale and the boy in tow.

To avoid arousing suspicion, she played the part of a slave owner. "Come on, boy. I'll take you to meet your new master."

He followed, shoulders slumped, gaze to the ground. Her conscience twisted. He had to be scared, feeling alone in the world. But she didn't know the rules here or how to play by them. If people knew she'd purchased him for his family members in order to set him free, would he be in danger of recapture? Best to continue to pretend for now.

She consulted the map and followed it down busy streets toward the river. She wrinkled her nose as they neared the wharf. Fishy. She'd gotten used to the smell of the river while riding upon it, but after a break from its constant assault on the senses, it hit her afresh. They walked down the riverbank until they came to a skiff with a sign posted nearby stating Floating Freedom School.

"This appears to be it." She squinted into the distance.

There, in the middle of the river, a steamboat was anchored. Bridge had explained Missouri had enacted a law a few years back that made it illegal to teach negroes or mulattos to read or write. In order to get around the law, a local preacher, Reverend Meachum, had created a steamboat school, technically outside of the state's jurisdiction. This had made it completely legal for him to hire teachers to educate hundreds of Black students who journeyed to the boat on skiffs.

She bent to meet his eyes. "You're free, Jimmy. Your family and friends bought your freedom. Now, you get to live with them and get an education at the Floating Freedom School."

His gaze narrowed in suspicion. "That's a cruel fib."

"It's true. I'm dropping you off here, and Marty will be here when school lets out to pick you up and take you home." She winked. "They might be preparing a party for your arrival."

His face lit up. "Truly?"

She laughed. "Yes."

"I ain't never been to a party before. I served in the kitchen during one, but I never got to go." The joy radiating from him made him look like a child for the first time since she'd laid eyes on him. She could imagine him running, playing, climbing, doing the things boys should do.

She pulled out a pen and his bill of sale and wrote a declaration of freedom on it using the words Bridge had given her, then she signed with a flourish. "Enjoy your new life."

As she lay in bed that night at the hotel, she basked in gratitude. She'd gotten the opportunity to play a small part in Jimmy's freedom. How glorious. She hadn't broken any laws—only social conventions—and hadn't put herself in any danger, and yet, she was a voice in the harmony of his freedom chorus. Adrenaline coursed through her from the whole experience, making it hard to fall asleep.

If freedom was a song that continually played, she couldn't wait to join in for her part again.

~

Claire's alarm went off at seven in the morning. She hit snooze and tried to drift back into her dream. A pleasant one this time. One where Neo held her in his arms like he had last night. Oh, the bliss of his soft touch, the gentle way he'd pried open pieces of her heart that had been hidden away for so long. After he'd filmed the video, they'd cuddled on his suite's sofa and talked until three in the morning.

True to his word, he hadn't even stuck his toe over the line of propriety. Their kisses had been sweet, light, and brief, interspersing deep conversation. He'd asked her to tell him a secret, and she'd told him about Troy. Afterward, it was as if he was trying to put as much distance as he could between himself and the handsy jerk from high school.

When she'd confessed how Troy had only dated her to win a bet that he'd be able to get her into bed, Neo's face twisted in disgust. "That's low," he'd said. "You didn't ..."

"No!" Her cheeks flamed. "I'm not that kind of girl."

"That's what I thought." He tenderly stroked her hair. "Good girl."

Why had she ever worried? Their evening had been chaste enough to write home about. And now she wanted to return to his arms via dreamland.

The alarm sang out again, and she shot up in bed. How could she have forgotten why she'd set an alarm in the first place? Their first port day! She'd finally get to feel the sand between her toes, hear the waves lapping the shore, lean back in the sun with a piña colada, and hopefully, shoot at least one video.

You need a lot of videos to make up for the lack.

At least one killer video.

No pressure.

She wasted no time changing into her swimsuit and plaiting her hair. Which cover-up should she choose? Comfy to accommodate the moderate amount of walking they'd need to do to get from the port to the beach or trendier but with straps that dug into her armpits? She had a similar decision to make on shoe choice.

She could nearly hear Trenia shouting, "Bring it, Claire!"

She clenched her jaw and stuffed the comfy choices back in the closet. If she wanted the big time, she had to up her game. And that meant making sacrifices. Goodbye, comfort. Hello, success.

"What are you doing?" Wendy rubbed her eyes and sat up in bed.

Oh, they were talking again. Thank goodness. The stalemate was getting old. "Just getting ready for today. Sorry I woke you."

"Ready for what?"

"The beach."

Wendy crinkled her nose. "We're not going to the beach."

"What do you mean?" Had she misread the itinerary? She could have sworn today was their first stop in Hawaii.

"What about Stella?"

Claire's ribs squeezed. *Stella.* If only Stella were here, they'd all three be laughing up a storm, cracking jokes no matter how early or no matter how late they'd stayed up chatting the night before. "What about her?"

Wendy flung an arm out. "We can't go galivanting around the beach while she's missing."

Was she saying … oh, heck no. Claire put her hands on her hips. "First of all, she's not missing. We know where she is. We know she's safe. Not dead. Not kidnapped." Wendy opened her mouth, but Claire pushed ahead before she could speak. "Secondly, what good is moping around the boat supposed to do for her? How is Stella served by us not going to the beach?"

Wendy was on her feet, face flushed. "We could use that time to research the *Arabia*."

"I've already scoured every online article I could find. I don't see how we're going to find any new information that will help. Besides, we're still waiting for her to write us back. We don't even know what to focus on until we hear from her."

Wendy averted her eyes and angled away. Her words rang defensive. "Wouldn't you feel guilty for going and having fun without her?"

"No. It's one hundred percent what Stella would want us to do. Do you know her at all?"

Wendy gasped. Claire's words reverberated in the small room like a slap. Wendy turned away fully, facing the wall.

Claire fumbled. "I didn't mean …"

But what did she mean? Did she truly think Wendy didn't know Stella as well as she did? That couldn't be true. Those two had been as close as twins from the first day they'd met. But it seemed Claire and Wendy each knew a different version of Stella.

She rolled her neck from side to side. How could she make this right? She tried again. "You're an amazing friend to Stella. You've always been there for her. Forever loyal. It's amazing you'd stick by her in this way." She ventured putting a hand on Wendy's shoulder. When her friend didn't shake it off, she let it linger and said a prayer for Wendy's peace even as she continued to speak. "I'm only saying I think Stella would want us to have fun until we know how we can help. If I could text her and ask her, I bet she'd tell us to *go*."

"But what if it's better for her if we stay?" It sounded like a plea.

"Better how? How could staying on this ship possibly help Stella get back? We've spent days researching, and it's gotten us nowhere." She could not conceive of any way that staying would benefit Stella, only of how it might alleviate Wendy's conscience.

Wendy didn't answer, only barraged Claire with soulful eyes. After a few minutes of the stalemate, Claire turned around and continued packing her bag.

Wendy sat back on her bed and wrapped the blanket around herself. So, she was going to mope when she didn't get her way. She had done that a few times in college as well. Used to running the show, she tended to either throw a hissy fit or wallow when control slipped from her grasp. Best to not cater to her. She'd get over it with time.

When Claire finished getting ready, she turned and forced cheer into her tone. "See you this evening."

Before she walked out the door, Wendy shot a reply. "You might know Stella, but you sure don't know me at all."

Claire shut the door on the odd remark. It had to be a ploy to get her to stay. A manipulation tactic. Because really, what didn't she know about Wendy?

~

Wendy threw herself back onto the bed and draped an arm over her eyes. What was wrong with her? So much for reconciling with Claire. Her parents had been right. She was brash with rough edges. Would those rough edges ruin every relationship? Not to mention her career.

She remembered looking up that word at twelve years old after overhearing her parents use it in reference to her. Brash—self-assertive in a rude, noisy, or overbearing way.

"Lorainne doesn't have much time left. I want them to end their relationship on a good note. I know Wendy can be a good sister if she tries."

Her mom had been wrong, apparently, because no matter how hard she'd tried, she couldn't seem to be soft enough for sensitive Lorainne. She hadn't been a good sister. Just like she hadn't been a good friend to Stella when her friend had needed her most. As Stella had watched her grandmother wither away from colon cancer, Wendy had kept her distance. Instead of pressing close as a best friend should, she'd avoided the glaring similarities between Stella's loss and her own. She couldn't do it. She couldn't face the reminder of her little sister's leukemia.

She'd failed them both.

But unlike Lorainne, Wendy had the opportunity to make things right with Stella. To show her friend she cared. Hence, this cruise. But of course, nothing ever went according to plan.

She sat up. Might as well go eat breakfast.

As she stood, a flash of bright turquoise caught her eye. Stella's phone. The giraffe case peeked at her. Claire forgot to take a phone? How'd that happen? The device was basically attached to the girl's hand. How long before she realized it was missing and came back for it?

Wendy grabbed it and swiped to see Stella's smiling face on the lock screen. She stood cheek to cheek with Everett, glowing with new love. Those two made the perfect couple. One could feel their devotion to each other from miles away.

A wave of homesickness for her friend rolled through her. Maybe looking through Stella's pictures would make her feel better. She entered Stella's birthdate for the lock code and smiled back at another picture of Stells and Everett. Too cute.

A text message popped up from Stella's mom asking how she was enjoying the trip. Wendy's stomach sank. If the woman only knew what her daughter was going through right

now. Best if she didn't. Stella could choose to tell her story—
or not—when she returned to them safely.

When the notification faded, the icon for text
notifications drew Wendy's eye. Fifty-seven texts? Who
were they from? Everyone should know she was on vacation
and off the grid. Curiosity pulled at her. What if something in
those texts offered a hint to help get Stella back? Or what if
there was an emergency? Friends didn't keep things from
each other, right? It wouldn't be a big deal to check.

She clicked on the icon to see the line of snippets. A few
mushy texts from Everett. She didn't need to dive deep into
those. A couple of ones from merchants highlighting sales.
One that looked like spam. Several from Trenia. Was she a
colleague at the paper? But the majority came from Stella's
boss at the paper, Randall.

A work emergency?

She should probably check. She clicked to view the
conversation. Her mouth fell open as she saw the N word.

> You were right. Those n*****s bought the building across from Tom's Bakery.
>
> I don't know what those black fools think they're doing. There's a certain way we do things around here.
>
> Found out they're opening a real estate business.
>
> We can't stand for this.
>
> Find the dirt. Take them down.

Wendy stared at the phone, willing the horrible words to
disappear. Stella's boss wanted to run Black businesspeople
out of town? Her throat tightened. He wanted Stella to help
him?

There was no way Stella would stand for this nonsense.
She must not have known her boss's true character, or she'd
never have taken the job. She was about to marry a Black
man. Their children, when they had them, would be biracial.

And after they married, Everett was moving to Stella's podunk town so she could keep her dream job while he worked remotely. Wendy had to warn her about her ignorant, racist boss. It could change their future plans.

Wendy nearly went for paper to write a letter, but a niggling doubt crept into her mind. How much was Stella aware of? Why had Randall said *You were right*? Instead, she scrolled up.

> Randall: Saw these n*****s waltzing around downtown. What are they up to?
> Stella: I can check.
> Stella: Two of them?
> Randall: Yeah.
> Stella: They were inquiring about the building for sale across from the bakery.
> Randall: There goes the neighborhood. How can we send the message they're not welcome? Ideas.
> Stella: Not sure. I'm about to leave for my cruise, so I'll touch base about this when I get back.
> Randall: Think about it.
> Stella: Will do.

Wendy reread the conversation again and again. There had to be another explanation. Her best friend could not be complicit in this kind of bigotry. But why hadn't she said something? Why would she stand by and allow such talk? She must have been offended. Was she planning on continuing to work for such a man? She'd said nothing about looking for another job. In fact, she'd touted this position as her dream job.

Where was this little Missouri town Stella had moved to for her dream editor job? She'd mentioned it was small, and even used the word "hick," but was it so White that two

Black people would be that easily noticed? How could two people of a different ethnicity cause such a stir? And poor Everett was about to move there. That place would eat him alive. Would Stella stand by and watch?

No. None of this made any sense. Right now, Stella was helping to cover for escaped slaves. She wasn't a racist. Not even close. She was one of the kindest, most compassionate people Wendy had ever met. She must have used leaving for the cruise as a cop-out to sort out how to address the topic with her boss. That had to be it. She was buying time. Creating a strategy. Only, why had she kept Wendy out of it all?

A sound at the door caused Wendy to click out of texts, lock the phone, and throw it back on the bed. She retreated to her own bed right before Claire breezed in, wearing her ginormous sunglasses.

"Forgot my phone."

"Stella's phone." The whole time Claire had been using it, Wendy had nearly forgotten it belonged to Stella. That it held clues about her friend.

Claire's brow scrunched. "Whatever." She took it and headed back toward the door.

"Hey," Wendy ventured. "You haven't seen anything … questionable while using Stella's phone, have you?"

"Questionable?" Claire peered over her shaded rims.

"Yeah, like any texts?"

"I don't snoop, if that's what you're asking."

Wendy went for an air of nonchalance, her shrug light and airy. "Just wondering."

Claire took another step toward the door. "Sure you don't want to come with me?"

Wendy folded her arms around herself, shaken inside. "Positive."

"Suit yourself."

As soon as the door shut, Wendy dressed. Stella wasn't the only one with a mission.

Chapter Fourteen

At noon the next day, Stella went to meet Dr. Duncan at the wharf as he requested. She saw him from a distance as he leaned casually against a crate on the dock. Roustabouts—as she'd learned deckhands were called—scurried back and forth loading cargo. One roustabout came to him, and they whispered back and forth as Dr. Duncan patted the crate. Then the man called someone to help him, and they hoisted the crate carefully.

Stella zeroed in on the scene. They handled that crate much more carefully than the other cargo, the majority of which the workers shoved and banged about.

She ambled up to Duncan, new reticule in hand. She smiled to herself. Reticule, that was the word. She was learning so many new words and felt nearly as smart as Wendy.

As she sidled up next to the doctor, she sobered. "Again with the precious cargo?" She trained her gaze on his expression. Were her suspicions correct?

Not so much as a facial muscle betrayed him, but he said, "That crate is of utmost value. Must be handled with care."

She raised a brow. "The same kind of care as the Frozen Charlotte dolls?"

His nod was barely perceptible. "Much the same."

"Are there precious loads of cargo on each trip?"

"Ah, Miss Lindy." He tilted his head. "You need only be concerned about the trips you are on."

She'd take that as a yes. Apparently, this was his thing. Rescuing slaves and mentoring time sailors.

He lowered his voice. "Might you be interested in assisting with the cargo?"

"Assisting how?"

His gaze darted around. A man stood a foot or so behind him, seemingly searching the horizon for someone. Stella alerted Duncan with a nod in that direction.

Duncan took her arm and led her away from the dock onto a secluded moss-covered pathway. After ensuring they were alone, he spoke. "Food and water. A mother with one boy and one girl. The father is the man I just spoke to. He's posing as a deckhand. It's too risky for him to deliver the nourishment. Authorities are looking for the family."

Her hand went to her throat. A mission. Could it finally be *the* mission? Her way back home? Only, was this mission a dangerous one? "What happens if I'm caught?"

He pursed his lips. "Six months in prison and a five hundred dollar fine."

Okay, that was better than hanging. But she couldn't stay in the past for six months. She had a wedding waiting for her. Except she likely couldn't get to that wedding without accepting the mission. *Oh, Lord. What should I do?*

In her mind's eye, she could see Jesus's gentle face giving her a raised brow, as if He were saying, *Do I really have to answer that?*

But God, I'm scared. You know me. You know I'm not brave.

His answer came so clearly to her heart, it was almost as if she heard it aloud. *That's okay. I am. Hold My hand. We'll do this together.*

She pictured those kind eyes again, full of love and understanding. She was right. He did know her. And He was inviting her into this anyway. Didn't that mean He would give her the power to overcome her fear? If she could draw courage from Him every step of the way, holding His mighty hand, maybe she could do this. Maybe her plus Jesus was enough to overcome her dismal history of freezing in fright when confronted with injustice.

"Okay." She nodded with more assurance than she felt. "What do I do?"

~

Claire took a sip of her piña colada and inhaled deeply of the salty sea air. Nothing better than a sunny, warm day on a white-sanded beach. Crystal blue waves crashed, seagulls sounded in the air. Everything was perfect—only she was alone.

This was certainly not how she'd pictured things going down. She'd been looking forward to cruising with her best friends. She'd pictured a trip full of laughter and chitchat. Doing each other's nails and catching up. The picture-perfect scene before her rang hollow without her favorite people next to her.

Life always seemed barren, like there was forever a proverbial empty seat next to her waiting to be filled. Always waiting. Never filled.

Where was Neo? Why hadn't he responded to her texts to spend the day with her? She'd poured her heart out to him last night. Had she said too much? Scared him away? He certainly hadn't bared his soul in return. Maybe she was destined to be alone. She took another sip. What a sad way to spend a beach day.

At least she'd gotten two videos recorded. They'd both turned out great, despite the fact Neo hadn't helped. She had the perfect backdrop and not too much wind ruining the sound. No editing them without her laptop program, but she could post them ASAP and call the day a win, right?

Sighing, she opted for a dip in the ocean. The hot sand scalded her soles as she dashed toward the crashing waves. A couple of guys whistled at her as she settled knee-deep into the cool water.

"Hey, pretty lady. Swimming alone?" a jock with a surfboard asked. "I could show you a good time."

She rolled her eyes.

"She's not alone. She's with me."

Claire turned at the sound of Neo's voice and nearly leapt into his arms, his very muscular arms. Oh goodness. Neo without a shirt was a sight to behold. Every inch of him was chiseled to perfection.

"You came!"

"Of course. I couldn't let you spend the day alone."

She'd spent *half* of the day alone, but she wouldn't focus on wondering what he'd been doing all morning. She'd relish the fact that he was here now.

The jock walked on, and Neo picked her up and twirled her around, splaying water in the air and sending her spirits soaring. When he set her down, he threaded his fingers through her hair and claimed her lips. Waves crashed against their knees, causing them to teeter, but his kiss held fast. She drank it in, thirsty for his affection after the lonely morning.

When they parted, he smiled adoringly at her. As if she were the most fascinating person in the world. Her heart warmed to match the sun that beat on their faces.

He grasped her hand. "I rented a wave runner. Come with me?"

"Of course." Nothing sounded better to her than wrapping her arms around this man while the wind coursed through her hair.

"The rental's not for another hour. How about a walk on the beach until then?"

"Perfect." Anything would be perfect with Neo by her side.

They withdrew from the water and walked hand in hand on the cool, wet sand, dodging joggers and laughing children and occasionally stopping to scoop up a seashell. Neo stored the shells in the pocket of his swim trunks.

"I appreciate you confiding in me last night. It meant a lot that you trusted me." He squeezed her hand.

"It means a lot to me that you're trustworthy." She returned the squeeze.

He extricated his grasp for only a moment to press a button on his smartwatch. Just those few seconds left her fingers cold and lonely, aching for his touch.

"So …" He turned that adorable grin on her. "Tell me another secret."

She giggled, but something inside prickled. It was sweet he was interested in her, but shouldn't it be reciprocal? Maybe she hadn't asked enough questions.

"You first." She gave him a playful nudge. "Tell me a secret of yours."

"Hmm." He looked to the sky as if the clouds would help him remember. "In my high school biology class, we were dissecting a cat. We were supposed to insert a straw into the cat's lungs and blow into it to inflate them, but"—he winced—"instinct took over, and I sucked in instead."

She dropped his hand to cover her mouth. "Oh my gosh. Gross."

"I know. Not my proudest moment."

"You drank cat guts? And I've been kissing that mouth?"

"It was years ago, and 'drinking cat guts' is exaggerating."

"Even so." She shuddered.

He took her hand again. "Still love me?"

Her heart tripped. Love? Did he just ask if she loved him? Way to make things awkward. She'd only known him for a few days. Surely, she couldn't claim love. Attraction, for certain. Admiration. Affection. But love? It was far too soon. But she couldn't say no. That would be hurtful, given the fact he'd shared such a humiliating moment and was likely feeling embarrassed.

He stepped into her hesitation, his eyes full of worry. "Oh no. Don't tell me I ruined this thing between us with that stupid story."

"Of course not." She shook her head. She had to put him at ease. "Yes, of course, I still love you."

He grinned and squeezed her hand again, harder this time. "Good. Now, your turn."

For a moment, she reeled inside. Was he not going to say it back? But that dimple and those laughing eyes put her at ease. "A secret, huh?"

"Yep."

Hmm. What to tell? Their arms swung together like a pendulum. A seagull dipped and dove onto the shore in front of them. They sidestepped two boys burying their father in the sand. He'd told her an embarrassing story, one he didn't have to tell. It was only right for her to reciprocate.

"I was at my older sister's high school grad party, and all my relatives and friends were there. My aunt says, 'Thank God Julie got a scholarship. That way you can save your money for Claire. You know, since she probably won't get one.' Then another aunt says, 'Is Claire even going to college?'"

"Oh no. They didn't."

"Oh yeah, they did. In front of my friends and everyone else. That's not the worst of it. My uncle waltzes into the room and says, 'Claire should model. She'd be good at that.' And everyone chimed in as if it was a brilliant idea. 'Oh yeah, she could make great money.' As if I would never be good at anything else. So, yeah, everyone thinks I'm nothing but a pretty face." She focused her gaze on her sand-encrusted feet.

"But you did go to college?"

"Yeah. I got a BA in kinesiology."

"You showed them."

"Maybe. I definitely didn't get a scholarship." Not to mention she didn't exactly take honors classes or ace the ones she had taken. "I'm up to my ears in college debt."

"You and forty-five million other Americans."

"The thing is, I can't help but wonder if they're right. What if this," she said, gesturing to her face, "is all I am?"

He stilled and took her cheeks in his hands. Caressing her jaw with his gentle touch, he looked deep into her eyes. "Oh, Claire, you are so much more."

She stood on tiptoe and wrapped her arms around his neck. How did he know exactly what she needed to hear? She thanked him with a passionate kiss.

Some teens behind them hooted and hollered. "Get a room."

Her cheeks warmed, and she broke away. "Anyway," she said as she resumed their stroll, "I guess my secret is I'm not smart, and everyone who knows me well enough knows it."

His brow furrowed. "I don't believe that for a second."

She sucked in her bottom lip, ignoring the burning in her chest. "I guess you don't know me well enough yet."

~

As if finding someone on a crowded ship wasn't difficult enough, Wendy set out to find Dr. Duncan on a port day. She rushed to his room and banged on the door. No answer. After another round of desperate knocks, she spun around to head to the dining area. No use wasting precious time. Perhaps he hadn't left the boat yet.

She nearly barreled into a steward.

"Excuse me, miss." The man looked as startled as she felt.

"No, it was my fault. Sorry." They stepped around each other, but then she turned. "Wait. Do you know the man who rooms here?" She pointed to Dr. Duncan's door.

"I service his room, miss."

"Do you know if he's left for the day?"

He smiled and shook his head. "He said he's been to Hawaii many times and didn't think he'd be getting off the boat."

Her shoulders sagged in relief. "Oh, good. Thank you."

"You are friends?" he asked warily, as if he wondered if he'd given out too much information.

"Oh yeah. Good friends."

It wasn't totally a lie. They'd shared a moment on deck. And they were about to become better acquainted. If she could find him.

She scoured the café and inquired about him in the restaurant. She searched around the near-empty pool and hot tubs, the coffee shop, and spa. The gift shop was closed, but that didn't stop her from looking around the entrance. No sign of him anywhere.

She would not, could not, get discouraged.

Her phone buzzed, and she checked the text. Grayson.

> We're headed to the beach now. Sure you don't want to reconsider joining us?

He'd attached a selfie of him and his dad. Man, Sam Hill even looked like a grump with a frown so deep it could have been chiseled on. She chuckled, imagining what he could find to complain about in gorgeous Hawaii.

She *could* join them. Meet Grayson's father and spend the day snickering at his complaints, when he wasn't looking, of course. More time with Grayson without research getting in the way? How heavenly. They'd both wanted to see the USS Arizona Memorial for those who lost their lives in Pearl Harbor. Besides, she'd already searched in all the common places for Dr. Duncan. If she hadn't found him by now …

No. She couldn't do that. Couldn't be like Claire and forget they were in the middle of a crisis.

> Sorry. Wish I could. Can't wait to hear all about it.

Now, where was she? Oh yes. She was about to search each and every deck.

By the time she made it to the top deck, her thighs and her chest burned. But there, Dr. Rodney Duncan stood at much the same spot at the railing as the first night when they'd spoken about his grandfather.

She schooled her steps to keep from ambushing the man and scaring him off. She approached casually, as if she'd happened upon him by chance. "Favorite spot?" Resting her elbows on the railing, she gazed out to where the aqua sea met near-white sand and tried not to hate herself for choosing to stay on the boat.

He glanced at her briefly, then made a soft sound in his throat that sounded something like an assent. "Are you a frequent cruiser as well?"

"No. Just couldn't stomach going on as if everything was normal without Stella."

"Ah."

She turned to him, pressing both hands together in a plea. "You have to help me."

"Help you do what?"

"I can't figure out how to get Stella back here, so I need to get to Stella."

His brow quirked. "Excuse me?"

"I need you to help me time-sail."

He reared back his head. "I can't do that."

"You have to." She took a step toward him, pleading with her eyes. "I need to get to my friend. She's not cut out for this. She needs me."

"If the other time called *her*, not you, then it's for a reason."

"But she can't do this alone!" Desperation clogged her throat. How could she make him understand? He didn't know Stella, didn't understand how ill-equipped she was for this. Tears pricked her eyelids. She pushed an explanation out through the threat of tears. "I have to be there for her. I haven't always been the friend I should have been. But I can do this for her. I can go to 1856 and help her. Tell me what I need to do to get there."

Dr. Duncan lifted a sad smile. "It doesn't work like that. Time-sailing isn't something we can control. A mission calls out to us; we don't call out to it."

"There's got to be something."

He shook his head. "Nothing that I know of."

"Ugh." She yanked at the roots of her hair. "This sucks."

She stomped away, arms wrapped tightly around herself, holding herself together. But she couldn't slam the door on this without trying one last time. She turned back toward his pained face. "Nothing. You're sure? Absolutely sure? You said you didn't remember much."

His voice dripped with regret. "I remember that much clearly. No one chooses to time-sail. It chooses them."

Okay, then. Door closed. "Thanks anyway."

She slunk to her room, drained and defeated. As she lay on her bed, staring at the drab white ceiling instead of crystal blue water, it occurred to her she had connections with someone far more powerful than Dr. Duncan.

Lord, once again, I tried to solve this problem on my own instead of going to You first. I guess You're used to that by now, huh? But You can do what Dr. Duncan can't. You can take me to 1856 to help her. You're the boss of time. So, take me there. Please, God. Make me time-sail to Stella.

Chapter Fifteen

Basket of provisions and lantern in tow, Stella exited her stateroom onto the moonlit deck. She ambled as if she were out enjoying the fresh air, nodding a greeting to a few men deep in discussion. Dr. Duncan had introduced her to the captain as his assistant. No issues there. Then they'd run into Bridge.

Stella had almost wrapped the woman in a hug.

Bridge curtsied, her eyes downcast. "Hello, ma'am. My name is Bridge. I'll be your chambermaid for this voyage."

Oh yeah. Bridge didn't remember her. Once Stella had stepped back onto the boat everything had been reset. All the history they'd built together had been lost when Stella returned to the boat. Bridge would have no recollection it was Stella who had aided in purchasing Jimmy's freedom. How had things transpired in the woman's memory? Stella frowned as she greeted her friend turned stranger. She'd have to wear her Jayhawks shirt in front of her to speed up their bonding.

After the introductions, Dr. Duncan had told her to visit the lower deck under the guise of checking on a sick traveler in deck passage.

Now her pulse thrummed in her ears and perspiration beaded the back of her neck as she descended the steps. *Don't get caught. Don't get caught.* Repeating that mantra only made her nerves go more haywire. She tried picturing Jesus walking next to her instead, holding her hand like He said He would.

Okay, yes. That helped. He promised He would never leave her or forsake her.

He was as close as her breath. She could do this because she wasn't doing it alone.

Once again, the scent of animal dung met her nose as her feet approached the bottom deck. She wove her way through kegs of butter, pork, and lard, past wicker baskets and coils of rope, past crates labeled Nails, Candles, and Catsup. She searched for the crate labeled Mirrors. Dr. Duncan had said it'd be in front of the cargo hatch next to the canned sardines and parallel to the first pile of lumber.

There! The lumber stood in a tall stack ahead of her to the left, its woodsy scent a welcome one. The clang of something falling made her stiffen and freeze in place. An empty bottle of whisky rolled in front of the lumber pile. She waited for its owner to make an appearance, ticking off the seconds in her mind. When a minute had passed without sight of anyone, she resumed her search with whisper-soft steps.

She smiled at the sight of the crate of canned sardines, then just as quickly wrinkled her nose at the awful smell protruding from it. No. Not from the sardines. From the box next to it. Just as Duncan had said, there was the crate labeled Mirrors. She'd made it without incident. *Thank You, God.* But that smell. Horrible. With the softest of knocks, she greeted the stowaways.

She set the lantern on top of the crate and felt around the side for the loose board. A gentle moan eked out of the container, followed by a shushing sound. When a board finally swung aside, she worked hard not to gag. Holding her breath, she brought the lantern down to view those inside and gasped.

A mother sagged against the side of the crate, her eyes sunken and listless. A petite child sat in her lap. The little one was the size of an infant, but Dr. Duncan had proclaimed the smallest one to be a two-year-old girl. Was she malnourished or naturally tiny in stature? Another child, this one older, so it must be the boy, huddled across from them, moaning. She reached out and felt the boy's forehead, anticipating a fever, but instead, his skin was unnaturally cool to the touch.

"You're sick?" she whispered.

In answer, the boy bent over and vomited into the chamber pot. She suppressed a wince. No wonder it smelled so bad. She felt the mother's and toddler's heads too. They were all cool to the touch.

"Oh man." What was she supposed to do about this? Three sick stowaways trapped in a suffocating space. She didn't need a degree in healthcare to know the closed quarters didn't make for a good prognosis.

First things first, she had to empty the chamber pot. Dr. Duncan had said to dump it into the river on the bow side. She hurried to do so, balancing her fear of sloshing the mess out of the pot and onto her clothes with the fear one of them would get sick without something to vomit into. "Jesus is with me. Jesus is with me." She mumbled the mantra with each step. The Son of God was born in a pungent manger, among filth and manure. He wasn't afraid of messy situations, and He was walking her through this. One step at a time.

She dumped the contents overboard and took a couple of gulps of fresh air before returning. *Okay, Lord. What next?* They were likely dehydrated. She took out the pitcher of water. She'd only filled it half full, afraid some would spill if she put too much in. Now, she regretted that decision.

She stretched the pitcher toward the mother. "Here. Take a drink."

But the woman didn't reach for it. Her hand lifted a bit, then dropped back into her lap. Was she too weak to take it? Stella did her best to reach the pitcher to the mother's lips and tilt it slightly, but the lack of room in the opening made the task difficult. Water dribbled from around the woman's mouth and onto her dress and her child's head, but from the way she gently smacked her lips, some must have made it into her mouth. Stella did the same with the toddler and then with the boy, each with similar results.

"Can you eat anything?" She broke off small pieces of bread and placed them into their clammy hands. No one took a bite.

Worry constricted around her heart like a boa. Were they going to die? And on her watch? God forbid.

She needed a washcloth to dab their faces with but had nothing. Reaching under her dress, she yanked on the bottom of her petticoat, ripping with all her might until she managed to tear off a piece. She dunked it in the pitcher and then used it to pat their foreheads. As she did so, the lantern light illuminated stains on their clothing. They needed to change. Bathe. But how could they while crammed into a crate?

She must find Dr. Duncan. After prodding each of them to take another sip of water, she repositioned the board and hustled back toward the stairs. Most of the food remained in her basket. No use leaving it there to rot.

As she rounded a barrel of cheese, she collided into a burly man with a scraggly beard. "Oh! Excuse me." Her eyes snapped to the revolver in his holster.

He eyed her up and down in a way that made her skin crawl. "What's a pretty lady like you doing wandering 'round at night by you'self?" The side of his mouth tipped in a slimy smile, and the scent of liquor leaked from him.

"I'm the doctor's assistant. Just finished tending to a sick patient. Now, if you'll excuse me." She made to step around him, but he blocked her path.

"You do Doc's errands for him, eh? Good at followin' a man's orders?"

Oh, heck no. This man would not bully her. Moxie solidified within her. She hardened her gaze and her voice. "If you touch me, I will claw your eyes out. I'll bite and scratch and kick so hard, you'll wish you'd never seen the light of day."

His eyes widened, and he flung his hands in the air. "Didn't mean nothing by it. Was only making conversation."

"Make it elsewhere." She shoved past him, and he moved out of her way, grumbling to himself as he did so.

Halfway up the stairs, a kickback of adrenaline hit her. Her legs weakened, and she dropped to her knees, trembling all over. Where had that bravery come from? She was scared little Stella, the one who cowered instead of standing tall, and yet look at her! She'd faced a man twice her size and won.

Lord, was that in me all along?

Elation at her victory propelled her to the promenade deck before the weight of the evening settled upon her again. Three lives hung in the balance downstairs. How could she help save them?

~

When Claire's alarm went off the next morning, she didn't bother with the snooze button. Another day at another beach with Neo. She sighed contentedly and stretched, then rose for a quick shower. But an envelope under the door stopped her.

"Wendy!" she shouted, snatching it. "Wendy, wake up! It's a letter from Stella. Finally. We've been waiting forever." She tore it open and plopped onto Wendy's bed.

Wendy sat up and rubbed her eyes. "Oh great," she said, but why didn't she sound more excited? "What does it say?"

> Hey guys,
> Thanks for the help navigating St. Louis in the 1800s. I couldn't have done it without you, at least not without looking crazy.

Claire stopped reading and looked at Wendy. "What's she talking about?"

Wendy shrugged.

"Strange."

"Keep reading."

> I have my own Frozen Charlotte doll now. I wonder if I'll get to bring anything back with

me when I return. Probably not. I'll have to find one on eBay.

Again, Claire turned to Wendy. "What's a Frozen Charlotte doll?"

"It was a porcelain figurine popular back then. I'll tell you the story later."

Maybe she was the only person who didn't know what one was. Still, the wording of the letter struck her as odd. She felt out of the loop.

> We set back off from St. Louis and are now on the ill-fated trip. There is another crate of enslaved stowaways, this time a mother with a toddler and a child who's maybe nine or ten.

"This time? She's talking like there was a last time, but we haven't gotten any letters from her since the first one. What's going on?"

Another shrug.

How unusual for Wendy to be so … unvocal. A dull ache crept up her temples. Was she the one going crazy? Or was it everyone else?

> We have a major problem, though. They're horribly sick. No fevers. Instead, their skin is cold to the touch. Their eyes are sunken and glassy, their skin wrinkly. They've been retching and have had diarrhea. The crate smells atrocious, but it's next to a crate of sardines, which disguises the smell somewhat. Dr. Duncan says they likely have cholera and to give them something called stomach bitters.

"Oh no." Claire winced.

"What?"

"Stomach bitters was a tonic given historically, but it's not the best. It was made with a large amount of alcohol. I need to write back and tell her better things to try."

Wendy raised her brows. "You know herbal remedies?"

What? Did she think Claire was only an expert on makeup and hair styles? "Of course. I read up on this stuff. Natural health is a passion of mine." Shouldn't she know that?

> Any advice you can offer would be appreciated. Hope you are well and you're enjoying Hawaii. Have a blast on those beaches and book an excursion. I want to hear all about it when I get back.
> Love,
> Stella

Claire shot Wendy an I-told-you-so look, then grabbed paper, pen, and a book to write on.

> Stella,
> Cholera was a nasty disease back then. It comes from drinking contaminated water or eating undercooked food. The main risk is from dehydration, so it's important to keep them hydrated. Do you have access to food and herbs? If so, here are some things you can try.
>
> > 1. Mash onion to make a paste. Add a pinch of black pepper and give a spoonful to them 2–3 times a day.

2. Give them a glass of lemon juice 2–3 times a day.

3. Boil a few garlic cloves in water and let this seep for two hours, then have them drink it throughout the day.

4. Make ginger tea and add holy basil, mint leaves, and black pepper.

5. Mix ½ spoonful of salt with 6 spoonfuls of water in 1 liter of water. Have them drink this for the electrolytes instead of straight water.

Let me know how those work.

Hawaii has been wonderful so far. It's beautiful here. Miss you a ton!

Claire looked over her shoulder. "Anything you want to add?"

Wendy frowned. "No."

Okay, then. Not her fault Wendy chose to mope instead of enjoying the island. She signed their names, stuck the letter in the envelope, and wrote Stella's name on the front. "I'll deliver this when I head out."

"Yeah, sure." Wendy hugged a pillow to her middle.

"You're staying on the boat again?"

"Guess so."

"Suit yourself." She had a delightful day in Kauai planned with Neo. They'd booked a downhill bike ride in Waimea Canyon after a helicopter tour of the Na Pali Coast. But first Neo would shoot a video for her on the beach. With such a deliciously long day ahead of her, she'd better get moving. "I'm jumping in the shower."

Wendy mumbled something unintelligible in response.

As Claire showered, she mulled over the odd wording of Stella's letter. She had to have written other letters. It was the only thing that made sense. They must not have been delivered. Maybe there were rules for the mailbox they didn't know about, times when it was off-limits and wouldn't deliver mail through time or something. Their Dr. Duncan probably didn't even know about it, or he'd have mentioned something. If only there was a way to find out.

Yet another mystery Claire was incompetent to solve.

~

Guilt gnawed at Wendy's gut. She was a horrible person. How could she have kept those letters from Claire? No wonder God hadn't answered her prayers to time-sail. She wasn't worthy of any special favors. She was the lowest of the low.

Her phone buzzed, and she checked the text.

> Pretty please come with us today. We're snorkeling, and you can protect me from sharks.

She snorted a laugh. She picked up Stella's letter and trailed her finger over the last paragraph. Did Stella truly expect them to get out and explore Hawaii without her? What would she think if she knew Wendy had been wallowing in their drab little room? She pictured Stella's horrified expression and how her friend would playfully slap her on the arm.

Ugh, Claire was right. Stella *would* want them to enjoy their time. How could Claire know their friend better than she did?

> Okay. Meet you in thirty in the café?

He answered with a thumbs-up emoji followed by three smiley faces.

She jumped up. That didn't give her much time to get ready. After a lightning-fast shower, she dressed, then styled and blow-dried her hair. Her gaze snagged on Claire's makeup littering the sink. Should she try some? She never wore makeup. What was the point of trying to impress people? But she wouldn't mind looking nice if that were possible for her. Sure, they'd be swimming, and she'd likely look a mess when the day finished, but what if Grayson's first impression of her today was impressive?

She scanned the labels, noting most everything was waterproof, and applied a bit of foundation, blush, and eye shadow. She blinked back at herself in the mirror. Wow. For knowing nothing about skin tone or application techniques, she'd done a remarkable job. She looked … attractive? Was that possible? She'd never put much stock into such things, but she had to admit, she felt pretty.

When Wendy walked into the café and Grayson's eyes widened in appreciation, every second she'd spent on her hair and makeup became worth it. No wonder Claire spent time on the routine.

"Good morning." He stepped forward and kissed the side of her head in greeting. For a moment, she froze. But no. It didn't mean anything. It was the sort of greeting one might give a sister or aunt. A friend.

"Good morning." She smiled up at him.

"This is my dad, Sam." He gestured to the man next to him. Sam's white shirt was half unbuttoned, revealing a thick, gold-chain necklace. His cropped white hair and goatee reminded her of snowy Astroturf. "Dad, this is Wendy."

She stuck out her hand. "Nice to meet you."

He fisted it and shook hard. "Heard so much about you."

She raised a brow. What had he heard? "You as well."

"Now, let's get breakfast so we can get out of this stuffy boat. Their eggs are dry, and the bread is stale, but at least the coffee is halfway decent."

She met Grayson's laughing gaze and tucked in her bottom lip to suppress a smile. Oh yeah. This was going to be a great day.

After consuming their *dry* and *stale* breakfast, they disembarked from the *crowded, gawdy* boat into the *stifling hot, far too bright* Hawaiian sun. They had a couple of hours of beach time before their snorkeling excursion. Sam Hill wasn't going swimming with the fish. He said the equipment was uncomfortable and fish were slimy and disease-ridden. Well, good. Wendy would have Grayson all to herself.

After Wendy lay in the sun chatting with Mr. Grumpy and Mr. Handsome for an hour, Grayson rose. "Let's get in."

Sam scoffed. "Saltwater dries out my skin."

"Will you come with me, Wendy?" He held out his hand.

She took it, allowing him to pull her to her feet. She slipped her cover-up over her head and then walked with him to the water. When her foot hit a rock, she stumbled, and he reached out and took her hand again. This time, he didn't let go.

Her breath hitched. *He's holding my hand. He's holding my hand!*

But only because she was a klutz, right?

"Thanks for putting up with my dad."

"Are you kidding? He's a riot."

"I'm glad you think so."

Did Grayson spend time at the gym? Those pecs couldn't come from reading history books. She tried not to stare.

"You look especially beautiful today." He smiled at her, the sun reflecting off his solid, bronzed chest.

She nearly choked on her own saliva. What had he said?

He chuckled. "Don't look so shocked. Has no one ever told you that before?"

"My mom," she spit out.

His chuckle barreled into a laugh. "Oh, come on. You've got to have a ton of guys vying for your affection."

"My students, but I think they're sucking up."

"Wendy, be serious."

"I am!"

"There's no special guy in your life? No boyfriend back home?"

She shook her head, too shocked to speak. Was this conversation really happening?

"That's hard to believe."

"None of the dates I've gone on have ended well. Apparently, I'm 'too much.'"

He interlaced their fingers as they stepped into the cool water. "Here, I was afraid to make a move on someone else's girlfriend. Turns out I had nothing to worry about."

"W-what?" she sputtered.

"Oh, am I not being clear?" His eyes twinkled. "I like you, Wendy." His thumb caressed hers as they stepped deeper.

She couldn't stop her grin from spreading. "I like you too."

"Good. We're agreed."

Chest deep in the sparkling water, they rode the waves hand in hand. Maybe there was a reason God hadn't answered her prayer to time-sail. It might not be a punishment. What if a good God had good things in store for her despite all the ways she'd failed?

Chapter Sixteen

Armed with the herbal concoctions Claire had recommended, Stella braved the light of day and made her way downstairs. She put on a chipper smile and greeted each first-class passenger she passed with "How do you do?" or "Lovely morning, isn't it?"

If she acted as if nothing were amiss, perhaps her heartbeat would follow suit and quit jabbing against her rib cage. When she reached the stairwell, she exhaled long and deep. So far, so good. But as she stepped onto the lower deck, she found it teeming with passengers. Several children with sooty faces raced past after a stray chicken. A group of women laundered soiled linens in buckets of murky water. Two men argued, one raising his voice and the other spitting a stream of tobacco directly onto the deck.

She skirted past them, attempting to appear as if she had important business to attend to.

A lanky man in an off-white muscle shirt and suspenders eyed her. "What are you doing here, miss? Ain't you supposed to be in first class?"

She'd rehearsed her line before leaving her room. "I'm Dr. Duncan's assistant. I'm here to search the cargo for medical supplies he requested."

"Can you ask Doc if he can take another look at Mary Jane? She ain't gettin' any better."

Stella frowned. "Yes. I'll do that." She had to remember. Too bad she couldn't set a reminder on her phone or shoot a quick text.

The man continued to watch her as she bustled off toward the box in question. The tightness in her chest eased when he was out of sight.

Now, safely shielded on all sides by crates and barrels, she found the sardines, and then the crate labeled Mirrors. Once again, an unbearable stench emanated from it. She hesitated before moving the board. What if one of them had died? God forbid. She wouldn't be able to handle it. She'd wither on the spot. But if they were all alive, they needed her. Urgently. She braced herself and scooted the barrier away.

She blinked, her eyes adjusting to the dimness inside. She held her breath, watching the mother's glassy eyes until they blinked. Thank God. The boy's chest rose and fell. Another mercy. The toddler in her arms let out a soft whimper that sounded like a hallelujah chorus to Stella's ears. All three of them were alive. Not well by any means, but they'd made it far enough for Stella to be able to administer treatments.

As soon as she'd received her friends' letter, she'd rushed to where Dr. Duncan sat playing cards and asked for the needed supplies. He'd seemed surprised and quite pleased by the suggestions. Perhaps these remedies hadn't been discovered yet. It had taken him only a trip to the kitchen and a few minutes to gather the ingredients, though boiling garlic cloves in water ended up being a bit of a chore.

Bridge had also provided her with a few fresh towels, so she wouldn't have to rip her petticoat again. Now, she dipped one in water and hurriedly went to work wiping faces soiled by sickness. As she did so, she whispered assurances. "I've brought you some things to make you better. Hang in there a little longer. You're going to pull through."

After emptying the nearly overflowing chamber pot, she spooned a bit of onion paste into the mother's mouth. The woman winced and turned her head from side to side. "I know. Not that tasty, but I'll give you something to wash it down with. Please don't spit it out."

She then helped the woman sip lemon juice, followed by ginger tea. Had Claire meant for her to try *all* those suggestions at once? This is where asking for clarification would have been helpful, but there'd been no time. She must do all she could.

"What's your name?" Stella asked, mopping the woman's brow.

She smacked now-moistened lips together a few times before eking out her answer in a gravelly voice. "Cora."

"Nice to meet you, Cora." Stella ran a hand down the toddler's limp arm. "What's this one's name?"

"Smitty."

"And the boy?"

"Timothy."

Speaking her children's names must have sapped all Cora's strength because she slumped against the side of the crate. Her eyes drifted shut.

Stella let her rest and followed the same procedure of liquids with the children, who squirmed a bit more but managed to get at least some of it down. Then, she repeated the sips of liquid again and again with all three of them.

"Now, how about some variety?" She helped each of them drink a bit of the clove water, followed by the electrolyte drink. When she tried for another round, the woman shook her head and put her hand over her mouth as if she were about to vomit. Point taken. That was enough for now.

Footsteps clomped close by, and male voices invaded their haven of privacy. Stella tucked herself into a small ball and held her breath.

"Yeah, back in March. Nearly hung the captain, I heard. Blasted abolitionists."

"They ain't allowed to bring weapons on this here ship again, is they?"

"Not a one."

"You think they'se followin' that rule?"

"Doubt it."

"What would happen if we searched these crates? Think we might find a gun or two?" Stella's eyes widened. Search the crates? Oh no. They couldn't. They'd find a lot more than they bargained for.

"Probably. Then what?"

"We'd put a bullet through whatever abolitionist brought them on here."

"Grab that crowbar, Bart. Let's see if this here is truly shoe leather."

Stella hitched a shallow breath as the sound of wood splintering mere feet away clawed at her senses.

"Looks clean."

"Did you dig all the way to the bottom? They likely hid weapons underneath other goods."

Beside her, Cora moaned. Stella widened her eyes, imploring the woman to keep quiet with her gaze. Was the sound swallowed up in their rifling? Apparently, because neither man so much as paused their task.

"Nothing. Let's move on."

"This one here says Sardines. You reckon it's true?"

Stella's stomach lurched. The men were at the neighboring crate! One sound and they'd be discovered. *Oh, Lord! Help!*

"From the smell of it, I'd say it's likely true."

They both snorted a laugh. Again, wood splintered.

A bell clanged from somewhere on deck, and shouts of "Grub pile" rang out.

"Hankerin' for breakfast?" one of the men asked.

"If I stay around this cargo much longer, I'll lose my appetite. What a putrid odor."

"Leave it for now. We'll search more later." Footsteps tapered away. "Maybe what we're smellin' is a rotten abolitionist."

Their snickers faded in the distance, but Stella couldn't seem to relax. This family wasn't safe here. But there were still five days until they arrived in Kansas City. And until the boat would sink. What would happen to them then?

Claire was in paradise. Seriously, was she even allowed to be this blissfully happy? Sitting next to the man of her dreams, soaring in the air above rolling green hills, majestic cliffs, cascading waterfalls, and whales swimming in water so blue there was no filter needed.

"How can I thank you enough for this?" She squeezed Neo's toned bicep.

He shrugged, as if shelling out hundreds of dollars to pay for a helicopter ride was no big deal. "I know the manager."

Oh yeah. He'd mentioned that. Maybe he didn't pay a ton of money for her excursion. Instead, he used his influence. Super suave. She jabbed his ribs. "Seriously? How are you so cool?"

"Just enjoy the view." He gestured to the window.

"You too."

"I am." But he was looking at her.

Talk about swoonworthy.

"Oh! That's Bali Ha'i!" She clapped, excitement overtaking her desire to look respectable to this man.

"What's that?"

"From *South Pacific*. You know, Bali Ha'i."

He raised a brow.

"You've never seen the musical *South Pacific*?"

"Noooo." He drew out the word. She was tempted to feel small because of it but squashed it down. He didn't mean anything by it.

"Stella, Wendy, and I love musicals. We watched them all the time in college. Bali Ha'i was this exotic forbidden island in the musical, but they filmed it here. There's a song about it and everything."

"Will you sing it to me?" That saucy grin was back.

After his less than enthusiastic response to her mentioning the musical? "Uh, no. I'm not much of a singer."

"Maybe some other time." He winked.

"No. I don't sing in front of people. Ever." She stuck to things she could do without publicly embarrassing herself.

"We'll see."

Hadn't her no been clear enough? Irritation rankled, but she took a cleansing breath. Let him think what he wanted to. What was the harm in that? And with the stunning scenery around her, how could she hold on to something so trivial?

Neo snapped a picture of her with a jaw-dropping view of the coast in the background. He showed it to her. "You want to post it, or do you want me to?"

"That should definitely come from me."

He texted it to her. "I'll send others tonight."

As the helicopter descended, she threaded her fingers through his. "I've been thinking."

He brought her hand to his lips and kissed her knuckles. "Yes?"

"It would make much more sense if I made you an administrator of my Facebook and Instagram pages. Then you could post pictures for me instead of sending them to me to post."

His face lit. "That's a great idea."

"I'll fix it tonight." She smiled up at him, and he captured her lips with his own. Oh, he tasted like magic. Like everything warm and good in the world wrapped in mint.

They exited the helicopter and took a cab to the beach for their last few hours before departure. "Want me to bury you in the sand?" Neo asked. "It would make a great picture."

She laughed. "Sure."

But a figure a little way down the beach caught her eye. Was that Wendy? No. It couldn't be. Wendy was back on the ship, sulking. Not sitting on shore, waves lapping her bare toes. Besides, that woman had a guy next to her, a guy who was *close*. Definitely, not her friend. But the hair sure looked like Wendy's. And the bathing suit was a matching style and shade. What a strange coincidence.

Wendy's impersonator had her back to Claire and Neo. Impossible to see if there was a facial resemblance. No matter, since it couldn't be her, and yet Claire couldn't seem to look away.

"Honey?" Neo's touch to her arm startled her.

"Hmm?" Wait. Had he called her honey? How sweet.

"You want to do it right here? Or closer to shore?"

"Right here is fine." That way she could keep her eyes on the mysterious Wendy look-alike.

~

Wendy relished the timbre of Grayson's voice as cool ocean water lapped over her legs and then receded again. The rhythm of the waves relaxed her, but not as much as the comfort of their conversation.

Snorkeling with him had been exhilarating and slightly terrifying when scores of fish had decided to nibble at her legs. She'd screamed and tasked Grayson with shooing them away from her. After all, they were there to *observe* the fish in their natural habitat, not become part of it. And while they'd seen enchanting sights and laughed until they couldn't breathe, this was the part of the day she'd hold closest to her heart. Simply sitting with him on the beach while the sun thought about setting, talking about matters of the heart hand in hand.

It turned out Grayson knew loss too. He'd lost his mother to a car accident. When he'd shared that corner of his heart, still raw and aching, she'd found the courage to broach the subject she'd never talked about with anyone, not even Stella.

"My little sister died of leukemia when I was twelve. She was nine."

His face crumpled as if the information pained him. "How terribly hard."

"I was sure she was going to beat it. I couldn't imagine things turning out any other way, you know? I saw myself as her coach in some way, like it was my job to push her to fight this monster that had invaded her body. My mom accused me of being a drill sergeant. I guess I took that job too seriously."

Her eyes misted. Where had the tears come from? It was so long ago, too far in the past to waste tears on now. She attempted to blink them away. "In the end, maybe not seriously enough because she died anyway, despite my coaching."

"Did you blame yourself?"

"Yes, but not because I didn't push her enough." She twisted her mouth, tasting the salt from her tears. She swiped at her eyes but stopped when she got sand on her cheeks.

"Here." Grayson pulled a clean towel from his beach bag and tenderly dabbed her face.

"Thank you." Her whisper came out hoarse. When was the last time someone had treated her with such tender care? She certainly didn't treat herself that way.

"If you didn't blame yourself for not pushing her enough, what *did* you blame yourself for?"

"For pushing her at all, I guess?"

"Sounds like you aren't sure."

"I'm not. My parents said I was brash and that wasn't what she needed. Problem is, I've spent the last decade trying to figure out how to stop being brash, and I can't seem to solve that puzzle. Seems like they wanted me to be less *me*."

"Ah. They wanted to de-Wendyize you." He nodded as if understanding completely.

"That's the only thing I can figure. I'm altogether too much."

He kissed the back of her hand, leaving a trail of sand on his lips. She laughed and tried to brush it off but only succeeded in leaving a larger sand trail. As he blew sand from his mouth, she grabbed the clean towel and shoved it in his face. "Here."

Laughter barreled out of him. He tackled her with a tickle, leaving her giggling and breathless on her back, his now clean face leaning over hers. "I'm glad they didn't succeed in de-Wendyizing you. I like you just the way you are."

Their smiles melted as their gazes tangled, questions lingering. She brought her hand up to trail his cheek with a featherlight touch. He moistened his lips, desire brimming in his eyes. She would have said, "Yes, Grayson. Yes, you can kiss me," if she could have forced out the words. Instead, she gave a single nod, and he responded with the ghost of a smile.

He brought his lips to hers, soft and sweet. She wrapped her arms around his neck, pulling him closer. The weight of his chest lowered onto hers, and his rapid heartbeat pounded a rhythm in tune with her own. His hands tunneled through her hair, a gentle caress. She clung to his neck, then explored his muscular shoulders while tenderly deepening the kiss.

"Wendy?"

Her lips froze midkiss. She placed her palms against Grayson's chest and gave a gentle push, scrambling to a sitting position, and looked into Claire's wide eyes.

"Oh." Wendy smoothed her hair. "Hi, Claire."

"Hi, Claire? Don't *hi, Claire* me. Who is this?"

"This is Grayson. Grayson, this is my *friend* Claire." She emphasized the word *friend* to remind Claire that's what they were to each other.

Grayson waved.

Claire sputtered, "What about the whole 'we have to focus on Stella' thing? You flipped out when you found me kissing Neo, and that was"—she twirled a finger in the air—"more than kissing."

Wendy's cheeks heated. "Was not." Had it looked like a sensual make-out session? It had been much more significant than that. Gentle, yet passionate. Tender, yet with a lingering promise. Unlike anything she'd ever experienced. Okay, maybe it *had* been more than just kissing, but not in the way Claire insinuated.

"Yeah. Whatever you say." Claire crossed her arms. "Looks like you've been keeping things from me. And I have a feeling your secret boyfriend isn't your biggest offense."

She spun and marched off, sand flinging with each angry step.

Wendy turned back to Grayson and cringed. "Sorry about that."

He took her foot in his hand and rubbed slow circles. "I'll forgive you as long as you say she's right."

"Her?" Wendy hooked a thumb over her shoulder.

"I want to be your boyfriend. Secret or not." He winked.

She grinned. "Okay. I'll concede to that."

"What other offense was she talking about?" He moved to massaging her other foot.

She shrugged. "No idea." Had she found out about the letters? Maybe Wendy hadn't hidden them as well as she thought. But why hadn't she come out and said so? It wasn't like Claire to hold back.

"No skeletons in that closet?" He smirked.

"None at all."

Chapter Seventeen

Stella moaned as her insides twisted. She barely made it to her chamber pot in time. She couldn't remember when she'd felt this awful, and at least then she'd had modern conveniences. She'd thank the Lord for running water and her own flushing toilet about now.

Is this what she got for helping others? Painfully sick? Perhaps this was the price of her mission, the price of getting back home. Now her stomach churned at a new thought. Had she only helped those people for selfish reasons? So she could return to her privileged existence? Would she have taken the risk—put herself on the line—for those three poor souls if there'd been nothing in it for her?

She couldn't think too hard on that. She didn't have the mental energy, wasn't thinking clearly with her body racked with pain.

How were the stowaways doing? Hopefully, she'd find them much improved after Claire's treatments. But how could she check on them in her condition? She nibbled her bottom lip as she remembered the men's threats to search through the cargo. If they went poking around anywhere close to that crate, they'd eventually realize the smell wasn't from sardines.

She needed to get down there.

She took a few steps toward the door and swayed, lightheaded.

There was no way she could go down there.

Why couldn't Dr. Duncan mysteriously appear at her door now? She had to tell him her predicament so he could check on the stowaways and bring her some of those remedies.

Lord, a little help here?

But no knock came.

The cramps intensified. Back to the chamber pot. She felt like someone was wringing her body over a washboard. There was nothing left inside of her to come out, right? She felt completely emptied, in more ways than one.

When that wave of torture subsided, she stumbled to her bedside table, grabbed her stationery and began a letter.

> Wendy & Claire,
>
> I'm sick. I've caught cholera from taking care of the stowaways. This is no joke. Y'all thank Jesus we don't deal with this beast in our time.
>
> I came across another issue. While taking care of them yesterday, I overheard men talking about searching through cargo for hidden weapons. They threatened to shoot anyone involved in smuggling them. If they start poking around, they'll find the stowaways and shoot me. If I don't die from cholera first.
>
> Any advice? Wish you were here. No. Wish I was there.
>
> Stella

Letter written. Now, how to send it? She cast a longing glance toward the door. She could almost hear her grandmother saying, "Where there's a will, there's a way." Good ole pull-yourself-up-by-your-bootstraps Grammy Rose. She hung on to her idioms until the day cancer stole her final breath. At least she went down swinging. Stella would too.

Leaning against the wall for support, she inched toward the door, then nearly tumbled into the main parlor. The first moments of the scene played out much like when she'd first stepped foot off the elevator into 1856. One by one, people stopped mid-conversation and mid-step, gazes fastening onto her. With a clamped mouth, she attempted a polite smile.

Bridge's wide eyes met hers from across the room, and the woman rushed over. "Can I help you, miss?" Something akin to panic warped her features.

Stella nodded and placed the letter into Bridge's hands. "Mail this for me, please." She spoke through dry, cracked lips. "Then fetch Dr. Duncan."

"Straight away, miss. But you truly should lie down."

Again, Stella swayed.

Bridge's arm hooked around her elbow in support. The maid guided her back into her room. "Is it the cholera, ma'am?"

Stella lay down and curled into a ball. She could only moan in reply.

"Doc says it's the bad air that spreads it. Them foul smells." She took the chamber pot out the back door and emptied it into the river, then returned. "Last boat I's on, the captain dumped six dead bodies overboard into the river. That cholera sucked the life out of them."

Stella stiffened. She'd thought she was being dramatic when she wrote to Wendy that she might die of cholera. Was she truly in danger?

"Aw, don't worry none. We's not going to let it happen to you. I'll fetch the doctor and get cloves boiling for you straight away. And you best be stayin' in your bed now, you hear? We can't let panic spread 'round the boat. It'd be sendin' all sorts of people in a tizzy."

"I'll stay here. But mail the letter," Stella croaked. "After you wash your hands."

Bridge's brow furrowed, but she said, "Yes, ma'am."

~

Wendy had tossed and turned all night, riding alternating waves of tension emanating from the bed across from hers and bliss from every second of her day with Grayson that did not involve Claire. She felt as wired as if she'd had twelve shots of espresso. Sleep held no appeal.

In lieu of the sandman, Wendy scrolled through Allison's pictures, scouring them for hidden details. What was she missing here? There had to be something that could help, some way to assist her friend. She couldn't be completely incompetent when it mattered most.

Around two in the morning, her blurry eyes grazed over a picture of a deck map. It had sections blocked out where different cargo had been found on the ship. How fascinating. And it showed where the snag hit, right in the upper left corner.

Wait. As quietly as possible, Wendy dug through her suitcase for Stella's letter detailing where the enslaved stowaways were. Hadn't she said their crate was by the sardines? In that case, they were right by where the snag would hit. Those people would be trapped in a box close to where water would stream in. They'd drown within minutes. From all the accounts she'd read, water had covered the lower deck in record time. There was no way Stella or Dr. Duncan would be able to free them fast enough.

News reports had said no one had died in the sinking. Did they know about the stowaways? Or had they covered their death up in the same way they had with the mule? Or perhaps if Stella hadn't been there, the runaways would have been discovered before now and booted off the ship before it could flood. Either way, she had to write to Stella and warn her to get them out of there before the crash happened. Maybe that was why God had placed her friend on that boat at that time. Stella's mission must be to save their lives.

Using her phone's flashlight, she rummaged for paper and a pen and crept toward the bathroom to write another letter. On the way, she spotted an envelope on the floor by the door. Stella had beat her to it.

She ducked into the bathroom and opened it without a second thought. Goodness. Stella thought she'd contracted cholera from the stowaways? That was what they thought back then, but it wasn't necessarily the case. Cholera spread through contaminated food and water. It wasn't an airborne disease. Although she could have caught it from not washing her hands properly after tending to them, it was far more likely it had come from dumping the waste of those who were sick into the river. The river they drew drinking water from. It was a wonder they weren't all ill. She needed to right that wrong as well.

After writing Stella, informing her of the facts about cholera and warning her of the location of the upcoming snag, she hurried to the mailbox to deliver the letter. Too late it occurred to her that she could have shown Claire this letter. Should have. Had keeping secrets become second nature to her? Too late now. When she returned, she slipped into her bed and waited for sleep to claim her.

She awoke to find Claire doing her makeup. Taking a deep breath, she jumped in to repair the newest breach between them. "Why don't you have breakfast with Grayson and me? I'd love for you to meet him."

Claire tossed a scowl over her shoulder, then returned to applying eyeliner. "Did you just meet the guy yesterday or what?"

Wendy squirmed but refused to look away from Claire's reflected gaze in the mirror. "No. We've been meeting each other in the library."

Claire's face lit in recognition. "At two o'clock."

"Strictly for research."

"Oh yeah? What were you researching last night?"

Her face flamed. "We slowly grew to become more than simply research partners." After all, she'd never lock lips with a guy within hours of meeting him, unlike some people in the room.

"Slowly?" Claire's gaze narrowed as she applied lipstick.

Comparatively. She bit down on the snark that threatened to spill out, clamping her jaw shut. Her mom used to tell her honey caught more flies than vinegar. She used to wonder who wanted to catch flies anyway.

"Will you give him a chance? Come eat breakfast with us."

Claire's deep sigh made her shoulders slump in an uncharacteristic slouch. "Okay." She ran a brush through her already silky, tangle-free hair, then turned with a mischievous glint in her eyes. "Is he a good kisser?"

Wendy covered her warm cheeks with her hands. "Oh my gosh, yes!"

"Well, there's that." Claire winked.

And with a rush of girlish giggling, they began to repair that bridge.

Wendy spotted Grayson the minute they walked into the café, but Sam Hill was nowhere to be seen. "Will your dad not be joining us?" Wendy asked as they approached.

Grayson placed a chaste kiss on her cheek and a hand on her back. "Not today. He found another golfer, and they're chatting up a storm about the best country clubs." He nodded toward a table in the far corner where Sam appeared to be in animated conversation with another older man.

"Oh. Bummer. I enjoy his company."

The corners of Grayson's eyes crinkled. "You'd be one of the few, but I'm sure he'll love to hear that."

She swatted at his arm. "Oh, stop. Be nice."

He turned his attention to Claire, who was scanning the dining room. Was she looking for someone? She wasn't still hanging around that guy, was she? Maybe she was nervous about having breakfast with the two of them.

"Claire, nice to see you again."

As if a camera had turned her way, she perked up, flashing a sunny smile. "Nice to see you too."

"I saved us a table. That one with three cups of orange juice on it." He gestured behind him. "If you don't like the juice, I'll drink all three."

A chuckle erupted from Wendy as if that was the most hilarious thing anyone had ever said. What was wrong with her? She must have "boy crazy" stamped on her forehead.

Claire rolled her eyes as she turned toward the buffet, but she had a shadow of a smile on her face.

They sat with their breakfasts and dove into small talk.

"So, Claire, how long have you and Wendy known each other?"

Claire smiled wide as she answered, but she didn't look at Grayson. Her gaze crested over his shoulder and to the left. *Odd.* She held the grin for a minute before answering. "Since college."

"KU, right?"

Claire nodded.

"What did you major in? Education as well?"

Now Claire tilted her head to the left and flipped her hair over her shoulder. What in the world was going on? Was she trying to impress him or something? Because that was not the way to go about it. "Oh no. I'm not nearly as intelligent as Wendy here. I got my bachelor's in kinesiology."

Grayson didn't seem to notice her strange behavior. He pushed his empty plate of French toast aside and slid the plate of eggs and bacon in front of him. "Where are you from?"

Claire cringed. "Gary, Indiana."

Wendy bit her lip, waiting. Here was the ultimate test of their compatibility.

"Like from *The Music Man.*"

She cried, "Yes," at the same time as Claire groaned, "No."

They both laughed.

"What?" Grayson pointed his fork at her, then at Claire. "Inside joke?"

"Just don't sing the song," Wendy quipped.

All of a sudden, Claire straightened, angled her head, and smiled like a model.

"Okay, what the heck?" Wendy looked over her shoulder to see Neo ducking behind a pillar. She sprung up and stalked after him.

"Wendy," Claire called behind her.

She knocked into the guy, bumping his phone from his hand. It thudded to the tiled floor. When he bent to grab it, she stepped in front of him. "Are you stalking my friend?"

"No!" Neo put his hands up as if claiming innocence, then ducked around her to retrieve his phone. "It isn't what it looks like."

"Really? Because it looks like you're a creeper."

Claire sidled up next to the psychopath. "He's not! I asked him to do it."

"To do what? Stalk you? Are you that desperate for attention?"

Grayson came to stand next to her.

"To take pictures of me for social media. I needed to increase my online presence. He's helping me."

Wendy eyed the two of them as if she was the parent of rebellious teenagers who'd sneaked out after curfew. "Do you realize how ridiculous this is?"

Neo put his hand out as if deflecting her verbal blow away from the woman next to him. "Respectfully, it's not ridiculous. You don't seem to understand Claire has a real career, and that career comes with certain expectations."

"A career?" Wendy scoffed. "Please. She does push-ups in front of a camera for already skinny, privileged women who don't want to inconvenience themselves by going to a gym. Half of her followers are probably men who only tune in for the eye candy." As the words spewed from her mouth, she tried to reel them in, but it was too late.

Claire blinked. Stepped back. Then screwed her face into a little ball of fire. "I knew that's what you really thought. And you wonder why I don't want to be around you."

"No, it's not …" But the eyes across from her blazed into her, so the lie died on her tongue. It *was* what she'd always thought about Claire's chosen profession. Did that make her a bad person?

She turned to Grayson with pleading eyes as if he could help her explain. But his face was etched with disappointment. "This is how you treat your friend?"

"No," she said, though he'd seen it firsthand.

"Yes." Claire wrapped her arms around herself. "All the time."

Wendy rolled her eyes. "Not all the time."

"Several times this trip."

"Come on." Wendy tossed her hand in Claire's direction. "She cares too much about appearances. It's all a bit superficial, don't you think?" Surely, she couldn't be the only one who could see the obvious. "And I don't trust that guy"—she pointed at Neo—"for one minute."

Grayson shook his head, disappointment radiating from him like summer heat from pavement. "You're not who I thought you were."

He ran a hand through his hair and walked away.

Neo wrapped Claire in his arms, leaving Wendy cold and lonely.

~

Claire shuddered before stepping out of Neo's embrace.

"Don't let her get to you." He squeezed her shoulders. "We have a romantic day ahead of us in Maui." The side of his mouth lifted. "Which always makes me think of *Moana*."

"*Moana* was set in Polynesia." At least, that's what Claire's niece claimed.

"Yeah, but Maui was the name of the demigod, so ..." He shrugged.

"Wait, how do you know about a Disney movie?"

"My little sister." He pulled out his phone, swiped a bit, then turned the screen so she could see a little girl with dark curls wearing a grass skirt and pink crop top. "She's obsessed. I took that picture at her *Moana*-themed birthday party after singing 'You're Welcome' for a bunch of six-year-olds."

"Aw." How sweet. The commonality endeared her to him.

"It's my favorite song to sing karaoke to. They have karaoke on the beach tonight. Want to go?" He slid his phone into his pocket and took her hand.

She wouldn't mind seeing him charm a crowd. "I'll support you, but I'm not singing."

He opened his mouth as if to protest but then closed it and nodded. "Fair enough."

Her phone buzzed in her pocket. A text from Trenia.

> You're killing it. This is what Fit TV likes to see. Great presence and engagement.
> Now, plan one final push for the end of your cruise.

One final push? What did that mean? Perhaps a stunning video she could record on the beach today and wait to post until they landed back in Washington. Her fingers flew across the keys.

> What kind of push?

"What's going on?" Neo's voice was laced with concern. "Something wrong?"

"No." She stared at her phone screen, waiting for a reply. "My agent says things look much better. Exactly what Fit TV wanted."

"Then why do you look like you're about to throw up?"

She did? It was the never-ending insistence that she continue to up her game. Her stomach churned. A deep, cleansing breath didn't help. "They want something more from me."

As always. There was always something else she needed to do, to give. It was as if she was forever on the cusp of her desires, a rabbit being led along by a carrot. Would it always be this way? Even after she sealed the deal with Fit TV, would pressure forever be nipping at her heels? *More. More. More. Give more.*

Finally. A reply.

> A giant Live video bash would likely seal the deal.

Okay, maybe now she *would* throw up. She cringed at the use of the words "giant" and "Live" in the same sentence. She kept her Lives small and simple. The fewer moving parts, the less chance of anything going sideways. But a *giant Live*? There were so many ways that could come crashing down around her. She showed the text to Neo.

"Oh, great! That sounds fun."

"Oh no. Not fun. Nerve-racking."

"Oh." His brow furrowed as he seemed to consider this. "What if we worked up to it. Today, you can do a small Live from the beach. When it goes well, it'll build your confidence."

She crinkled her nose. "How small?"

"Instead of a recorded video, we could do it live. Same routine. Same plan. You're already ready to go."

They'd recorded the past two days of videos without a hitch. Her shoulders relaxed. "Seems safe enough."

"Totally."

Then why did the glint in his eyes unnerve her? She shook off the feeling and focused on the beautiful day ahead of her.

Hours later, she emerged from the bathroom at the beach to find Neo talking with some guy. Who was he? Between the sun hat hiding his face and the glare in her line of sight, she couldn't make out details. Neo passed a few bills into the man's hand and clasped him on the shoulder before he retreated.

She drew near. "Who was that?"

He startled at her words. "Oh, that? A friend."

"What were you paying him for?"

Neo appeared to be fighting a grin. "He's doing me a favor."

She quirked an eyebrow.

He waved her off. "It's nothing, really."

Odd, but okay. He had mentioned he'd cruised here before. Often enough to have friends in the area? Whatever, she wouldn't pry. No need to be *that* girl.

Soon, she sat cross-legged on her mat on Kaanapali Beach, crystal clear water in the background, Neo standing barefoot in the soft, fluffy sand, camera in hand.

"Ready?" he asked.

"Set. Go." She grinned wide for the camera, and he gave her a thumbs-up, the sign to begin. "Hi, everyone. Today, I'm doing an intermediate-level floor workout Live! I hope you'll join me. If you do, make sure to let me know in the comments, then grab a water bottle and your mat, and let's get to work."

A young family walked onto the beach and set down their towels and a bucket of toys only a few feet away from where she was filming. She shook off the distraction. She had to stay focused on the camera and let the rest melt away.

"We're going to start by lowering ourselves onto our mats one vertebrae at a time." As she did so, a red beach ball came flying and smacked her in the face.

"Oh, I'm so sorry!" The mom rushed over, straight into the video, and snatched the ball from where it had landed in front of Neo. "Edward, apologize to the poor woman."

Claire remained frozen in a crunch position, the last of her vertebrae suspended in the air by her ab strength. She forced her grin back to the surface. "It's fine," she said through gritted teeth.

"Oh, no. We always make him apologize. Must teach proper manners."

She tried to catch Neo's gaze with inconspicuously widened eyes, but his mirthful eyes remained pinned on the boy and mother.

The mom took her young son's hand and nearly dragged him over to her. "Edward, say you're sorry."

He dipped his head and didn't reply.

"Edward." Her voice held warning.

"It's fine," Claire said, lowering onto her back.

"He really should apologize," the mom insisted.

"Okay, but," she said, motioning to Neo, "we're filming a video here."

"Oh!" The woman covered her mouth. "Sorry." She backed away, tugging her son along.

Claire looked back at the camera. "Sorry for the interruption. Let's continue." Was her face as beet red as it felt? How mortifying. *That* was why she opted for recorded videos over Lives. Hopefully, Fit TV wasn't cringing right now. She went on with the plan, leading her virtual audience in crunches, leg lifts, and leg circles. She had to speak up to make sure they could hear her above the playful shrieks of the boy a few feet away.

Occasionally, she was conscious of people walking on the beach behind her, but she was determined not to let them distract her. However, as she switched to plank position, she saw a couple stroll by and stop directly behind her. Right in the shot. Before she returned her attention to the camera, they locked lips.

Oh, great. Now there were people making out in her live video. Well, at least maybe that would increase the views.

Before she could give instructions on what her viewers should do next, the guy spoke. "Alisa, will you marry me?"

She snapped her head in their direction. Sure enough, he'd lowered to one knee. He held out a black ring box, and the girl covered her mouth with her hand. "Oh, Mike. Of course, I'll marry you."

Goodness, what should she do? Continue with the video like nothing was going on behind her? Congratulate the happy couple? Address the utter craziness with her audience of this attempt at a Live and call it a day?

Before she could decide, the guy sprung to his feet, lifted up the girl, and swung her around. Sand flung in all directions, pelting Claire in the face. Then, the girl's foot knocked into Claire's head. Ouch.

Claire scrambled to stand from plank position, clutching her aching forehead. The girl must have been too blissful to notice. She didn't apologize or even acknowledge Claire's existence.

She looked to Neo, who still held the phone up. Apparently, this video continued to roll, no matter how humiliating. What to say? What to do? Her head pounded. The boy's lighthearted screams drilled into her skull. She couldn't keep pushing through this lunacy.

On trembling legs, she stood and stumbled toward the camera. She dug deep for a cheerful voice. "Well, wasn't that exciting? Congrats to the happy couple. I think we'll call it a day. If you'd like a more extensive workout, please check out my channel." She waved goodbye.

Neo put the phone down, then burst into laughter. "Oh my gosh, that was great."

"Great? Are you kidding me? It was a disaster. Nothing went as planned."

But Neo smirked, looking entirely too pleased. What was that about? Worry wormed its way inside of her, but she stomped it out. This was probably something she'd laugh about too at some point. A point far down the road when the humiliation wore off. Maybe it wasn't a huge deal. Maybe Fit TV wouldn't see it as a fail, but as her being authentic. That was trending, right?

Still …

No. She wouldn't doubt Neo's intentions. He was the best thing that had happened to her in a long time. Any doubts that arose were simply her insecurities, and she needed to squash those flat.

Chapter Eighteen

An hour later, Bridge returned with onion paste and clove water. Stella gagged at the taste of the paste, then retched again. She couldn't seem to keep the clove water down either. She writhed in pain from intense cramps.

"Oh my." Bridge dabbed her head with a cloth. "Dr. Duncan should be here shortly. He was seeing to another patient."

The stowaways or someone on deck? She'd completely forgotten to convey that man's message to the doctor regarding Mary Jane. Hopefully, Stella's slight didn't land someone else in peril.

Did this other patient have cholera too? She'd heard whole shiploads of people had died from this disease, but surely, that couldn't happen to them. But the history books proved otherwise. Unless …

What if she'd altered history by transmitting the disease? Scenes from *Back to the Future* flashed through her mind. Oh no. Maybe history would have been better off without her.

Just like Everett.

"Oh! I almost forgot." Bridge's voice filtered through the haze of depressing thoughts. "I have a letter for you."

Stella perked up, lifting her head from her pillow. "A letter?" she rasped.

Bridge placed it in her hand. "You can read it later. Rest now until the doctor comes."

Stella nodded, though she had no intention of waiting a minute longer than necessary to read Wendy and Claire's letter. As soon as Bridge closed the door, Stella ripped it open.

Stella,
You probably didn't catch cholera from caring for the stowaways, at least as long as you're washing your hands well. Back then, they thought the disease spread through airborne particles, "bad air" or "bad smells," but we've since learned it comes from either eating undercooked meat or drinking contaminated water, though it's possible to catch it from contact with the bodily fluids of those who are infected if you're not careful about hygiene. You're drinking straight river water, aren't you? Ugh. Nasty. Who knows what's been dumped in that water.

Stella cringed. She knew. She'd dumped the contents of foul-smelling chamber pots in there.

I'll be praying for you to recover quickly and for the stowaways.
I need to tell you the snag is going to hit the upper left side of the boat, and the bottom deck will fill with water within minutes. If the stowaways are in a crate nearby, and I think from what you mentioned, they are, then they very well might drown. You need to get them out of there before the crash.
Ask me any questions you have.
Love,
Wendy & Claire

Her pulse raced as she pictured Cora, Timothy, and tiny Smitty trapped inside a flooding crate, groping for a way out, panic fumbling their fingers. Yes, they had to get them out of there, but how? Where? If they sneaked them off the boat during wooding, they'd remain in slave-controlled territory. The chances of their discovery and recapture were high. But they couldn't be among those rescued when the boat sank. Trevor could blend in with the other Black male roustabouts, but as Dr. Duncan had said, there were no other Black women and children, besides Bridge, and they'd stick out like a birthmark on a queen's face. After they came all that way, endured the unthinkable, the thought of them returning to bondage was incomprehensible. There had to be a different way.

She refolded the letter but paused and unfolded it again. Something seemed off. What was it? She scanned the text again. The wording, *I* and *me*, jumped off the page at her. All the previous letters had said *we*, clearly coming from both Wendy and Claire, but this one seemed to be from Wendy alone, even though Claire's name graced the bottom. Surely, Wendy hadn't written it without Claire. But where were the telltale signs of her friend's influence? Claire's distinct voice was absent in this letter.

What was going on with her friends back in the present? Were they getting along? Wendy could have sharp claws at times, but she'd never use them on Claire.

Another wave of cramps rolled through her, and the letter crumpled in her grasp. She'd better live through this so she could smooth any rough waters between her friends.

A knock sounded, and Dr. Duncan spilled inside her room, his hair standing on end, his shirt even more rumpled than usual. He took one look at her and mumbled, "Oh no." He shut the door behind him and paced the length of her room.

"What? That bad?" Her attempt at humor fell flat as pain squeezed her abdomen. She moaned and rolled to her side.

"This isn't good, Miss Lindy. It's definitely not good if you die."

Die? Was it truly a possibility? She shuddered.

He scrubbed his face. "I've never lost a time sailor before. I'm not certain how that will affect things."

"Lose me?" She propped onto one elbow. "Oh no. You can't lose me. I can't die. You have to do something. Make me better somehow."

"I can try." He ran his hand through his hair.

"I need you to do more than try. There's got to be a remedy."

"You know more about remedies than I."

The hairs on the back of her neck prickled. "You're a doctor. Do something."

He frowned, his shoulders drooping. "I don't know what to do."

"That doesn't exactly inspire confidence in your doctoring abilities."

He let out a long exhale. "I'm not a doctor."

She blinked back at him. "What?"

"It's a ruse. The only way to justify my presence on these boats, the only way I can watch over time sailors."

"You're not a doctor." She shook her head, betrayal slicing her heart. "You lied to me."

His deep sigh rippled between them. "Not intentionally."

This was too much, entirely too much to process when her body ached and her strength faded.

He came to her bedside and helped her sip more clove water. This time, it went down without threat of coming back up. She closed her eyes, desiring nothing more than to fade away from this nightmare into the escape of sleep.

"My mother was a time sailor."

She pried one eye open to find him looking pensively out her back door. He'd said he would tell his story in his own time. Was this it?

"She crossed the waters when she was heavy with child. I was born here, in this time, then she was taken back to hers." His voice sank low, mournful and forlorn.

He turned to her and met her gaze. "I have time sailor in my blood. They pull me to them whenever they arrive in this time. I feel it my duty to look after them, care for them until they can return to their time. I've guided more than a dozen, and I've never lost one." His features hardened with determination. "I can't lose you."

She spoke past the lump forming in her throat. "That's good because I can't die. I have a fiancé to marry."

He gave a decisive nod. "Then let's get you well."

She frowned. "There's something else. The stowaways are in danger. You can't lose me, and I—" Her voice cracked. "I can't lose them."

~

Wendy should have been exploring the dormant Haleakala volcano and majestic Maui rainforests with Grayson. Instead, she ordered another Coke from the Tiki bar.

"You sure this is all you want?" The bartender's brightly flowered shirt and leis did little to lighten her mood.

"Yeah. I don't drink." Unfortunately. She wouldn't mind numbing the pain about now.

"Suit yourself." He set the Coke in front of her and moved on to a more lucrative customer.

Behind her, a man cleared his throat. When she met his gaze, he nodded to the full bar and lifted his brow as if to say, *Really? You're taking up space at the bar for that?*

Okay, she could move to a table and order food. Nachos sounded good anyway. Nothing like drowning her sorrows in cheese.

She shot the man a sarcastic smile as she hopped off the bar stool and headed for an outside table. There, she sipped on her Coke and stared at palm trees until her eyes blurred. Her stomach growled. Where was her waiter? If she didn't get served soon, Yelp was going to hear about it.

Finally, a woman with a swishing high ponytail and a notepad approached and asked for her order.

"I want the Beach Nachos, but with just cheese. Nothing else."

The waitress scrunched her cute little nose. "No pico?"

"No. No pico, no sour cream, no cilantro, no ava crema. Just cheese."

Her expression twisted in a grimace, and her lip protruded in a pout as she wrote the order, then sashayed away.

"Tell me how you really feel," Wendy mumbled.

Her glass now empty, she slurped loudly through the straw, hoping Miss Judgy would get the hint. All that accomplished was making her cheeks sore.

She pulled out her phone and checked her texts again. Nothing from Grayson. Maybe she needed to make the first move. She could admit she'd overreacted. Again. But he had to agree the whole Neo-taking-pictures thing was next-level creepy. Someone had to say something. She was the only *someone* who could. He couldn't stay angry at her for that, right? Guilt pooled in her gut as her own words echoed through her mind.

A career? Please. She does push-ups in front of a camera for already skinny, privileged women who don't want to inconvenience themselves by going to a gym. Half of her followers are probably men who only tune in for the eye candy.

So maybe that didn't need to be said. Why did she keep spewing thoughtless words like an active volcano? Discontentedness bubbled under the surface, abrasive and sinister. What would it take for the harshness to grow dormant inside? If only she could be different. More like Stella.

She stared at Grayson's name on her phone. Maybe she could even call? No. Too scary. But a tentative text? She could brave that.

Can we talk?

She sucked in her bottom lip as she waited for a reply.

Depends. I'm not okay with how you treated Claire this morning. Want to talk about that?

So, he wasn't going to let her avoid the subject. There'd be no pretending the blowup had never happened.

Sure. I'm sorry.

More loud slurping. *Come on, Grayson. Forgive me.*

I'm going to need more.

More? What more? She'd given an apology. A sincere one. What else could she give? She started to type as much when another text appeared.

Wendy, I've loved spending time with you, but I don't think you're ready for a relationship right now. You've got stuff you need to work out.

Moisture pricked her eyes. What? He'd just said he would talk about this, and now he was shutting down the conversation? How unfair.

Her throat burned from holding her emotions at bay. She attempted another drink only to growl in frustration when nothing came out. Where was her waitress? What kind of place hired such incompetent staff? She slammed her glass onto the table.

Finally, the waitress scurried out, tray in hand. "Oh! You need a refill?"

Wendy rolled her eyes. "You think?"

"I'll get that right away." She placed the basket of nachos in front of Wendy and turned back toward the kitchen.

Heat climbed Wendy's face as she stared at the green and white dollops on the dish in front of her. "What is this?"

The waitress pivoted back to her, ponytail bouncing with the movement. "Your Beach Nachos. Is something wrong?"

Seething rage rose inside her chest. Nothing today was how it should be. Anger spewed from her tone. "I said cheese only. Cheese only. How hard is that? Are you completely incompetent?"

The woman's jaw unhinged. Her bottom lip trembled. "I, uh—"

"You wrote it down. Didn't you check your little cheat sheet when you put the order in?"

"I'm sorry." Her voice wavered. "It's my first day."

"Yeah, well, maybe it should be your last."

As the waitress hurried off, a wave of regret crashed over Wendy, like it always did *after* an outburst. Always after. Never before. *You've got stuff you need to work out.* She buried her head in her hands. What was wrong with her? She'd never been able to control her tongue. Why couldn't she be a decent person? *Lord, is that too much to ask? Can't You transform me into someone more like Stella.* Heck, she'd even take being more like Claire at this moment, minus allowing creepy guys to stalk her.

"I saw everything."

Wendy's head snapped to look toward the sound of the semi-familiar voice. Mrs. Gardenia glowered at her, hands on her hips.

Oh no.

"I watched you go off on the poor waitress. I knew I was right about you. Someone who can treat people like that shouldn't have influence over young people."

Wendy put her hands out, scrambling for a semblance of explanation. None came.

"I caught your little hissy fit on video, and I'm sending it to your boss. We'll see how the school board appreciates it."

Wendy launched to her feet, clasping her hands together in a pleading gesture. "This isn't necessary, is it? Everyone has bad days."

"Apparently, you're the cause of quite a few people's bad days." Her scowl drilled into Wendy's conscience.

Ouch. *Oh, God, is it true? I don't want this to be who I am.* Mrs. Gardenia's eyes narrowed. "Stay away from my daughter."

Okay, now, wait. The lady made it sound like Wendy had been stalking Allison or something. Mrs. Gardenia was the one taking secret videos.

Wendy lifted her hands. She'd admit to many things, but … "I'm her teacher."

A vein bulged in Mrs. Gardenia's neck, and tight lines accentuated her mouth, causing her to look older than Wendy knew her to be. "Not for long."

Wendy's stomach plummeted. It was true, wasn't it? Her teacher gig was up. Maybe it was for the best. Her students deserved better. Better than her big mouth and volatile temper. Better than *her*.

Everyone did.

~

Claire dug into her taco salad at the karaoke bar and grill, closing her eyes as she relished the taste. There wasn't anything particularly healthy on the menu, and she hadn't indulged in something this decadent in ages. Oh my word, she missed the taste of fried tortilla shell and sour cream. Hopefully, this wouldn't do a number on her waistline.

"A piña colada for you and a margarita for me." Neo placed the drinks on the table and sat across from her.

"Thanks. One is about all I can handle. I'm a lightweight." And she hardly ever drank.

But after they'd finished their meals, he came back from the bar with another drink in hand. "You've got to try this peach daiquiri. It's amazing."

"Okay. I'll take a sip." Only he was right. It tasted delightful. She took another drink, closing her eyes and letting the flavor settle on her tongue.

He chuckled. "You enjoy that one. I'll get my own."

And she did enjoy it. Along with the Miami Vice and Isle of Islay swizzle he brought next. She was on vacation, after all. About time she acted like it. She'd been wound tighter than a corkscrew. It felt good to loosen up for a change.

By the time he went to the mic to sing "You're Welcome," she was floating in a happy bubble. He looked good up there, sounded good. She hooted and hollered her appreciation as he bowed.

He grinned at her. "Your turn."

She pointed to herself. "Me?"

"Yeah, you. Get up there. Let yourself go. You'll feel better for it."

"Oh no. I don't sing in public."

Laughter bubbled around her. The upbeat music threatened to make her soar with its beat. She drained the rest of her Halo-Halo cocktail.

Neo smirked. "You would have this crowd spellbound. Why not try it? You'll never see these people again."

That was true. What would it hurt? If she completely humiliated herself, it wouldn't go any farther than this room of drunken people who couldn't sing much better themselves. They were a supportive bunch, all cheering for each other. She had yet to hear anyone hurl insults, even when people missed the pitch entirely. What would be a safer space than this?

"Okay." She smacked her hand onto the table. "I'll do it."

"You will?" His grin spread. "What song? The one from that musical?"

She wrinkled her nose. "No. No one will know that one. What about 'Girls Just Want to Have Fun'?"

"Perfect."

Wild, nervous energy pulsed through her as she told the DJ her selection and waited for her turn. She was really doing this. What had gotten into her? Alcohol, no doubt, but she hadn't had *that* much. And nothing too heavy. Perhaps Neo inspired courage within her. With him by her side, she could be brave and try new things. She could be a bolder, more daring version of herself.

She liked this version.

The DJ called her name, and she made her way to the mic to the sound of applause. She'd apply her philosophy on Pilates videos here: go big or go home. Better to make a bold mistake than to appear timid and unsure. Dozens of faces zeroed in on her, expressions eager. They wanted to hear from her. She'd give them a show.

She belted out the lyrics from the get-go. No, singing wasn't her strong suit, but it felt good to let loose, to not have to be perfect at something before diving in. She spent much of her life making sure everything was *just so*. Her poses were carefully crafted. Her social media was pristine. She never did anything she wasn't sure she could succeed at. But this?

This was free-falling. And it felt good.

She lost herself in the music, in the beat, in the moment. She closed her eyes and *lived* it.

She opened her eyes and smiled at Neo, only to falter. Her voice cracked as she stared at the phone in his hand. He was recording her, eyes mirthful behind the screen. Was he making fun of her, or simply enjoying the moment with her? And was the video for their eyes only? It had better be. What were the words to the song? Her tongue tripped over itself. *Get it together, Claire. Bring it.* Sweat beaded at the back of her neck. She sucked in a sharp breath and recovered the beat, the words, her composure.

As the song wound down, she forced a final smile for the crowd and then stumbled back to the table and snatched the phone from Neo's grasp. "No one was supposed to see that," she said as she shut off the record button. Her eyes widened as she looked closer. The whole thing had been live streamed on her page.

Chapter Nineteen

Stella had no doubts that Claire had saved her life. She certainly couldn't credit nondoctor Duncan. But now, with twenty-four hours of clove and electrolyte water, ginger tea, and nasty onion paste inside of her, she was finally turning a corner. Though she hadn't recovered full energy and she still felt shaky after standing for a few minutes, determination propelled her from her stateroom and down to the lower deck.

She gripped the railing for support and stopped to catch her breath three times before she reached the bottom of the stairs. "'I can do all things through Christ who strengthens me,'" she whispered to herself. Then she prayed for His strength to fill her. She couldn't collapse and quit. This mission was too important. Lives were on the line.

Duncan had assured her the stowaways were alive. He and the woman's husband had been taking care of them during Stella's illness. That arrangement was far riskier, especially with threats to search through the cargo, but so far, they hadn't been caught.

Now, she crept toward the precious crate, the need for proof of life churning within her. She had to see with her own eyes that they were okay before she could rest easy. But as she neared, someone else hunkered next to the crate in question. Panic surged. She dipped behind a barrel and eyed the scene.

The man had his back to her. All she could make out was black pants, a black suit coat, and a bowler hat. What was he doing? Had he sensed something amiss and gone to investigate? She looked around for a weapon. Perhaps she could sneak up on him, whack him in the head, and make off with the stowaways before he could turn them in. A crate nearby was labeled Blacksmith's Tools. Surely, something in there would do the job. If only she had a crowbar to open it. Then again, if she had a crowbar, she wouldn't need anything else.

The man turned, and she spied his profile. Tension released from her body. It was the woman's husband, the children's father. She recognized him from the day Duncan had spoken to him on dock, and he'd taken the crate with utmost care.

She approached with gentle steps and spoke in a hushed voice. "Are they doing well?"

He startled, then his eyes alighted on her. "Miss Lindy? I've heard much about you."

She smiled back at him.

"Thank you for everything. I owe their lives to you, I hear."

She waved him off. Without Claire's wisdom, she wouldn't have had a clue what to do. "They're okay?"

"Much better." He swiped his hat from his head and mopped his damp brow. "See for yourself."

She bent near and peered inside. All three had far more color. The boy grinned up at her. The little one bounced on the mother's knee.

"I'm glad." But they were far from safe, which is why she'd come. "Is there a place we can talk privately?"

His smile dimmed, but he nodded. "Follow me." Pausing every so often to scan the area around them, he slunk around the boat through piles of cargo until they were on the other side, safely secluded by three walls of lumber. The pile on the bottom was slightly wider than the ones above it, creating a sort of bench to sit on. "No one comes over here."

Easy to see why. There was hardly any space to maneuver with the cargo packed so tightly together. But here, in this little triangle, he'd created a small haven.

"I'm sorry. I don't know your name."

He eyed her warily for a minute. Of course, as a runaway, he wouldn't trust easily. He shouldn't. But he had credited her with saving his family's life. Finally, suspicion melted from his features, and he answered, "Trevor Daley, miss."

"Nice to meet you, Trevor." She stuck out her hand. He stared at it for a full thirty seconds before taking it and shaking.

"We need a new plan." She lifted herself onto the makeshift bench, a bit high for her, as her feet dangled a couple of inches from the ground when sitting. "I can't disclose why, but that crate isn't safe for your family. They are at great risk by staying there more than another couple of days."

He crossed his arms. "Why?"

"I can't tell you why, but you must trust me. We need to get them out of there."

His frown created deep rivets on his face. "What do you suggest?"

"I'll sneak them to my stateroom and hide them there. Bridge will help keep the secret, I'm sure. The tricky part will be getting them off the boat without anyone noticing. I haven't figured that part out yet, but I will."

The worry lines spread to his forehead. "You must. We must. My family is my world, Miss Lindy. Freedom ain't freedom without them."

She swallowed a wave of longing for Everett's arms. "I understand."

"Do you? Do you have children, Miss Lindy?"

She shook her head.

"Because until you see fear spark in your little boy's eyes while he puffs out his chest, yearnin' to be a man, and a lion rises inside you, ready to pounce on anything that would snuff out that courage or would dare raise so much as a hand against your boy, I don't believe you do. Until you watch your baby girl, as tiny as a fairy, toddle after a fluttering butterfly, and you know you will kill any man—Black or

White—who dares lay an unkind hand on her, I'm not sure you can. And until you've felt your blood burn with jealousy because the one you love ain't yours to claim—there's a deed of purchase stating someone else owns them—don't you be telling me you understand."

She couldn't speak. She knew nothing, nothing at all, of the type of love and sacrifice and pain this man had experienced in his life. She bowed her head, throat thick and scratchy.

"How would you get them to your room?"

At his question, she looked up. Under his earnest gaze, she explained her plan. When his mouth unhinged, she scrambled to justify why it was the best method. Finally, he joined her on the bench, leaving a wide berth between them. "I don't got much choice but to trust you, Miss Lindy. But you've got to tell me, why are you doing this? You could get in a heap of trouble if you'se caught."

She tucked her bottom lip between her teeth, considering what to share. What would it hurt to tell the truth? "I'm engaged to a Black man."

A whoosh of air left his lungs. Of course, this must sound ludicrous. He didn't know she wasn't from this time period. White women didn't marry Black men in 1856. Still, she fought the urge to backpedal. The truth burned on her tongue. She needed to unburden her soul to someone. He trusted her to be a safe place. The least she could do was trust him to be the same.

"My boss is blatantly racist. I knew that, and I took the job anyway." She lowered her gaze. "I chose my dream position as an editor of a paper over my loyalty to Everett." Shame burned within her chest. "He said some things—used filthy, racist language—during my interview. I should have walked out right then, but I didn't. I kept my mouth shut. Worse, I *smiled*. As if I agreed with him. All because I wanted that position, even if it was at a small paper in a podunk town. Beats covering bland stories and spending years working my way up at a bigger paper, right? I mean, how could I pass on this opportunity? Who gets the chance to be an editor that soon after graduation?"

She shook her head. "But it's not just my boss. It's the town. On my way to the interview, I passed a huge Confederate flag flying in someone's yard." Wait. The South hadn't seceded yet. Trevor wouldn't know what she was talking about. "Never mind." She kicked her heels against the lumber.

"You'se trying to make up for your wrongs, I take it." Trevor nodded as if he understood.

"In a way, I guess I am. Though I'm not sure I ever could. This mess with my job isn't the first time I've failed to stand up for what's right."

His sympathetic gaze lacked judgment, and she found herself spilling more of her story to him. The story about Zarina poured out, each detail vivid in her mind.

How Mrs. Randolph stopped her as she brushed by the teacher's desk on the way to her seat. "Stella, I have a favor to ask you." The older woman smiled at her as if she already knew Stella would say yes.

Stella looked at her expectantly.

"We're getting a new student today. Zarina. Will you show her around? Help her feel welcome?"

Stella nodded. "Of course." She always did. She was the go-to for that kind of thing at Ridgecrest Middle School, which was fun because she made all kinds of new friends.

"I knew I could count on you," Mrs. Randolph said.

She filed to her seat and pulled books and notebooks from her backpack. Her eyes kept roaming to the front door, eager for a glimpse of the new girl, but the bell rang without a sight of her.

Mrs. Randolph was halfway through the pre-algebra lesson when the door opened, and a dark face with dozens of braids popped through the doorway. Was that her?

"Am I in the right place?" the girl asked.

Whispers and snickers erupted across the room.

"You must be Zarina." Mrs. Randolph's voice was kind, but concern pinched the lines of her eyes.

"Yeah." She stepped inside and surveyed the room, her eyes narrowing as she looked around. Was it obvious to her? That they'd never had a Black student in their class before? Last year, there was a Black boy in the grade below them. He came for a couple of months, then stopped coming for some reason. But in their grade? Only White kids.

"Welcome. You can sit by Stella." Mrs. Randloph pointed to the desk to her right.

Stella ignored the snickers and smiled at the girl, trying to put her at ease. What would it be like to be in her shoes? To be different from everyone else in the school? Being the new kid was hard enough. A warm bubble filled her chest—a desire to be someone Zarina could trust. Someone she could count on. She wanted to know all about her. She envisioned Saturday night sleepovers and swimming together at the lake.

"Hey," Stella said as Zarina sat beside her.

"Hey," she replied.

As she pulled out a notebook and pencil, Stella jotted her number onto a scrap of paper and passed it to her.

She smiled slightly as she took it. "Thanks."

When class let out, they walked together to the locker they'd share. She showed her the trick—how to push the door in before yanking it open so it didn't jam. Zarina laughed at the picture of Stella's boy band crush hanging in the locker.

"I know. Lame, right?" Stella giggled at herself. Who was Zarina's crush? She couldn't wait to find out.

Murmurs alerted her to a group approaching. Hopefully, not the jock jerks. Her shoulders relaxed to see it was her friends Lexie, Summer, and Britt. But they looked less than friendly as they stepped near.

"Ugh. Sorry you have to drag her around." Summer scrunched her nose as if Zarina smelled like trash.

Stella's mouth parted. Did she just say that?

"What's your name again? Zariba?" Lexie joined in on the mean girl routine.

Zarina crossed her arms, stared Lexie down, and stated her name.

"Oh yeah, I knew it was a Black girl's name. Nothing normal." Lexie spit out the word Black as if it were contaminated.

Heat simmered in Stella's chest. She opened her mouth to tell them to stop, to shut up, but nothing came out.

"Did you get bussed to this school?" Britt asked.

"No. I live nearby." Zarina tossed Stella a look as if she had a life raft she could hand over if she wanted.

Her heart thrummed wildly. She didn't. She couldn't speak. Couldn't say anything. Couldn't stop this.

"What, at the trailer park?" The words barely made it from Britt's mouth before the three girls broke into laughter.

Stella's eyes burned. She wanted to cry, but instead, something far worse happened. A giggle squeaked out of her mouth. Nervous laughter scrambled up and out of her with a mind of its own. She clamped her hand over her mouth to stop it, but it was too late. Hurt flashed across Zarina's face. Betrayal lanced the air between them.

With a look full of venom, Zarina spun around and marched away.

No! If only Stella could run after her, explain she didn't mean to laugh. That she sure didn't find it funny. It was just something she did when nervous. But even as the scenario raced through her mind, the truth caught up with her. Even if she'd never cracked a smile, she had said nothing. She didn't stand up for Zarina when it counted. She'd thought she was a decent person, good-hearted and kind, but it turned out she was a coward. She didn't have what it took to stand up for what was right.

Not then. Not years later.

"What about now?" Trevor's deep voice broke through the haze of her memory. He'd listened attentively, without a trace of disgust on his face, though confused lines had appeared with the mention of certain phrases such as *trailer park*, and he probably had no idea how she'd gone to school with a Black girl.

She inhaled deeply, the scent of the lumber beneath her filling her nostrils. She was still afraid. Terrified, really. But now she wasn't willing to let fear stop her. She closed her eyes and pictured Jesus beside her, holding her hand. *"Be strong and courageous. Do not be afraid or terrified because of them, for the* Lord *your God goes with you; he will never leave you nor forsake you."* She might not have the courage in and of herself, but she could glean courage from One who had an infinite supply.

"Now I'm going to draw strength from the Lord and do what I feel He's calling me to do."

"Which is?"

"Get your family safely to my stateroom."

His brow creased. "And you're sure this will work? That both my family and you will make it through safe and well."

How she wished she could nod and assure him all would be well. "I don't know. I have no guarantee. God hasn't promised me safety or success in this. All I know is I won't be alone."

His lips firmed into a thin line. "And that's enough?"

Now, she could nod. Smile, even. "That's enough."

~

Claire pushed last night's spectacle out of her mind. She'd spent hours vomiting throughout the night and awoke with a massive headache. Wendy had to be judging her in her perfect little head, but she'd said nothing snarky. Instead, she'd wordlessly handed her a couple of ibuprofens and a cup of coffee.

Claire needed no further reminders of why she didn't drink. She definitely didn't need to check her page for any more comments. It seemed the whole world was laughing at her atrocious singing and moronic behavior. Neo had sworn he hadn't meant anything by it, that he hadn't known she wouldn't want him to film it. He'd looked innocent enough, and she hadn't explicitly told him not to. Guys were clueless about a lot of things. She'd have to be a lot more specific about what was and was not okay to post since she *had* made him an admin of her page. In retrospect, that would have been a good conversation to have before jumping to that move.

But today was a new day. Their last port day. She covered the bags under her eyes with makeup and dressed in her favorite bikini. Her phone dinged. Neo?

No, Everett for Stella. She kept forgetting she had Stella's phone.

> You OK? Thought I'd hear from you by now. Miss you and love you.

Her fingers itched to reply, to assure him that Stella was alive and well. However, did she even have such assurance? They hadn't heard from their friend in days. The last they'd heard, the stowaways were sick. Had the herbal remedies she'd suggested worked? If only Stella had given a recent update. She had no guarantee to offer Everett. How horrible to leave him worrying though. What should she do?

She glanced at Wendy, who was twirling her hair while staring at the ceiling. If only they were talking. How to respond needed to be a mutual decision. But venturing into a conversation right now was like swimming in shark-infested waters. She'd steer clear and enjoy the day with more pleasant company.

The tropical foliage of Hilo welcomed her and Neo as they made their way off the boat hand in hand. "This is gorgeous." She took in the bright blossoms filling the landscape.

"You're beautiful." His fingers trailed her shoulders, then down her backbone to her waist, sending tingles to her toes.

"I feel like enjoying the day for a bit first before filming a video." For once, they'd planned no excursions. They had nothing on their agenda except for relaxing on the beach. What an ideal way to end their time in Hawaii.

"Sounds perfect."

And it was. They chose Richardson Beach from a dozen tempting choices and lay on towels discussing their favorite college classes and what made good professors good. Those types of topics always made Claire feel smart and bolstered her self-confidence.

She raked her fingers through the dark green sand. "This is amazing."

"The olivine crystals give the sand its color."

Whatever olivine crystals were. Neo sounded super smart himself, rattling off random trivia facts like that.

"So, why'd you pursue kinesiology?" he asked. "What type of job did you hope to land with your degree?"

She prattled on about her desire to connect with people, to give them hope after an injury, and about her fascination with the body's ability to heal.

"You're really passionate about this, aren't you?" His sunglasses hid his gorgeous eyes from her.

"You sound surprised." Surely, he didn't think she was only a pretty face.

"Why is this the first I'm hearing you talk about it?"

She shrugged. "Everyone thinks it's boring." People's eyes tended to glaze over when she talked about anything she found interesting. She'd learned long ago to keep her thoughts to herself.

"Well, I don't." He reached over and ran his hand up her arm and to her neck. His mouth twitched in a smile. "Ready to get in?" His voice had turned husky.

Her belly quivered. Oh yeah. She wanted to get in the water and kiss this man until they were both senseless. She stood and gave his hand a tug. It didn't take much. He lunged for her, and she laughed, sprinting for the water. He chased her, picking her up and twirling her as they reached the placid bay.

She stepped in. "Oh my gosh! Fish!"

Tropical fish. Everywhere. Brilliant colors swirling in the water like a watercolor painting come to life. No wonder so many people were snorkeling around them. What exquisite beauty.

Neo didn't so much as look down. He fiddled with his smartwatch, and then his mouth met hers in a hungry kiss. Refocusing, she returned the kiss with fervor. He nudged her deeper into the water until all but her shoulders were covered. His mouth trailed her jaw, her neck, her ear as his hands explored her back. Too much. This was too much. She needed to put a stop to it before they got carried away.

"Neo? We should—"

He covered her words with his mouth. She moaned. If only he didn't taste so good. But they needed distance between them. She put her hands on his chest to gently push him away. Except he crushed her body closer to his, melding them together. Heat spread through her.

He nibbled her earlobe. "I love you, Claire."

Her heart thudded. Her mind swirled. Was this love? Dizzy euphoria threatened to overwhelm her senses.

"Say you love me too."

He kissed her deeper, and she couldn't find words. Did she love him? She wanted to be with him, didn't want to be without this giddy feeling of delight. "I-I …"

"Say it, Claire." He fiddled with the strap of her bikini top, twisting it in his fingers.

An uncomfortable sensation wedged its way through the euphoria, clearing her head. She inched his hand away from her strap. "I … like you. A lot." Her words came out in a pant.

His eyes flashed, hot and angry. He mashed his lips against hers as if he owned them. She winced. His hands dropped to her bikini bottoms, and he toyed with the strings. What was he doing? She swatted at his hands, but with his mouth pressed against hers, she couldn't breathe and couldn't stop him from undoing the strings.

In a flash, he ripped her bikini bottoms off and held them triumphantly in the air.

"Neo!" she screamed.

He laughed and backed away.

She dove for her swimsuit, but he dangled it out of reach. She swam toward him, clawing, grasping, jumping, but he evaded her, backing farther and farther toward shore until she could no longer follow him without exposing herself. She stood stuck in the water, arms wrapped tightly around herself, as he laughed and taunted her with her bikini.

Then, to her horror, he pulled out his phone.

~

Wendy was sitting in the near-empty ship café working on her third ice cream cone of the day when Grayson's text came through.

> You were right not to trust that guy. Check out Claire's Facebook page right away.

She stared at the message. What in the world? What guy? Her mind tripped through their last interaction. He must be talking about Neo. But why was Grayson hanging out on Claire's social media? Weird.

> Why are you on Claire's FB?

Then, she hopped on Facebook and clicked on Claire-ity Fitness. His reply came while it was loading.

> To see if you had a point. You do.

Her jaw dropped as a live video came on the screen. There was Neo, holding up Claire's bikini bottoms, telling everyone to stay tuned if they wanted to get a good look at Claire.

"She's got to come out eventually." He smirked for the camera, then panned to Claire.

She looked pale and near tears, her arms covering as much of her body as possible. Oh, Wendy could spit fire about now. That jerk. How dare he do something so heartless.

She ditched her cone in the trash and flew toward the elevator, texting as she went.

> Omgsh, thanks for the heads-up. On my way to grab her another swimsuit now. Can you meet me there for backup?

As soon as she figured out where they were. How many beaches dotted Hilo's shoreline? Once in her room, she threw both of Claire's other bikinis in a bag and got her own suit on. Her phone buzzed.

> He said they're at Richardson Ocean Park. Be there in ten.

Thank God. Though fully confident in her ability to tell the lamebrain off, if he attempted to get physical, she had no recourse. It wouldn't come to that, would it? Then again, who knew what someone who was capable of that level of cruelty would do. She hailed a cab as fast as she could.

Wendy spotted him from a distance, still talking into that stupid phone. Thankfully, Grayson and Sam stood a few yards away, arms crossed, looking ready for a signal to barrel the guy to the ground. She caught Grayson's eye and gave a little wave. They approached at the same time, from different directions. Good, they'd gang up on the sleazeball.

"You've seen her in leggings and a sports bra, but you're about to see her in hardly anything at all. Get ready." Neo's cocky smile filled the screen in front of him.

Wendy stepped forward and smacked the phone from his hand.

"Hey, what's your—" His eyes widened as he took her in. If she looked half as enraged as she felt, he had every reason to fear. "Not you."

"You better believe it's me. Were you about to ask *me* what *my* problem is?"

He pursed his lips and stepped backward. "Just having a little fun. It's a practical joke."

"Um, no. It's sexual harassment, and I'll report it as such."

"Oh, please. It's not—"

"Yes, it is." Grayson stepped next to her, bent to retrieve the phone to turn off the recording, then stood to his full height. "It's despicable and disgusting. Didn't anyone ever teach you to treat ladies with respect?"

Neo snorted. "Come on. She threw herself at me from the first day I met her. She was asking for it."

No one saw Sam's punch coming. When his fist collided with Neo's jaw, Wendy's hand flew to cover her mouth. Speckles of blood dotted the dark sand.

From where he hunched over, Neo looked up with wild eyes. "You are all crazy." He snatched his phone from Grayson's hand and stalked away.

"I love your dad," Wendy mumbled. Then her gaze found Claire's. "Coming!" she shouted. She grabbed a bikini bottom from the bag and waded into the water. Her friend was shaking violently when she reached her. "Oh goodness. It's going to be okay. Here." She handed over the swimsuit and turned around while Claire put it on. Good. No sign of good-for-nothing Neo anywhere.

Claire's arms wrapped around Wendy in a tight embrace that Wendy returned. She held her friend as her body trembled with tears.

"He ruined everything."

Wendy stroked her hair. "No. Everything will be okay. He didn't … take advantage of you before going to shore, did he?"

Claire shook her head. "No, thank God."

Truly, thank God. "Good. See? It's all fine."

Claire sobbed harder. "The job. I'm sure I won't get it now."

Wendy pulled back and searched Claire's face. "What job?"

Chapter Twenty

Bridge agreed to help with Stella's plan, that is, after spouting off about how it was dangerous and foolhardy. Perhaps it was. If she'd had time, she'd have run it by Wendy and Claire to see if they had any better ideas, but she couldn't wait. Maybe those men were all talk in their boasts to search the cargo, but she couldn't take the risk.

In the privacy of Stella's cabin, Bridge stripped from her uniform and slipped into one of Stella's dresses. It wasn't a perfect fit, but no matter. It was only so she'd have something decent on in case she needed to make a run for it in an emergency. If all went as planned, she'd be changing back into her own clothes within the hour. The bigger question was whether the other clothing exchanged would fit, and Stella had only her vague recollection to go on.

As if reading her mind, Bridge thrust a shawl into her hand. "In case it won't fasten in back."

"Good idea." Stella folded it and added it to the ample woven basket where she'd nestled Bridge's uniform underneath some linens. The basket had a handle on each side and wedged nicely on her hip, though it looked awkward with her attire.

Bridge eyed her again, and she could almost hear the woman doubting the believability of her running this errand in a fancy hoopskirt.

"I was about to join the women in the ladies' cabin when I got called away to aid a sick passenger." She blinked innocently.

Bridge shook her head with a heavy sigh. "I'll be praying the whole time."

"Me too." With every step.

The chambermaid's parting word of "Godspeed" ushered her out the door and into the twilight.

Since she was supposed to be on an urgent errand for the doctor, she had reason for hasty steps. She greeted the passengers she passed with a brief smile and nod but didn't linger. Hopefully, no one asked Duncan about her errand.

He didn't know a thing.

Anger still simmered inside her at what he'd done. He'd lied to her, pretended to be someone he wasn't. She'd trusted him. To think that trust could have killed her, could have killed the very people he was trying to protect. Okay, he had taken care of them when she was too ill to do so. And he had helped to take care of her. She wouldn't stay mad at him forever. She just wasn't ready to fling open her arms to the man right now.

She was on her own.

No. She had Trevor. And Bridge. And Jesus.

Yea, though I walk through the valley of the shadow of death, You are with me. You are with me. You are with me.

When she made it to the stairwell, she wrangled the basket against her side with one hand and gripped the banister with the other until her knuckles whitened. Was she truly going to do this? Her? Scaredy-Cat Stella? But as she descended one step at a time, it became clear this had nothing to do with her and what she hadn't been able to do in the past. She pictured the faces of this mother and her children. Their lives were at stake. They were worth the risk.

So, though her knees trembled, she pushed forward. Once among the cargo, she slunk along the shadows, creeping from crate to crate until she reached theirs. She slid the board to the side. "You ready?" she whispered.

Cora squinted into the faint light, brow furrowed. "What?"

"Are you ready?" Stella asked again, slower.

"For what?"

Stella's pulse ratcheted up a notch. Trevor was supposed to relay the plan to his family so they would be prepared. They were to be ready to spring into action. She didn't know? What had happened?

Stella scanned the area to ensure no one was around, then explained what was going on. The more she talked, the wider and more fearful the woman's eyes grew. Oh no. She looked like she was going to be sick again.

"Can you do this?" Stella asked, then she clenched her jaw. It wasn't a question. It wasn't an option. She put her hand on Cora's shoulder. "You can do this."

Using the hammer she'd packed at the bottom of the basket, she pried off another nail and took off the board, allowing Cora to exit with Smitty in her arms.

Stella couldn't keep her mouth from falling open. Huddled in the crate, the woman had appeared small, but Stella had assumed it was only because of the cramped space. Standing before her, Cora looked gaunt and frail, barely able to heft Smitty, who was but a wisp of a thing herself. Stella covered her shock with a tight-lipped smile. Timothy scrambled out of the crate. She led them to the secluded area where Trevor had taken her the day before and handed the woman Bridge's dress in exchange for the child. Smitty whimpered in her arms, clearly not used to being away from her mama. Stella shushed and bounced the sweaty bundle.

Cora emerged with Bridge's uniform hanging off her as if she was a child playing dress-up. Oh dear. Had she always been that thin or had she lost a lot of weight during her sickness? Regardless, they wouldn't be needing the shawl. Would she even have enough strength to carry the basket? If not, Stella would need to do it, but that would make maneuvering difficult. One step at a time.

You are with me. Lord, help us.

"Okay, we got the largest basket we could find. Smitty will fit just fine, but she's going to need to be still." Stella winced as she spoke. What an unreasonable request. She handed the child back to her mom and took all but one linen from the basket, leaving a bottom cushion.

She left the mom to get the little one situated and turned to the older child. "Do you understand what to do?" Though he nodded, she continued, "You must hug my leg and move with me every step. Do everything you can not to fall. And don't make a sound."

He nodded solemnly.

"Okay." She lifted her hoopskirt, exposing her skinny jeans underneath. "Get in."

The mother grasped her arm. "You sure about this? It's mighty inappropriate. A colored boy and a white woman."

Her hand instinctively went to her neck. Could she be hanged for this? "I know." Well, she probably *didn't* know. Not as well as this woman did. "But we don't have much choice. Let's go, *Bridge*."

Baby in basket and boy clinging to her leg, they started off. Shoot. She hadn't thought about the sound of extra footsteps.

"You need to take your shoes off," she whispered.

His mom repeated the command, and they waited while Timothy did so. She tucked the worn shoes in the basket under the linens.

They made it a few more awkward steps, Stella and Timothy working to walk in rhythm, when the baby whimpered, tousling the linens covering her. Fear stole Stella's resolve. This was impossible. How had she ever thought this plan would work? They'd barely made it a few feet, and everything was falling apart. She looked ridiculous. Anyone who saw her would know something was off. She looked as if she were walking with a charley horse in her leg. Poor Cora's arms already hung heavy with the weight of the basket. How would she make it all the way upstairs? And she didn't look a thing like Bridge. Anyone from first class would be able to spot her as an imposter.

She dragged in a ragged breath, tears hovering around the edges. She couldn't do this. Why had she ever thought she could?

Cora frowned at her, then set down the basket and took her hands. "Let's pray." Her grasp was warm and firm. Despite the woman's petite frame, strength flowed from her. "Lord Jesus, we ask for Your help. Blind the eyes of those who would seek to harm us and send Your angels to aid us. If You could part the Red Sea for the Israelites, we reckon You can make the way clear for us to get to safety. In Jesus's mighty name."

"Amen." Stella's shoulders relaxed. If she truly believed the songs she worshiped to at church, she could be confident their safety didn't hinge on her perfect wisdom or execution of a plan, but on God's power and faithfulness. And He was with them, no matter what happened.

They walked forward.

Just as they were emerging from the cargo, the two men Stella had seen days before rounded the corner, nearly colliding with them. One with a mustache tickling his lower lip tossed Stella a saucy smile. "What's a fancy lady like you doing down here?"

"I came to attend to a sick patient and am now on my way back to my cabin upstairs. I bid you farewell, gentlemen." She gave a curt nod and took another step, only the boy stumbled beneath her, nearly causing her to lose her balance. The man caught her arm and stabilized her.

"Careful, little lady. I have a tendency to sweep women off their feet." He winked.

She suppressed the urge to cringe and forced a tight, polite smile, but she said nothing. A soft cry sounded from the basket.

"What's that?"

"Hmm?"

"Did your colored woman say something?"

"We must be going." All she could think to do was hum to cover up any further sounds. And the only song that came to her mind was "ABC" by The Jackson 5. It was something, at least, and she ascended the steps in slow, awkward motions, accompanied by her loud humming. Well, that was one way to ward off any advances from the horrible men below. When she glanced back down, they'd disappeared.

They reached the top of the stairs, and Stella's shoulders sagged in relief. The deck was clear. And what was that sound? Music? It came from above.

"A calliope band." Cora's voice was filled with wonder. "Praise be."

A nervous laugh spilled out of Stella. She didn't have to hum any longer. The band covered the baby's soft whimpers. The boy sneezed against her leg. And that. The band covered that too.

They were almost to her door. A grin spread at the end in sight. Her plan had worked! They were going to make it. No one was getting hung tonight. But then a shadowy figure stepped out of her room onto the deck. Out of her room?

She stopped short, causing the boy to stumble and fall. She cringed and flared her skirt behind her to cover where his leg peeked out. She squinted into the emerging darkness, pulse swooshing in her ears. She couldn't hide, couldn't pretend she hadn't seen the person. Best to put on bravado, even as she trembled.

She tilted up her chin. "Who goes there?"

"Miss Lindy." Duncan spun toward her, expression stern. "You've got some explaining to do."

~

Even fully clothed and wrapped in two blankets, Claire felt naked as she huddled at the corner of her bed. She kept reliving that nightmare from two days earlier of being exposed and alone in the water and the walk of shame afterward. Though Wendy had come to her rescue with another swimsuit and though she'd wasted no time in slipping on her cover-up and wrapping a towel around herself, it seemed like every eye was undressing her as she slunk back to her room.

It had to be all in her head. It wasn't like everyone on the beach and on the boat was glued to her Facebook page. Even the people nearest to them likely hadn't a clue what had happened. Everyone was in their own world. But no amount of logic could evict the creepy crawly feeling from underneath her flaming hot skin. She'd never live down the mortification.

And though she'd probably never drown it with chocolate lava cake either, she was sure going to try Wendy's suggested remedy. After all, there was no use trying to stay trim now. Her Fit TV career had gone down the drain with Neo's dirty trick. Might as well enjoy sugar if she couldn't take pleasure in anything else in life right now.

Wendy had gone to get her a slice of cake. Claire didn't plan on leaving their room again until the steward kicked her off the boat. Even the remote possibility of seeing Neo sent her into shallow breathing.

Her phone dinged. Should she check it? Ironic how she'd never asked that question before. Checking every notification was a given, but now ... What if it was Neo texting something nasty? Or what if it was Trenia telling her what a failure she was? She hadn't heard from either of them since *the incident* two days ago. Not that she expected any word from Neo, but it was only a matter of time before the proverbial Fit TV shoe dropped. The sooner, the better.

She reached for her phone. A notification for a Facebook message from someone she didn't know. She normally ignored those. They were salesy at best and vulgar at worst. But curiosity niggled. She clicked to open it.

Check out the group Celebrity Prank.

That was it, the entirety of the message from someone named Chris with a profile picture of a cat. The group? Did they mean a Facebook group? She typed the name in the search bar. A public group. She hit join. Her pulse began to thrum as she scrolled, then dread spread through her body. There, front and center, was a picture of Neo holding up her bikini bottoms, with her looking small and broken in the background. The post had 297 likes and laughing face emojis.

Tears filled her eyes. What kind of cruel, heartless group was this? She started to scroll farther down, but Wendy burst through the door, distracting her.

"Sorry it took me so long. They were out of lava cake but were in the process of making more, so I had to wait for it to come out of the oven." She stilled halfway to the bed. "What's wrong?"

Claire couldn't speak past the lump in her throat. She turned the phone around so Wendy could see for herself. Wendy sat next to her and exchanged the phone for the plate. Claire downed half the cake in one bite, salty tears mixing with the chocolate sauce.

"Oh my gosh. The jerk." She scrolled down. Claire caught glimpses of her face, but Wendy kept scrolling. "There. His first post about you. 'Met this pseudo famous YouTuber on the cruise I'm on. She seems super gullible and would be fun to prank. Ideas?'"

Claire slammed her eyes shut. From the very beginning? He had never cared for her, not even a bit. How could she have been so naive? She opened her eyes and spoke with a shaky voice. "Pseudo famous. That means fake famous, right?"

"Yeah. Kind of." Wendy winced. "It means you have some kind of celebrity status, but you don't deserve it because you haven't done anything special."

"What'd people suggest?"

"Are you sure you want to know? Maybe it's better if we get off here."

"I want to know." She had to peel back the curtain and expose every piece of this nightmare.

"Let's see. Make her think she's uber famous and popular. Get random people to ask for her autograph or for a picture with her."

Claire dropped her face into her hands. "Oh no. The impromptu exercise class on deck. I bet it was all a setup."

"The one I walked in on?"

"Yeah. I'm so stupid." Claire pounded her fists onto her legs. "Why did I think all those people wanted pictures with me? No wonder he kept laughing. I made a total fool out of myself." She rubbed her palms onto her forehead. "Are those pictures on there?"

Wendy scrolled up and flashed one of Claire and the old lady.

"I'm going to die. Literally, going to melt into this bed and die of embarrassment."

Wendy rubbed her back. "The only people who know about this are those who are in this group. That's only"—she scrolled up—"thirty thousand people. You have way more followers than that."

Ugh. Thirty-thousand group members and whoever they've told.

"Ohhh." Wendy's shoulders slumped.

"What?"

"Neo's a moderator. Maybe even the founder? It's hard to tell. Either way, it looks like he's using this group to build a following of his own."

"Great. What else? How else did he humiliate me?"

"I don't think we need to deep dive into this. Eat more cake."

Claire forked another piece into her mouth and spoke around it. "What else?"

Wendy sighed, finding that first post again. "'Ruin one of her live videos.'"

"Check."

"'Get her drunk and video her embarrassing herself.'"

"Check."

"'Get her to tell you a secret. Something no one else knows.'"

She choked another bite down with a sob. "Check."

"'And record her confessing her love for you.'"

She straightened. "That's why he kept pushing me to tell him I loved him. But he was recording?" That stupid smartwatch. "The twirp."

Wendy scrolled until she came to an audio clip. She pressed play.

Claire's voice sounded from the phone, muffled and scratchy but clearly hers. "Yes, of course, I still love you."

Claire palmed her forehead. It would take too much mental energy to explain the way he'd trapped her with his words after telling her his secret. She scoffed. Cat guts. It probably never even happened. Only, how could he make something like that up?

"In the comments, people said it didn't count because it sounded coerced."

She threw back her head. "Because it was!" But that explained why he'd tried again to get her to say those words. And why he'd fiddled with his watch in the water. Only … "Did he record me telling a secret too? His watch must have had an audio recorder."

Wendy scrolled again. A few seconds later, Claire's scratchy voice filled the space between them once more. "I was at my older sister's high school grad party—"

"Ugh." She pressed the pause button to make herself shut up like she should have done at the time. Why had she blabbed everything to him? Whatever. It didn't matter anymore. What was done was done.

"That's it?" She cringed with her question. Could it get any worse?

"Well, and 'Get a picture of her naked.'"

Claire shuddered to think how close he'd come to that one. How before he'd gone for her bikini bottoms, he'd gone for her top. He'd probably intended to take them both. Thankfully, God had at least protected her from that fate. A picture like that circulating around the internet would be disastrous for her on many levels.

Wendy put down the phone. "Enough of that. Nothing good can come from rehashing what a jerkola that guy is. Are you ready to tell me about this whole job situation now?"

Claire hadn't been willing to talk about it, or anything else, after the fiasco on the beach. Now, though? Yeah, unburdening herself would be good. She slid the last bite of cake into her mouth and actually tasted the flavors this time as she nodded.

With Wendy sitting so close their knees brushed, it was as if they were on the same side for the first time since college. Wendy's expression didn't hold a trace of judgment as Claire recounted Trenia's first mention of Fit TV's interest in her and then their two-week watch period.

"Why didn't you say anything? I could have been helping you this whole time. Maybe then you wouldn't have turned to creepy Neo."

Claire shrugged. "You kept saying this trip was about Stella. I got the message loud and clear. It wasn't about me."

Wendy tossed her arms in the air. "I didn't know your entire career was on the line!"

"Would you have cared if you knew? I wasn't under the impression you thought my career worth saving. Or that you would even categorize it as a career."

Wendy's face crumpled at Claire's assessment. "I'm sorry. I keep letting my jealousy of you get in the way of our friendship."

Claire pointed to herself. "*Your* jealousy of *me*?" Why would someone so brilliant be jealous of her?

Wendy nudged her knee. "Yes. You're gorgeous and popular and successful."

"I'm not—"

"Don't even try to deny it." Wendy pulled her mass of curls into a messy ponytail. "Truth is, I'm in a bit of a career crisis myself. I might lose my job."

Claire's mouth parted. "Seriously?" Her view of Miss Perfect skipping down an idyllic life path fractured. How could it be? Brilliant, witty, perceptive Wendy fired?

"Yep." Wendy recounted the whole story, from Mrs. Gardenia complaining about her at the school board meeting to her boss telling her she was on probation to Mrs. Gardenia filming her going off on the poor Hawaiian waitress.

"Oh no. I'm so sorry." Her friend lacked a filter, but there was no doubt she was an excellent teacher. She didn't deserve to be fired. Claire laid her head on Wendy's shoulder. "I'll pray you get to keep your job or that you get another one you like even better."

"And I'll pray the perfect opportunity opens up for you."

Claire found a smile, despite the dried tears crusting her cheeks. "Doesn't it feel good to get everything out in the open? No more secrets between us."

Wendy's voice was soft, almost unsure. "Yeah. No more secrets."

~

Guilt churned Wendy's stomach. She needed something to do besides sit here in this little room with Claire who thought all wrongs had been righted between them.

They hadn't. There was one secret still eating at her. Was it worth disrupting this blessed peace and budding connection to unburden herself?

No. She couldn't do it.

"Do you want another piece of cake?" Wendy rose, heading for the door. "I'll go get one for you."

Claire grabbed her middle. "Oh gosh, no. I haven't indulged in that much sugar in years. If I eat another piece, I'll be sick."

Okay. "Something else? A celery stick?"

Claire giggled. "No. I don't need anything. How about …" She tilted her head as if considering options. "Why don't you let me paint your toenails?"

That was not what she'd had in mind.

"Come on. It'll be like old times."

Claire's hopeful expression pierced her resistance. They had enjoyed these sessions in college. A lot of great conversations had drifted through polish-scented air.

"Okay. But no crazy bright colors."

"Deal."

Claire was on her second toe when Wendy's phone dinged. She frowned. "It's Everett. He's worried about Stella. Has he been texting her phone?"

Claire threw her head back. "Yes, I meant to talk to you about it, but we weren't exactly talking. I didn't know how to reply, so I never texted back. I don't want him to worry, but what can I say? I thought about texting back as Stella, but that could get weird."

"Yeah. It could traverse into awkward territory fast. Maybe I can say that Stella lost her phone, but she's fine?"

"So, do the thing where you don't technically lie, but you don't tell the truth either?"

Wendy gave her a side-eye. "If you want to explain to him what's going on, go right ahead."

She finished the last nail on that foot and waved her hand over them to create a breeze. "No, it's okay. Your almost honest method is fine."

Another text notification sounded. "Okay, Everett, we get it. You love your fiancée."

Except it wasn't Everett this time. It was Allison. How'd she get Wendy's number? Oh yeah. She'd texted pictures to herself from Allison's phone.

> Dillon Lane asked me to go to the movies with him. Should I go? Is he one of the good ones?

"Oh no. My student is asking my advice on boys."

Claire chuckled. "That's cute."

"No, it's horrible. This is the girl whose mom hates me. I have to steer clear of her, not become her bestie." Wendy showed Claire the text.

"Aw. She knows you're a good judge of character. Which is true by the way. Good thing she didn't ask me. I'd steer her wrong. But you? You snagged the most decent guy on this ship."

Wendy snorted. "Snagged is a bit of an exaggeration. I don't know where Grayson and I are exactly. He was pretty ticked at how I treated you."

Claire pointed the fingernail brush at her and smirked. "That's why he's decent."

"What do I do? Reply that it's inappropriate to text your teacher?"

She started on the other foot. "Answer her. Some girls don't have mothers they feel like they can talk to about that kind of stuff. She's asking your opinion because she trusts you. Do you think this Dillon guy is a good kid?"

"Yeah. He is." Smart. Respectful. Kind.

"Then tell her so. You never know how much she might be hungering for a bit of mentorship."

Wendy sighed and replied to Allison. Hopefully, Claire was as good at advice as she was at pedicures.

Chapter Twenty-One

Duncan paced the length of her room, hands tugging at his wild hair. "Do you have any idea the danger you've placed us in?"

Stella crossed her arms and stared him down. "No, but I have a pretty good idea of the danger I saved them from." She cast a glance to where the stowaways lay side by side under her bed.

"How do you expect to get them off the boat? Not quite as simple as unloading their crate anymore."

She opened her mouth to answer, but nothing came out. She didn't have a plan for that yet.

He continued, "The cook caught Bridge sneaking an extra portion onto your breakfast tray this morning and gave her quite a tongue-lashing for it. He's likely to fire her."

Stella winced. She certainly hadn't meant any harm to come to Bridge.

His gaze narrowed. "And the talk around the breakfast table was about a new soft crying sound coming from the right side of the boat."

"The baby wasn't used to her new surroundings."

He stuffed his hands in his pockets. "Well, there are no boiler noises to disguise children's sounds up here, are there? Funny you didn't think of that before you concocted this foolhardy scheme."

If only she could defend herself with the real reason their move had been necessary. News that this boat would sink tomorrow burned on her tongue, but she held it back. If she told, could they possibly avoid the snag and subsequent sinking? Then there'd be no excavation over a hundred years later. No museum in Kansas City. No window into the past.

What else would change? Best not to tempt fate and find out. She twisted her lips and buried the truth inside.

With a huff, he marched to the front door, then spun around. "Rumors are flying. Do your best to keep the children quiet and to appear as though all is well. I told everyone you were under the weather this morning, but you must join the other passengers for dinner and supper to avoid suspicion."

"Can't you tell them I'm too sick to come to dinner?"

"No! That wouldn't do. They're already wary. They must see your face to put the rumors to rest."

She cast a glance to the expressive eyes peeking out at her. "But what will they eat?"

"Expect a delivery of herbal teas once per day." A mischievous glint replaced the aggravation in his eyes. "Make what's within last."

She nodded, but she'd have to see what he'd supply. She wasn't above stuffing hunks of bread into her blouse at mealtime to sneak back to her room. Once, at a buffet, her grandma had wrapped a slice of peach pie in a napkin and slid it into her purse. Stella smiled at the memory of Grammy Rose pulling the pie out, extracting the breath mint that had glued itself to its side, and digging in with her fork. Stella may not have learned lessons on integrity from that woman, but she sure did have endearing memories.

Once again, the ache of missing her grandma twinged in her chest. What would Grammy Rose think of this strange predicament Stella found herself in? She likely wouldn't understand it, wouldn't get why Stella was risking her well-being for these enslaved people. *Formerly* enslaved people. Thank God. With the Lord's help, they would never return to bondage.

No, Grammy Rose wouldn't understand. She had been born in a different time. At least, that was the excuse Stella had always made for her. Because Grammy Rose's words hadn't differed too much from Stella's boss's slurs.

The memory was seared into Stella's mind of when a Black family had moved in a few houses down from Grammy Rose. *There goes the neighborhood. Pretty soon, we'll have to move. This will turn into a ghetto.*

Stella hadn't disputed Grammy Rose's racist words. Not then, not ever. How could she have? She loved her grandma with everything in her. And Grammy Rose was a *good* person. The most tenderhearted person she'd ever known. If anyone was in trouble, Grammy Rose had rushed to their aid, giving her money, time, and resources to help in whatever way she could. She'd prayed for a solid hour each night, while knitting in her rocking chair. There was no one with a truer, kinder heart.

So how could she not have seen that the color of a person's skin didn't make them less worthy of kindness?

People were complicated. Was anyone all good or all bad? Weren't they all a mix of beauty and faults, strengths and weaknesses?

She had loved Grammy Rose fiercely despite this glaring character weakness. And she was learning that Jesus loved her ferociously despite the fact she'd failed to stand against injustice time and time again. And in His gracious love, He was giving her another chance.

No matter how many times she'd failed before, no matter how many times she hadn't spoken up when she should have, His mercies were new this morning. This was a new day, and on this day, He was making her more like Himself.

Praise the Lord.

That morning, Stella told the children stories in hushed tones and did her best to clean their faces and hair with water from her basin. If only they could run around and expend some energy, but other passengers were sure to hear the commotion of extra footsteps. They had to remain still and quiet. Maybe at night, the calliope band would play again, and they'd have an opportunity to move about.

When it came time for the noon meal, Stella gave the children paper and pens to draw with before she left to join the others in the main cabin for a meal of roasted duck and asparagus. Never having seen a ballpoint pen before, the children squealed with delight, making it hard to tear herself away.

But now she sat next to Mrs. Braiden and Mrs. Scott, two women whose husbands had set out west before them to get settled and had now sent for them to follow. She'd found these women to stick to safe subjects, do most of the talking, and not ask intrusive questions. The best type of travel companions when one was trying not to spill a secret.

"Did you hear about the boiler explosion on the *Ancient Treasure*?" Mrs. Braiden shook her head before munching a piece of duck.

"Those poor people." Mrs. Scott put her hand over her heart. "Such a tragedy."

"I heard it was them firemen's fault."

Stella reoriented her confused thoughts to the time and place she currently resided in. Here, firemen weren't men in boots and red coats who blasted burning buildings with powerful hoses. They were the dock workers who kept the boiler fires fueled with wood day and night. She'd gathered that much from eavesdropping.

"The darkies they had stoking the boilers overloaded them and caused them to explode. Some of those boys don't have a lick of sense." Mrs. Braiden tsked.

Heat surged in Stella's belly. Were these privileged women really blaming the Black workers for the explosion? She hadn't a clue how boilers worked, but considering those explosions weren't unheard of on riverboats, it was doubtful the cause could be as simple as worker negligence. "I don't think that's true." She spoke before she even realized what she was doing.

The women blinked at her, looking as stunned as she felt.

"What do you mean?" Mrs. Braiden sat back in her seat. "It's a known fact. Careless firemen cause boilers to explode."

If only she had research to back her point, but she wasn't an expert here. All she had was a vague feeling that their reasoning was off. "Firemen have a difficult and dangerous job, and I doubt they take it lightly. I think it has more to do with captains pushing the boats too hard to drive profits." She dabbed her mouth with her napkin.

The women exchanged a baffled look. It was as if no one knew where to go with the conversation after that. Great. She was supposed to be appearing as normal as possible. Would this odd conversation arouse suspicions?

Bridge approached, worry lines creasing her forehead. "Miss Lindy, may I have a word?"

Stella placed her napkin on the table and stood.

Mrs. Scott huffed at Bridge, her expression pinched in disdain. "I beg your pardon. What is so important you must interrupt this lady's meal?"

Lord forgive her, she could slap this woman. Instead, she inhaled deeply and forced a smile. "I'm sure it's of utmost importance." Is that the way these uppity women would put it? She put a hand on Bridge's arm and directed her away from curious eyes and ears. "What's going on?"

"It's Dr. Duncan," Bridge whispered. "I fear he might be in a heap of trouble. These rough-looking men came and talked in his ear, then next thing I knew, he was walking with them downstairs, all stiff-like."

"Stiff?"

"I think they had a pistol to his back, hidden 'neath a jacket."

A pistol? Stella sprung into action, rushing to her room, then barreling through it and out the back door to the promenade deck. She had to find him. But then what? What was she going to do when she came across two rough-looking men with a gun? She paused and wrung her hands. She needed a weapon. Something. Anything. She stepped back inside her room and searched. The only thing that caught her eye was a stack of books. She grabbed a hardback and raced out the door. "I'll return shortly," she whispered as an afterthought to the family under her bed.

She was nuts. Absolutely insane. Going into a gun fight with a novel? But adrenaline propelled her forward, and she took the steps two at a time. She heard voices before she saw their figures.

"Where are they? Tell me."

She stilled, blood cooling, reason returning. She couldn't barge into an altercation between these men. She needed a plan, but how was she supposed to develop one when she didn't have a clue what was going on?

"I'm afraid I don't know what you're talking about."

Stella's ears perked at the sound of Duncan's voice. She put her book down on a barrel and peeked around its rounded edge. The three men came into view. Her breath lodged in her throat. The man who'd spoken to her when she'd been sneaking the stowaways upstairs had a gun to Duncan's head, and they were standing before the empty crate where the family had stayed.

"You know something. I heard you'se a dirty abolitionist."

He snorted. "Hogwash."

The gun cocked.

Lord, help her. She had to do something. She sneaked back the way she'd come, then emerged from the shadows with urgency. She put on an ignorant tone. "Dr. Duncan? Are you down here? Dr. Duncan?" She made a show of looking here and there, even bumping into cargo.

The man mumbled, "You." The man lowered his pistol to his side but made no attempt to hide it. His gaze narrowed. "What do you want?"

"Oh." She put on a smile. "Dr. Duncan. There you are." Duncan's eyes widened, but she continued, "I've been looking all over for you. Mrs. Scott is feeling dreadfully ill. Bad duck, I'm afraid." She put a finger to her chin. "Do you think so? I hate to accuse the cook or whoever purchased the meat, but I fear she's only the first of many to come down with it. Please come quick. We're about to have a doozy of a crisis on our hands."

Did people say *doozy* in this time? Hopefully, she sounded convincing. She was putting her full weight behind the assumption these men were deck passengers who wouldn't know the goings on of what happened upstairs and, therefore, wouldn't be able to call her bluff.

The men eyed her suspiciously.

"Sorry, little lady," the one with the gun said. "We weren't finished with your Dr. Duncan."

"Oh, dear." She bit her lip. "Please hurry. I'm afraid everyone is in a tizzy upstairs."

The other man nodded to his partner in crime. "She's been down here. Maybe she knows something."

"That's right." Gun Man's smile spread wide and slimy. "What do you know about this here crate?" He kicked the side of it.

She frowned at it, tilting her head as if inspecting it. "It appears empty." She opened her mouth wide as if shocked. "Are you investigating a robbery? Did someone steal the contents of a crate of cargo?"

Gun Man snickered. "Don't worry. We'll find them. And when we do, we'll shoot you and dump your body in the river."

Was he talking to Duncan or her? She shivered.

She schooled her face into continued innocence. "I haven't a clue what's going on, but if I can have Dr. Duncan's assistance upstairs, that would be most appreciated."

"Sure." His oily smile remained. "He can go with you'se upstairs. But we're coming too."

"Oh, good. If it *is* the duck, we may have many needing help to their rooms."

Their cynical chuckles came as an answer.

She walked toward the stairway, her mind scrambling for a way out of this mess. Perhaps she could hum again. It had worked last time. *Oh, God. Oh, God. Oh, God.* No other words came, but once again, she pictured holding Jesus's hand. Was she walking with Him to the cross or to safety? Either way, He was with her.

The three men filed behind her. She discreetly grabbed her book as she passed the barrel where she'd left it and slowed her steps to where Duncan walked next to her, the other two men directly behind.

She caught Duncan's eye and mouthed, *Catch me*, as they ascended the steps. His brow furrowed, and she mouthed it again and again until understanding dawned in his expression. *Here goes nothing.* At the landing, she bent forward. "Oh goodness. Oh no. I feel ill. Must be that dreadful duck."

She moaned. Then, book in her left hand, she swung her arm backward in a dramatic gesture, whacking the gunman solidly in the side of the head with the hardback. She stumbled back a step, as if she were about to faint, and jabbed the other man in the ribs, knocking him off balance. Duncan caught hold of her arm, keeping her from falling. Both men tumbled into each other, then down the steps, a thud sounding as their skulls met the deck.

She looked at Duncan with wide eyes. By all appearances, both men were unconscious. But for how long? "What now?"

He palmed his forehead. "You get upstairs. I must get off this boat."

"Off the boat?" Now *she* grabbed *his* arm, truly feeling off balance. "But you're my guide. How will I know what to do without you?"

"You never truly needed me." A sad smile lifted the edges of his mouth. "But it looks like I needed you."

~

Somewhere between having Claire paint her toes and do her makeup, Wendy and Grayson called a tenuous truce. His text made her smile because it sounded like something she would write.

> Forgive me for jumping to conclusions? Bad habit.
> Of course, I forgive you. You weren't entirely wrong. I had a lot to apologize to Claire for.

And apologize she had. Crazy how when they peeled off the outer layers, both of them had an idealized version of the other that had created underlying jealousy. And how, underneath it all, they were both riding the struggle bus in remarkably similar ways.

> Want to meet in the library later? Kiss and make up?

Her anxiety over their mishap unfurled at his words. Would she ever! But one glance at Claire scanning eye shadow shades had her typing a reply she didn't regret in the least.

> Maybe another day. Claire needs me right now.

His reply came so fast, she didn't have time to put her phone down.

> Sounds good. You're worth waiting for.

Warmth melted through her chest. Somebody pinch her.

Maybe Claire was right, and Wendy was a good judge of character. Of course, they hadn't really addressed the issues looming between them. Mainly that he'd said she wasn't ready for a relationship, and they lived in different cities. Was there a future between them to be had? Still, he seemed legit to the core. Even if nothing more came from meeting Grayson, she was thankful she'd met him.

Lord, thank You for putting Grayson in my life. But could You bring someone decent for Claire? Why did her friend seem to attract the jerkiest guys on the planet? It didn't seem fair. If Wendy got a good guy, and Stella too, why not Claire?

Stella.

Wendy straightened with a start. "It's September 4."

"What?" Claire paused, the applicator halfway to Wendy's face.

"In Stella's time. It's September 4. The boat sinks tomorrow."

Claire lowered the mascara, eyes wide with alarm. "Oh my gosh. And we've heard so little from her. We don't know if she's found out her mission or even if she's still okay."

Though Wendy knew a lot more than Claire, she hadn't heard from Stella in some time. Hopefully, that meant their friend was busy saving the 1856 world and earning the right to return to them. Unless it meant something horrible had happened to keep her from communicating. The last she'd heard Stella was sick, after all.

"I'm scared." Claire's voice trembled.

"Me too."

"Maybe she'll write tonight, knowing it's her last chance."

Last chance. Wendy swallowed. "Yeah. Hopefully."

She should have suggested they both write Stella that instant and mail the letter together. But the train of her deceit of keeping the letters from Claire was so far down the tracks, she didn't know how to reverse it now. She'd have to wait until Claire was asleep and pen a letter by herself.

Claire implored her with misty eyes. "Can we pray together?"

Way to make her feel like the lowest of the low. Here she was plotting further deceit and Claire was turning to the Lord. Why had Wendy ever thought her shallow?

She forced a smile. "That'd be great."

They joined hands and together lifted their hearts to plead for their friend. The moment would have felt almost holy without the weight of deception on Wendy's shoulders.

Once Claire drifted off to sleep, Wendy snuck to the bathroom to pen one last letter.

> Stella,
> This will probably be the last letter we'll get to write you, and we wanted you to know we love you with all our hearts. We hope you are safe and well and that you are accomplishing your mission there. Return to us soon. It isn't the same without you.
> Love,
> Wendy & Claire

She wiped a stray tear from her cheek. So stupid to keep this letter from Claire. They could have easily written it together. It didn't incriminate her at all. And what if Stella didn't return to them and this was their last chance to say goodbye? What if Wendy had stolen that from Claire? She sniffed and patted another tear dry with her shirtsleeve. Too late now. What was done was done. She needed to mail this and get to bed.

She crept out of the room and to the mailbox. Again, there was hardly anyone around. An easy errand. But as she turned to retrace her steps to her room, realization dawned, and dread pooled in her chest. Her key.

She'd forgotten her key.

~

The click of the door had startled Claire from sleep. She rubbed her bleary eyes and squinted as they adjusted to the dimness. Where was Wendy? The bathroom door stood ajar, light off. She must have left. That had to have been what woke her. But why would Wendy leave?

Propping herself onto her elbow, she flipped on the desk light. It wasn't like she could go back to sleep now. She'd been resting fitfully anyway. She kept imagining Stella's ship sinking in the morning.

She scanned the room while stretching her arms wide. In college, it hadn't been unheard of for Wendy to go grab a middle-of-the-night snack if she couldn't sleep. Maybe that was where she had gone. But her opened suitcase stuck out from under her bed, blanket strewn around it. Why would she be riffling through her suitcase in the middle of the night? An eerie feeling settled within. Something was off.

Dropping to her knees, she pulled the suitcase fully free from the blanket entanglement and bed frame. A mesh laundry bag of dirty clothes sat on top. She moved it aside to find a Bible, a couple of books, and … letters? She took out the papers and held them toward the light.

Stella's handwriting graced each page. Claire read a few lines. Sifted through the papers. Read more. This didn't make sense. These sounded like Stella writing from 1856, but they'd only received two letters. There'd been more letters? All these? And Wendy had kept them from her. Why? Because she wasn't smart enough to be in on planning Stella's escape? Because she wasn't a good enough friend to keep her in the loop?

With as many tears as she'd cried in the past couple of days, she should have dried up, but her eyes misted yet again. She was forever left out, always on the outside looking in. Now, her two best friends had joined forces and left her standing out in the cold. Maybe this was her lot in life, to be utterly and completely alone.

Either the letters hadn't been in order, or she'd messed up the order when she'd looked through them because everything was haphazard. She began piecing them together and laying them sequentially on Wendy's bed. How much had she missed?

Footsteps in the hallway caused her to still. The movement thundered in comparison to the quiet night. Was Wendy about to come flying through the door? Would they have another altercation just when they'd finally found common ground? Nothing but silence now. She must have been hearing things. She went back to ordering the letters. But then a tentative knock sounded.

Claire padded to the door. "Who is it?"

"It's me, Wendy. Forgot my key."

She swung the door open and waited for an explanation.

Wendy fiddled with her hair. "Glad you're up. I didn't know what I was going to do."

No excuse as to where she'd gone? Interesting. Maybe she'd met her quota of deceit for one trip. In a few steps, the letter-strewn bed came into view, and Wendy froze.

Claire wrapped her arms around herself, willing her voice not to break. She had to be strong. "No more secrets, huh? Well, this is a big one. Why? Why would you keep this from me?" Pain leeched into her words. So much for her armor.

Wendy's face crumpled, and she collapsed to her knees. "I don't know. I'm so sorry."

With her head bowed, curly hair formed a curtain hiding her face, but sniffles punctuated the air around them as her shoulders shook.

Claire stared, dumbfounded. That certainly wasn't the response she was used to. Around Wendy, she was always braced for a fight. And she could use one about now. A target to lash out against. But this broken, tearful person before her? What was she to do with this?

Claire swiped at her wet cheek. "I'm too stupid to be in on the whole mission thing. Is that it? I know nothing about history and am no help in finding solutions to get her home. Might as well leave me out of the loop." She shrugged as if she could bounce the hurt off her shoulders.

Wendy looked up, and her brow pinched. "What? No, not at all." She scrambled to her feet and put her hands on

Claire's shoulders. "Why in the world would you think you're stupid? You probably saved that family's life. You might have saved Stella's life." She gave Claire a little shake. "You're brilliant, Claire. Don't you know that?"

Brilliant? Yeah, right. Nice try, but those pep talks didn't work on her. She had decades of experience with the truth.

"Look, I made a dumb mistake." Wendy dropped her arms from Claire's shoulders and sat on her bed. "One night when you were asleep, I saw a letter from Stella. I didn't know whether to wake you up or not, but since you were sleeping so peacefully, I decided to read it myself and let you read it in the morning. But then I got excited because she was asking questions I knew the answers to. Finally, I could help her. Be there for her, like I had failed to do for the whole past year. I've been trying to make things up to her, you know? So, I jumped the gun and replied, and then I mailed it, which started a whole train of responses I didn't know how to stop. I never set out to keep you out of the loop. It just happened."

Claire shook her head to erase the last of the sleepy fog. "Wait. Make what up to her? You've said something like that before. I don't get it."

Wendy brought her knees to her chest and wrapped her arms around them. "I ditched her. This whole last year when her grandma was suffering and dying from cancer, I bailed. Friends are supposed to have their friends' backs. 'A friend loves at all times,' right? Only I didn't. I made one excuse after another to not visit. I barely called or texted. I straight up *avoided* my best friend, right up until the funeral. What a loser I am."

Understanding dawned and Claire sat next to Wendy, knees propped in the same position. "You couldn't deal with it. Not after your sister."

Wendy shook her head. "I should have been able to. For a friend like Stella, I should be able to do anything. But I couldn't take the reminders of Lorainne's decline. It hurt too much."

Stella hadn't mentioned a thing about Wendy not being there when she'd needed her. "I'm sure she understood."

"That doesn't make it okay."

"You're so hard on yourself." Claire tucked one of Wendy's curls behind her ear. "I bet that's why you're hard on other people. You might seem critical of others, but you're not nearly as critical of them as you are of yourself. Maybe if you learned to give yourself grace, you could give others grace too." She sucked her bottom lip in between her teeth. "Actually, I bet you have trouble receiving God's grace for yourself. You can't give something to others you don't receive first. Do you feel like you have to do penance?"

Wendy groaned. "Always."

"Then that's something to talk to God about. I'll pray He helps you to receive His grace so you can give it freely to others."

Wendy's eyes glistened as she looked heavenward. "See? You're brilliant."

She'd let that one lie. She was done arguing for now.

Chapter Twenty-Two

Stella's room was surrounded. As daylight waned, she paced, scouring her mind for every available option. At any moment, one of those rough-looking men could barge through her door. No matter that she'd locked it and angled the desk chair underneath the handle. It wouldn't take much to bust through. Or they could break the glass and come through the back. Either way, it would take them but a moment to find the stowaways hidden under her bed.

From what she could make out among the shouts and mumblings from both directions, they were searching for Duncan, not for her specifically. But they wouldn't find him on this boat, and when they didn't, they'd likely question her as she was the last person seen with him. She hadn't come out of her room for breakfast or dinner. It was anyone's guess whether that was the right move or not. It might have created more suspicion than it squelched.

She just had to hold them off until the boat crashed. Then the ensuing mayhem would take everyone's mind off her and Duncan and the missing "cargo." How long did she have? Minutes? An hour? And then what? All the passengers would file onto lifeboats. All the *White* passengers. And all the Black crewmembers were male, save Bridge. It's not like she could sneak them onto a boat along with everyone else.

Someone pounded on her door. "Open up. You're needed for questioning."

She froze. What should she do? Play dumb again? Pretend she wasn't there? Prepare to fight?

The Lord will fight for you. You need only to be still.

The pounding intensified.

"Okay, Lord," she whispered. "Let's see what You can do."

The doorframe cracked and splintered. Stella spread her feet, bracing herself for whatever was to come. The dinner bell chimed in the background, and a murmur of voices rose from the main hall. The doorknob rattled. The chair shook.

"I'm warning you, open up."

Stella breathed deep and exhaled long. A soft whimper sounded from behind her feet. "It'll be okay," she promised.

It probably sounded like an empty assurance, but it had to be true. Had to be.

The chair burst apart as the door slammed open, revealing the reddened face of a beefy man who reminded Stella of a bodyguard. The temptation to wilt in fear rushed at her, but she held strong. *The Lord will fight for me. The Lord will fight for me.*

He strode toward her, fist clenched, when the boat jostled, then tilted to the side, sending both of them stumbling. Screams echoed from all directions, as did the scraping of chairs, stools, and tables tumbling about. Stella's senses tingled with awareness while the meaty bodyguard's eyes widened in alarm.

"What in the blazes?" He rushed from the room.

Stella peeked into the main hall to find mass chaos. The room was a flurry of pandemonium, people jostling one another as they scrambled for the promenade deck.

"We've hit a snag! Water's already covering the bottom deck!"

Stella closed her splintered door and turned toward the family scrambling up from underneath her bed. "Hurry. We've only got minutes before this entire boat will be under water." She slung her already packed bag over her shoulder and ventured a glance out the back door.

The boat was leaning left, and it seemed the passengers had all gone right to wait for lifeboats in the safest above-water spot. "Can you swim?"

The mother, looking flushed and faint, shook her head. Of course not.

"Follow me." She thrust open her back door to reveal water already creeping up the deck. No time. They had no time. *Please, God! Help!* Back pressed against the boat, she inched away from the swirling water. She reached out a hand and took hold of the boy's arm as he emerged from the room. The mother followed, holding the baby. She'd thought the river looked placid compared to the vast ocean she'd left, but now it seemed to be a vicious monster seeking to devour them. Its murky depths hid all sorts of secrets, and the clutches of its current were unforgiving. She couldn't let it steal Smitty. Timothy. Or Cora, weak with fear.

Muddy water swirled around her ankles and nearly reached the boy's knees. They had to move faster. She picked up the pace, but her foot slipped, and she fell to one knee, scraping her leg. She bit back a flinch at the pain and willed herself to focus. The current tugged at her, but she resisted and pulled herself to standing. What to do? How could she get three people who couldn't swim to shore? No lifeboats would be coming to this side of the boat, even if they were desperate enough to risk capture by using them. While lifeboats would scurry the rest of the passengers about as far as the length of the boat itself, Stella would need to usher her bedraggled crew to the opposite shore to avoid detection, a distance at least twice as far.

Her gaze alighted on a piece of driftwood slinking by. Was it large enough? It would have to be. "Wait here," she said, as if they had anywhere else to go. She sloshed through the water, climbed the railing, and swam toward the board. Fishy water seeped into her mouth and something mossy tangled around her ankle. She bobbed toward the board and grasped it with one arm. Pain sliced her hand as splintered wood rubbed against it. Gritting her teeth, she turned and kicked with all her might against the current back toward the woman and children waiting for her.

She got as close as she could. "Grab on," she called to Timothy.

He looked to his mother, asking for permission. She nodded, and he took a flying leap into the water, arms outstretched toward Stella. Floundering to keep hold of the board with one arm, she grasped his wrist as his head bobbed under and yanked him upward, placing his hand on the board.

"I didn't expect you to do that."

He gasped and then smiled impishly. Boys.

"Now, you have to help me hold on to Smitty carefully so your mama can get on here safely."

His goofy grin melted into a solemn nod.

"Hand us the baby." She reached out one arm.

Cora's eyes filled with worry as she gawked at the treacherous waters.

"I know it's scary, but you don't have a choice." She stretched her hand out farther.

Cora angled forward and released her baby with a sob. Stella grabbed hold of Smitty's upper arm and pulled her onto the board. "Hold her other arm," she instructed Timothy. With the baby secure on top of the wood, Stella coaxed Cora into the water and directed her to grab hold of the other side of the board. Then, using every ounce of energy she possessed, Stella paddled them to shore.

~

Wendy was a pile of nerves all day as images of a sinking steamboat flashed through her mind. She needed to get out of their small room before she went mad from being trapped like a caged animal, only Claire still refused to leave. And how could Wendy abandon her?

She tried again. "What if we went to the library? Neo wouldn't go there."

Claire shook her head. "I might run into him on the way. Or someone who saw what happened."

This wasn't healthy. Clearly, fear's iron grip clenched her friend. Understandable, but not okay. How could she help?

"I need to find Dr. Duncan. I have to know how this works, what it looks like for her to come back to us. Come with me. Please?" She held out her hand as a lifeline.

Claire bit her lip.

"Where's Neo's room?"

"Twelfth level, left side."

"Nowhere near Dr. Duncan's room. We'll steer clear of the common areas."

Claire tilted her head. Wavering, perhaps?

"You can wear a disguise." Wendy grabbed Claire's ginormous sun hat from the closet and plopped it on her head.

A hint of a smile rewarded her. "Okay."

"Okay? Great." She slipped on her flip-flops and headed toward the door before Claire could change her mind. "Let's go."

When Claire dragged her feet, sulking behind, Wendy looped her arm through her friend's arm and propelled her forward. "Want to take the stairs instead of the elevator?"

Claire sniffed. "I first met Neo on the stairs."

Okay, then. Elevator it was. Wendy did her best to block everyone's view of Claire, not that anyone was paying much attention. People talked amongst themselves or scrolled on their phones. No one seemed to be on the lookout for the subject of the latest celebrity prank.

They exited the elevator and made their way down the hallway littered with discarded food trays.

"I think I'm going to shut down all my social media." Claire sounded on the verge of tears. Again.

Wendy slowed her steps. "Shut it down? What about—"

"I was waiting to hear from Fit TV. I haven't yet, but that's got to be the right thing to do. Bow out of it. Say goodbye to the ridiculous rat race."

"But this is your livelihood."

"Not anymore, I'm sure." She dabbed at the corner of her eyes with her pointer fingers. "Maybe I could work at a health food shop. I'd like that."

Wendy put a hand on her shoulder and bent to meet her eyes. "You're giving up? Because of one jerk face?"

"I don't see any other way."

Oh, heck no. There was no way she was letting nasty Neo ruin her friend's future. She cast a glance toward Dr. Duncan's door. But this was a longer conversation for another time and place. "We'll talk about this later." She gave Claire's shoulder a squeeze, then closed the distance and knocked on the door. And knocked again, harder.

No answer.

"I bet he's on the top deck."

Claire lifted a brow.

"He's always on the top deck." Oh yeah, that was another thing she'd kept from her friend, though not intentionally. "I had a whole conversation with him one night up there, not to mention the one on our first port day."

"You what?" Claire's mouth dropped open.

"I'll fill you in on the way." She expected Claire to protest, considering venturing to the top deck meant passing all sorts of people who might know about the incident at the beach, but apparently, her friend's curiosity overrode her inhibitions. Wendy told her about both conversations with the mysterious descendant of Stella's Dr. Duncan as they made their way upstairs.

"You were going to ditch me for 1856? Leave me here all by myself?"

Wendy winced. "You seemed content."

Claire shuddered. "What would I have done if you hadn't come to my rescue on the beach?"

Good question. Maybe God knew what He was doing after all.

They approached the infamous top deck railing of her previous encounters with the doctor, but he wasn't there.

Wendy stared at the empty space as if he might materialize before her eyes.

"What now?" Claire asked.

"I have no idea."

"You didn't exchange phone numbers?"

Wendy snorted out a laugh. "Didn't even think of it. That's where your input comes in handy."

"We could wait here for a bit. See if he shows up?" Claire turned her face to the sea breeze. "It feels good to be out of that stuffy room."

It sure did. Sitting in the sun was as good a plan as any.

They found lounge chairs and leaned back, basking in the warmth. Too bad they hadn't dressed for this. Then again, it might be a while before Claire would wear a swimsuit in public again.

Claire pulled out her phone. "Okay. I'm going to do it."

"Do what?" Wendy sat up, ready to swipe the phone from Claire's grasp if she meant what she thought she meant. She'd throw Stella's phone overboard again if it meant saving Claire from throwing away her future over a stupid boy.

"Delete— Wait, what's this?"

~

Claire's thumb hovered over the private Facebook message request. She didn't normally pay them any heed, but it was a good thing she'd read the last one that had tipped her off to the celebrity prank group, even if the realization had been intensely painful. But this message was from an Angelica *Duncan*.

She couldn't *not* read it.

"What's what?" Wendy asked.

She held up a finger and clicked on the message.

> I saw your video asking for information about the *Arabia,* and I'm curious as to why you're interested. One of my ancestors was on that

boat when it sank, and our family has a long history of maritime travel. Might you have a personal reason for asking about it? Something about a mission?

Claire catapulted up and grabbed Wendy's arm. "It's a Duncan."

"Huh?"

"I got a message from a Duncan. She knows. She knows about time-sailing." Claire read Angelica's message to Wendy.

"Oh my gosh! We need to talk to her. Can we video chat?"

"Maybe tomorrow when we get to Canada. We won't have a strong enough signal while at sea."

"Ask her!" Wendy scooted next to Claire on her lounge chair, looking over her shoulder.

"Okay, okay."

Yes, I have a personal reason for asking, and yes, it involves a mission.

Wendy's hair brushed Claire's shoulder. "Ask her to video chat."

"Let's see how she replies to this first." Just in case.

Wendy made an exasperated sound. "She obviously knows."

"Forgive me for wanting to be a bit more cautious, considering everything I've been through."

"Okay." Wendy gave her a side hug, and Claire's defenses fell. The fight leaving Wendy so easily was new. Nice.

We've encountered people who have had friends and family disappear while on boats. The missing person ends up in a different place and time. Is this what happened to someone you know?

Wendy shoved her shoulder good-naturedly. "See?"
Claire typed a reply.

A friend started on this cruise with us and then vanished. She sent a letter saying she's on the *Arabia*. Can you video chat tomorrow?

"Is that okay? What if I misinterpreted her message? If she doesn't know anything, she'll think I'm crazy."

"How could you misinterpret that? It's pretty clear. Send it."

When Claire hesitated, Wendy pushed the send button. "Guess you're going to have to wait to shut down your social media." She shot Claire a smug grin.

"I could close down everything *but* Facebook."

Wendy placed her hand on Claire's and squeezed. "Please don't. Sometimes you just need a little more time to gain a different perspective. Wait."

Claire closed her eyes and nodded as she filled her lungs with fresh, salty air. If only she could believe a new perspective, a new life, waited around the corner.

Chapter Twenty-Three

It was remarkable how fast the boat she'd been standing upon mere moments before sank beneath the water. Stella had thought the fathomless ocean depths formidable, but this river must be raging over quicksand. Wendy's claims had seemed exaggerated until the Muddy Missouri devoured the *Arabia* before her eyes. It'd been a handful of minutes, ten at most, and only the pilot house poked up through the current. But they'd all survived. Thank God, everyone had survived.

Wendy was right. If those stowaways had been in that crate … She shuddered. She looked at them, drenched and shivering. Cora clung to her children, smothering their dripping hair with kisses. Stella wrung out the hem of her dress, casting glances across the river to the opposite bank where Mrs. Scott exited a lifeboat, sobbing dramatically. She scoured the shoreline for Trevor to no avail.

What now? This poor family remained in a slave state, and the mother and children were separated from the father. Nothing about this situation proved safe. Where were they? Wendy had said somewhere outside of Parkville, wherever that was. It was anyone's guess how to get them to free Kansas from here. But Kansas was west of Missouri, that much had stuck from geography class. So perhaps all she needed to do was follow the direction of the rapidly setting sun.

With a deep sigh, she took a step forward. *You're still with me, right, Jesus? If You want to redirect me, this is a great time.* Grammy Rose had always said it was easier to guide a moving ship. Of all the idioms Grammy had spouted, that one perhaps rang the truest right currently. Stella's ship had been stuck in the harbor, afraid to move.

"Follow me." Hopefully, her proffered smile looked more confident than she felt.

Cora held Smitty in her arms while Timothy clung to the fabric of her dress. Darkness drank up the air around them, and they stumbled over rocks and tree roots. Mosquitos buzzed, making Stella's skin itch with the sound. Beside them, the river that had just monstrously gulped their boat now hummed a placid melody.

Did she plan on walking all night in inky darkness? Until what? She passed a Welcome to Kansas sign?

Lord, I have no idea what I'm doing. Help!

A dark figure emerged from the shadows ahead, face shrouded by the night as well as by a black hat. Stella gasped and flung her arm out in front of Cora, as if that alone would protect her. "Stay behind me," she whispered. "And play along."

She'd pretend like they were her slaves, and they had every right to be with her, though what kind of story could she concoct as to why they were wandering by the riverbank late at night? And sopping wet? If asked where she was from, she didn't know the area well enough to say. *God, don't let him ask many questions.*

The figure drew nearer, but with tentative steps, not the bold ones of an accuser. And this was a dark-skinned man. Her shoulders relaxed. He shouldn't cause them any problems … unless he was out for the bounty.

"Cora?" the man rasped.

"Trevor?" Cora's voice wobbled.

Stella squinted through the darkness and nearly squealed when he took off his hat and revealed his face.

"Daddy!" Timothy ran to his father and threw his arms around his legs.

Trevor's soft chuckle melted into the night as his wife joined in the embrace.

"How'd you find us?" Stella leaned in for a side hug, her smile broad.

"I saw you'se swim to safety from the other side, but I had to go downriver a ways to find someone who'd help me cross. You'll never guess who I found." His white teeth gleamed in the moonlight.

She narrowed her eyes. "Who?"

"Dr. Duncan. He's set up a contact for us to help us get the rest of the way to freedom. He's waiting for us downriver."

Of course, it was him. Good for them. A bubble of satisfaction filled her chest. This was her mission. It had to be. And she'd accomplished it. This family was alive and well and headed for freedom, and she'd gotten the chance to play a small but important part in their journey. She wasn't the hero of their story—they were the ones who deserved such a title—but she'd done her part, and she was thankful for the opportunity.

But a question poked at her. She stepped closer to Trevor and spoke softly so Timothy wouldn't overhear. "What happened the day you were supposed to warn them?"

"Got caught up. Some scoundrels sectioned off us colored workers and pelted us with questions, trying to find out who had abolitionist ties. Even after they was done with me, I couldn't risk going to my family. They was watching us all."

The gravity of what they'd been through, what could have happened, peppered her arms with goosebumps. "Good call."

Thank You, Lord, for keeping everyone safe.

She hugged each one of them goodbye. Was that improper in this time period? She didn't care. After what they'd been through together, she couldn't imagine doing less. "I'll never forget you." She fought back against the surge of emotion threatening to spill forth.

"You don't want to come with us to Dr. Duncan?" Trevor asked.

She looked back to where the remnant of the *Arabia* shown in the distance. To get back to her life didn't she need to stay close to the boat?

"No, thanks."

"Okay, then." The four of them clung together, offering her parting smiles and waves. "Thank you for all you'se done."

She could say it was nothing, that she'd only done what anyone else would have, given the circumstances, but she'd be lying. Maybe she'd only done what anyone *should* have done, but this assignment had changed her. It had turned her inside out and caused her to confront the fear lurking inside. Had it transformed her into who she'd always wanted to be? Or unlocked a piece of her always there but held captive all her life? Either way, it wasn't nothing.

She watched them disappear into the distance, surrendering to the trees' shadows until they emerged to fill what looked to be a fishing boat. *Lord, continue to keep them safe. Protect them all the way to freedom. Let them live a long and happy life.*

She hugged herself, now chilled by the evening breeze whipping against her still-damp dress. Wisps of hair, having been released from her bun, tangled into her vision. What now? She was utterly alone in 1856, without Duncan, Bridge, or any other friend. Without a mailbox or a way to contact Wendy and Claire. Without a boat. She'd accomplished her mission—surely she had—and yet, here she was. Still here. Still stuck.

What if Duncan had been wrong and there was no going back? What if this was her life now? No marrying Everett. No returning to her friends and family. Her job. Her life. What if she had to make a new life for herself here, in Missouri before the Civil War?

Just the thought of it made her head throb. She rubbed her temples and turned around to walk back the way she'd come. She could barely make out the *Arabia* now. Talk about a fast sinking. To think they'd made a three-hour movie about the *Titanic* going under. If the *Arabia's* demise were turned into a motion picture, it'd be more like commercial length.

A wave of dizziness washed over her, and she stilled, trying to regain her bearings. She hadn't eaten all day and had drunk little. After the life-threatening ordeal she'd undergone, it wasn't a surprise her body protested. Still, with no restaurants in sight, it didn't look like that problem would be remedied anytime soon. This is where DoorDash would come in handy.

When she started to walk forward again, she swayed. Okay, this wasn't good. She couldn't faint in the middle of nowhere on the riverbank. She clenched her teeth against the pounding in her head and sat on a rocky section of the bank. Rubbing her hands against her shaking legs, she fought a swell of panic.

She couldn't stay here all night, but where could she go? She searched the horizon for any hint of hope. There wasn't a person to be seen or heard on her side of the riverbank. Perhaps she *should* try to find Duncan.

Across the river, faint firelight shone. The other passengers perhaps. Were they camping there? She was tempted to smile at the thought of those proper first-class women reduced to camping in primitive conditions. But loneliness and worry engulfed her, and she couldn't make her mouth turn upward.

But wait. What was that? Moonlight illuminated what looked to be a small rowboat tied to a nearby pole. For some inexplicable reason, it drew her. Was it simply because she'd spent so much time on the water as of late that land felt oddly motionless to her? The need to get into that boat clawed at her until she could no longer sit still. She stumbled toward it, head aching, vision blurring. She would appear drunk to anyone who looked on, but of course, there was no one. No one to observe her blatantly trespassing. What had gotten into her?

Lord, forgive me. I don't want to steal this boat. Just sleep in it for the night. Yes, that was it. She yawned and stepped into the boat, falling to her knees. The vessel swayed on the water, droplets of moisture splashing upward, but it didn't capsize. It smelled heavily of fish, but it wrapped her in a feeling of warmth and safety as she lay down, using her bag as a pillow.

Fatigue gripped her, pulling her down into a drowsy abyss. She would gladly give in, but something stopped her. There was something she needed to do.

Everett. She forced her eyes open. She needed to make things right with Everett. Which was crazy because she had no way of contacting him, but still, she had to try. She dug through her bag, pulled out Claire's phone, and powered it on. This was ridiculous. Of course, she wouldn't get a signal. Obviously, a text wouldn't send. But the burden of her heart begged to be released.

> Everett, it's Stella. I need to tell you how I've wronged you and that I'm so very sorry.

She proceeded to pour out the whole wretched story via text, tears punctuating her sentences as they hit the screen. From the first hint she had that something was off with the job to the last jerky thing her boss had said that she'd never spoken up against. She confessed it all.

> I do love you. I'm sorry I haven't spoken up when I needed to. I was afraid. I think that's changing.

She inhaled a shuddering breath. It was, wasn't it? She'd done numerous things these past two weeks that would have had her deep-diving into sheer panic before. *Please, Lord. Let this be a lasting change.*

> I hope so. And I hope you can find it in your heart to forgive me.

Finally, when she futilely hit send, she felt lighter somehow. If only she could really tell him. But if God would get him this message and allow her confession to clear her conscience, maybe they could start afresh. Or maybe he'd never forgive her. Either way, it had to be better than living under the weight of guilt.

Now released, she gave in to her heavy eyelids and the fatigue that pressed on her. Perhaps she could face this new reality far better after a good night's sleep.

~

Wendy had barely relaxed her head against the lounge chair next to Claire when Dr. Duncan bustled up to them.

"There you are. I've been looking for you."

She launched forward as if someone had pressed a lever to straighten a recliner. "You've been looking for us? We were looking for you."

He ran a hand through his hair. "I remembered something."

She flashed a wide-eyed glance at Claire before turning her attention back to Dr. Duncan. "What?"

"The lurching—do you know about the lurching?"

She nodded. "It fast-forwards time."

"Yes, but *not* if someone is in the middle of completing their mission. The mission supersedes everything. So, if someone lurches in time, they weren't in the process of their mission yet. And if there's a snag, and they don't lurch, they were."

Wendy threw her head back and groaned. "That would have been helpful to know earlier. Stella thought she'd missed her mission because of the lurching."

"Not at all."

"Now you tell us," Claire mumbled.

He stuffed his hands into his pockets. "Sorry. These fragments of my grandfather's conversations are coming back to me little by little."

"Anything else? Anything about how time sailors get back?"

He tilted his head up, as if he could find the answer among the clouds. "I think they just have to be on water to return."

Wendy stood and paced, nervous energy pulsing through her. "On water. What does that mean exactly? Will she be able to return once her boat sinks?"

"She'll have to find another boat."

"Another boat?"

Claire stood and planted her hands on her hips. "What kind of boat? A steamboat?"

"I don't think it matters. She just needs to be on the water. But don't worry. She'll get there. Grandpa always said when it was time to go, it was like a magnet pulled the time sailor toward the water. They were powerless to resist. Like how salmon return to their home stream."

Wendy narrowed her eyes at him. "You're only now remembering this?"

He shrugged. "Like I said, it's coming back to me."

Okay, fine. She'd take what she could get. "But does it ever not happen? Does anyone not return home afterward?" She braced herself for an answer she might not want to hear.

He rocked back on his heels. "Every story Grandpa told had a happy ending. Maybe he left the sad ones out." A wistful smile played on his lips. "The idealist in me would like to think that's just how things happened. Each with a satisfying conclusion."

So, they'd sit back and trust salmon-level instinct to guide Stella to a boat so she'd return home? With only one full day left of the cruise, she'd better find a water-faring vessel quickly.

"Thanks," she offered weakly. His information had been helpful, even if she would have appreciated it much earlier.

He gave a nod, clicked his heels against the deck, then turned.

"Wait," Claire called.

He stopped and faced her.

"How are you related to Angelica Duncan?"

His face wrinkled. "No idea. But I never made it to any family reunions. I have a flock of second and third cousins I've never met. Could be any number of people."

He turned again and made it a few steps before Wendy called after him, "Wait."

This time, humor lit his eyes as he faced her, brow lifted.

"Are you a real doctor?"

"PhD in marine biology." He winked.

Wendy and Claire exchanged a smile as Dr. Duncan strode off. He was linked to the water in his own way.

Maybe after this trip, they all would be.

~

Claire ducked her head as they followed the waiter to their table for dinner. How had she let Wendy talk her into going to the restaurant? At least Neo had always passed on formal dining in favor of the casual atmosphere of the café. She wouldn't likely run into him here. But what about people who had seen what happened? Her cheeks burned.

They sat, and Claire hid behind a menu.

Wendy gave her hand a squeeze. "Relax. No one's watching."

If only she could relax and forget everything that had happened. Not anytime soon. But at least she wasn't holed up in her room any longer. Progress.

Wendy gently pried the menu from her grasp. "You know what I think?"

Claire winced. Did she want to know?

"I think you think you're unintelligent."

She feigned a jaw drop. "Wow, Sherlock. How long did it take you to crack that case?" The sides of her mouth twitched upward.

"I'm serious. I haven't a clue why, but you think you're stupid. That changes how you act toward people, how you respond. And it changes how people respond to you."

Claire bristled. "What's that supposed to mean?"

"You attract loser guys like that salmon magnetic thing."

She couldn't argue there, but … "Are you saying that it's my fault?" She crossed her arms.

"I'm saying … What am I saying?" Wendy paused and closed her eyes. When she reopened them and spoke again, her words rang with clarity. "Why do you think you're stupid? Who told you that?"

She raised her brows. "Literally everyone."

Wendy pointed a finger at her. "Not true. Try again."

"My parents. Blake Adams. Troy. Ryan."

"Okay, hold on. Blake the Snake. I remember that story. So, Blake tells you to wear a sports bra and look hot for a picture for the class project, and you believed that was the only thing you were good for?"

"Not exactly." But at least somewhat. Had he planted the seed or only watered it? Either way.

"When did you start dressing like that?"

Their waiter came by, but Wendy waved him off, asking for a few more minutes.

"Like what?"

"Don't get me wrong. You can pull it off and look amazing. If I wore what you do, I'd look like a before picture in a weight loss commercial. I'm not trying to judge here. I'm just wondering why you show so much skin. If you don't want people to focus on your body, why do you highlight it?"

Her question, though spoken kindly, stung, and Claire scanned the menu selections to avoid the ramifications. When Wendy's hand covered the salad choices, Claire met her eye. "It's expected in my line of work. I have to dress for my job."

"Of course." Wendy nodded. "I guess I'm wondering if doing YouTube videos is actually your ideal job. When you were young, what did you dream of doing with your life?"

Claire shifted her jaw. Good question. One with many answers. "A holistic doctor. A chiropractor. A missionary. A nutritional scientist."

Wendy grinned and patted her arm. "That's it. I knew it was in there. And somewhere along the line, people like Blake the Snake convinced you that you weren't good enough for any of those things. Except I think you are."

If only it were that simple, but Claire cracked a smile for her well-meaning friend.

"If you were a nutritional scientist, would you show up to work in a crop top and leggings? Heck no. Why don't you start taking yourself seriously? Then maybe other people will take you seriously, and you can get out of this rut." She threw up both hands. "Unless you truly want to do the YouTube thing. I will support you in whatever. You've got a gift for connecting with people and building a following. I'm sorry for not appreciating that sooner."

She had to laugh. She covered her mouth with her hand but couldn't suppress her giggles.

"What?"

She shook her head, unable to speak. Wendy was still fully opinionated Wendy, but the way she'd just expressed herself was thoughtful and kind. But also direct. And sweet.

After they ordered, she continued to ruminate. "I've thought I was dumb for years. Years, Wendy."

"Do you think Jesus would agree?" Wendy skewered her with the intensity of her gaze.

"No," she whispered. She splayed her hands on the table, clarity dawning. "No. I don't think Jesus thinks I'm dumb."

Wendy placed her hand over Claire's and squeezed. "Of course, He doesn't."

Claire grabbed on and squeezed back. "Seriously, this is a revelation. I never thought to ask Jesus what He thought about me. Have I been going through life harboring an opinion about myself that is directly opposite to Jesus's opinion?"

Wendy tilted her head, squinting. "Technically, I don't think Jesus has opinions. Whatever He thinks is true, so He only has facts."

Well, there was a thought. What facts did Jesus know about her that she hadn't considered? Unconsidered possibilities unfurled with promise inside of her as they ordered and began to dine. She couldn't wait to spend time alone with the Lord and journal all He would surely reveal to her.

Claire had just forked a bite of salad into her mouth when her phone rang. Wait, what? Rang? She stared at the device open-mouthed. Angelica's Facebook profile picture flashed on the screen along with the green phone icon to answer her video call. But they weren't close to Canada yet. How was she getting a signal?

Wendy nudged her shoulder. "Answer it!"

"Here?" Claire looked around the dining room filled with tuxedoed waiters serving tables of chatting guests.

"Hurry. Before she hangs up."

Claire swiped the answer icon as if it might bite. "Hello?"

A friendly-looking blonde with thick, wavy hair smiled back. "Hi, Claire? It's Angelica Duncan. Is this a bad time?"

Was it? Just seeing herself in the little box on the phone screen caused apprehension to rise.

Wendy slid into her hesitation, scooting next to her on the bench seat. "No, not at all. I'm Claire's friend Wendy. We were just finishing dinner. It's nice to meet you."

Claire cast a glance at her half-eaten salad. Finishing up? Maybe she should enjoy her meal and call back later. After all, she hadn't planned out what to say. She should at least have a list of questions to ask.

"It's nice to meet you as well." Angelica's warmth sought to put Claire at ease, but anxiety hummed a steady background rhythm inside of her. Would she ever be free of it again? "I hope you don't mind, but my brother, Bearett, is with me here. He wanted to join in on our chat." She angled the camera to the side, and a man's face came into view.

A freshly shaven, good-looking face.

What was wrong with her? She had to be devoid of brain cells to be looking at any man with an ounce of interest after what had happened with Neo. She needed to swear off men indefinitely. Buy a cat. Learn to knit sweaters.

Wendy waved at the camera. "Of course, we don't mind. Nice to meet you, Bearett." She gestured for Claire to get up, and with a pouty face toward her salad, Claire did so. The two walked out of the dining area and to a couple of chairs in an alcove where they sat.

"Tell us everything you know," Wendy said.

Seriously? Here? This part of the boat didn't get much traffic, but it wasn't exactly private. What if people overheard this conversation about time-sailing and thought them crazy? "Maybe we should—"

Wendy silenced her with a hand to her arm and a subtle headshake.

Claire sighed. Why did she care if people thought she was crazy anyway? Other people's opinions didn't truly matter. Hadn't she just learned that?

"We grew up with our dad telling us stories of people he called time sailors." The siblings shared a conspiratorial grin. "He heard these stories from his father, who heard them from his father, I guess. Stories about people disappearing from boats and ending up somewhere on a different boat in the past."

Claire found her voice. "Did you believe the stories?"

Angelica shook her head. "Not at first. But then—"

Bearett joined in to finish her sentence. "We kept running into them." They both laughed, then he continued, "Not the time sailors themselves, but friends and family who said their loved ones had disappeared." His kind eyes sought out Claire's. "Is that what happened to you? Did someone you love disappear while you were on the cruise ship?"

"Yeah. Our best friend."

"Did you find out about the mailbox? There's always some kind of mailbox."

She nodded. Crazy how tears wanted to slide out now, of all times. Maybe it was the feeling of being understood by these people.

Wendy jumped in. "We think she discovered her mission and was in the process of completing it, but she hasn't returned yet. And now her ship has sunk, and there's no way to get ahold of her."

"The *Arabia*," Angelica said to her brother.

"Oh yeah. That's right."

"Wait," Claire said as she straightened. "Why do you keep running into time-sailing situations. That's strange, right?"

The two shrugged at each other before turning back to face them.

"I don't know. It's the way it has always been with our family. Our dad and grandpa had run-ins with time sailors too," Angelica said.

Bearett brushed a lock of blonde hair from his face. "At first, we thought those were merely more stories, but after we had experiences of our own, we believed them."

"If it was a family thing, it would explain Rodney," Wendy mumbled.

"Do you know a Rodney Duncan?" Claire asked. "He's on this cruise."

"Rodney?" Angelica's brow furrowed. "Let me check the family tree." She disappeared for a moment, leaving Claire with a clear view of Bearett's sun kissed face.

"She's into all that genealogy stuff." He gave an adorable what's-a-guy-to-do shrug.

A moment later, Angelica filled the screen, papers in hand. "Does Rodney look to be in his early fifties?"

Claire and Wendy nodded.

"Then it looks like his grandfather Roy was brothers with our great-grandfather Andy."

For some reason, Claire's shoulders relaxed at the news. "So, you *are* related. And he knows what he's talking about?"

"Appears so."

She let out a deep breath. "Because he said she'd be magnetically drawn to a boat when it was time to come back. He said the instinct would be so strong she wouldn't be able to resist." She fiddled with her hands in her lap. "We've been so worried about her. We want to make sure she gets back okay."

"I'm sure." Bearett leaned toward the camera. "It's got to be nerve-racking, what you're going through. It's a test of faith, for sure. Do you mind if we pray for you? I don't know if you're into that kind of thing or not—"

"We're believers. Christians." Claire laughed. Of all the bizarre connections to make on this crazy trip, had they connected with the family of God? True brothers and sisters, not pretenders? "Yes, please pray."

Wendy grabbed her hand and squeezed as Angelica's sweet voice and Bearett's rich baritone covered them in prayer and peace.

Claire's smile as she thanked them when they finished was full and genuine.

Bearett returned it. "Keep in touch, you guys. Please. Let us know when she returns."

When she returns.

For the first time in days, Claire was filled with hope for tomorrow.

Chapter Twenty-Four

S tella shifted her position, eager to ease the pain in her cramped back. Was it morning yet? She blinked open tired eyes, expecting either twinkling stars or a shaft of sun to greet her. Instead, white blurred in her vision. She rubbed her eyelids. White plastic? And not five feet above her.

Her heart pounded with sudden adrenaline as she scrambled to a sitting position. Where was she? What had happened to her boat? She slapped at the white walls that encased her. She'd been lying on a bench, using her bag as a pillow. The pounding of her hands on the walls echoed in her ears as she surveyed rows of sterile benches. A lifeboat? How ironic.

There. Behind her and to the left was an opening to this … whatever this was. She grabbed her bag and stumbled to it, starving for oxygen. She poked her head outside and gulped in fresh air, relishing the sunshine on her skin. Was that music? She looked down.

A white ladder separated her from a strip of deck below. A familiar-looking deck. She squinted in the direction of the music. The "Cupid Shuffle"? Her eyes grew wide. Was she back? The insignia on the side of the ship proclaimed it was true. She stifled her cry by covering her mouth. She'd never been so happy to hear modern dance music in her life. She sniffed the air. She'd never been so delighted to smell breakfast tacos either.

Wendy. Claire. She had to find them ASAP. She only needed to figure a way down from … Where was she? Another glance around and she laughed out loud.

She slung her bag over her shoulder, and carefully descended the ladder. As her feet hit the deck, an older man stopped directly in front of her.

"What were you doing up there? They didn't make an announcement, did they?" He cast a worried glance at the cloudless sky.

"No." She tried for a reassuring smile. "Just a safety check. Everything looks good."

"Okay, then." He nodded and moved on.

Now, where could she find Wendy and Claire? What time was it anyway?. She should have regained the ability to use Claire's phone with her arrival. She pulled it out and turned it on. Eight in the morning. They might be in their room, or they could be at breakfast. As she considered what to do, the phone blew up with notifications.

After two weeks away from technology, the barrage of chimes overstimulated her. She couldn't deal with it, not right now, and she was about to stuff the phone back in her bag when Everett's name caught her eye. He'd texted this phone.

Apprehension surged with the memory of how *she* had texted *him* last night. But it didn't go through, right? It couldn't have.

With a trembling finger, she expanded the text.

> Stells, thank you for telling me. I know that must have been hard for you. I can't say I'm not hurt or disappointed in what you did. I'm also proud of you for confiding in me. Let's talk when you get back, and we can face this together. Love you, Ev.

Stella's throat burned. Did that mean he forgave her? The burden she'd been carrying since her first meeting with her boss slid off her shoulders. Yes, they still had decisions to make, perhaps hard ones. But if they were making them together, she'd be okay. *Thank You, Lord. You knew what You were doing when You told us to confess our sins to one another so that we could be healed.* He was pretty smart like that. To think each day was an opportunity to grow in trusting Him more.

She closed out of the text thread, ready to rush to the café to see if she could spot her friends, but another text caught her attention.

> Hi, it's Aubrey from Fit TV. We've loved what we've seen this week and provided you can pull off that big Live event Trenia mentioned, we're ready to offer you the deal. Our office will give you a call in a few days to work out the details.

Wait, what? Claire was going to get picked up by a TV network? Stella nearly squealed. How amazing for her! What in the world had she missed in these past two weeks? She rushed toward the elevators to get to the café but then pivoted around toward the stairwell. Better not take any chances, considering how her last trip in an elevator had gone. She wasn't going to let anything get in the way of her connecting with her friends this time.

~

Wendy hovered in front of the elevator like a lunatic, ready to pounce on Stella should she be one of the people to step off. Her friend *had* to return today because they disembarked tomorrow morning. And there was no way Wendy was getting off this boat without Stella.

"You don't think this is the least bit ridiculous?" Claire asked, leaning against the antique mailbox.

"Not at all. We lost her at the elevators, so it only makes sense we'll find her at them. And the mailbox has been our point of contact the entire time."

"Yeah, but what if she shows up on the top deck where she was supposed to meet us in the first place."

Okay, she had a point. What had made Wendy sure this was the best spot to wait for Stella's return? She'd claimed instinct, but perhaps it was only desperation. She had to do something, wait somewhere.

The elevator chime dinged, and the doors slid open. Wendy scanned each face and tried not to let disappointment take hold when Stella's wasn't among them. They had all day. *Lord, please don't let it take all day.*

A notification of a Facebook message sounded from both her and Claire's phone at the same time. She pulled her phone from her pocket and smiled at the group message sent from Angelica to Bearett and the two of them.

> Please let us know as soon as she arrives. We're praying.

She met Claire's eye and nodded for her to reply with their thanks.

Oops. She'd missed a text from Grayson.

> Good morning, beautiful. Isn't your friend supposed to get back from her mission soon?

She wasn't ready to answer that one. Stella would get to decide who knew her story, and if she didn't want Grayson in the loop, Wendy would respect that. She wasn't quite sure how she'd *not* tell him, but she'd figure out a way.

She hadn't left Claire's side since *the incident* and thus hadn't gotten to indulge in any more of Grayson's scrumptious kisses, but he texted often enough. That was promising, right? If he meant to taper off their relationship in preparation for a full-scale breakup, he had a strange way of going about it.

The elevator opened again, and another wave of disappointment met her. No Stella.

Claire sighed. "This might be a long day."

"No kidding." Maybe it was a stupid idea.

A few people brushed by, and recognition lit at the girl's straight brown hair. "Hi, Allison." Wendy spoke without thinking it through, without considering who was walking next to her student.

Allison turned and offered a shy wave, but Mrs. Gardenia pivoted around and shot Wendy a fiery glare. "You."

Wendy swallowed, then forced a polite smile. "Hello, Mrs. Gardenia."

She stalked closer and pointed a finger at Wendy's face. "I've been meaning to talk to you."

Wendy stepped back. "Oh?"

"I told you to stay away from my daughter. I made that crystal clear. And yet, what do you do? You text her." A vein throbbed in her neck. "You carry on an inappropriate texting relationship with my twelve-year-old daughter."

What was she insinuating? Allison had asked her advice about a boy's character, and she'd given it. That was all. "Hardly inappropriate."

"Considering I had expressly commanded you not to communicate with her, *any* contact would have been inappropriate. And the school board is going to hear about it."

Wendy inhaled slowly through her nose. This had to stop. *Lord, give me the words.* The words of a verse, "A gentle answer turns away wrath," came to mind. Could she give a gentle answer? The Lord sure was gentle with her when she was far from deserving of such tender treatment. She calmed at the thought.

"Mrs. Gardenia, I'm not sure how we got off on the wrong foot, but I want to apologize. I think I must have said something that offended you."

"Everything that comes out of your mouth is offensive."

No, she would not take the bait. "Can you tell me specifically what I said or did that hurt you?"

The woman flinched at the word *hurt*. Was that what was at the heart of the matter? One eye narrowed. "I know all about teachers like you. You think educators know more about the children than parents do, and you're out to strip parental rights away." Her voice hitched on the last word.

Wendy's mouth parted. Where had she gotten that?

"I learned about it in a parent advocacy group," Mrs. Gardenia said, as if Wendy had spoken her question out loud. "Your name is on the list of teachers to keep an eye on, which makes sense as outspoken as you are. You'd have no problem steamrolling over parents' wishes—our rights and responsibilities—to achieve your own agenda." She huffed.

Wendy closed her eyes briefly, putting the pieces together. Of course. She'd heard rumblings about the group among the staff as well as PTO members. Though the group was founded with good intentions, a few of the members seemed to be on a witch hunt for people to blame. Apparently, they'd named her among the guilty because she had a loud mouth.

"I assure you, that's not the case. I am one hundred percent on your team as a parent, Mrs. Gardenia. I believe I cannot do my job as an educator without having a healthy partnership with those at home. I'm not sure what I said that gave you that impression, but I promise you, I meant nothing in that vein."

The woman opened her mouth as if to respond but closed it again. Allison stood in the background, watching wide-eyed.

Wendy's heart filled with compassion for this mother who took her position seriously and didn't want any educational system to strip away her rights to the daughter she loved fiercely. A mama bear if there ever was one.

"I'm not your enemy, but I *am* a good teacher. I'm good at what I do because I care tenaciously for my students, and I push them to be their best instead of allowing them to take the easy way out." She winked at Allison. "Before advocating for the school board to fire me, please take time to consult my colleagues and students. And please consider that in vying for a replacement for me, you might be filling my slot with the kind of person you're hoping to avoid."

Allison came up next to her mom. "She really is a great teacher. I learned the most in her class."

Mrs. Gardenia put her arm around her daughter, her face far less red than it had been. "Thank you for clarifying." She tucked her hair behind her ear. "I'll take what you've said into consideration."

"I appreciate it."

While she didn't exactly smile as she walked off, she wasn't frowning or huffing out threats. Wendy would count that as a win.

Claire walked up and wrapped Wendy in a hug. "Wow. You handled that so well. I'm super proud of you."

Wendy squeezed back. "I did, didn't I? It felt good."

"Hey, I hope you saved some hugs for me." Stella's voice startled them apart.

Wendy turned toward the elevators, only to realize the sound had come from the other direction. She spun around, and there was Stella, wearing the same sundress she'd worn the day they'd last seen her.

"Stells!" Wendy nearly tackled her friend to the ground a second before Claire joined the huddle.

Stella hung on tight. "Oh my gosh, I missed you both so much."

When they almost knocked into an elderly couple, Wendy linked arms with both friends and steered them toward the sitting area outside. "You have to tell us everything."

"Same." Stella grinned.

Wendy checked her watch. "We have almost twelve hours before we dock in Victoria, so that should be plenty of time to catch up."

As they all sat around a table, Stella propped her elbows on the tabletop. "Okay, but when do you do the big Live bash, Claire?"

Claire stared back at her. "How'd you know about that?" Before giving her a chance to answer, she shook her head. "I'm not doing it. I'm going to quit my channel."

"What?" Stella pulled Claire's phone from her bag. "Fit TV wants to sign you. They just need you to do a big Live bash to seal the deal."

~

Claire stared at her phone in Stella's hand. "What?"

Stella lifted a shoulder. "You got a text. Sorry to snoop. Curiosity got the best of me." She slid the phone across the table. "Here. Read for yourself. Then please explain."

She picked up the phone and read. Her hands flew to the top of her head, then to her cheeks, her mouth, and her head again. "She sent this after the whole debacle on the beach. I still have a chance. You've got to be kidding me." She searched Wendy's beaming face. "What if they don't know yet, but they hire me and then find out?"

Wendy shook her head. "They know. It's their job to find out everything about the people they hire. She looked between her two glowing friends, then down at the text. "I don't know. It's exactly what I wanted, but now I'm torn." She bit her lip. "I'm not sure I want it anymore."

Stella put up her hands. "Hold on. You're going to have to tell me what in the world is going on because two weeks ago, there was no way you'd turn down an opportunity like this."

Claire explained the entire mess, with Wendy interjecting an occasional quip or comment. When she got to the fiasco on the beach, she waited for shame to coat her afresh, but strangely, it had lessened. Was it her conversation with Wendy yesterday that had made the difference or the one she'd had with Jesus last night? Well, one had led to the other, so she was thankful for both.

Stella's face pinched into a tight, red ball. "Will you point this Neo guy out to me? Because I want to punch him in the face."

Claire sat back in her chair. "Really?"

"Yes, really. What a jerk!"

Wendy started to giggle, and Claire followed suit.

"What?" Stella asked.

"That's not what I expected you to say." Claire's shoulders shook with her laughter.

Stella cracked a smile. "What did you expect?"

Claire pictured Stella speaking with a serene smile about the virtue of forgiveness. "Something about loving your enemy and praying for those who persecute you."

Stella waggled her head. "Yeah, well. That too."

Wendy gave Stella a playful punch on the arm. "Eighteen fifty-six made you go all mama bear."

"Or friend bear," Claire quipped.

Stella brought her fist to her chin. "Is there another word for it that doesn't make me sound like a Care Bear?"

Wendy snorted.

Claire had to concede. "Mama bear does sound far more intimidating."

"I'd like to think I gained a *boatload* of courage during my little trip." Stella gave an exaggerated wink.

Wendy rolled her eyes. "But apparently not a better sense of humor."

"I want to hear all about it. Tell us everything." Claire sat on the edge of her chair, ready to take in every detail of the wild adventure.

"Wait. We need to figure out what to do about your thing first," Stella said. "I think you should do it."

No, she couldn't. Just the thought of all those eyes on her gave her the willies. It would only bring back memories of the last time there was a Live on her page. And the comments. How could she brave them? There were bound to be rude and vile ones. Not to mention the huge risk of something going wrong. She could embarrass herself all over again. Hadn't she done that enough already? "I can't."

Wendy placed a hand on hers. "Hear me out. I agree with Stella. I think you should do this, even if you don't end up taking the Fit TV job."

Claire reared back. Why in the world would she go through that if not for the job?

"If you don't do it and you quit your channel, the last memory you'll ever have of this season of your life and career will be what Neo did to you on that beach. But if you do the bash, you'll always have *that* as your last, best memory."

"Unless it goes sideways." She cringed.

"It won't." Wendy squeezed her hand.

"Yeah, it won't." Stella grinned at her. "Because we're going to help you."

Claire looked back and forth between her friends. They sat on the edge of their chairs. If she only said the word, they'd be off and running to do whatever they needed to do to make her bash a success. What if she made a comeback from the Neo disaster? That would be far better than allowing his cruelty to cage her in fear and more satisfying than watching Stella punch him in the face. Well, almost. Could she rise above what he had done to her and come out bigger, better, and braver than before?

She managed to return their smiles. "What do I have to lose? It literally can't get any worse." Well, hopefully not.

"Yes." Stella made a cha-ching motion. "All right, let's make a plan."

For the next half hour, they discussed possibilities and developed a task list for each of them. It would, unfortunately, mean waiting a bit longer to catch up, and they'd have to let Stella out of their sight. She wouldn't disappear again, would she? She insisted she wouldn't and was adamant about this plan. They couldn't help but agree and trust it would all work out.

If Neo could convince people to participate in a workout session on the top deck to make fun of her, surely, they could get people to participate under the allure of a minute in the spotlight. It was going to take every ounce of courage she had, but she could do this. After all, she was smart enough. And capable. Jesus thought so, and His opinion trumped everyone else's.

Armed with their tasks, they reluctantly split up with plans to meet by the pool in an hour. And no one was to take the elevators.

After asking around twenty people if they wanted to participate and receiving a handful of affirmatives, Claire got Stella's text that she'd obtained permission from the cruise director to do the video on the stage by the pool. Great news. Now, there'd be upbeat music to add to the excitement. Go big or go home, right?

When the friends reconvened an hour later, they'd gotten over eighty people to agree to participate between the three of them. Everyone had been told to meet by the pool at two o'clock, which gave them time to figure out camera angles then grab a bite to eat and listen to some of Stella's story. They'd have to hear the rest later.

"Ready for this?" Wendy asked as they looked up at the stage at a quarter till two.

"I'm not sure. I guess we'll see."

Stella shuffled waiting participants into their places.

"She came back at just the right time," Claire mused. What an amazing friend. What amazing *friends*. She bumped Wendy's shoulder with her own. "Thank you for doing this for me."

"Are you kidding? I get to star in a workout video. When will I get this opportunity again?" Wendy's eyes danced with her tease. "You are putting me front and center, right?"

"You'd better believe it." She nudged her friend forward. "Go take your place."

Wendy started toward the stage but stopped and waved to Grayson and Sam in the crowd before finding her towel.

Stella handed Claire the wireless microphone headset. "They said you can use this. Go for it."

"Here goes nothing." Claire took a cleansing breath and put the mic on. She smiled and jogged up the steps. Their happy expressions and buoyant chatter brought an energy to the crowd, which pulsed through her. She welcomed everyone and explained how the video was going to work. Surveying the massive crowd, she estimated more than eighty people. She bounced on her toes. This was going to be a blast.

After Stella maneuvered people around a bit more, she gave a thumbs-up, and Claire started the countdown. Wendy angled the camera at her and nodded.

"Hi, everyone. It's Claire from Claire-ity Fitness here with eighty or so of my new friends—" Shouts erupted around her, and she waited for them to die down. "And we're here to do an amazing workout. Grab your mat, or towel, and join along."

Music emanated from the speakers, elevating the festive atmosphere. As she led everyone through the workout, elation filled her. How amazing was this, interacting with people and exercise in this way? She couldn't imagine giving this up to work behind the counter at a health food store. Though helping customers find the right products would be fulfilling, it was clear it wasn't what she was made to do. For her, it would be akin to hiding. God had made her beautiful. Maybe instead of seeing that as a bad thing, she could use the influence it brought for good, to combat the Enemy's lies with God's truth. She could speak hope. Be a light on a hill. Being seen didn't have to be a bad thing. Why had she thought she couldn't be both smart and beautiful?

About halfway through the routine, the music suddenly stopped. After a few awkward seconds, "Girls Just Want to Have Fun" blasted through the speakers. The same song she'd embarrassed herself with while doing karaoke. She froze. It had to be Neo. She scanned the area and found him standing at the bottom of the steps to the stage with his arms crossed, smirking back at her. He wanted her to freeze. To crumble. To fail.

Okay, change of plans. She'd been about to lead everyone in a kneeling side kick, but instead, she stood. She needed the leverage, the feeling of rising above. "Okay! We're going to do side-kick squats. These are going to work your quads, glutes and thighs while increasing your flexibility." The saucy smile she tossed at Neo before turning toward her audience was one of triumph. He'd tried his best, but he hadn't crushed her. She was having the time of her life with her friends and a mass of camera-hungry strangers.

"As we do this rep, belt out this chorus." Voices rose all around her, some good and some not so good. What did it matter? They were on a cruise, having a blast while working out together. She threw back her head and laughed, then sang along.

Chapter Twenty-Five

Wendy jumped up at the sight of Grayson entering the café. She waved her arm erratically until his gaze connected with hers. He smiled and sauntered her way. This was her last chance to see him. They were disembarking in an hour and then what? Would his gentle, probing eyes and soft touch be merely a memory? They hadn't spoken in person since their argument. Where did things stand between them? She needed to find out, so she'd asked Stella and Claire to wait for her text of "all clear" to come and join them for breakfast.

When he reached her, he wrapped her in his arms and kissed the top of her head. "I missed you," he whispered into her hair.

"I missed you, too."

When he pulled back, she gestured to the table. "I got you breakfast." Hopefully, it was still warm.

He chuckled. "Am I that predictable?"

"You like everything, so I got it all." She smirked.

"You're not eating?"

"Already ate." She'd only been able to stomach a bagel, knowing this conversation was coming.

He rubbed his hands together and sat. "Thanks. Might as well enjoy my last meal here, I guess."

Her smile fell. Would this be the last meal they ever shared? She should come out and ask, but she might not like the answer.

Grayson puffed out his cheeks. "Before I dig in, let's clear the air."

She stilled.

His shoulders dropped with his sigh. "I was a bit hasty and jumped to conclusions"—his gaze flew skyward before falling to hers once more—"again. It's one of my worst traits. The Lord and I are working it out, but you should know that about me up front."

Because? She sat forward, lured by the prospect of a future, however messy, with him.

"I said you weren't ready for a relationship because you had stuff to work out." He chuckled and pointed to himself. "I have stuff to work out too. Everyone does. If you boarded this boat completely healed and whole, you wouldn't be human. Expecting perfection is unrealistic and unfair."

Her hand went to the base of her throat. Was he saying …? She couldn't speak. Wouldn't allow her big mouth to ruin this moment.

"What I'm trying to say is I'm sorry for judging you harshly. I can't promise we won't ever fight again or have misunderstandings, but I would like the chance to see where this goes."

"Where this goes?" she echoed in a shaky voice.

His eyes were tender, pleading. "I'm asking for my boyfriend status back. I don't know—"

"Yes."

"Yes?"

"Absolutely."

The side of his mouth quirked upward. "I was going to say—"

"That you don't know how it will work with us living in two different cities. Blah, blah, blah. Whatever. Yes. Absolutely. One hundred percent, let's give it a whirl."

His grin spread. "Yeah?"

She slapped her leg. "Yes, okay. Now get over here and kiss me already before I hop over the table and spill your orange juice."

In the span of a moment, he knelt in front of her. Threading his hands behind her neck, he leaned in for a kiss she felt all the way to her toes.

"I gather it was an okay speech?" he asked when he pulled away, resting his forehead against hers.

She raised her brows.

"I practiced it for days in the mirror. My dad could have given it just as well after listening to me over and over, but I thought it would mean more coming from me."

She threw back her head and laughed.

"Man, I love that laugh. And the cute little snort thing you do afterward."

She covered her face.

"Yeah, that. And the fact that I always know what's on your mind. Your strong, bold opinions. Gosh, they're fascinating."

"So, you don't want to de-Wendyize me?"

"Not a chance."

What a dream come true. Someone who cared for her just the way she was without trying to force her to change. Someone who made her want to be more like Jesus because of the way he cared for her. Someone to pour herself out for.

She claimed his lips again, filled with gratitude. Who knew when she'd set off on this cruise she'd find exactly what her heart had been longing for all along?

God knew.

Thank God.

~

Claire paused from packing her last things when Stella called her name.

Stella emerged from the bathroom, phone in hand. "I think this text was meant for you. It's from someone named Bearett." She handed her phone to Claire.

Checking in. Did she make it back?

Claire palmed her forehead. With all the excitement of Stella's return and then the Live, she'd forgotten to update him and Angelica. She typed a quick reply.

Omgsh. Yes! Sorry. It's been a whirlwind.

"So … you told some guy about my little adventure?" Stella rolled her suitcase toward the door.

"Just Bearett. Did we even tell you about him and Angelica? They're descendants of your Dr. Duncan and relatives of our Dr. Duncan."

Stella dissolved into laughter. "Do you realize how ridiculous that sounds?"

Claire chuckled. "Now that you mention it, we do sound crazy."

Are you free to video chat now? I'd love to hear about it.

Was she? She scoured the room with her gaze, ensuring she hadn't forgotten anything, then checked the closet and the bathroom. Nope. All packed. And right now, they were waiting for a text from Wendy to let them know to join her upstairs in the café. Hopefully, she was patching things up with Grayson, and Stella would get to meet Wendy's new man.

Stella stepped into the bathroom. "I'm going to take a quick shower, and I'll be ready to go. I'm all packed except for the few things I need to get ready."

"Bearett wants to video chat. Mind if I go up a few levels where I get a better signal?"

"Not at all. I'll be quick, then I can meet you and Wendy, and hopefully Grayson, for breakfast."

"Sounds good." She grabbed her phone, typed in his contact info, and messaged as she walked.

Hey, it's Claire. I'll call from this number in just a sec.

Wait, he'd said nothing about Angelica being in on this call. Only him. How did she feel about having neither

Angelica nor Wendy as a buffer? She pictured Bearett's piercing green eyes. She didn't mind, though she probably should, considering everything she'd been through this past week. His gentle demeanor put her at ease. Still, she had no right to trust her judgment when it came to men, even if the relationship was platonic.

He probably had a wife or girlfriend. She checked his Facebook profile for his relationship status. Single. Seriously? That did not help to settle her nerves. *Lord, give me discernment. And help me to look at this guy as Your son, not anything more.* Not now, at least.

She found a quiet spot on the fourth deck and dialed. His eager smile greeted her after the second ring.

"Hey, Claire! Thanks for calling."

"No problem." She grinned back. "It's been crazy, but yes. Stella came back yesterday." She explained about the phone switcheroo. "Anyway, we had a lot of catching up to do."

"I bet. So, what was her mission?"

His inviting green eyes drew her in, and she found herself spilling the story, at least what Stella had given her permission to tell. She left out info personal to her friend's past and present.

Bearett ran a hand through his hair. "I can't believe it. My relative was a secret freedom fighter before the Civil War? That's amazing."

"I guess the family tree Angelica documented didn't tell that much?"

"No." He laughed. "And you can't get that information from a DNA kit either."

"Oh, and get this." How could she have nearly left out the most relevant part for the man she was talking to? "The Duncans are drawn to time sailors because you have time sailor in your blood." She relayed Dr. Joseph Duncan's tragic tale of being separated from his mother by over a hundred years.

His mouth parted as he blinked an unfocused gaze. "That explains so much." He scrubbed the back of his neck. "I wonder if the freedom fighting is in our blood too. I mean, everyone who time-sails does so to complete some sort of mission. It would make sense if those in my family are mission-minded as well."

"Are you?" She studied his pensive expression as he processed.

"Yeah, I think so. Not in the same way as Joseph Duncan, though."

"What cause are you passionate about?"

His expression turned bashful. "Orphans. Children in poverty. It breaks my heart to see, yet my church's mission trip to Guatemala is the highlight of my year every time." Pain flashed across his face. "I wish I could do more than throw money at the crisis."

"I used to want to be a medical missionary." Claire spoke softly, almost as if to herself. The desire to travel to third-world countries with aid for curable diseases and prayer for those who could only be healed supernaturally had lain dormant for years. But if she stoked that fire, she had no doubt it would roar to life within her once again.

"Now there's a way to make a huge impact." He chuckled. "If only I would have thought of that before investing my life in the water. I'm a charter boat captain, and I just can't seem to get away from my boat."

She laughed. "Of course not! You're a Duncan."

He pressed his hands together and extended them toward the screen. "Thank you so much for telling me. It's such a gift to have someone to talk to about all this. Someone besides my sister, I mean."

"Of course."

A text from Wendy came through, letting her know they were clear to come meet her and Grayson in the café. Thank God, they'd reconciled that relationship. They were good together.

"Hey, Bearett, I've got to go, but it's been great catching up." A pang of regret hit her at the realization this would likely be their last conversation.

"Yeah, it has. Hey, if you're ever in Chicago, look me up."

She sat forward. "Chicago? Seriously?"

"Yeah. Why?"

"I'm from Gary, Indiana. It's like thirty-five minutes away."

He scrubbed his clean jawline "I thought you were from Kansas City."

"No, Wendy is. I'm not far from you."

"Well, then." His face lit up. "Let's keep in touch."

Anticipation stirred within her. "I'd love to."

~

Stella stood on her tiptoes, searching the busy port for Everett. She bit her lip. If only she were taller. But then, the crowd parted, and his handsome face came into view. Suitcase forgotten, she raced toward him and flung herself into his arms

"I love you." She was breathless and not only from the short jaunt. His strong arms around her felt like heaven. "I've missed you so much."

He kissed the top of her head. "I've missed you like crazy." He tilted her chin up and captured her mouth with his in a sweet, lingering kiss. "I love you, too."

She sighed and rested her head against his chest.

"How was Hawaii?" he asked, squeezing her tight.

"Well ..." She had much to tell him, so much she couldn't explain through text. *Please God, let him believe me and not call off the wedding because he thinks I'm a lunatic.* Hopefully, with Claire and Wendy vouching for her, he'd believe the impossible. She'd considered not telling him what she'd been through over the past two weeks, but secrecy was no way to start a marriage.

Wendy and Claire neared, hauling their suitcases along with Stella's.

Wendy winked. "You forgot something."

"Sorry." Stella scrunched her nose.

"It's okay. Being in love makes you do crazy things." From the dazed look on Wendy's face, she was falling herself. Grayson seemed to always be on her mind. How sweet.

"Okay, ladies." Everett took the heavier suitcases in hand. "My future mother-in-law is excited to see you all and has a plethora of plans. Dress alterations tomorrow, I think, and I don't remember what else."

Claire narrowed her eyes. "You're saying our time of rest and relaxation is over. It's time to get ready for this wedding."

Everett nodded. "Pretty much."

Rest and relaxation over? She'd barely gotten an hour of it. No matter. She'd received something far more valuable: the peace that only comes when you know you're in the center of God's will.

She threw her head back and laughed. "Goodbye, vacation."

Epilogue

Stella's misty gaze locked with Everett's. She stood across from him on the church's decorated stage. Bouquets of white roses dotted the end of every other aisle, perfuming the packed sanctuary with their heavenly scent and adding to the ethereal beauty.

The pastor smiled at the bride and groom. "You may now kiss the bride."

With great flourish and fervor, Bearett dipped Claire and kissed her thoroughly. Hoots and cheers sounded around them. Stella clapped, then wiped stray tears away as the newly married couple exited the room.

She met Everett at center stage and took his arm. "Wasn't that beautiful?"

"Reminds you of our wedding, huh?"

She nodded. Was it only two years ago when they'd walked down the aisle? "I'm so happy for them."

"I was thinking the same thing," Wendy said from behind them where she held on to Grayson's arm. "I couldn't help but think of our wedding and how amazing it is we all got to be bridesmaids for each other."

Wendy and Grayson had tied the knot six months prior in St. Louis. They'd had the rehearsal dinner at The Screaming Peach. How wild.

As Stella glided down the aisle, she waved to her daughter, Bridgett Rose, where she bounced on the pew between Stella's parents. A few rows back sat Dr. Raymond Duncan, who winked at her as she passed.

After the guests had filed through the reception line and showered the newlyweds with bubbles, the wedding party piled inside the limo for the ride to the reception.

Stella looped her arm around the bride's shoulder. "Claire, you are absolutely glowing. What a perfect wedding."

Claire pressed her palms onto her cheeks. "It *was* perfect, wasn't it?"

"Like a fairy tale."

"Who knew a happily ever after existed for me?"

"I had a feeling God wasn't going to pass you by." Stella gave her friend's shoulder a squeeze. Of course, trials were bound to come. Such was life. But gratitude filled her that all three of them had godly men by their sides who would remind them to cling to the God of all hope when times got tough.

The reception was filled with delicious food, moving toasts, and much dancing. When "Girls Just Want to Have Fun" blasted from the speakers, the three best friends hit the dance floor.

Stella had to shout to be heard above the music. "Wendy, don't think I missed you not sipping your champagne during the toast. Is there anything you want to tell us?" She narrowed teasing eyes at her friend.

Wendy's cheeks reddened. "I didn't want to take away from Claire's special day."

"You're pregnant!" Claire and Stella cried out at the same time.

"Sh." Wendy laughed. "We haven't told anyone yet."

The news called for a group hug and a few happy tears. Wendy and Grayson had been trying to get pregnant for several months. The transition to her new St. Louis home and job at a middle school there had been equal parts bumpy and exhilarating. What a joy for her to have this new development to celebrate.

"Congratulations," Stella whispered.

"Thanks." Wendy beamed, then turned her attention to Claire. "You do realize when you have children, they'll have time sailor in their blood, right? They'll be drawn to time sailors. How cool is that?"

Claire's eyes twinkled. "I know. It's fascinating to hear Bearett's stories. I wonder what adventures we'll face together."

They'd bought a lake house in South Haven, Michigan, and Bearett had secured a job as a charter boat captain there. He couldn't seem to get enough of the water. Claire had decided she'd had her fill of the limelight. Though her YouTube channel got plenty of views, she hadn't posted a new video in months. Instead, she taught Pilates classes at her local YMCA while she studied to become a homeopathic doctor.

Bridgett ran onto the dance floor and twirled around.

Claire put a hand over her heart. "She's adorable."

Stella had to agree. "Isn't she, though?"

"Have you guys decided what you're doing?" Wendy asked.

Stella held out her hand to Bridgett and spun her little girl around. "Yes. We're staying where we are."

It had been a grueling decision. Their little town wasn't an easy place to have a racially diverse family. Some people were stuck in their ways, and change was sluggish. In the end, their commitment to stay put hadn't been about Stella's position at the paper at all. Though it was ironic how the more she pushed back against her boss's racist remarks, the more she seemed to thrive there. "Whether or not they want Everett there, they *need* him. There is a wealth to be gained by diversity. He shouldn't have to pay the price for their ignorance, but in the end, he decided it was worth it. He feels this is where God is calling us, at least for this season."

"Good for you." Pride radiated from Wendy's grin. "You are so brave."

She was, wasn't she? Her courage came from holding His hand in the journey. With her Savior by her side, she could brave strange waters.

The End

Look for the next Time Sailors book *Braving Fiery Waters*.
Did you enjoy this book?

You might also enjoy these other books by Sarah Hanks:

The Mercy Series
Mercy Will Follow Me
Mercy's Song
Mercy's Legacy

The Sister in Arms Collection
A Battle Worth Fighting
Fall Back and Find Me

Stand Alone
Awakened to Life

Author's Note

The idea for this story came to me while cruising with my bestie and another friend in January 2023 on a ship with retro decor and an antique mailbox. We realized the cruise ship didn't list a thirteenth floor—it skipped from floor twelve to floor fourteen—and joked about what could be on the mysterious missing floor. As we were taking the elevators up to the top deck, for some reason, my friend Rene and I got into one elevator, and Michelle got into the other. When we reached the fourteenth floor, we waited for Michelle to step off the other elevator and greet us. Only she didn't. As we continued to wait, wondering what was taking her so long, I started rambling about how she probably ended up on the mysterious thirteenth floor, which was actually a time portal that sucked her back into time onto an antebellum steamboat. (If you've read my Mercy series, you know I have a thing about steamboats.)

While Michelle did turn up a bit later, proclaiming she'd hit the wrong button and then gotten turned around, the story idea had taken off like a snowball rolling downhill. Rene and I had visited the Arabia Steamboat Museum in Kansas City together when I was researching for my Mercy series. It seemed a natural fit. And thus, my first time-traveling novel was birthed.

Yes, the *Arabia* was a real steamboat that sunk in the Missouri River on September 5, 1856, with over two hundred tons of cargo on board. You can visit the museum and see the cargo for yourself as the mud perfectly preserved it for over a hundred years. Maybe when you visit, they'll still show the same video both Grayson and Wendy viewed to explain the excavation process and how they tasted the pickles they unearthed.

It's also true that Border Ruffians raided the ship in March 1856 and discovered one hundred Sharps rifles and two cannons in a box marked Carpenter's Tools destined for Kansas territory. A letter dropped by a Massachusetts man tipped them off. The border war between Kansas and Missouri created a tense environment during that time, and many consider what happened between these two states to be the spark that lit the Civil War.

That's where historical accuracy wanes and creative license takes over. There is no evidence any slaves were smuggled on board the *Arabia* en route to Kansas territory, although slaves finding their way to freedom on steamboats among cargo and even inside crates was not unheard of. The *Arabia* also did not have a calliope. It was a sidewheel packet boat, built for cargo first and passengers second, unlike some other types of steamboats. Also, 1856 was a bit too soon for the calliope to be commonplace. However, since the instrument was such an important part of steamboat transportation, I chose to include it in this story.

I've been asked why I choose to write books that touch on the subject of racism. I'm not sure how to explain it other than to say the Lord has gripped my heart. I, like Stella, lived much of my life in a White bubble. When loved ones made racist comments, I did not speak up at first out of fear. Instead, I made excuses. They were a product of their generation. They didn't know better, etc. As long as I wasn't the one making the comments, it was okay to let it slide, right? The people speaking were people I loved. People who loved me. Good people in all these other areas. How could I risk our relationship by opening my mouth.

It's a long story of how this changed for me, but what gave me hope is that I learned I could speak up. The Lord could help me be bold and yet kind. He could help me speak the truth in love.

For all my beautiful Black and Brown brothers and sisters who have been the subject of racism, I'm deeply sorry for the way I and others like me have kept our mouths shut instead of speaking the truth from the heart of Jesus. With the Lord's help, we will stay silent no more. No longer will we stand by while anyone made in the image of God is degraded.

I hope you received from this story the truth that transformation is possible through the power of Jesus. We no longer have to be shackled by fear. Jesus is with us, as close as our breath, and through His strength, we can brave any waters.

Sarah Hanks

But now, this is what the LORD says—
he who created you, Jacob,
he who formed you, Israel:
"Do not fear, for I have redeemed you;
I have summoned you by name; you are mine.
When you pass through the waters,
I will be with you;
and when you pass through the rivers,
they will not sweep over you.
When you walk through the fire,
you will not be burned;
the flames will not set you ablaze."
Isaiah 43:1–2